"Seeped in mystery, Lily's story unfolds as readers keep peeling back layers of her tortured past. The amazing young woman works out of her comfort zone for women's suffrage, always concerned for her loved ones. Author Linda Brooks Davis has a beautiful gift with words, putting me in mind of Jane Austen."

—**CARYL MCADOO**, Christian author of multiple genres
including historical family sagas

"Years after reading Linda Davis's first book, *The Calling of Ella McFarland*, I still recall the characters and many of the scenes—a sure indication of the vividness of Linda's writing. Now that I've read her second book, *The Mending of Lillian Cathleen*, I know it too will stay with me. If you want to treat yourself to a compelling and memorable read, this is the book."

—**ANN TATLOCK**,
acclaimed novelist, editor, children's book author

"In *The Mending of Lillian Cathleen*, Linda Brooks Davis delivers a story rich in characters who will tug at readers' hearts set against a vast historical backdrop that includes the beginning of World War I, the women's suffrage movement, and the ugly sex trade of young girls. Davis's lyrical writing allows us to see this world through the eyes of a woman who must overcome a horrific start in life to fight against an overwhelming evil to save others and ultimately herself. The icing on the cake is a sweet, satisfying romance. *The Mending of Lillian Cathleen* is a keeper."

—**KELLY IRVIN**, bestselling author of *Through the Autumn Air*

In this thought-provoking tale, Linda Davis takes us from the tiny town of Needham, Oklahoma and into the bustling metropolis of 1914 Fort Worth, Texas, where we get a bit of mystery, a bit of history, and a harrowing glimpse at what it meant to be a woman without a voice. With unflinching commitment and compassion the author speaks for all the generations of sisters who came before us. In *The Mending of Lilian Cathleen*, she introduces a heroine who is a true force of justice, with a fragility running just beneath her freckled skin.

—**ALLISON PITTMAN,** author of *The Seamstress* (Tyndale, 2019)

Praise for
The Calling of Ella McFarland
by Linda Brooks Davis

"I couldn't be more proud of Linda Davis. You'll find it hard to believe The Calling of Ella McFarland is a debut novel. Linda handles every nuance with the aplomb of a veteran, having honed her craft and polished her skills. It's her first, but I'm confident it won't be her last."

—**JERRY B. JENKINS**, *NY Times* best-selling author

"Not only a fascinating love story, but also a thoughtfully written and historically accurate novel featuring important themes. This debut will satisfy on many levels."

—**JAN WATSON**, award-winning author of historical fiction

"Davis demonstrates a talent for developing appealing characters with whom readers can connect . . . A top choice for those who read for character and enjoy a well-developed historical setting."

—**LIBRARY JOURNAL**

"A masterful story of a woman who stumbles onto a need to empower women while reaching out in love and sacrifice to help other afflicted women. This debut novel shows the excellent craftsmanship of author Linda Davis. We'll be seeing more of her!"

—**DIANN MILLS**, best-selling author of
historical and suspense novels

"The characters race across the pages carrying the story with them. Some of the twists and turns surprised me, and Ms. Davis was able to bring them to a satisfying conclusion."

—**LENA NELSON DOOLEY**, best-selling, award-winning author of the McKenna's Daughters series

"A charming story of family and a young woman's courage to be obedient to God in the face of adversity. I loved the historical detail. Choose a long, quiet day to curl up with The Calling of Ella McFarland. You'll want to finish it once you get started."

—**CARYL MCADOO**, author of historical and contemporary Christian fiction

"Davis knits together an intricate, multi-level tale, leaving open threads for more . . . a book where the author and the characters share flesh and blood and story, and the reader gets folded right in."

—**ALLISON PITTMAN**, award-winning author of historical fiction

". . . Ella McFarland . . . a woman worth knowing . . . a complex character filled with the strength of her convictions, but tethered by the same human frailties as the rest of us. I found myself transported to turn-of-the-century Oklahoma Indian Territory . . . Davis does a beautiful job of weaving together a lovely romance and a powerful message of God's enduring, steadfast love in even the most trying of times. The Calling of Ella McFarland is a powerful debut effort."

—**KELLY IRVIN**, best-selling author of The Beekeeper's Son

"It's easy to see why this book won First Place in Jerry Jenkins' Operation First Novel. The characters captured my imagination right from the beginning and drew me into this wonderful story. Linda Brooks Davis is definitely a talented writer and I hope to see many more books from her!"

"This is an amazing book. It reminds me of books I read as a child—ones that kept me turning the pages, enthralled with the story and captivated by the characters. It is beautifully written . . . I found the book inspiring . . . **This is a jewel box of a book**—a love story, a story of trial and heartache, but also of victory and joy. I highly recommend it.

"I received this book as a gift and had intended for it to get me through those sleepless nights with a newborn. I finished all 357 pages in two days! I was enraptured by Ella's fierce spirit, faith in God and passion for the underprivileged. Linda did an excellent job giving life to each character and successfully transported me back to the early 1900's. Not only was it easy to read, I found myself deeply connecting with the characters of the book through the triumphs and trials of their faith. The end brought me to tears. Amazing read. Hope there is a second in the works!"

THE MENDING *of*
LILLIAN CATHLEEN

LINDA BROOKS DAVIS

BROOKSTONE
PUBLISHING GROUP

Brookstone Publishing Group
P.O. Box 211, Evington, VA 24550
BrookstoneCreativeGroup.com

ISBN: 978-1-949856-00-2 (print), 978-1-949856-01-9 (epub)

Ordering Information:
Special discounts are available on quantity purchases by corporations,
associations, and others. For details, contact
Brookstone Publishing Group at the address above.

Cover art by Carpe Librum Book Design: carpelibrumbookdesign.com

IN MEMORY

Daddy

Wilson Freeman Brooks
1914-1971

You were my prince.
You healed my spirit with the touch of your hand.
Your nobility in suffering taught me to trust the Lord.
You were the closest I'll come to Jesus this side of Heaven.

DEDICATION

To my brothers

Jerry, Dalton, and Dale Brooks

Princes, all

We share a common love
and a button box of memories.
I love you.

Tell Me the Story of Jesus

622

Fanny J. Crosby, 1880

John R. Sweney, 1880

PART

One

... MY GROANINGS ARE
POURED OUT LIKE WATER.

JOB 3:24B

CHAPTER 1

*M*a resisted a drunken beast as long as she lived.

I lower my head to the barren table and run my hands along its blackened surface, as nicked and pitted as my mother's skin. She fed her brood atop this slab. As best she could.

My fingers coax from the wood's crannies a lifetime of embedded moments, photo cards in a parlor viewer.

Long extinguished firelight shimmers in the table's gentle slopes, back light for a promenade of memories.

Pressing my ear to the hardened plane, I capture a fleeting accompaniment, a dirge played on a broken heart. Tin plates clatter. Bean juice sizzles. One corner of the table rocks atop a nail keg. And hands etched with grime grip spoons as if they're brooms.

My imagined viewer clicks, and a bitter Oklahoma winter arrives. A blowing rain. Work-roughened hands upend the table and slide it into a rectangular frame, our shanty's one door, Ma's feeble attempt to batten her family against storms.

The scene shifts, and a distant Christmas glows in the wood's warp and woof. Ma sits alone, abandoned to die. I find her. Feed her. Dress her in decent nightclothes. And spread fine quilts over her skeletal frame.

But she disappears without a word, save a penciled note.

> *Go back to that fancy college, Lil'. Make somethin' of yourself,*
> *somethin' I weren't able to do. Fly. For me.*

I trace a fingertip along the board's undulating lines. Love beyond measuring is ground into the wood grain.

Clenching my eyes shut, I glimpse my mother stumbling through a counterpane of snow. To the blacksmith's shop. And parts unknown.

One photo slide supplants another, and I'm returning to college on rail tracks headed south. For Ma's sake.

I blink, and the meager lights darken, stirring scraps of a lonely memoir created months ago. Ma and I enjoy a handful of hours in the deep of night, she on one bank of Rock Creek and I on the other. We whisper secrets across the water and hide from the monster she married.

The table's wooden canvas darkens to black, save a lone, ghastly figure. A feather pillow in his tobacco-stained hands. And Ma, spiritless in death.

I should have killed him.

Curling my fingers around the table edge, I wince. A rough-bored hole has nipped my fingernail, peeling it back. I staunch the scarlet bloom, but what's to be done for the borehole cruelty carved in my heart?

Today's announcement in downtown Needham will render the first stitch.

Lifting my head, I lean against the sycamore chair back. Hand-carved and rough as a cob in winter, its bumps and bulges poke at me, prod me to cast aside the haunting photo promenade and to stand.

"Ma would've judged this day hotter 'n a billy goat in a pepper patch, Lil'." Donnie, my bowlegged brother, leans against the door frame and stares at his meager world outside. Stones encircle an abandoned campfire beneath a stubborn black walnut tree, witness to decades of thunderstorms and lightning, droughts and wildfires.

And tumults of a different sort under our tin roof.

He clumps onto the slanting porch. Rickets has stolen his mobility.

I join him. "It's a hundred and six degrees."

"You reckon that's as hot as Ma's billy goat?" He runs grubby fingers through the thatch he's chopped neck length with rusted shears.

I grin and ruffle his coffee-black mop. "I reckon so. It's out of the ordinary for sure."

But this is no ordinary day.

The jury has reached a verdict.

"Gotta run, brother mine."

He peers at me, telltale curiosity rimming his black-marble eyes. "Where ya goin', sis?"

How much do I reveal? Depravation has cast his mind in a limited mold. "I'm going into town. But I'll be back later on. With some news."

"What kinda news?"

I tweak the tip of his nose. "The good kind. The kind Ma would whoop over."

He slaps a thigh and chortles. "I'll be watchin' for you then."

Striding toward the meandering stream behind the shack I once called home, I halt in the tinder-dry brush. And turn for another glimpse of my brother's gap-toothed grin.

Joy crests near my heart. Good tidings await my brother and me— and our departed ma—the other side of Rock Creek.

CHAPTER 2

*P*erched on an old church pew in the main courtroom, I ignore the cramp in my lower back and focus on Judge Wilson Fulbright.

"Gentlemen of the Jury, I'm told you've reached a decision." The silver-haired jurist scrutinizes the panel under eyebrows laced with steel.

The foreman stands with a tug of his vest. "Yup. Got us a verdict."

The crucial document crackles as it passes to bailiff and thence to judge, a journey mirroring decades of such treks in Glover County's airless hall of justice.

No prior rendering has wielded such power over my family as this one on the twenty-eighth day of July 1914. A guilty decree will bring justice to my mother and send her murderer to prison. It'll free Donnie from the clapboard prison he calls home.

The announcement will tie off a loose thread for the community of Needham, but will it alter folks' opinions of me? Or will my past forever define me?

Dabbing at perspiration on my chin, I slide my trembling hands to my sides and clench the edge of the pew. My nails press half-moons into the wooden underbelly.

"The Lord will bring justice." Ella Evans, my dearest friend in the world, whispers at my right. If her brother were present, he'd echo her sentiment.

Fidgeting, I glance over my shoulder. Where is Cade?

Seated to my left, Adelaide Fitzgerald—my heiress friend and benefactor—releases a mint-tinted sigh. "That no-good'll get what he deserves at last." She shakes a lace handkerchief and scatters the aroma of violets.

More like elder sisters than mere friends, these two dear women have served as my ever-present supports throughout the trial.

At a table just beyond the bar, the accused twirls an ink pen between fingers as steady as granite. His ace-black thatch bristles from a cowlick at the crown of his skull, and a newly cropped strand laps his collar.

Judge Fulbright smooths the certificate atop his elevated desk. Perspiration has plastered his frosted mop across his pate and sapped starch from his shirt.

He raises his eyes and glowers. "Defendant, stand up."

The defense attorney rises and adjusts his tie. His client poses beside him, bantam rooster-like.

Hand fans flutter, stirring damp tufts beneath ladies' hats but little else.

"Publish the verdict." The jurist passes the form to the Clerk of the Court and swipes a handkerchief along his neck.

My pulse quickens, and my cheeks flame. My breath catches like a hare in a trap, and I force it between tightened lips.

I'll survive this day with grace—as Ma would've.

The lead juryman, the town's blacksmith, repositions his spectacles. "As to the charge of Murder in the Second Degree, we, the jury, find the defendant, Walter Sloat . . ."

Hand fans still, and the air congeals around us.

The worn-smooth pew bites into my back.

". . . not guilty."

A collective gasp claims every speck of oxygen.

"No." Ella grabs my hand. Her head jerks forward, wobbling the straw headpiece perched atop her topknot of golden spirals.

Addie wads her kerchief into a clenched fist. "It can't be." She presses whitened knuckles against her lips. A mahogany-toned tress escapes its comb and dangles above an arched eyebrow.

The judge scowls at the jurymen. "So say you all?"

The foreman squares his shoulders, straining his vest buttons. "Yup. We all agree."

Each man replies the same. Each, save the foreman, averts his eyes.

Would they have reached the same conclusion if *their* daughters had testified?

Judge Fulbright turns to the clerk. "Make the finding a part of the record." He fixes a whetted glare on the defendant. "Walter Sloat, you've been found not guilty of the murder of your wife by a jury of your peers, a rendering I find profoundly shameful. See that you use your freedom wisely. Or *I* will."

He hammers the gavel atop its block with such force it cracks. "Court adjourned."

Like gunfire penned in a valley, commotion bursts through the gallery. Citizens shout and point at the jury. Newspaper reporters flee with pencils and notepads in hand.

The vile perpetrator turns and ogles me with a grin that bunches his sideburns.

Nauseous, I can only stare. "I saw it with my own eyes. Why didn't they believe me?" Disbelief holds me immobile.

With multicolored eyes flashing, Ella releases my hand. "It appears the eyes of a woman can't be trusted."

Addie's dark-chocolate stare spears the jury members filing out. Her peacock blue suit shines bright against her reddening skin. "They're a rotten bevy of mealy—"

"The murderer's going home." The words rattle off my tongue. "What about Donnie?"

My benefactress helps me to my feet. "Let's get out of here. The stench is repugnant."

The courtroom spins, but my friends' strong arms steady me.

"Stiffen your spine." Ella whispers at my ear. "You've a spirit as fiery as your mane." Her tone has hardened. "Fortitude's in your very marrow, lass."

A stranger leans toward me. "Foolhardiness, you mean."

Addie jerks around. "How dare you. Lily traversed oceans when she crossed Rock Creek!"

The matron throws us a disparaging glance and slithers alongside the evildoer's attorney.

Ella's eyes flash an array of colors above cheeks blazing bright peach. "Nothing but rubbish. Pay them no mind."

How often have these two friends admonished and defended me? Ella saved me from my father's cruel hands and taught me to read. Addie moved me into her fine estate, Broadview, and sent me to college.

But none of it matters here at home. The Sloat name has clotted into a byword.

Still . . . My friends insist I'm more than my name implies.

Besides, haven't I been associated with honorable names the better part of a decade?

I force back my shoulders. "I'll defend Donnie, no matter the cost. If that's foolhardy, so be it."

Straightening my cotton bodice and skirt, I toss aside the barbs and stride down the main hallway. Thankfully, I chose a wide hair band, not a hat with folderol. Even a conservative plume like Addie's would feel out of place . . . now.

My friends' heels pound like a quartet of hammers alongside the muted cadence of my soft-soled pumps. Their hobble skirts swish, but mine hangs limp around my legs. Planning a day of celebration, I embroidered collar and cuffs in bright green. To match my eyes.

The cheerful color mocks me . . . now.

My friends push through the front portals.

I step into the blazing heat and shade my eyes.

Even the sun's rays beset me.

The finger of a gentle wind trifles with my skirt hem, but the crowd musters around me, blocking every vestige of breeze.

"Best beware." A matron in a broad-brimmed hat tilts her head at a decisive angle.

Is it pity or recrimination that draws her eyebrows into wavy slants?

A bowler-hatted man points his cane. "How can you live with yourself, lying about your own father?"

"What'll you do now?" another shouts. "Run away with your tail between your legs?"

Addie raises a hand. "Silence—"

"Wait." I wouldn't have dared interrupt, nor spoken to an assemblage, in bygone years. But am I still that cowering ragamuffin? Haven't I learned to speak my own thoughts?

Indeed.

"The Good Book says . . ."

A side door bangs open, and the twelve men file out. Some hail cabs. Others clamber into automobiles. The rest duck their heads and slink away.

I restrain the storm of censure tumbling through my middle. Best not plow a field yet to harvest. "We're to seek justice and correct oppression."

Voices dim.

"My mother suffered the worst kind of oppression." I move my focus from one spectator to the next. Mellowing my tone, I hook a thumb toward the courthouse. "But Ma received not a whit of justice today." I point at the crowd. "Women are denied more than votes."

Ladies at the back raise their hands and call out their agreement, but the circle of townsfolk tightens. Truth be told, they thirst for my blood.

"Back up, everyone." Addie elbows a pathway through the crush.

I stand erect and descend the stone steps toward her apple-red Cadillac. We three friends thought we'd celebrate at Sweet Shop, but now . . .

The crowd stirs.

Ma's murderer steps into my path. "Your lies've found you out." His graveled tone picks at my spine.

Bitter memories flash.

A hot poker. The stench of burning flesh. The pain.

A bridle, bit end. A horse whip.

Worst of all, a pillow. And Ma, pale and lifeless.

Marshaling my confidence, I dig beyond my urge to retreat. "You've done all you'll do to me or Ma." Try as I may, I can't control the tremor in my voice. "But if you lay a hand on—"

"You ain't gonna turn Donnie into no upstart like yourself. I'm your pa. Won't allow it."

"You're no father to me. I haven't wrapped my arms around you a single time, even as a child. I'll call you Walter . . . abuser of children . . . murderer . . . anything but Pa."

A murmur creeps through the crowd.

"You're fit for nothin' but a cotton patch, girlie." The cur leans backward and guffaws. His derby hat plops to the ground, stirring dust.

Repulsed, I pull away and restrain an urge to slap the miscreant. Has this man's blood tainted me?

"Outta the way!" Cade McFarland materializes from nothing but my longing, it seems. He tosses the weasel aside like a bundle of broomcorn. "Lily has none of your heart or soul. Stay away from her."

Half a foot shorter and sixty pounds lighter, the older man skitters aside, possum-like. "Look—"

"No, *you* look." My defender raises a fist. "Get!"

Smirking, Walter snatches his hat and flicks off dust. Reshapes the dent. Pops it atop his head. And strolls away, whistling.

The bully's a coward at heart.

Cade, a prince among men, takes my hand. "I'm sorry I didn't make it in time." The skin above his golden-brown eyes furrows. "You don't deserve this, Lily."

I duck my head and lean against his shoulder. "I must get Donnie away." But how?

He thrusts a folded square of paper toward Addie. "This wire came for you."

She unfolds the message and pales. The space between her dark eyebrows contracts.

My stomach knots, and I move to her side. "Who's it from?"

"Herr Romano." An aspiring opera singer, Addie has long planned to pursue the opera in Italy. She announced weeks ago she'd be leaving for Europe soon. But her departure plans have remained a mystery.

I can't imagine Broadview without her. Dare I hope the maestro has called off the production? I capture a calming breath. "What's the news?"

"Austria-Hungary has declared war on Serbia." A spot at the base of her throat pulsates. "Russia has mobilized."

Ella stares, trance-like. "Lord, help us. The world's about to catch fire."

CHAPTER 3

*B*y midday, the weather thermometer has crept to one hundred eight degrees, mirroring our shared ire.

"I won't stand for it!" Cade strikes Broadview's kitchen table with a powerful fist. "First the foul verdict." He scowls at Addie. "And now you're running off to Europe?"

Petite Ella raises a calming hand. "Simmer down, brother. You'll be a boon to no one if you lose your head. We must be as wise as serpents, as gentle as doves." She's gathered her irascible golden curls into a topknot of damp spirals.

I bolt upward, rocking the ladder-back chair. "Ma was gentle, friend. Where'd it get her?"

She anchors me with a hand on each shoulder. "What pain you've endured." Lines of her telltale compassion crease her brow.

"What pain *Ma* endured, you mean." I step away and spear Addie with a glower. "Now *you're* courting danger."

She lifts a shoulder, breezy-like. "Italy's not involved in the Austria-Serbia conflict."

My curly-haired friend nibbles on a thumb nail. "The Lord has a plan."

I expel a huff. "A plan for suffering like Ma's? For war and death and destruction?" Ordinarily I smooth out wrinkles between folks and avoid turmoil, but this is no ordinary day. "For what purpose, for pity's sake?"

"Only God knows." Staring out the window, she murmurs, as if to herself.

Sometimes my friend's dogged faith crawls under my skin. "Can't God work out a plan that doesn't include such misery? Now that Walter's loose, who knows what agony he'll wreak?"

Cade growls. "If that no-good sets foot on this acreage to do you harm, I'll—"

I seize his forearm. "Don't fall into Walter's pit. If you suffer on my account, I'll never forgive myself." I turn a piercing gaze to my Europe-bound friend. "Speaking of suffering—"

"Italy will never join the fray." Her vigorous head shake threatens her mahogany-brown chignon. "Herr Romano says so."

"We'll see, won't we?" I snap a nod.

The air all but crackles.

Margaret Gallagher, Addie's lifelong housekeeper, steps into the kitchen and removes a pitcher from the ice box. "A cool glass of tea'll settle our nerves." Forever serving others, the dear woman wet-nursed the orphan heiress in infancy and in time became more than a housekeeper. She's a surrogate mother.

"Good idea." Addie opens a pastry tin. "And there's scones."

"I'll have coffee." My rugged protector peaks as with grit in his throat. "Make it strong."

We sit without speaking, fingers drubbing the tabletop and sighing. Soon the percolator's blub-blub abates, along with the tension.

My thoughts return to the vile verdict. I swipe the table with a kitchen towel. "How did those right-minded men find Walter not guilty?"

"They're a *wrong*-minded bunch, that's how." Ella locks her arms over her chest.

"Come to think of it . . ." I reach across the table and squeeze Addie's hand. "How can a *right*-minded woman like yourself traipse off to Europe with a war on?"

She shrugs off my concern. "No more than a local conflict. It'll blow over."

"So why has Russia mobilized?" He demands with a pound of his fist.

"Just cautionary. Be that as it may . . ." My beautiful, Europe-bound friend swishes out the kitchen doorway. "I'm leaving soon, war or no war." Her voice tumbles along the hardwood floor from the direction of her study."

My generous benefactor speaks the truth. She set aside her dreams on my account nine years ago. But must she troop off to Europe? At a time like this?

"I need some air." I whirl around and flee the household's emotions, as thick as yesterday's oats.

Threading my way toward the graveled pathway, I stumble but right myself with a hand on a statuette. I long for my place of solitude, the gazebo. My prayer closet, my friends claim. I'll accept the label if it'll help.

The summerhouse nestling in a glen near the creek far exceeds the quality of my childhood home. Constructed of brick and mortar with arched side openings, its cedar-shake trellising matches the roof. An irrigation system waters the foliage that fires the retreat with seasonal color.

I fall to my knees at the structure's bench. "According to Ma, I can trust You. But how can I after today?" I lay my head on the hardened slats. "But how can I correct the injustice? Protect my brother? Or keep my friend at home? I'm barely out of girlhood and haven't a penny to call my own.

"Will Needham forever remember me as the young'un from the other side of Rock Creek and as uneducated as a stump? Perhaps I *should* run away with my tail between my legs."

"May I join you?"

Cade.

My breath catches, and I squelch my eyes tight. His voice is at once ever so welcome and saber sharp. If he knew how far into darkness my troubled past reaches, he wouldn't allow me near. Battening my defenses, I snatch a handkerchief from a pocket and dab at moisture lining my nose.

He extends a hand, and I place my palm on his, noting anew the work-roughened skin, so unlike his tender heart.

"Troubled about your brother?" He settles us onto the bench, gentleman-like.

"Yes. He's crippled in mind and body. And at the mercy of a murderer."

"Shh." He places a fingertip on my lips and wraps an arm around my shoulder.

I flinch.

"We're friends, Lily. For life." He cups my cheek and nudges me toward him.

My head comes to rest on his broad shoulder. How soothing, the scent of starch and shaving cream. I'd remain at his side forever—as more than a friend—if I could.

My insides tangle into knots, and I groan. Never can I call this man mine. And I haven't the strength to tell him why.

He tightens his hold. "According to Mama, tears heal."

A breeze rattles the jasmine vine and sprinkles its sweetness around us. But warring thunderheads brew inside me.

His freshly laundered shirt would welcome the tears pressing against my eyelids. But life has molded a dam around my heart, holding them in check.

He draws me closer. "I want to comfort you as—"

"Well, well, well. What do we have here?"

The grate of an unwelcome voice brings this dear man's comfort to a standstill.

Tall, proud Sabina Gallagher, Maggie's daughter, leans against the gazebo's arched entry like a cat with a secret. She has forced her thin, wispy hair into a tight bun. As colorless as dust, it swallows the light, leaving a dull patina of pewter, neither silver nor gold.

The odor of counterfeit gardenias—her ever-present perfume—erases the garden's delicate aroma.

I hold a hand under my nose. Now I must dodge contentious barbs?

"Oh, my dear." Maggie squeezes past her daughter, and my comforter relinquishes his place beside me. "I'm very sorry." Her tender reach is broad enough to include her daughter, Adelaide, and even me.

"It was a shock."

"Aye, for us all." Mercifully, she withholds her thoughts of God's mysterious plan.

My bold advocate stomps like a stallion rearing for freedom. "Let me get my hands on that—"

"You'll do nothing of the sort." I must settle this firebrand of a man before the Sloat curse mars him.

His hands fist. "Someone needs to. They freed a murderer today."

Sabina crosses her arms over her bosom. "Twelve upstanding jurymen disagree." Possessed of neither Addie's generosity nor Maggie's warmth, she snarls, and her features pinch. "Frankly, your devotion to Lily astounds me." She ekes a tightened gaze from my head to my feet. "Or is it pity?"

His fists tighten and open, tighten and open.

Undaunted, she continues. "Nor do our fine Glover County citizens agree. A witness who lies under oath should be jailed. If the Women's Club has its way—"

My champion snorts. "They'll exact the kind of injustice the jury rendered?"

"They'll rewrite their bylaws to exclude such riffraff." She snaps her eyes toward me. "Club officers are convening in the morning, matter of fact."

I hold my tongue. Returning cruelty for cruelty feeds malice.

Her mother points toward the house. "Go, daughter. You've become a shrew."

Her daughter huffs. "I've better things to do than reason with the unreasonable anyway." She shoves aside the vine and ignores the shower of blooms, trampling the delicate petals as surely as the garden's tranquility.

"I'll be going now, Lily." My handsome companion expels a deep breath, whips a turn, and trounces westward toward McFarland acreage.

"Tea and scones inside." Maggie shoos me, mama hen-like.

I check my pendant watch. Two o'clock. "I haven't a speck of appetite. Slept poorly."

She aims for the house and calls over her shoulder. "Holler when you're hungry, lass."

Alone again, I slump onto the bench and lean against the trellising. This day's torrid event has cinched me tight. Like kneading fingers, the nearby stream's gurgles and the sweet fragrance of jasmine and honeysuckle soothe me.

But the storm in my mind refuses to be quelled.

Here I lounge in luxury while my brother sits in squalor just down the way. In a shack that squats in the center of a cursed piece of sod. My gut grumbles, and I wad my lightweight skirt front into two fists.

What good am I? Am I like the chameleon skittering through the vines? He darkens to his ivy surroundings and lightens in the summer-dried grass. Do I, like this lowly creature, adapt but never truly change?

The good Lord saw fit to set you on the other side of Rock Creek. For His purposes. Ma's words . . . her voice . . . swat me alert.

An idea, a sense of purpose twitters up my spine. I'll slip down to the creek after dark. Give the flycatcher's call. If Walter isn't around, or if he's passed out drunk, Donnie'll join me creekside.

Forcing myself to my feet, I trudge toward Broadview, the mansion I now call home.

Maggie greets me mid-garden with a folded scrap of paper and a broad-brimmed straw hat. "Special delivery from Blossom." She whips a turn. "I'm fixing supper."

I unfold the note from the second of Ella's five adoptive daughters.

Emergency! Mama's summerhouse! Immediately!!!!

Six exclamation points? Seems the thirteen-year-old's aflutter. Again.

My watch hands point to four and twelve. Four o'clock already?

Addie asked to speak with me before supper.

Best hurry.

CHAPTER 4

*E*ager to dispense with precocious Blossom's request, I strike out on the pebbled pathway skirting Broadview's garden. A plow and planter sit idle, and a breeze wafts the musky odor of the fertilizer silo my way. An animal skitters through tall prairie grass, and brush grabs at my simple skirt.

I swirl into Ella's summerhouse and come to a standstill.

No sign of the child. I search for a note hidden amid the honeysuckle vines—treasure hunts and mysteries, her favorite past time of late.

Have chores waylaid my young friend?

Following the path toward the Evans cottage, I pause at a fork and swipe a handkerchief across my forehead. The brutal sun extends not a speck of mercy. I release the floppy bow beneath my chin and cinch the ribbons tighter. The wide brim collapses against my cheeks, fair and freckled and apt to burn.

To the left, the split path meanders through a copse to the McFarland farm, Ella's girlhood home and where Cade lives with their parents. Might Blossom have hiked to her Grandma and Grandpa Mac's? Unlikely, considering the elderly couple's failing health.

No doubt the child's busy at the cottage. Distractions hound her, it seems.

A dog barks in the distance, the sort of yelp that signals alarm. My eyes snap to the right where the path points like an unambiguous arrow to Rock Creek.

"Help!"

Cupping my hands around my mouth, I break into a run. "Blossom!"

The Evans's canine foundling, Wally—a hulking mongrel sprouting honey-colored sprigs from head to tail—springs from the brush.

I raise my hands to ward off the distressed mutt. "Stay!"

Halting in a flurry, he all but topples me. He traces a circle around me and bounds toward the brook, baying as if to the moon.

The canine tears through the bushes, and his baying turns to sharp, staccato barks.

"Hurry, Lily!" The youngster's tone has sharpened.

I push aside the brambles and stumble onto the creek bank.

"I fell in." She sputters and clutches the fronds of river fern, her ivory skin whitening above the murky water. Her guard yips and whines and leaps into the creek alongside her.

I kneel on a rocky outcropping. "Here. Take my hand." Our fingers interlock. "I've got you." I raise her over the slippery slab, and we collapse against a great water oak.

Wally paddles downstream and claws up the muddy bank.

"You can't swim, young lady." I puff a breath through stiffened lips. "Which is why your mother insists you stay away from the creek. What're you doing down here?"

Creek water dribbles from her hairline along her cheeks and onto her sopping wet play dress. She nods toward her Brownie camera lying on its side beside her shoes and stockings. "Taking pictures. Tossed it aside just in time." Her perpetually animated tone seems to have survived her harrowing experience.

"Pictures of what?"

She shrugs. "Creek critters."

"Why, for pity's sake?"

She moves her eyes in a full circle, as if memorizing the scene. "They live in a whole other world."

Puffing in exasperation and stirring loose strands at my hairline, I bump a shoulder against hers. "A world your parents have forbidden you to visit alone." No doubt the meandering stream woos Blossom to its banks more often than any of us want to consider.

Slobbering, Wally lumbers up and halts beside us. He shakes, head to paws, and his thick fur scatters muddy droplets across my bodice and face. "Silly goose! Look what you've done now." I swipe my sleeves along my cheeks.

The mutt pants and plops onto the ground. His tongue lolls to the side, and his broad chest heaves.

Blossom snatches up her camera, aims it at the dog loafing beside her, and snaps.

I unfold her scribbled message. "You sent a dispatch worthy of six exclamation points."

She jerks around, and her eyes and mouth stretch wide. "Oh, Lily. I forgot."

I remove my hat and soft slippers. Dangling my legs over the edge, I immerse my feet in the cool water. "What's the emergency?"

"The verdict." She secures her canine friend with a leash and moves her picture-taking box away from us. "Been talking it over with Donnie." She tips her head toward the far bank.

Unease creeps up my spine. I scan left and right for signs of the murderer who claims the land just across the creek. One arm of the water oak stretches skyward and joins hands with a sycamore on the other side. A tattered rope slouches overhead, remnants of a makeshift bridge that in former days provided a daring short-cut over the bedraggled acreage and into Needham.

The gap above the bridge of my nose pinches, a line that's grown ever-more permanent of late. It defies my looking glass. "That has to stop. Walter's back."

She glances sideways. "I hear Mr. Sloat's bad. But I think he's nice."

A strand of dread curls in my middle. "Have you met him?"

"Just once." She touches the twig to the water, sending ripples in ever-widening circles. "Before he went to jail. Came crashing through the brush, hollering how he'd wallop Donnie good. But he stopped and . . . smiled at me. Made a bit of conversation."

Goosebumps pebble my skin. I rub my hands over my arms and turn to her with a scowl. "Does your mother know you're down here?"

"She thinks I'm at the summerhouse . . . with you."

"Oh, dear. Why do you lie to your mother?"

Ignoring my query, she swishes the tip of a twig in the water and flicks droplets skyward. "Donnie's different from the rest of us. He's crippled. Doesn't read or write. Or do figures. He's what folks call simple minded, isn't he?"

And easily molded by his no-account pa. "His thoughts do tend toward the simple."

"Why'd the Lord give him such a mind?"

Why, indeed? "Can't answer that."

She stares across the creek, as if imagining what might lie on the other side. "Your brother's my friend. He believes in my dreams."

"Sounds like a friend to me."

"Will Mr. Sloat take him to a doctor? And to school?"

The no-account help his son? Thanks to his neglect, Donnie was stricken with rickets. Cooped up within four clapboard walls, his mind hasn't developed. "We grown-ups will figure it out. Meanwhile, answer my question you so handily avoided. Why do you lie to your mother?"

Her lips draw into a pink drawstring pouch. "I know how she'll answer." She flicks a stream of driblets. "Sometimes I feel like running away."

This girl and her adoptive mother share not a shred of bloodline, but they possess twin independent streaks.

"You've a bright, curious mind and a sensitive spirit, Blossom Evans. Like your mother. Who, by the way, deserves the truth. Had I dreamed you'd—"

"I have a dream." She clenches my arm and angles her eyes upward, as if witnessing her vision unfolding. "Gonna be a newspaper reporter. Like you." She laces her fingers as if in prayer. "Take me to Fort Worth. I can learn from you. On your job."

Truth be told, newspaper reporting requires a level of boldness I fear I lack. I haven't shared my uncertainty with a soul, but I'm just that— uncertain. "They won't let a thirteen-year-old accompany me place to place. Besides, now that the trial ended . . ." I picture my brother's grin of expectation. Why did I mention good news? My shoulders collapse, bowing my back. "I'm not sure I'll work so far away."

The youngster releases a heavy breath, and the corners of her mouth droop. "Mama wouldn't permit it anyway. She expects a coming-out. But I'm not interested in marrying. I'm gonna see the world. Snap pictures for newspapers. Papa bought me a developing box so I can print photographs anywhere."

"A world traveler like yourself will need such a device." I wink, but unease bedevils me, camped as we are so near Sloat land. I should take my young friend home.

She lifts a nonchalant shoulder. "No one would marry me anyway. I'm skinny. Plain as a fence post. And as flat-bosomed too."

"An awkward colt often becomes a beautiful horse. Besides, you're perfectly lovely. Your hair's the color of . . ." I run a finger through a pale blonde strand draping Blossom's shoulder.

"Not copper colored like yours, that's for sure."

A lone sunbeam shoots between foliage, and her hair flares with light. "You've a patch of corn on your head."

"I what?"

"It's like corn silk. And your eyes . . ."

"Bleached. Like Papa's drawers on the line."

"For heaven's sake. Your eyes are . . . They're pale blue crystals."

"I'd rather they were like what Uncle Cade calls yours—green as the foxfire's light." She holds a hand over her chest and gazes upward as if dramatizing a romance.

My cheeks warm. This child and her uncle are cut from the same pattern—romantics, both.

I wrap an arm around my young friend. "Let's hurry home. Your mother's hosting a group of suffragists. And your father's taking you and your sisters to town for ice cream."

We replace our stockings and shoes with her mongrel friend panting in anticipation.

She points toward home. "Go, boy." Howling, he gambols through the brush and out of sight.

She slips her camera strap over her shoulder and pats the gadget. "I keep it with me." Her tone has turned ever-so-serious. "Never know when I'll find something newsworthy."

Creek critters quiet and flying creatures still. The sudden hush gives me pause. Shuddering, I glance around. "Let's get outta here." Cursed Sloat land's a stone's throw away.

CHAPTER 5

$\mathscr{R}$eturning to Broadview with a smooth brow, if not a smile, I change into a wrapper and sit at my dressing table with a brush in hand. The handle is silver, of all things.

Surely I can convince Addie to remain at Broadview. At least until the European conflict is resolved. I must corral my emotions and present my arguments in a reasoned manner.

She peeks into my bedroom. "A cold supper's prepared. It's in the ice box. Have time for a chat first?" Her hair, as dark as the Blood Rose, hangs loose around her shoulders. Her dressing gown grazes her house slippers in emerald-green folds. Lovely.

"Of course." I set aside my brush.

"See you in the study." She strides down the hallway toward the stairs.

Why the study? We always chat in her bedroom suite. Peculiar.

Tying my mane into a tail with a berry-brown ribbon, I drape it over my shoulder and descend the stairs on feet as bare as the day I was born. The carpet buries my toes in luxury.

The study lies at the end of the east wing. Its expanse of floor to ceiling windows affords early morning light for reading and writing. And in the late afternoon, it overflows into the hallway, highlighting my way.

The mistress of Broadview sits in a wing chair at a window, her tea table arranged for two. I claim her chair's twin, my curiosity stirred.

Butterflies flash beyond the window glass. An azure creature flits amid buttonbush blossoms, and scissor-tailed flycatchers swoop. The garden stretches across the lush landscape to the creek.

"Blackberry." She sips her tea with her gaze fixed on the butterfly show.

I pour a cup. A spot of cream. A lemon wafer. An embroidered napkin in my lap. I lean into the plush upholstery. "May I—"

"I have news, Lily."

I straighten, my curiosity piqued.

"As you know, I received a letter from Herr Romano some weeks ago offering me the role of Magdelone in *Amica*, small production in Milan to revive flagging interest."

"Yes. And you accepted. You're departing in two weeks."

"Three days ago, I received a telegram confirming travel arrangements."

My curiosity curdles. "I fear my grand plan to convince you to cancel your Italy trip is disintegrating. When will you leave us?"

"Thursday."

"In two days?" My tea cup rattles in its saucer.

"I delayed telling you. Due to the trial. You've had enough on your mind." She raises her palms toward the ceiling. "The jury's ruling is shameful. A crime. Still . . . I must go."

I can't imagine Broadview without my angel friend. But I've stood in her way long enough. Resting my head on the chair back, I allow my breathing to normalize. "This is the opportunity you've waited for. How long will you be away?"

Her eyes cut back to the butterfly display. "At least a year."

I press my hands over my grumbling middle. I've a distasteful lump to swallow. "I'll have my things out before you leave."

She grabs my hand with the fierceness of a trap. "You'll do nothing of the sort. This is your home. Not your temporary abode. Nor the home of a friend. *Your* home." Her remarkable eyes flash burgundy.

"Broadview was built with Fitzgerald earnings. For Fitzgerald descendants. Not Sloat. It's *your* birthright, not mine."

"A birthright I can share with whomever I please."

"Living here when you're away would be unseemly."

"To you alone, my friend." She makes her way to her fine mahogany desk. "I anticipated your response." She extracts a large envelope from the lap drawer and motions to the leather armchair at the desk. "Please join me."

With equal parts anticipation and dread warming my cheeks, I lower myself into the cushioned seat.

"Perhaps this will make my request more palatable." She removes paperwork and slides it toward me. "This gives you power of attorney over my affairs."

"What in the w—"

Her raised hand halts me. "Only you and Maggie love this estate as I do. I choose you."

"Maggie's been by your side since you were an infant. She's like a mother."

"Indeed." She gazes into space. "When Mother died, she wet-nursed me. And after Father's fatal accident, she created a real home. Far more than a housekeeper, Margaret Gallagher's all the mother I've known."

"All the more reason—"

"For your service in my absence, I'm offering a stipend. Should there be need of more, the bank will transfer funds into your account." She nudges the paperwork. "Please read it."

Addie spoke those words when she insisted I'd read Louisa Mae Alcott's *Little Women*, like it or not. She taught me to speak properly and to function admirably in social circles. Now she's asking me to sign my name to a document giving me control of Broadview.

Has she lost her mind?

"I know nothing about running an estate, friend."

"I've laid out a plan for banking and legal support. As you know, Maggie looks after the household staff. And Vernon Yancey's overseen this estate since I was a child. I need you to represent me at the monthly managerial sessions. And settle any disputes that may arise."

Ma's long-ago pronouncement surfaces, as if from a dream.

. . . the grace of Almighty God . . . set you amidst plenty. For His purposes.

Ma's God and His purposes leave me confounded.

"But any number of able businessmen would—"

"I want someone who loves Broadview as I do. That's you.

Furthermore . . ." She presents a second document. "I'm naming you my heir.

My mouth slackens further.

"And one thing more." She slips a single sheet of paper from a right-hand drawer. "This springs from love. It goes for Donnie, too."

I read and re-read the words, and my head snaps side to side, as if of its own accord. "I can't wear the Fitzgerald name. I'm not worthy."

"I'm an unmarried thirty-two-year-old woman. I have no offspring." She enumerates on her fingers. "My parents're dead. So are my grandparents. I've no siblings. I consider you my sister. So, you're my heir. I'd be honored if you'd bear my name as well."

Addie's heir and name bearer? Control of Broadview? When she opened her home nine years ago, I was a battered girl of thirteen. Illiterate, scarred, and afraid of shadows. She devoted herself to me, but can a Sloat wear the Fitzgerald name?

I double over with my head in my hands.

She whisks to my side. "I meant no offense, dear."

I fight to catch my breath. "Offense? Of course not."

Three documents lay before me: power of attorney for Broadview; a contract for services; and a single sheet of paper changing my name from Sloat to Fitzgerald.

She removes the pen's cap and holds it out. "I've signed. Will you?"

This woman taught me to write my name with a flourish. And now . . .

Grasping the fine writing implement with a trembling hand, I tap down the barrel sleeve to extend the nib. Touch the tip to the blotter. And the ink flows.

First, the power of attorney. Am I as capable as my mentor friend claims?

I move my focus to the contract. The stipend's a fortune, enough to furnish Donnie every advantage. But is Broadview my future? Or Fort Worth and a career?

My hand trembles and the pen with it as I move to the third signature line. Lily Sloat or Lily Fitzgerald? Can I discard my birth name and assume the Fitzgeralds'?

Changing my name won't alter who I am. Not a whit. Nor does my heart desire Addie's responsibilities. Broadview is her inheritance, not mine. The stipend is a fortune, but it would tie me to this place where the man I love longs for me just the other side of the rise, a love I never can claim.

The import of my decision can't be overestimated. My loved ones will be affected in varying degrees. Letting the pen fall to the carpet, I sit back and look her square in her burgundy-brown eyes. "I can't sign these. I'm sorry."

She slumps against the desk.

"Walter's loose and capable of any sort of violence. I keep Donnie away from him."

"How do you propose to do that? The good-for-nothing is his father."

"I could make a home for us far away."

"You'd leave Broadview . . . permanently?"

I square my shoulders. "If I must. For Donnie."

She returns to her desk chair. "This has been your home for nine years. It can be your ancestral home—and Donnie's."

Broadview, my *own*? Could it be a true home—not a charitable dwelling place—to someone like me? "A Sloat is hardly worthy of this estate. Fitzgeralds helped create laws. Sloats break them and run."

"According to our dear Irish surrogate mother, 'No matter how tall— or short—your parents, you must do your own growing.'"

We snicker at the housekeeper's proverb in spite of the serious subject matter.

"I can never be sure of Donnie's safety with Walter nearby. So I'll take him with me."

She rests her head on the tufted chair back. "I wouldn't ask you to give up your dream. My attorney has agreed to assume the role if you decline."

Indeed. Such a professional can trusted with everything she owns.

"I'm leaving in two days." She swooshes around the desk, and we embrace as sisters. her chest trembles in sobs, and moisture bleeds onto my shoulder.

"I love you and Broadview, but Donnie's on the brink of manhood. His future will be little changed from his past without an education. I have an idea or two other than a tutor at Broadview."

She holds my face in her hands. "I know."

"You do?"

"I know *you*. Family comes first. But I insist on the stipend."

"But—-"

"For Donnie."

I expel my relief. "I won't dip into it unless I must. I'll be earning a salary." I glance down at my hands and the hangnail I've been worrying. "I can't wear the Fitzgerald name."

She inhales audibly. "And why not?"

"Sloat's the name I was born with. Like it or not, Sloat blood runs through my veins. Fancy clothes and name can't change that. Besides, I'd be pretending."

She plucks a kerchief from a pocket. "If you insist . . . May the Lord bless and keep you."

Do I pray the same? Would her Lord hear me? "Please be careful in that foreign country. I don't know what I'd do if . . ." Words fail me.

In my bedroom alone, I question my decision, and my mind races. What's best for Donnie? Should I abandon my own dream to remain at Broadview? Or head to Fort Worth for a career I fear I haven't the stomach for?

The little mocker chirrup-chirrups outside, but he offers no wisdom.

Still, I must remain steadfast.

CHAPTER 6

*D*eep in the night, I fling aside the sheet. I've lain between lavender-scented bed linens as long as I can bear.

Placing my bare feet on the cool oak floor, I don a split skirt. Button my shirtwaist. And tiptoe to the stairs.

At the clink of brass fittings and a gentle whir, I pause with a hand on the banister. The regulator wall clock strikes once. Ten more will muffle my footsteps. I make short work of the remaining treads, avoiding those I've learned will complain.

Moonlight spills through the front sidelights, brightening my way across the foyer. No time for shoes. And no need. I'm a sharecropper's daughter.

With a turn of the brass knob, I slip onto the veranda.

A sliver of light peeks from between Sabina's closed drapes. I wait, my senses sharpened. The light fades and blinks out.

Padding along the broad porch, I round the corner. Pause. Listen.

Critters' songs blanket the night scape. Tree frogs. Cicadas. Crickets. The *hoo* of an owl. A coyote's *yip* to the south.

As a girl I lay awake many a night in the old shack, listening to creatures on both sides of the creek. They made the same sounds, even harmonized.

Why can't human beings do the same?

Remembering my brother in Walter's clutches, I run like my mare Daisy. Through the garden. Across the pasture. Down a bridle path. And a footpath.

A thicket has long hidden Sloat acreage from Fitzgerald, Evans, and McFarland eyes. But in times past, when Walter was away or stone drunk, Ma, Donnie, and I sat on opposite banks and visited.

Even the densest grove can't bar love.

Shoving aside brush for the second time today, I step into the tranquil world of Rock Creek. The brook babbles over boulders farther upstream. It swishes around hairpin curves and swirls in eddies where water abuts soil, a backdrop to the night songs of the hovering residents.

I scale a buckeye to a low-hanging branch. Cup my hands around my mouth. Mimic the scissor-tailed flycatcher's call. Wait. And call again.

The brush rattles, and Donnie emerges on the far bank. The moon shows me the crippled brother I love. His skin, sun-darkened to shades of roasted black walnut shells, blends into the shadows. His eyes are blinking fireflies.

As thin and fragile as a dry reed, he plops to the bare sod near a black haw shrub. "What're you doin' here?" His meager voice spans the night stillness with ease.

"Checking on you."

"I'm fair to middlin', I reckon." He inhales a stiff, noisy breath. "What's the good news you promised?"

"It didn't develop as I thought it would. I'm sorry."

"Ain't nothin' to be sorry for. Good news is plumb hard to come by some days."

"I'm scared spitless for you, brother."

He snaps a black haw twig. "Nothin' to be scared of 'round here, Lil'." He chuckles. "No such thing as a boogeyman."

I perch on one bank; my loved one sits on the other. And Rock Creek, as stubborn as the locks on women's clubs' doors, yields not an inch between us. "Cross over, Donnie. Come to me."

"Why should I? Pa and me're goin' into bi'ness. He's off to Tulsa tomorrow. And then we're packin' to Fort Worth."

I jolt, and my perch bounces like a fishing bobber. "I won't let you."

Donnie holds his body taut. "Don't come over here. Pa's shotgun's at the ready."

"I'll never call the man Pa again."

"Ma said he's my pa, and I was to act like it. No matter what."

A finger of guilt picks at my scabbed-over innards. "But he killed Ma."

"Pa says you lied. Jury said so too."

How was I to counter? "I saw it with my own eyes."

"But Pa—"

"He's a liar. And a murderer."

"I won't listen. Hush up." Bending his curved legs beneath him, he sits on his haunches.

"All right. Have it your way. Where's Walter now?"

"Sleepin'."

"Drunk?"

He shrugs.

"Let me help you."

"Don't reckon I need your help, Lil', what with Pa tendin' to bi'ness."

"I might as well be whistling jigs to a milestone as to be talking sense to you."

"Don't know nothin' 'bout no milestones." Grabbing a haw branch, he stands.

"There may still be time for your legs to straighten a bit. You're not quite grown. If you were to be fed nutritious meals—"

"Corn pone does me fine."

"The right food'll provide what your bent legs need."

"Pa's gettin' me a operation. And I'm gonna dance a jig."

My head falls forward. The bark scratches my cheek. "Will nothing change your mind?"

"Naw."

"Don't leave without talking with me again. Promise?"

"Do my best. Ma'd want me to." His voice thins as he melts into the murky gloom.

"Can't depend on that man's promises, Donnie Sloat! I'll make you understand."

The brittle rattle of brush serves as my brother's response.

The wrong committed in the courtroom must be righted and this innocent boy championed. I must find a way to stop the insanity.

Maggie awaits me in the garden with lantern in hand. "Where've you been, my girl?"

"Checking on Donnie. Sorry if I woke you."

Gathering me under an arm, she turns toward the house. "Insomnia's the blight of old age. Let's have a cup of chamomile. 'Twill soothe our spirits."

"They're leaving."

"Who?"

"Donnie and Walter."

"Where to, in heaven's name?"

"Fort Worth."

"Cowtown." Her pace slows. "That's where Sabina lived."

I've been spared the details of the heartache Sabina brought her mother, but the furrows around Maggie's eyes have deepened in recent years.

The querulous young woman surprises us at the back doorway. Attired in her azure dressing gown, she strikes me as a cranky blue jay. Her gown's flimsy fabric swirls in the night breeze, revealing her rawboned shape. "What nefarious activities have you two been into?"

Her mother's body tenses. "I'll not stand for your derision."

"Look at you, Mother." Sabina lets loose a humorless chuckle. "You're wrapping your arm around the infamous false accuser. You'll be the talk of the town."

"Enough of the barbs, daughter. 'Tis time for peace. If it can be had."

The crotchety jay flounces away with a pointed-beak glance over her shoulder.

In the kitchen, I'm struck by the aroma of the morrow's rising bread, at once fomenting and soothing. Rather like the day's emotions.

Maggie settles just-washed teacups into the oak cupboard, rattling the fine porcelain. I compare favorably to the solid stoneware pieces. Not so,

Donnie, as fragile as delicate bone china that lets the light show through. Tugging off my ragged shawl, Ma's patchwork of tatters, I'm reminded of the mishmash of blotches I conceal. Neither would garner praise in the Needham's Women's Club. How do I prevent such maltreatment of my brother? He won't listen. And Walter's about to whisk him away besides.

I join her at the table. "How do you retain your gentleness before Sabina's . . ."

"Heartlessness?" She sets her cup in its saucer and searches my features. "How did your mother?"

Warmth rises from my midriff to my face. "For love." Of course. "I'm sorry."

"Nay, 'tis I who's sorry. Sorry for my daughter's spitefulness. You're a dear, and she has no call." She pats her lips with a napkin.

I blow a steady breath over my cup, scattering tendrils of steam. "Where's cruelty born?"

"From the devil himself. Parent abuses child; child grows to do the same—unlike yourself." Focusing beyond me, she traces her cup's rim with a fingertip. Do the shadows conceal her distant secrets? "Liquor gets the best of some. Others, like my daughter, God alone knows."

"I'd be her friend if she'd let me."

"You and my daughter live in the same house, but you're worlds apart in spirit." Her gaze wraps me in tenderness. "Since my daughter returned from Texas, her bitterness has deepened."

"I'm sorry for you. And for her." I swallow a turnip-sized lump in my throat.

She flicks away my concern. "Enough pondering. Let's enjoy our tea."

Soon the entry grandfather clock strikes midnight, and we set our dishes into the sink.

She gives me a one-armed hug. "I'm off to bed. Sleep well, child."

In my four-poster bed, I yank the sheets to my chin, pondering my life. Ella snatched me from a lion's jaws and taught me to read. Addie wrapped me in sachet-scented sheets and sent me to college. All the while, I've not known fear. Until today.

Staring past the gloom around my bed, I focus on the bead board ceiling. Donnie's face appears. His eyes, chunks of ebony, fill. Tears creep over pebble-sized freckles and fall in great lobs onto his scrawny chest.

I grew careless while in college in Texas. Didn't protect my loved ones. Shall I simply hold onto my regret? Or do something?

Donnie insists Walter is taking him to Fort Worth. And *Caller* has offered me a position, a task I'm not sure I have the stomach for, but I'll accept for my brother. Bits of ideas attach to one another, slivers of steel drawn to a magnet.

"Keep your intentions a mystery, God of my mother." I claim a double portion of night air and heave it out. "I'll work out my own plan."

CHAPTER 7

I don my dressing gown and greet the morning at my window. Scissor-tailed flycatchers chitter and swoop in the garden, scooping up their breakfast buffet—flies, mosquitoes, and nameless midges. Where will I find views like this apart from Broadview?

"You're leaving *tomorrow*? How can you?" Sabina's shriek blasts from the kitchen up the stairs, obliterating the agreeable aroma of frying bacon.

Cringing, I tighten my sash and turn from the pleasant outdoor scene. No doubt breakfast is prepared and growing cold. I must hurry.

"Not giving us much notice, are you?" Silence. "Well? Answer me." The household's resident blue jay is jabbering at her provider, for pity's sake.

I pause on the second-floor landing. Should I remain upstairs and avoid the woman's fury? She mentioned a Women's Club appointment, so she might be leaving soon. Still, I'd like to discuss my plans with Addie and Maggie, and I haven't much time.

"Can't be helped." Addie's tone conveys a hint of irritation.

Sabina snorts. "Thankfully, I've lived under this roof all my life. So I know how things are done. I'll assure all runs smoothly."

I clench the balustrade and creep down the carpeted treads.

"That'd be a fine kettle of fish." Her mother mutters the words, as if to herself.

"What's that, Mother?" The woman's tone is sharp edged, caustic.

"Daughter, this estate requires—"

"I know what it requires. It's my home, after all. Furthermore, a fine school back East is my alma mater. I've a head for business."

"I've asked Lily to oversee Broadview." Addie speaks in a conciliatory tone.

"A dirt-poor sharecropper? A lousy Sloat?"

"I'd appreciate a cooperative attitude on my last day at home. Lily has declined. So my attorney will have charge."

"A hint is sufficient for the wise, daughter."

"So now I'm an uncooperative fool?"

"You're putting words into our mouths. Calm down. Can't you support Addie, the woman who's provided for you all your life?"

My presence would only add to the turmoil. I turn to retrace my steps.

"I'll calm down when I'm given some respect. Harboring this foul—"

"I'll not have you speaking ill of that dear girl upstairs. Shall I call her?" Addie's volume has risen.

Mounting the stairs in leaps, I halt on the landing.

"For pity's sake. Has that Sloat foundling stolen your good sense?"

"Daughter, you know better—"

"I do know better, Mother. It's you two who don't."

"That's it!" A fist pounds the table. "I love you, but I won't allow your impudence. Be gone before I lose every shred of control."

Bless Maggie, torn between two daughters she loves.

Sabina stomps outside, and the door slams shut.

I peek out the window that brightens the landing. Sabina's marching toward the horse barn pounding the air with her fists. Hopefully she'll postpone her poor mare's currying.

"What's behind her animosity?"

"'Tis anger for herself, I fear. She who loses her reputation loses her shame."

Venturing into the kitchen, I find a downcast Addie at the table and Maggie adding steaming water to the sink. "Sounds like Europe's not the only battle site this morning. Why all the ruckus?" I pour my coffee and fill a plate with scrambled eggs and crumbled sausage.

Maggie turns from the sink. "Morning, lass."

I claim a chair at the table and look from one to the other. "What's behind Sabina's animosity?"

"'Tis anger for herself, I fear," dear Maggie mutters as if to herself. "She who loses her reputation loses her shame."

Addie expels a deep breath, shaking her head and planting an elbow on the table. "Can't I leave for Italy knowing this household is at peace?"

"No peace can be found without unity, lass."

Fiery Sabina represents disunity in spades.

How am I to maneuver the strife? I stir cream into my coffee, pondering the quandary. "Perhaps I should leave right away. For the sake of unity."

"What?" Addie's eyebrows pinch together, and her back straightens, as if for onslaught.

"And for peace."

"*You* aren't the problem." She lunges to her feet and stomps toward her study. "I've appointments in town."

My appetite destroyed, I nudge cold scrambled eggs from one side of my plate to the other. "Should I try to reason with her?"

Maggie spoons a generous helping of fruit onto my plate and chuckles. "Don't give cherries to pigs or advice to fools."

I smile at the dear woman. "Much of life would be tasteless without your Irish seasoning. Thank you." I run a fingertip along my cup's rim. "You deserve a home at peace. Your daughter's bone of your bone. You belong together. I can care for myself."

"Broadview is your home, too, lass."

"Let's discuss this later. Judge Fulbright sees unscheduled clients beginning at eight o'clock."

She leaves off questions about my visit to the judge and returns to her kitchen chores, her expression pensive.

What a perfectly miserable morning. And it isn't yet seven o'clock.

Vexed, I return to my room with my mind aswirl and my bag of worries bulging. There's the outrageous verdict. Donnie's welfare and my planned request of Judge Fulbright. Sabina and Maggie. Addie's venture into danger. My oversight of Broadview. Even Blossom.

I mustn't let household quarrels delay me.

Making quick work of a bath, I consider my wardrobe choices. A torrid day such as this one calls for lightweight cotton. The peacock-blue blouse and simple skirt make a sensible choice. And provide the right amount of dignity.

Slipping my feet into plain pumps, I lift my jewelry box and remove a tray. A three-emerald ring lies alone in a velvet-lined compartment. Cade's gift three Christmases past, it was intended as a friendship, for-get-me-not piece while I was away at college. But living among society girls woke me up, revealed the wide the chasm between us. I've not worn it since I returned from Texas. Hasn't seemed right, some how.

The jewels stir turmoil in my heart.

Returning the finery to its private nook, I tug on navy cotton gloves and inspect my reflection in the floor mirror. Is the blue too bold? The bun at the back of my neck too loose?

I stretch to my full height and raise my chin. No, it's perfect.

"Well, well," Sabina purrs behind me. "Where's our little humming-bird off to?"

I whirl toward her. "Why must you do that?"

"Do what? Notice you?" Her gray eyes swallow the light.

I snatch a straw headpiece from an armoire hook and attach it with a hat pin. "I apologize. I'm jittery."

"What in the world for?"

Will it matter if she knows my destination? How can she interfere in my plans?

"I'm speaking with Judge Fulbright." I aim for a casual tone as I wrap my handbag's braided strap over my shoulder.

She chuckles. "Didn't get enough of the man in the courtroom?"

This woman won't exasperate me. "It's a matter altogether different."

"So mysterious. Perhaps I should inquire elsewhere."

I reach for her. "Please don't."

Her eyes constrict to slits. "What can be so important Wilson

Fulbright would give Lily Sloat the first hour of his day?"

I brush past her into the hallway. "I'm getting my brother out of Walter Sloat's reach."

Her footsteps follow. "Why would a man of influence listen to a nobody?"

Why, indeed?

I wheel around. "I've learned a host of lessons from Adelaide Fitzgerald—like how to speak properly."

She folds her arms and slants an eyebrow.

"She trained me to sit at a table and use a napkin. And speak to people of importance."

"Without her, you'd still be barefoot and pulling a cotton sack."

I lift a forefinger. And pause. What's the good in a pointed finger? Best aim for peace. I entwine my fingers at my waist. "I towed a cotton sack . . . when I was a girl. Now I sport hand-tailored dresses. But either way, I matter. Same as you.

"Now, please excuse me." Tucking paperwork into my satchel, I snap it shut and brush past my tormentor. My skirt swishes against the balustrade and my insides wobble, jelly-like, but I descend the stairs with my spine erect.

A white Buick roadster awaits me in the drive. Will I ever feel comfortable with luxury? Or with generous gifts like this one?

Pitching my satchel and purse onto the front passenger seat, I plop inside and slam the door. My hat wobbles, and I reattach the long pin.

Heat has risen from my belly and pooled on my face. No need to inspect my reflection in a mirror. Two bright spots will linger on my cheeks well into today.

I must catch Judge Fulbright before his first appointment. I check the dash clock. A quarter of eight. Not a minute to spare.

"Come in, Miss Sloat." Judge Fulbright greets me from his office doorway.

"Thank you for seeing me, sir." I pause to marshal my confidence. "Please call me Lily."

"Lily it is." He gestures to a pair of tufted-leather armchairs facing his desk.

Seated with satchel at my feet and handbag on my lap, I gaze around the room. How delightful, the redolence of old leather. Book bindings. And pipe tobacco. My eyes feast on the three walls of floor-to-ceiling bookcases, surely as much knowledge of the law as can be found in all of Oklahoma.

But does the man possess an equal measure of wisdom?

The jurist grabs the chair beside me. "I've received more visitors from your locale this morning than in months. Miss Fitzgerald just left."

"Addie?"

He nods but keeps his counsel.

I put aside my puzzlement. No time for questions.

"What can I do for you, Lily?"

My fingers tighten around my purse. "It's my brother, Donnie."

"You have a brother?"

"Yes. He's kept at home most of the time."

He leans forward with his elbows on the arms of his chair. "And?"

"He's in danger."

"From whom?" His gaze tightens.

"Walter."

"Your father?"

"He's Walter to me."

"I understand." He lowers his eyes. "I've expressed my opinion of the man." He clears his throat and brings his gaze back to mine. "Does this have anything to do with the verdict?"

"Only indirectly." I catch the inside of a cheek between my teeth.

"Go on." The dark pupils of his steel-gray eyes flash.

"I ask to be named Donnie's guardian."

He leans forward, his gaze unwavering. "On what grounds?"

"Walter's a cruel drunk."

"You made that clear at the trial. Do you have new information?"

I pause for a fortifying breath. Angling my head to the side, I open the neck of my bodice, exposing the dark welt. "He used a horse whip on me." Shame tugs my head lower. "There are more besides, products of a whittling tool and a branding iron."

He steeples his fingers at his chin and gazes at the ceiling. "Why did you not testify to this in court?"

I stare at my gloved hands. A decorative stitch is coming loose. Will I come apart too?

"You weren't here nine years ago, Judge . . . when Walter beat me to the edge of death."

His shoulders round, collapsing his proud posture. His eyes close, and his fingers knead his lined brow. "Why wasn't he arrested back then?"

"My mother and the sheriff worked out an understanding."

"What sort of understanding?"

"Charges were dropped. In exchange, he let me live with Ella McFarland."

Judge Fulbright's hands fist on the arm rests, and his jaws clench.

I lower my head at a renewed wave of remorse. "I was too ashamed to share . . . his mistreatment of me . . . in open court." I straighten and lift my chin. "I never dreamed he would be acquitted."

His gaze roves the rows of law books. "How old are you, Lily?"

"Twenty-two."

"And your brother?"

"Nineteen."

He grunts and runs a fist over his whiskers. His lips draw into a pouch. "Not yet twenty-one. Still . . . he's all but grown."

"Not really. Donnie's . . . impaired."

"In what way?"

"He has the mind of a ten-year-old." I curl my handbag's strap around my fingers.

"Granting guardianship to an unmarried woman when a parent lives is unorthodox." He taps a finger on a knee. "Have you asked Donnie to live with you?"

I lower my gaze. "He refuses."

"Why?"

"He thinks Walter'll get him an operation. To straighten his legs." My cheeks burn. "Walter failed to put decent food on the table. And Donnie suffered from rickets."

The judge's eyebrows lift, creating beds of furrows on his forehead. "How do you propose to care for your brother? You have a connection with a newspaper in Fort Worth, if I remember right. Are you employed as a reporter?"

"Not exactly." I clear my throat and snatch a letter of intent from my satchel. "I interned at *Caller*." Enthusiasm for this position has been trickling from me, but I staunch the leak with a hiked chin and a mind anchored on my brother. "They offered me a position."

"If your employment isn't yet settled . . ."

"On the other hand . . . " I show him the paperwork. "Adelaide's going to Italy. She asked me to assume power of attorney over Broadview. I declined, but if remaining at Broadview improves my case for guardianship, I'll do so."

He scans the document. "Miss Fitzgerald thinks highly of you. Are you willing to forego your newspaper plans?"

I snap a nod. "I will."

He gestures left and right in an arc. "No matter my personal opinion of Mr. Sloat, I must abide by the law."

"I understand, sir."

"Before I can remove an underaged boy from his home . . . aged nine or nineteen . . . I must be satisfied it's unlivable. I must speak with the boy."

"Walter's in Tulsa now. Donnie's alone."

Standing, he tugs down his vest. "Time to visit then." He cancels his morning appointments and escorts me to his four-seater Oldsmobile. He tosses his Homburg into the back and roosts in the driver's seat.

"It's best Sheriff Dawson accompanies us." He parks alongside the sheriff's office and hops out. "Won't be but a minute."

I stuff my gloves into my satchel and run the back of my hand across my damp forehead. If I'd testified to Walter's treatment of me . . . to everything, Donnie might be safe at Broadview.

But I'll make it right today.

The two men step from the sheriff's office to the brick walkway. Nodding to me, Sheriff Dawson adjusts his Stetson and mounts his horse.

Sitting straight as his Fiberloid collar, the judge aims his Olds toward the Sloat place.

CHAPTER 8

$\mathcal{R}$uts crease the overgrown drive and test the Oldsmobile's springs. The dirt troughs carve a lopsided grin around the shanty's face.

Judge Fulbright brakes, and a dust cloud billows around us. Sheriff Dawson reins in and dismounts. No sign of Walter's old truck.

"The place has shrunken." I've viewed it from the back side and through brush and the veil of night the past nine years.

"Your vision has expanded."

"Soil's as stone hard as ever. Still no sign of a garden."

The lawman comes alongside the car. "Walter Sloat ought to be ashamed of himself."

I nod. "For this and much more."

A scrawny rooster raises his head and eyes us. With a twist of his neck, he resumes his meandering around a barren chicken yard.

This hovel was once my home? The sight threatens to shroud me in darkness, but I refuse to let the old shack bring me down. I'm here for Donnie.

My escort steps past the car's running board and retrieves his valise from the back seat. I step out and scan right to left and back again, the scene at once family and stranger.

Attired in faded, over-sized shirt and patched trousers rolled into wide cuffs, Donnie steps off the stoop, and the screen slaps shut.

I run to my brother and embrace his sharp-angled frame. "I've missed you."

"Better git, Lil'. Pa said—"

"This is Judge Fulbright, Donnie. And Sheriff Dawson."

The law officer removes his hat and proffers a hand. "Pleased to make your acquaintance, Mr. Sloat."

Donnie ducks his head and picks at a button's loose thread.

"May we come in?"

"Nobody darkens our door when Pa ain't around."

The lawman gestures backward with his hat. "A *judge* has come calling. That's different."

"Different how?"

"Gotta do what an officer of the court requires."

"I have to disobey my pa? "

"Either answer our questions here and now. Or I'll take you into town."

Donnie's tongue glides between his cheek and teeth, creating a bulge that circles left and right. Whirling, he flings open the screen and merges with the dim interior.

The judge grabs the screen door before it can swat shut and directs me inside with a nod of his head.

I gather myself and enter the old shack.

A familiar stench greets me. Accumulated grime. Overripe food scraps. And under-tended floorboards. Was this Ella's experience the first time she visited me?

The sun lays a shaft of light across the worn-smooth floor I swept as a girl.

What's happened to the fine furniture Broadview supplied four Christmases past? No doubt Walter sold it, leaving little else changed. Same grimy firebox and hearth. Mattresses on the floor. Homespun garments on hooks. Ma's shift, threadbare as an old tea towel.

My heart twists.

Donnie perches on an upended log at the three-legged table I wiped clean for years. Nail kegs still support the table top that serves as a door in winter. A yellowed-glass bottle in the center sprouts a handful of wildflowers.

Four years ago, Addie and Maggie supplied a solid table and a fine bed, Christmas gifts. But Walter had gotten his hands on them.

The men hang their hats on wooden pegs. They choose two of three sycamore chairs and gesture for me to follow suit.

I ease into the third chair. The dim interior thickens with the weight of years and tears. My straw hat with the simple ribbons has assumed the density of an anvil, forcing my head downward. Unpinning the headpiece, I snatch it by its brim and fan.

"We can have us a drink, if you're of a mind to." Donnie thumbs toward the pump.

The judge smiles. "I need to wet my whistle."

"I'll get it." Facing the old memories head on, I scoot to the tomato crate nailed to the wall, two chipped glasses and two tin mugs its sole occupants. Half-empty bean and rice sacks slouch below it. Wild onions and a potato have sprouted inside a basket woven from dried reeds.

I lay my hat atop the crate. Lifting a glass to the light, I smile. Donnie washed them. He can do little about the flies crawling through the torn screen. Years ago, I paid no heed to the creatures. Now I recoil. How can I serve these gentlemen in unsanitary conditions?

I remove the wash pan from the wall and place it under the pump head. Heaving the handle, I rinse the glasses and cups, fill them with well water, and place them on the table.

"Where's your father?" Judge Fulbright lifts a beaker to his mouth.

"Gone to Tulsa."

"He leave you often?" Sweat inches down the man's temple and into his whiskers.

"Why not? I'm near full growed."

The older man downs the water in gulps that bob his Adam's apple and wipes his mouth with a handkerchief. "How do you feed yourself when your father's away?" He opens his satchel and lays writing materials on the table.

"Slingshot. Fishing line." Donnie nods to the burlap sacks. "Beans. And corn pone."

The jurist scrawls in a ledger. "Ever have milk?"

"Nanny goat out yonder gives a tad. When there's rain and Indian grass grows tall."

"Any vegetables and fruit?"

My brother and I exchange glances, and I'm unable to suppress a wry grin. Clearly, this man wasn't reared a sharecropper's son. "Still fix collard greens, Donnie? Chickasaw plums?"

"Ever now and again. And there's what I work for in McFarland fields."

The judge harrumphs. "Seasonal, at best. You read and write?"

"Naw. Pa ain't never seen the need."

"Oklahoma has compulsory education laws."

"Com . . . What's that again?"

"Lads like yourself are to attend school. It's the law." He leans forward with an elbow on the table. "Has your father ever struck you? Not a swat to your backside. Has he ever struck you with a fist or something else?"

Donnie's skin reddens. "Pa ain't hurt me none."

"I need the truth." The man's tone has assumed an edge of authority.

Dark-lashed eyelids ease upward, and slivers of light flash bright black in the pupils. "Why you asking? Pa in trouble?"

He waves away the question. "Our job is to assure your safety."

Donnie's eyes flick side to side. A deep furrow plows across his brow.

I refuse to back down. "Answer, brother."

Donnie pushes to his feet and waddles to the doorway. Sunlight casts the shadow of his legs, like parentheses, on the pine planks.

Are you watching, Ma's God? Do You care?

Donnie turns back and faces us. "Don't wanna leave Pa."

I collapse into the chair back with my face in my hands. I can't let mulishness go unchallenged. "He killed Ma. Almost killed me. You'll be next."

"Like I told you before, Ma taught me better 'n to desert my pa."

Judge Fulbright clears his throat. "Would you give us men some privacy, Lily?"

I stiffen. "Why—"

"Wait outside." He glances around the one-room cabin. "Or by the hearth."

Donnie plops down at the table with his chin hiked and his shoulders stiff. But a smile bunches his cheeks—a *smile* of all things. At a time like this? The three men huddle around the table, mumbling.

A heavy darkness descends. Inexplicably dizzy, I stagger. This house brings back memories that rattle like nails in a tin box.

Nabbing a swatch of broomcorn, I swipe at ashes in the firebox. I cough and stumble to an open window, and my lungs seize clean air. My head clears, and I return to the corner beside the hearth, the limited world I inhabited as a girl.

The faded outline of what once sat beside the hearth—Ma's sea chest—encircles me. She'd never been anywhere near the sea, so I question its origin. Supposedly handed down from a distant relative, it has sat like forgotten kinfolk as long as I can remember.

Time to open the chest . . .

I turn back to Donnie. "Where's the chest?"

"Ma said take care of it for Lil'. Moved it out yonder to the coop. Key's on a nail."

Key's in the cleft of the rock, Lil'. Christmastime 1910.

"The coop's not much better than under a tree."

"Pa was gonna chop it up for firewood."

Cogitating, I cross my arms on the wooden plank that serves as a mantel, half listening to the drone of conversation.

Ma showed me the contents that snowy Christmas Eve of 1910. Has Walter discovered her keepsakes and destroyed them? Perhaps I should investigate.

Slipping outside, I enter the lean-to, and the heavy, earthy aroma of a chicken coop greets me. I allow my eyes to adjust to the dimness and nab the key, the same one Ma hid years ago in the cranny beneath a window seal, her cleft of the rock.

Donnie has turned the old coffer into a roosting ledge for a trio of bedraggled setting hens. Their eggs have helped keep him alive, so I don't begrudge them the space. I shoo them away and plunk down their nesting boxes.

Working the trunk away from the wall, I shove it into a patch of light and run my hands along the lid. It's the same old chest I opened three Christmases ago. The wood has darkened. Scratches mar what once was a smooth surface, but some long-ago bog darkened the wood and made it almost indestructible.

I trace the carving in the lid:

RLD 1775

My family name's been trampled by time. Ma whispered words, as if they were stolen secrets. Someone named Rachel owned the chest. But Ma was ill. Time was short. And the tale slipped away with the years.

Now Walter Sloat has trampled our family name to dust.

The key turns the lock with a rasp and a clunk. I lift the lid, and the old trunk's mouth gapes through a haze of dust motes.

I remember the contents, remnants of a former life in a tumbled array. The dogeared Bible. Finely stitched quilts. Trimmed and embroidered handwork.

A mound of baby clothes. A stuffed doll with spool arms and legs.

The needlepoint miser's purse and cameo brooch I discovered in these depths years past now lie in my jewelry box at Broadview. For scooped-neckline bodices, I tie the carved ivory image at my throat covering the clot of scarring.

As before, I wonder where these items come from. Are they part of Ma's roots? And why did I not care when she lived?

But time's fleeting. I'll examine these items later. I close and lock the lid, and air surges. The old trunk has maintained a seal. But the contents won't last forever. Should I cart it to Broadview?

This sea chest is yours, Lil'. Ma made her intentions clear.

Puzzling anew over my find, I button the key into a skirt pocket and shuffle back to the old house.

Judge Fulbright's voice brings me to a halt at the stoop. "I admire your loyalty, lad. Uncommon in a young person."

"But we have a duty to keep you safe." The sheriff has stepped in, his tone gruff.

"Your sister has petitioned the court for your custody."

"Them's fancy words, Judge. What do they mean?"

"You'd live with her. But you'd have to cooperate."

"Co . . . Operate." Improved humor brightens my brother's tone. "Pa's gonna get a doctor to operate on my legs."

I scramble inside, no longer able to corral my emotions. "This is your chance to be free of . . ." I gesture to the surroundings. "This pigsty."

Donnie scowls. "Ma lived here. She never called it a pig pen."

My brother's observation stuns and shames me to silence, but I recover straightaway. "Ma—"

"He's your *pa*, I know." I lift pleading hands. "But he'll kill you if you don't—"

"Like I said, he ain't hurt me."

"What do you call the condition of your legs?" Crumbling into a chair, I cross my arms on the table and lay my head atop them.

How can I reason with a limited mind like Donnie's?

Sheriff Dawson's gaze tightens. "Need I remind you of what your sister endured several years ago?"

"Naw."

"It's by the grace of God she lived."

Donnie's chin quivers in a single spot. The tremor inches to his lips. He brings his elbows to the table and covers his face with his hands. His shoulders shake. Teardrops creep between his fingers and splat onto the table.

I wrap my arms around my brother. How frail. A front tooth is chipped. "Please hear us. Pa or no pa, this place isn't safe."

He leans toward me. "Ain't right to leave Pa. 'Sides, he's gonna get my legs fixed."

Judge Fulbright sighs as if he carries an anvil in his lungs. "Young man?"

Donnie swipes the back of a hand across his nose, smearing mucous. "Yes sir?"

"Promise me any time you feel afraid, you'll let your sister know."

"I reckon I can do that."

"Mighty fine. I'll be checking on you." He returns his supplies to his office satchel. "We must be going. I've afternoon appointments waiting."

"That old trunk." I draw the man's attention to the chicken coop. "Mind hauling it to Broadview?"

"My pleasure." He snatches his hat and steps outside.

The men wedge the old heirloom into the Olds's back seat. The sheriff mounts his stead, and the judge starts the Olds engine. "Ready, Lily?"

I pause before speaking. "I won't be going back with you."

CHAPTER 9

"Where you goin', Lil'?" Donnie bends his head to the side as if confused.

"Thought we'd sit at the creek awhile." Might I coax him across?

"Why you wanna do that?"

"Why not?" I shrug. "It's cool down there." I dab a kerchief above my upper lip. What I'd give for a breeze.

The judge scratches his neck. "Your car's at my office. I'll come get you later on."

"No need. I'll walk into town."

He points to my feet. "In those fine shoes?"

"No. Barefoot." I remove my shoes and toss them into his Olds.

Sheriff Dawson winces. "You propose walking down Main Street . . . barefoot?"

"That's how folks view me anyway."

"You're wrong, Miss Lily." He moves his focus to my brother, who's doodling a bare toe in the dirt. "Your father's gone to Tulsa, son?"

"Left 'fore sunup." Donnie continues his toe drawing.

The men exchange glances. Clear their throats. And share reluctant nods.

I flash a confident smile. "Thank you for your concern, gentlemen, but we're fine."

The men depart, and Donnie retrieves a blackjack walking stick he whittled himself. Tagged by some as hard as cast iron, the wood matches Donnie's will.

I consider changing into Ma's old shift but decide against it. I'll leave the garment where she last hung it.

"Ain't crossin' over, Lil'." Donnie insists as we stroll. Cord grass and bee balm have all but overtaken the path.

"I understand."

"Don't be thinking to change my mind."

"I won't." But I never promised I'd not entice you, brother mine.

We push aside the thick brush and step onto the creek bank. Water rushes from an underground spring farther upstream, but it meanders among reeds along the horseshoe enclosing Sloat acreage.

Frogs and crickets halt their racket. The world holds its breath, it seems.

I point to a rocky, moss-covered outcropping. "Let's sit."

Setting his cane to the side, Donnie plops down and rolls his cuffs to his knees.

I turn my eyes from his bowed legs. He hasn't grown to the size of most nineteen-year-olds. But perhaps there's still time.

We dangle our legs over the ledge with our feet in the water. "Ahh. Still cool."

Across the way lies the spot where Blossom and I spoke. Was it only yesterday?

"You visit with Blossom here, brother?"

He scowls. "Where'd you get that idea?"

"She told me."

He harrumphs. "Was to be our secret."

I lean against him. "I won't tell."

"I hear there's a big world out yonder." He tips his head toward the far bank.

A shaft of sunlight breaks through the foliage. "Indeed."

"You ain't gonna get me into that world. Scares me."

"It's only different. I'll introduce you a little at a time."

He tosses me a rare smile and stirs the water with a toe.

I swat a mosquito. "Blossom told me about your damselflies. You've learned a great deal on this rocky perch."

"See them circles?" He nods to a placid pool etched with round ripples. "Damsels're dancin'. I'm gonna dance like that one day. After my operation."

Walter and that operation again. "Oh, Donnie. Come with me. With proper nutrition, there's no telling—"

The putter of an engine snaps our heads around.

"What's that, Lil'?"

"An automobile. Could be Judge Fulbright. We'd best—"

The car engine dies, and a whine of rusty door hinges keens in the distance. Never knew Walter to oil them.

The judge wouldn't walk inside with no one around.

Has someone made themselves at home?

The silence stretches thin.

The door gives another screech.

"Donnie!" Walter shouts.

My brother grabs my forearm. "It's Pa."

"Gonna tan your hide, boy!" Walter's graveled voice bodes ill.

"I'll look yonder in the shed." I recognize the voice. It's the jury foreman. He's associating openly with Walter?

"I'll check the creek."

Donnie wrenches away. "He's coming."

"Hurry!" I jump into the creek and motion for him to follow. My skirt billows around my waist.

"No." He folds his legs under him and uses his cane to stand. "I'm going back." He chin nods to the far bank. "Go." He turns toward his decrepit home and dissolves into the brush.

"Donnie!" I whisper-shout, treading water.

"What're you doing out here, boy?" Walter's voice has neared.

Should I follow?

"Just sitting a spell, Pa." Fear has strung Donnie's voice tighter than a clothesline.

Little help I can yield with nothing but my bare hands for defense.

"I told you to stay inside, young'un." Walter's words slur. He's been drinking.

"Been looking for hoppers." Donnie's strained-thin voice grabs my core.

Whack!

"Ow, Pa."

I stroke toward my brother. But what can I accomplish with no weapon?

"Whose hat's in the house? 'Fess up, boy!"

Ice-like fear grips me. I forgot my hat.

Donnie squeals as if in pain.

"That's a gal's get-up. Who'd you let in my house? Speak up or I'll get my razor strap."

"All right. Don't hurt me." His plea squeezes my innards. "Lil' came to call."

Silence.

I must go for help. Re-crossing the stream, I gain footing and claw onto the Fitzgerald's slippery bank. My cotton bodice clings to my heaving chest.

Donnie's yelp tightens to a thin squeak.

I can't leave him alone with these men. I ready to dive—

The click of a pistol hammer holds me in place.

Stepping through the brush into view, Walter tosses my hat aside and holds a steely bead on me. "Trespassers are shot around here."

"Why would anyone care to step foot on your wretched acreage?"

"You tell me, missy?"

How I've longed for a father to love me. For gentle hands to soothe my hurts. A tender voice in the night. What is it that draws rancor from the man who gave me life? "You're a low-down drunkard."

"I don't give a care what you think, girl."

I fist my hands. "You care what Judge Fulbright thinks?"

"To him you're a false accuser and I'm an upstanding businessman." He kicks my hat into the creek. It circles atop an undercurrent and disappears.

"You conduct business in shadows. Transact in back alleys. Deal under tables. You'll be hearing from the sheriff." And I'll seek help in ways Walter never dreamed.

He guffaws. "I look forward to it, you upstart you."

I shove through the thicket and run across the pasture to the house. Trembling at the thought of Walter's fist—or worse—aimed at my brother, I bound up the back steps. "Maggie!"

"Over here." She peeks out the larder. "What's got you in a stir?"

"Walter's got Donnie." I run for the stairs.

"Lord, no."

I lean over the railing. "Sheriff and Judge Fulbright can intervene."

Tossing aside my wet clothing, I don a dry riding skirt and shirtwaist and carry my boots down the stairs. "Walter and his blacksmith friend rode up." I pull on my boots at the entry bench. "Donnie ran back." My hands fist. "Walter slapped him. And threatened a shaving strap. No telling what he's done by now."

She gazes toward the heavens. "Lord, surround Donnie with Your angels."

"I possess no wings or halo, but I'll be Donnie's angel all the same. My roadster's in town, so I'll ride Daisy." Grabbing a riding hat, I aim for the barn.

Daisy has grown from a skittish filly into a sturdy mare. She lifts her muzzle and whinnies. I saddle her, and we head toward town. My grip on the reins tightens with each thought of Walter.

Tethering Daisy behind the legal office where she'll be spared automobiles' sputters and fumes, I remove my hat and smooth my hair. Surely I look a fright, just out of the creek and clothing thrown on without a care. I check my buttons. Tug down my blouse. And straighten my shoulders.

The judge's assistant greets me. "May I help you, Miss Sloat?"

"I need to speak with the judge. It's an emergency."

"I'm sorry, but he was called into court."

"I'll find him."

"But, ma'am . . . "

I swoosh outside and let the door close of its own accord, drowning the man's voice. Not that it matters. Nothing will stop me.

Striding down the planked sidewalk and skirting storefronts, I round the corner at McFarland's General Store and stumble into the president of the Women's Club.

"For heaven's sakes, watch where you're going." The lady frowns.

"Excuse me." Sensing the woman's disapproving stare at my back, I cross the street and enter the town square.

Judge Fulbright is descending the courthouse's stone steps.

"Your Honor!"

"Hello." He doffs his headpiece. "We moved your trunk to Broadview's parlor."

"Walter's back." I cough the words between ragged breaths. "With the jury foreman."

"The foreman at his own trial?"

"He's a bad one. Donnie ran back to them, and Walter walloped him. He threatened a razor strap and brandished his rifle at me. I told him he'd be hearing from you and the sheriff."

His gaze tightens. "Come with me." He leads me across the square to Sheriff Dawson's office and swings the door wide. "We're needed at the Sloat place."

The sheriff motions to a pair of chairs. "Have a seat."

We explain, and the lawman nods his understanding. "I'll head out there now."

"I'm going with you." The judge and I declare our intentions in unison.

The sheriff studies me. "Got a firearm?"

"Sworn off 'em." I could have used one facing down Walter, but I won't admit it now. I lift my chin. "But I have a responsibility to help my brother."

He taps down his Stetson. "Stay in the car and follow instructions."

The judge motions me to his Oldsmobile, and we putter out of town at a quick clip. The sheriff follows on his stead.

The automobile comes to a standstill outside the old house, and my driver, the dignified jurist, removes a shotgun from under the dash.

Our lawman escort strides to the stoop and knocks.

A patch of sunlight flickers in the shadows beyond the screen.

He knocks a second time, rattling the flimsy frame.

The old rooster lets loose a half-hearted crow. A pair of trousers snaps on the clothesline. A blackbird caws and flaps his wings.

"Walter Sloat, this is the sheriff." He draws his pistol. "I've had a report of a disturbance out here. Come out now."

No movement. Or sounds.

He opens the door, and it releases a rusty wail. "I'm coming in. Put up your hands."

He passes into the shadows.

Judge Fulbright levels his shotgun, and I level my gaze.

Will my heart pound out of my body?

The sheriff's boots tap the planked floor from one side of the cabin to the other. He steps to the stoop. "No one's here. Come in."

The judge directs me into the shack. Signs of a hasty departure—an overturned chair, a spilled jug of milk, a biscuit tin on the floor. The tomato crate had been torn from the wall and lies in shreds, the glasses shattered, the tin mugs missing.

Regret rears its ugly head. "If I hadn't waited so long—"

"This isn't your doing, Lily."

A scrawny finger of a breeze flicks the hem of a tattered flour-sack curtain. Ma dyed the embroidery threads with buttonbush, mulberry, and marigold blossoms. Years of wind and rain have demanded their toll.

Fresh blood splatters stain the wall above a pile of quilts. Bound to be Donnie's.

The same wall absorbed other grisly blotches over the years. Mine. And Ma's.

Clutching my middle, I collapse into a chair at the table. Memories of savagery bat through a flood of rage. And terror. I rest my head on the slab, the second time in as many days.

Love, longing, and heartache force tearless sobs from the grim darkness within me.

These fine gentlemen who've known me on the periphery of life hear the lament of my soul. Neither priests nor preachers, simply good men, they lean close, and I absorb their warmth.

A hand pats my head. Another cups my fist. One man murmurs, his words unintelligible. The other moans as if caught in my dirge. Their empathy touches my heart, but tears refuse release.

If only. If only. If only. Oh, the agony of regret.

At length I straighten and wipe perspiration from my forehead with a sleeve. "We have to find Donnie."

A groan answers from across the cabin. And the pile of quilts shifts.

CHAPTER 10

I stumble to the mound and throw aside the quilts. "Donnie."

The sheriff squats beside me. "Let's turn him over. Easy."

My brother's nose is smashed to one side, turning blue, and swelling. The flesh around both eyes is discolored. Blood trails his cheeks and oozes from his mouth. But he's breathing.

I shove his mop from his forehead and dab the blotches with my handkerchief.

He winces.

"It's Lil'. The judge and sheriff are here too. We're taking you to Doc."

His lashes flicker, black moth-like, and his head droops to the side.

The men hoist him outside and lay him in the car's back seat.

I claim the front passenger seat and slam the door. I'll build a wall of defense around my beloved brother one brick at a time if I must.

Ever vigilant, the officer of the law trots alongside us into town.

The *Open* shingle in the town physician's front window welcomes us.

My escort parks in the alley, and I bound into the office. "Doc, it's Donnie."

His assistant holds aside the back door. "Bring him in."

A mother and daughter gape at us in the waiting area. I'm struck by the contrast between this girl's childhood and my own. I first visited Doc shortly after I turned eighteen. Addie insisted, and I relented, though mortified.

"I'm issuing warrants." The sheriff's heavy-heeled exit snaps silent with the slamming of the door.

"I'll wait in the sheriff's office." The judge nods a farewell and departs.

Doc rolls up his sleeves. "Let's see what's under here." He unbuttons my brother's shirt, revealing sharp angles but no scars. And no marks, aside from his battered face.

I exhale my relief.

The medical assistant positions a privacy screen between us. Waiting in a straight-backed chair against the wall, I recall my dire past: Walter's whiskey breath; his ire, never extinguished, only banked, until liquor enflamed it.

At length, the physician peeks around the screen. "You can join us now."

I stand at my brother's dirt-caked feet.

"He's been manhandled and struck about the head. His nose is broken." Doc forces his eyelids open and flicks a lighted instrument side to side. "His pupils respond, so there doesn't appear to be a concussion. One loose tooth should tighten. The gash inside his bottom lip will heal. But mainly, this boy suffers from long-term malnutrition."

Calm and steady, he applies ointment to contusions. "Gave him aspirin and laudanum, so he should sleep. But use the laudanum sparingly. Instructions are on the bottle. There's bleeding from his nose, so prop his head with pillows. Ice'll help the swelling. Bring him back in three days, and I'll set his nose. Don't be alarmed by discoloration. It'll worsen."

Scalded-milk fury in my gut threatens to boil over. But it's the lawmen who can do something about this. "I'll fetch the sheriff and judge." I step outside and signal to the men.

On either side of my semi-conscious brother, they raise his arms over their shoulders and guide him to the car.

Moving alongside them, I monitor the transport. "May I ask you to ride ahead of us, Sheriff? Maggie needs to prepare a room."

"Happy to." He trots off with my Daisy on a lead rope.

I hold Judge Fulbright's satchel on my lap in the front passenger seat. He starts the engine and steers his car toward Broadview.

What a welcome sight, the estate's entrance pillars. Silver-haired Vernon, ever the vigilant overseer, stands watchman-like on the veranda.

Loyal to a fault, he welcomes us with a frown. "Walter Sloat ought to be—"

"Getting the boy's testimony is the first step." The judge punctuates his words with a sharp head nod.

The men maneuver Donnie down the east hallway to a guest suite where the aroma of sandalwood greets us.

"Vern's cologne." Maggie smiles and whispers behind a hand. The dear pair have prepared as if for a prince. The coverlet and sheet have been turned down and the pillows fluffed. The windows are thrown open, and a breeze tickles the sheers.

"I'll take it from here, ladies." Broadview's faithful estate manager assumes oversight of a boy ignorant of life beyond his deprived world. He removes a night shirt from the armoire, and the rest of us meander to the veranda.

The kind caregiver joins us momentarily. "He's awake. Not speaking, but I wager he's wanting his sister, don't ya know."

I scamper inside and find my battered loved one propped up on fine feather pillows. Between sheets scented with sandalwood. "Need anything?"

He shakes his head, and his focus flicks toward the window. His expression reminds me of former days when he feared for Ma and me. He needs reassurance. "Mr. Yancey's fortifying our boundary lines and hiring more fence riders. Walter won't step foot on Fitzgerald land. He knows what's waiting for him. "

I ease away, but he grabs my arm. A single tear bleeds from his eye. "The men are leaving soon. I'll be right back."

Stepping onto the veranda, I lean against a post with my arms crossed at my middle. "He's still not speaking."

The judge nods. "There's no physical reason. It's the trauma. He needs time."

The sheriff dons his hat. "Anything I can do, ma'am, you know where to find me."

The men shake hands and separate, one astride his horse and the other tramping inside to extract relevant information from one Donnie Sloat. Daunting.

An hour crawls by, and Judge Fulbright returns to the veranda. "I wasn't able to coax a word from your brother, but it'll come in time." He slips an envelope from a coat pocket. "Meanwhile, I prepared guardianship papers. And a restraining order for Mr. Sloat."

I hold the paperwork against my bosom. "Thank you."

He cranks his car and putters away, and I mull over present affairs that are pulling me in opposite directions.

Find justice, Lil', and take care of my boy. Ma calls to me from . . . somewhere. "You'd offer a bit of wisdom if you were here, Ma. How I miss you."

"'Tis a lovely heirloom in the parlor. Shall I polish it?" Maggie has joined me.

"Thanks, but I'll do it." Perhaps I'll feel closer to Ma.

"I set out cleaning supplies." She scurries inside and rifles through a sideboard drawer. "There's a crocheted doily around here somewhere."

Ambling into the parlor, I focus on the old chest aligned with the interior wall. I kneel and scrub with a concoction of vinegar and a well guarded, secret ingredient. Decades of soot come away, blackening the rag. Gradually the grain appears, undulating like ocean swells. Beeswax enhances the lines, and the engraving emerges, crisp and clear.

I'll not cover the surface with a doily and photographs. It must be allowed to glow. I gave the contents only a cursory examination in the chicken coop. Perhaps now's the time . . .

An automobile engine purrs in the distance. Is Addie returning from her appointments? She'll find an altered household.

I step outside, and we exchange waves as her automobile jounces toward the car barn.

"Time for supper." The warm herald draws me inside to the kitchen

Like it or not, I must wait to reopen the chest.

My Europe-bound friend accepts my brother's arrival with her usual aplomb. "Keep him away from the creek. And that monster, Walter."

Wafts of stewed chicken greet us in the kitchen. Maggie sets a basket of fruit on the table, and we take our usual places.

Laying my napkin over my lap, I nod at the empty place. "No Sabina?"

"Temperance League." Maggie shakes her head as if befuddled.

The lady of the house chuckles. "Oh, to be a moth hovering around a wall sconce."

"Aye, no telling what schemes those fancy hens'll hatch."

"Let's speak of happier things." I force brightness into my tone.

"How about chicken pie?" The preparer of the delight ladles the savory pastry into three bowls. "I saved a goodly portion for our young man." She points with her chin toward the east wing.

Addie inhales the heady aroma and smiles. "A soothing balm for my spirits."

"'Twas the same for me at my mother's table." Our cook harrumphs. "We can use some soothing with Walter on the loose."

"Let's lay it before the Lord."

We join hands for a prayer of gratitude, but my eyes stray to the vacant place at the table.

Sabina's.

How might I befriend her?

At our collective *Amen*, I reach for a plum. Biting into the fruit, I wipe juice from my chin. "At times I feel there's hope for friendship with Sabina."

"Beware. 'Tis for her own good the cat purrs." Maggie blows across a steaming spoonful of the concoction, and the rich sauce drips into her bowl.

A shroud of disquiet laps around our shoulders, and we finish the meal without speaking.

Soon spoons clink in our empty porcelain bowls. "Care for tea, my girls?"

Addie dabs her lips with the napkin. "Perhaps later? I've work in my study, but first . . . "

Now what?

"I saw to last minute business details in town. My attorney will be in charge of Broadview while I'm away."

A load lifts. One less worry. Still, how can I summon a goodbye for my dear friend?

"Did you leave any for me?" Sabina has slipped in unnoticed. Dressed in a bold black and white-striped suit and a headpiece of ruby-red silk roses, she leans against the door jamb with a fist at her waistline and an elbow jutting to the side.

Her mother jolts. "For heaven's sakes, give us warning."

"Surely you were listening for me. It's after eight o'clock." She flips her hat to a hook and tugs off her gloves.

Her mother glances at the clock. "It is at that. Care for chicken pie?"

"No. We had a feast." She yanks a pin from her topknot, releasing a wispy tress.

"You joined the League?" Addie's raised eyebrows tug her eyes wide.

"Surprised I'd assume the cause?" She removes a second hair pin, and a flimsy strand falls down her back. She ducks into the hallway. "That's not all that would surprise you if you noticed anyone but Lily." Her heels clack on the hardwood floor toward the stairs.

We three recoil.

Addie waves away the barb and sets her empty bowl in the sink. "I'll be in my study if anyone needs me."

Maggie prepares dishwater and calls to me over her shoulder. "Back to your task, lass. I'll feed our boy his supper."

Returning to the parlor, I graze a hand over the chest's gleaming surface. *Are you hiding secrets here, Ma?* I tug, but the lid refuses to budge. It's locked. Of course. I secured it myself.

My thoughts race. I buttoned the key in a pocket before crossing the creek. What if . . .

CHAPTER 11

I dart to the utility room and fling a mound of dirty laundry from the wash tub. Snatching my riding skirt, I examine the pockets.

Empty.

As deflated as an empty wind sock, I collapse onto a ladder-backed chair. I was certain the key would remain secure in the buttoned pocket.

Have I no choice but to force open Ma's heirloom? And destroy the lock?

I scoot into the kitchen. "Did you find a key in my skirt pocket, Maggie?"

She turns with a puzzled frown.. "No, lass. I moved your things straightaway from the chute to the tub."

"But I didn't toss my clothes down the chute." I lean against the kitchen dresser with my arms crossed over my midriff. Realization dawns. "But I know who did."

Peeved, I peek out the window. Sabina's striding toward the barn like a vexed plow horse. Is she constantly angry?

"Has that girl of mine been snooping again?" She clangs aside her shelling bowl and peers through the window. "There's no way to know what's in the pot 'til the lid's lifted. I'll search her room."

"What if she returns?"

"There's no better judge than the battlefield, my dear. Time to enter the fray."

"Who's doing battle?" Addie's voice whips us around.

"Heaven preserve us. Didn't hear a peep."

"Our minds've been elsewhere. I can't find the key to Ma's chest."

She hikes a fist to her waist. "Let me guess . . . Sabina."

"I'm afraid so. I'll wring it from my her hand if I must."

"She's coming back." Addie points through a sidelight.

We step to the porch, barring the entrance.

"Out of my way." She shoulders between us.

Addie crosses her arms. "I suspect you have something belonging to Lily."

"Can't imagine what."

"Lily's key. Give it to me."

Snarling as if repulsed by an odor, the agitator exposes her pocket linings. "Why would I have a phantom key belonging to a Sloat?" She turns a hardened gaze to me.

"It was in my skirt pocket."

"That sopping wet skirt you left on the floor? The one *I* dropped down the laundry chute? Surely you know the key's at the bottom of that stream, silly girl."

"Your mother made the pockets exceedingly deep."

She shrugs. "Perhaps Mother's not the seamstress she claims to be."

"Your mother's stitches are worthy of royalty. And I'd know if my riding skirt was in need of repair." I extend a palm. "All I want is the key. No questions asked or charges leveled."

"How many times do I have to tell you? I don't have it."

"I don't trust you as far as I can pitch you." Addie's hands have fisted.

She spits out a brittle snicker. "Don't trust me? Oh, dear. Whatever will I do?"

"Trust is earned, as we both learned at your mother's knee."

She hikes her chin.

"So I'm sure you won't mind if we conduct a search."

Fury burns in her eyes. "This isn't right."

I'm overcome with a sudden sense of futility . . . and wrongheadedness. What are we thinking? Granted, reasoning under these circumstances is as useless as hoeing with a dull blade, but we're behaving despicably ourselves. We've allowed one bitter woman to create a war zone.

"You're correct." I back away. "I need the key, but if you won't give it to me, I'll have another made."

Retreating to my room, I sense three sets of eyes at my back. I close my bedroom door and lean backward against it, searching my memory for clues.

I sped from the creek earlier today and shed my wet clothing beside the dressing screen. A faint circle of dampness remains on the wooden floor.

Kneeling between dressing screen and mirror, I place an oil lamp on the floor and lower my head for a fresh perspective. Hair pins are lodged beneath baseboards. A cotton ball hides behind a dresser foot. And among the clumps of dust under my bed . . . the key.

Holding the subject of the evening's turbulence in the palm of my hand, I lower my head in a moment of self-reflection. Household turmoil has unearthed a hard truth. Sabina's rage knows no boundaries. It has flamed and growled in recent days, but what have I done to quell the strife?

Maggie deserves a home at peace. I must be gone.

I awake and turn toward my windows. Morning has yet to dawn in full, but it appears a clear day will accompany us to Fair Valley. From there, my Italy-bound friend will travel to Kansas City and then to New York City where she will board the ocean liner, *Vaterland,* bound Hamburg, Germany. She will proceed to Rome by train.

If war permits, that is. A coil forms in my core, but I push aside the sensation.

An insistent whistle sounds from downstairs. The kettle.

Tossing aside my sheet, I dress in a wrapper and descend the broad staircase. Is Donnie awake?

Luggage is piled in the entryway, and a travel hat hangs on the hall tree, a Prussian-blue felt that hugs the traveler's head. It sports a conservative brim, a bow, and a wired frill resembling a feather. Her handbag and gloves lie on the entry table.

I enter the kitchen as a flycatcher calls. Distant barking reaches through windows.

"Top o' the morning to ya." Maggie chimes her greeting with a broad smile. "Vern's with our young man."

"I never dreamed he'd prove such an asset with my brother." I sigh. "We've come to the dreaded day of departure." I look around. "Where's the world traveler?"

"In her study. Tending to last-minute details."

Taking my usual spot at the round oak table, I stir milk into my coffee and sip. "Just a scone, please. My stomach's turning flips."

She sets out a bread basket and cups and saucers. "My daughter packed up and disappeared in the night."

I start at the unexpected news. "I'm sorry. Where will she go?"

She joins me and pours herself coffee. "Fort Worth, I reckon."

"I hope she finds contentment. For her sake and yours."

"'Tis my daily prayer." Buttering a warm plum scone, she hums as if welcoming this day. "Where's your smile off to, my girl?"

"Not much to celebrate with our dear mistress of the estate leaving. How can you smile with your loved one who knows where?"

"If I dwell on what's passed me by, I'll not enjoy what's hovering near. According to my dear mum, continual cheerfulness is a sign of wisdom. 'Tis a truth as old as the mist and older by two."

"How do you maintain your cheerfulness on a day like this?"

"By setting my thoughts on Addie."

"She's all I can think about. I hardly feel like smiling."

She reaches across the table and takes my hand. "Ponder her *joy*, dear girl. 'Tis contagious."

"Equal parts joy and fear have claimed me. I'm happy her dream's within her grasp. But what about the war?"

She eyes me over her cup rim, one eyebrow peaked. "What were you saying about joy?"

I toss her a grin. "Let's see . . . I'm grateful to be free of overseeing Broadview."

She nods but offers no response.

"But there's Donnie to consider. And my job offer in Fort Worth, of course."

"'Tis a knapsack full of possibilities. You must decide what you'll carry and what you'll leave aside."

I bite off a corner of the scone. "Delicious. You have yet to teach me your secret."

"Hunger's a tasty sauce." The dear woman's homespun bromides season life with wisdom and cheer. I'll miss her.

Addie steps into the kitchen. "We must leave for Fair Valley." Her eyes snap to the wall clock. "In less than an hour." She swirls out the back door.

"Run along now, child. I'll tend to our boy."

I guzzle the last of my coffee and scamper upstairs. Pots clatter in the kitchen. Addie instructs the gardener near my window. The little mocker chatters. The sounds, like threads on a loom, weave a design called *Home*.

A wren has need of naught but her nest, according to Maggie. Broadview has been my nesting place nine years now. I'll be lonely in a big city with no friends nearby.

And without the man I love.

Bending over, I force back a sob. Will the unrelenting throb consume me?

No. I won't let it. I must remember Blossom. My brother. And justice for Ma.

I choose a simple gown of lightweight lawn for the journey to Fair Valley. And string the trunk key on a satin ribbon that I wear around my neck. Tucked beneath my high-necked blouse, the cool metal brings unexpected comfort.

With the sun barely pinking the horizon, Vernon stacks luggage into his Ford truck. Donnie's tucked into the cottage with Ella's husband Andrew and their six girls. The drive to Fair Valley whips us about, but we anchor our hats with wide scarves and laugh at the wind.

Ponder Addie's joy.

I will try.

We chat on the depot platform while Vernon checks the luggage. Our always fashionable traveler has chosen a Prussian-blue traveling attire with a narrow skirt and narrower hem. A pleated peplum reaches to her knees in back, and she gleams in the new sun. Off to Italy and her dream come true, hasn't she every right to sparkle?

I focus on her eyes. Burgundy lights flash. "Stroll with me a bit?"

She tucks my hand into the crook of her arm, and we meander to an isolated spot.

I steel myself and gaze into her eyes. "You're the picture of grace."

"How's that?"

"As I see it, mercy is the withholding of punishment, even if it's deserved. And grace is adding a gift into the bargain."

She nods.

"Walter punished me without mercy, and Ella removed me from the defilement. That's mercy." My throat tightens. Has my inner dam developed a chink?

I suppress insistent tears. "You moved me into a palace. Dressed me in fine clothing. Seated me at your table. Even offered your name. All, gifts of grace."

"You've been the gift to me, dear girl." She dabs the corner of an eye.

I raise a hand of protest. "I want to repay you."

"A gift isn't a gift if it's paid for."

I stand erect. Resolved. "As much as I want to repay, we both know I can't."

She smiles. "Not even by overseeing my affairs in my absence. But the offer will stand. Always."

"You've done it again."

"What's that?"

"Given me a gift. The gift of wings."

Our treasured heiress, whose generosity knows no limits, boards the train and finds her compartment. She lowers a window and reaches for us. We three touch her fingertips and blow kisses, and my two companions dry tears. At the blast of the train's whistle and the belch of steam, I cover my ears.

The train chugs forward, and we jostle beside it, waving. The dark-haired beauty leans out the window, her hat askew, and flutters her handkerchief. We respond with hankies of our own.

Vernon offers a single-fingered salute and plods to his truck with his shoulders slumped.

And then she's gone.

Ella dabs at tear tracks. "Don't know if I can bear it. Addie . . . gone again?"

"'Tis best she seek her dream." Maggie stares after the train.

"If only her dream were here at home . . . " My eyes claim custody of the caboose, a pinprick on the horizon.

Fort Worth Caller awaits me.

Walter and justice hide just around the bend.

But first, I must assure Donnie's long-term safety and education.

CHAPTER 12

I drive the sedan back to Broadview, and Vernon follows in the truck. The auto's empty interior mirrors my heart.

Now I must settle my own travel plans.

I brake at Broadview's grand steps, and Maggie dashes inside.

Ella and I sit immobile, staring through the windshield.

"Look." She points at her husband and five stair-step girls dotting the hillock. "Where's Blossom?"

"And Donnie?"

The girls run toward us, shouting and flinging their hands above their heads.

"Something's amiss." Bounding from the auto, she skids on pea gravel and flies to her family.

The flustered father jogs alongside his children. His typically placid expression has wrenched into harrowed lines.

"Mama! Oh, Mama!"

"Blossom's disappeared."

"Where could she have gone?"

"We've looked everywhere."

"She was here. And then she wasn't."

"Thank God you're home." Andrew gathers his wife into his strong arm.

"What's happened?" She pales and pushes him away with wide-eyed alarm.

He runs his fingers through his ebony-dark hair, and the sun flashes in his sapphire irises. "We finished breakfast. The girls and Donnie went to the gazebo—"

"Where were *you*, for pity's sake?"

"In my study. Not twenty yards away. I was preparing my sermon, and the girls—"

"We were playing charades, Mama. As we do with you."

"She told us to close our eyes."

"I told her we weren't playing hide-and-seek. But she—"

"I heard her running down the path."

"Oh, Mama."

Sobbing, they wrap their arms around their mother.

Ella snaps her focus to her husband. "How could a girl disappear playing charades?"

He hangs his head. Despair has ravaged his features.

The girls whimper and sniffle.

"Have you checked Mama's and Papa's?" She shoves curls from her sweaty brow.

"First place we looked, dear. Cade's combing the woods."

"And elsewhere on the estate?"

He clasps her shoulder. "We're all searching, including the gardener and housemaids."

Seemingly confused, Donnie hobbles from the bridle path with a cane. The skin around his battered eyes has blackened.

I point him toward the house. "Find Maggie. Tell her I'll be there in a minute."

Nodding, he limps toward the rear entrance.

"The rest of you, keep looking. But stay together." I pivot. "Vernon!"

"What is it, Miss Lily?" He secures the auto shed door and plods to me.

"Blossom's missing."

He recoils. "How can I help?"

"Alert the workers and send everyone out." Cold, hard fear ripples through me.

Taking off in a hard run, I charge past Maggie and Donnie. "I'm changing into a bathing costume."

"What for in heaven's name?"

"Hear that?" A dog bays long, low and desolate. "Wally's at the creek."

With my bathing attire askew and my water shoes laced tight, I race through the garden, cross the pasture, and sail over fences, my arms pumping and my lungs heaving. I'll avoid the briar patch by swimming through the reeds.

Splashing into the creek, I stroke around the first bend and through the cattails and undergrowth into the clear pool at my brother's mossy ledge. Wally's stationed near the buckeye, but no pale-haired youngster perches beside him.

But she's been here. Wally announces it with each breath.

I tread water, my heart racing. "Blossom!" Swimming toward the west bend, my eyes dart left and right. "Where are you, child?"

I circle back and climb onto the ledge, gulping air. The child wouldn't have jumped into the creek. She can't swim. Has she fallen in farther downstream? Is she lying alone somewhere, struggling for breath? Or worse?

My gaze snaps toward the old shanty. Did she make it across somehow ?

Swinging my feet from the water, I careen through Sloat brush and into the clearing and aim for the decrepit abode.

A breeze stirs. Tattered curtains flap out the kitchen window. I slam aside the screen door and barrel inside, dripping water and scanning left to right. "Blossom?"

Unearthly silence answers. Even the blackbirds still.

I stumble outside. No scrawny goat. No hens or old rooster. I turn a full circle but find no sign of life.

Wally barks, and girls shout across the way. Panic is setting in.

I cross the creek with my mind swirling and pause on the bank to catch my breath.

Wally whimpers and scratches around exposed buckeye roots. A glint of metal draws me forward on my hands and knees.

"What'd you find there?" I smooth his riotous coat and ease him away.

A black box has been discarded among the roots—the sweet child's camera. Did she forget it? Or hide it?

"Good boy." I take hold of the strap as if I'm latching hold of her hand. Shuffle to my feet. And hurdle through the wildwood, heedless to the brambles. Wally gambols at my heels, hollering.

Blossom has been to the creek. We must organize a search party. Now.

Sheriff Dawson organizes the two dozen men. The expected one hundred eight degrees will not deter them.

The Brownie focuses the search on the creek. Led by the sheriff, the men spread across Broadview property, each combing a section of the creek on each side the reedy bend.

Determined to join them, Ella proceeds to her horse barn to saddle her mare, and I follow.

Will every single one of my loved ones march into peril?

"Where are you going?" A storm cloud has settled around us, but I must make her listen to reason.

"I'm going with the men, of course." She jerks the tie strap through the girth ring.

I tighten my gaze, hoping it will pierce her iron will. "You have five daughters crying their eyes out." I point to the cottage.

Ignoring me, she cinches the strap tighter. "The sooner Blossom's home, the sooner her sisters' tears will dry. Our housekeeper and Nell, the nanny, are seeing to them."

I grip her shoulders. "You're acting precipitously. Have you forgotten all the times you've—"

She jerks away, but moisture has gathered in her eyes. She leans her forehead against the mare's shoulder. "How does a woman of action sit by and watch others—men or nay—do her job? I should've stayed home today. Should've spoken with my daughter two days ago. I should've—"

"Listen to yourself, taking the blame when we don't know what's happened yet."

"We know my child's disappeared!" She breaks into sobs.

Her agony brings a Bible verse to mind, one my mother sometimes quoted: *My roarings are poured out like the waters.*

"Come to Broadview. The girls can play parlor games. Chase butterflies. Anything to distract them from the wait."

Catching the hem of her skirt, she wipes away tears with its underside. "Never have a handkerchief when I need one."

We chuckle in spite of the consuming terror.

She turns her focus toward Broadview. "Getting out of the cottage will distract the girls. But there's Wally. He's distraught like the rest of us. And he hasn't eaten."

"Bring him and his bed."

The girls welcome the world of diversions Broadview offers. But once inside the grand house, they and their mother collapse into a sobbing heap in the parlor. Maggie hovers on the fringes of the group. I join the wail in spirit, but my eyes refuse to release their moisture. Has my spring dried up?

"We have to find our sister, Mama." Fear casts a shadow over the deep blue of the eldest's eyes.

An expression of dread, even horror, flashes on her mother's face. "The men are doing everything they can, dear."

I reach for the child's hands. "We won't quit until we find her."

Ella tosses her soggy handkerchief aside, and all five daughters offer her their hems.

"Thank you, but I've a hem of my own."

They weep into their cotton skirts, and my friend offers a muffled supplication to her God. If He's what she claims, He can hear her just fine.

Raising her head, she clenches her fists. "I know I can be as stubborn as a wooden goose sometimes. But I simply won't believe my dear one's come to real harm. I'd feel it otherwise."

Hooves thrum, and automobile engines putter outside.

I peek between window sheers. "Maggie, please prepare refreshments for two dozen."

On the veranda I light the porch lamps to ward off the lurking dusk.

We eight females stand shoulder to shoulder as the two dozen males approach.

CHAPTER 13

$\mathcal{A}$s the sun dips out of sight, it brushes the horizon with swatches of orchid and pansy-purple. Riders rein in, and automobiles brake in Broadview's circular drive.

Covering my nose and mouth against the dust, I thumb toward the rear. "Refreshments on the veranda, men."

They thank me and stride toward the back.

Sheriff Dawson, Andrew, and Cade dismount and slog toward us.

I steel myself at the sight of Ella's broad-shouldered brother, his trousers trail dusty and his warm brown eyes chocked with fatigue. He slaps his Stetson against his leg.

"What've you learned?" My voice shakes, and I clear my throat.

Stepping onto the veranda, Andrew swipes his sleeve across his face and locks gazes with his wife.

Trembling, she claims his hand. "Tell me."

"We found no sign of Blossom in or around Rock Creek. Or in Needham."

She slumps against him.

I raise my hands, flashing my palms. "Surely her camera—"

"A lead that's come to a stand still." Cade's expression is grim. "There are others, but . . ." One eyebrow crooks downward, a sign I recognize as tenderness.

Tamping down discouragement, I gesture to the sitting area.

Ella and Andrew take the swing, and he holds her beneath his arm.

The other two men settle on the railing with their Stetsons, crowns down, beside them.

Leaning forward with his elbows on his knees, the lawman focuses on the grieving mother. "I feel confident your little girl didn't fall into the creek. But we did find this, Mrs. Evans." He tugs a yellow satin ribbon from a vest pocket.

Gasping, she grabs it. "It . . . It matches the trim on her dress."

Her husband leans his cheek against her head. "Found it in a ditch. South of town."

"Might your girl have run away?" The sheriff speaks in a tender tone. "Has anything been troubling her lately?"

She shakes her head. "No more than any other thirteen-year-old."

"She has been troubled, Sheriff." I speak before giving it a thought.

The child's parents stare as if I'm an apparition, and the peace officer draws a tablet and pencil from his pocket.

I anchor my mind on my young friend's message two days ago. "Blossom has a mind of her own . . . an independent spirit."

Swishing a hand, he encourages me to continue.

"She asked to speak with me . . . the day before yesterday . . . after the verdict. I found her at the creek."

"In what way was she unsettled?"

"She talked about Donnie. And Walter. And the photography she loves. Claims she'll work for a newspaper. She's impatient to start."

"Go on."

"She asked if I'd take her to Fort Worth."

"What?" Her parents spout in unison.

"I told her it was impossible."

"She's been trying to interest me in her photography. But all I've had time for is the suffrage club." Ella collapses against the swing back.

The sheriff worries a cupped hand over a fist. "I'll wire the authorities at Fort Sill. And the communities south and east to the rail line at Ardmore. And beyond."

"Dear God, return our child." Ella whimpers and leans into her husband's side.

"What's next?" Andrew's solid gaze pleads with the lawman.

"Search teams will fan out toward Oklahoma City, Fair Valley, and

Westwood. We'll reassemble at my office in two hours. Every man will bring his own searchlight."

Andrew prepares to stand, but the peace officer stops him. "You're needed here." His focus alights on Ella. She has wrapped the yellow ribbon around a finger and is tugging on the end as if to compel her child to return.

"Ma'am, we might need that ribbon." His eyes snap to the worried father. "To show witnesses."

"No need to spare me." She releases the strand of yellow into his broad hand. "I'm neither weak-kneed nor unrealistic. It could be used to identify a body . . . the clothing."

Settling his Stetson, the sheriff taps the brim and joins the men out back.

Ella and Andrew embrace, and the swing rocks in a rhythm the two of them seem to know. He prays in low, gentle tones.

Cade turns to me. "Care for a walk?"

I can't bear to stroll alongside him. What if our hands touch? I might lose every shred of self control. "You're bound to be exhausted." I point to a conversation grouping. "Let's sit a bit. Then you need some refreshment."

Settling into a chair, I take a steadying breath. "What did you learn in Oklahoma City? Any news from Europe?"

He bends a leg and rests his ankle against the opposite knee. "Rumors of impending all-out war. Troop movement in Germany. Troubling."

I scrape my lower lip between my teeth. "Surely she'll return when she hears."

"She might be forced to. Ocean liner travel is halted for now."

"Her ticket is for *Vaterland*."

He nods. "German. It'll be detained."

"If there's a single ship setting sail for Europe, she'll be aboard."

"All we can do is pray."

Silence as fragile as rice paper stretches between us. "Try to get some rest." He excuses himself and rounds the corner toward the back garden.

Dread has sapped me of my strength. I rest my head in a hand and knead ropes of worry along my brow. How I long for Cade to hold me the way Andrew holds Ella. Battling hopelessness, I step inside and pass through the entry, past the dining room and kitchen, to the back sidelights.

Everyone has gathered on the rear veranda. The girls chatter on the broad steps. Exterior lamps spread a warm glow over their heads, and June bugs and moths flick here and there.

They've all found a spot to light. Where do I belong?

And where—oh where—is Blossom?

The men resume their search as planned. I attempt to join them, but Sheriff Dawson claims I'm needed at home. I suspect his denial has less to do with my friends and more to do with my gender.

I accept his decision with reluctance. "Call as often as you can then. Please."

Cade agrees with a nod.

Insisting she needs time alone to pray, my sad-eyed friend sets off for her summerhouse, and her loving husband escorts their brood to the cottage.

I see to my brother and the dog that has claimed him, feeding the sad-eyed mutt and moving his bed next to his new friend's.

Maggie closes the house for the night and retires to her suite. All the while, she speaks to herself. Or to the Almighty.

Dressed in nightgown and duster, I settle in the veranda swing and stare into the surrounding blackness. Deep in the night the telephone rings, and I scramble to it. "Have you found her?" The question has forced itself beyond the boundary of my lips of its own accord.

"No sign of her from Needham to Oklahoma City." Cade's breathless response, though welcome, serves to deepen my dread. "I'll call again in Norman."

Returning the earpiece to its cradle, I collapse on the parlor divan with a sense of impotence. If I believed in a God who cares, I'd cry to Him for mercy. But my gaze falls on Ma's sea chest instead.

The old trunk seems to call to me.

The lone wall sconce in the entry provides little illumination, and I have no desire to flip on the overhead light, brittle and unwelcome on this dismal night. Instead, I rifle through the butler's pantry and choose a fat beeswax candle in a copper chamber holder. Its glass sleeve multiplies the light.

Kneeling beside the old coffer, I bump against a side table and rock a vase of neglected roses. Wilted petals shower the tabletop. I clear a spot for the candle and realize the scrubbing has revealed an extraordinary grain. Ma said the wood cured and hardened in a bog. But where?

I finger-tame loose strands of hair behind my ears and sit with my legs crossed. Working the beribboned key from under my gown, I insert it into the lock. The mechanism unlatches, and I let the lid rest against the wall.

A familiar, welcoming sensation harkens to my former examinations of the trunk and draws me to the heirloom's innards.

I focus on the Bible. Turning to the births and marriages record, I graze a fingertip over names and dates written in a bold, cultured hand. They date back to 1753 but include neither a Ruby nor a Walter.

I know nothing of Ma's background. She was more refined than her crude husband, but where and from whom did she learn?

Flipping through the tome's crackly pages, I find passages underlined. And notations in the margins, some in the same bold hand, others in Ma's scrawl.

My dear mother's fingers turned these leaves and smoothed their crinkles.

Splotches mar a few pages.

Did her eyes shed the tears?

Who scratched the notes?

I bring the light nearer and flip to the back flyleaf.

Strange symbols have been printed in the margin: ברכה.

Odd.

Ma's treasured book sat in arm's reach as I matured. Its nearness spared us not a speck of Walter's cruelty. But did its contents strengthen her in ways I haven't learned?

My eyes prickle. Tears threaten, but I bat them away. I won't fall to pieces like the roses. I'll batten down the hatches of my sentiments.

Laying aside the tokens of a past life, I examine the trunk's interior. Screws secure the bottom to what I assume are braces below, but veneer has curled in one corner. I press it down, but it refuses to stay. I run a finger under the loose edge. My nail catches on what feels like fabric.

I retrieve a screw driver from the household tool box. With considerable pressure the fasteners spiral out, and a false bottom releases. Setting it aside, I discover relics tucked into the space. Someone hid them, but why?

There's pair of brass candlesticks atop a square of lace. A velvet drawstring bag enclosing an oblong object. An old journal bound in surprisingly supple leather, sheepskin no doubt. And a roll of vellum tied with ribbon.

I open the pouch and remove a palm-sized wooden implement, double layered with a needle-like point. An empty thread bobbin is positioned between the layers. I hold it to the light. It's inlaid with the same symbols scrawled in the Bible—ברכה.

Peculiar.

The first page of the old register bears a single line of print, a pale duplicate of the initials and date carved into the chest's lid. I hold in my hands an account of someone's life. No, more than one person. Several.

Some pages have stuck together, and the parchment threatens to split. Perhaps I can soften the fibers with steam.

Setting the memoir aside, I untie the roll of vellum, spread the delicate folds, and bring the lamp closer.

I squint, and a sketch emerges. A tree. With a furrowed trunk. And deep roots. Heavy branches. A canopy, thick and full

Names have been worked into the wood grain. I recognize none of them.

Curiosity whispers. What have I stumbled upon?

Reattaching the bottom, I lay my finds atop the other keepsakes and lock the chest. The ribbon slips over my head, and the key lies cold against my skin.

I'll reexamine the peculiar trove in tomorrow's light, but I mustn't lose sight of what matters most—Blossom. Her disappearance has altered everything.

CHAPTER 14

*M*orning raindrops as fat as tadpoles plop onto dry grass beyond the veranda, hinting at cooler temperatures. But the shower abates, dashing hopes.

"I was plagued with bad dreams, Maggie." Weary and out of sorts, I finger-comb damp strands from my cheeks.

"Have a bite to eat." She spoons cooked oats into a bowl. "Tell me about them."

"I don't recall. Just that they were bad." Frowning, I shiver in the kitchen's damp heat.

"Dreams aren't to be taken seriously."

I stir brown sugar and cream into the oats. "Ma spoke of omens, but I never put stock in them."

"Nor should you. Nothing but old country and mountain tales."

Still, they bedevil. I wash my bowl and spoon. "I'm going for a walk."

Burdened, I wander across the estate. Has Blossom's body floated downstream to Red River? I all but retch at the thought. Her parents insist they will trust the Lord, but surely their terror exceeds my own.

Our beloved traveler wired us from Guthrie. But we've heard nothing since. Has she met with a trans-continental accident?

Finding Cade perched on the veranda railing enjoying a tall glass of water, I release a breath of relief. He's home safe.

He sports the fiery imprint of his hatband around his forehead, his Stetson nearby. A layer of trail dust covers his denim trousers, and sweat outlines his cotton shirt's underarms and front placket. Weariness coats him.

I resist an urge to rush to him and settle into the swing instead. "Any news?"

Folding his frame into a sturdy iron chair, he gulps the last of the liquid and swipes a bandana across his mouth. "Sheriff and a couple of his men went as far as Fort Sill and from there to Ardmore. I rode to Chickasha and OKC. Rest of the party covered Guthrie, Fair Valley and Westwood. Two headed to Ada and Tulsa."

He crumples forward with his head sagging. "A telegram arrived from the sheriff. I left it with Ella and Andrew."

"How're they doing?"

"Andrew's an oak." He harrumphs. "And you know Ella as well as I do."

Pea gravel crunches, and our heads snap around.

Ella tramps toward us, her stride long and her steps solid.

He meets his petite twin sister at the bottom step. Cut from the same bolt of cloth, they're stitched in contrasting designs. Her honey-golden curls shine next to his dark-walnut thatch streaked with gold. Her eyes give off multi-colored glints, and his flash warm brown. Her exuberance draws folks' eyes more readily than her brother's studied sobriety. But their iron wills stand like twin towers.

I meet my distraught friend at the top step and note a tremor in her hands.

"Sheriff Dawson called. Word's getting out. The rest is in God's hands."

I curl to a wicker chair. "Where was God . . . *before* your daughter disappeared?"

Ella plops into the swing. "He was beside her then. And now. And with us." Her eyes show telltale signs of fatigue, but she's bearing this burden better than I imagined. What has changed?

She continues. "I spent most of the night in prayer, and . . . I just know she's alive."

One of Cade's eyebrows arches into a point.

"I must trust God. Or lose my mind." Her head plops forward, and she kneads her corded forehead. "Bring us news, Lord."

A car engine drones in the distance.

"Someone's coming." He returns to the steps, and we join him.

Sunlight flashes on a shiny black surface, and a familiar Oldsmobile putters through Broadview's gates.

We greet Judge Fulbright at the circular drive, and Cade opens his car door. "What've you heard?"

"I've come to visit with Donnie, but I'm also bearing news. Besides a financial crisis on Wall Street that's closed down the stock exchange— troubling, to say the least—I received a phone call from the governor. Russia's announced full mobilization. Europe's in for all-out war."

"Dear Lord, no." Ella speaks barely above a whisper, but her words are powerful.

We gather on the veranda, and he motions for us ladies to be seated. "I've been thinking Miss Fitzgerald's on a fool's mission since the steamer she booked to Europe—*Vaterland*—has been removed from service."

Cade nods. "I spoke again with to the train master. Seems her route changed. From Kansas City, she was scheduled for the craziest knot of connections you ever heard. She was to lay-over in Nashville and Atlanta both."

I shake my head at the troubling news. "Determined to make it to Italy, no matter the cost."

Clearing his throat, the judge straightens in his chair. "I thought she was on a fool's mission . . . but then I heard from the governor."

I cock my head. "What's the governor got to do with Addie's plans?"

"This is to go no further than these two families. Matter of fact, the governor preferred I keep it even from you, but I . . . I just couldn't." He glances at Ella. "Not with all the uncertainty at present.

"Quite simply, he asked Miss Fitzgerald to serve as his eyes and ears in Europe. She's sailing on a government transport straight to Naples. He's providing security, by the way."

Ella presses a hand against her chest. "Thank the Lord."

I mull and give voice to my thoughts. "She might be in more danger than if she were a simple troupe member. As a private citizen performing in an opera, she'd be looking for ways to avoid trouble. But with a mission, she might endanger herself unnecessarily."

My friend expels a deep breath. "You're right. We must be on our knees for her."

"And Blossom?" I'm miffed that we're worrying about Addie before the lost child.

My friend sets her eyes firmly on mine. "Half of Oklahoma's looking for our child. Besides, the Lord's working out a plan through her." She flings a hand upward. "Don't ask me how or why." She clenches a fist at her bosom. "I just know it."

"Speaking of missions . . ." The judge pokes a forefinger. "Mine is to ferret out information from a certain young man inside." He grabs his hat, "Oh. I all but forgot." He removes an envelope from a coat pocket and extends it to me. "Postmaster caught me on my way out of town."

I tear open the envelope and devour the message. "*Caller* wants me to cover the Women's Society page." I will be forced to shoulder past society dames' stiff necks and withering glances, a proposition that leaves me nauseous.

The judge places his hands on my shoulders and tightens his gray-eyed gaze. "You're standing at a crossroad. May I offer some advice?"

"Of course."

"*Caller* puts you in a position to shine a light on issues important to women—including the all-important vote. No one knows the needs of women better than Ida Tate." He punctuates his declaration with a blandishment of his hat. "She has quite the history, you know."

Without knowing it, the judge has spoken a name that's been dancing on the fringes of my mind. Ida served as the headmistress of Jackson Academy, a home for Chickasaw orphans, the better part of her life. With Oklahoma statehood in 1907, the property passed into the private arena, and she purchased it herself.

The older man tosses me a sharp nod. "Her influence extends beyond Oklahoma. I suggest you discuss this newspaper assignment—and Donnie's education—with her."

"But until Blossom's located . . ."

"It's time you leave Blossom to Oklahoma's powers that be . . . and the Lord, young woman."

I blanch. "So I'm to abandon the search?"

"Not exactly. You're broadening the search area. To Texas. Remember . . . a press pass will admit you to society circles. But with a reference from Ida Tate, you can find yourself visiting working families' homes, tenements, hospitals, even prisons. To how many such environs would you have access on your own?"

None, the man knows well enough. But I see myself among working families and combing tenements, not society's soirees.

"That's what I thought. So rub elbows with the high and the lowly. Ask questions but turn over clues to local law enforcement. Do not endanger your own safety." He strides into the house to speak with my recalcitrant brother.

Ella bounds to her feet. "It's a sign. I just know it. You've not a moment to waste. So get some rest. I can see you're bone weary." She gives me a hug, and she strides toward the rise with her brother.

He turns at the crest and waves.

Dazed, I return his gesture and enter the house.

Maggie and the judge are conversing in the entry.

He adjusts his hat at the mirrored hall stand. "Couldn't coax that boy to speak. Maybe Ida will have better luck." Pausing at the doorway, he turns back. "That hound's good for the boy. Neither wants to lose sight of the other. I wouldn't make them if I were you." And with that he departs as efficiently as he arrived.

I aim for the telephone extension in the study. "Best call Ida right away."

"I'll bathe the canine member of the family." Maggie swishes off to retrieve Wally.

Ida's gracious reply confirms the judge's assessment. On the hallway settle, a Fitzgerald family heirloom, I weigh the puzzling developments.

Maggie joins me. "Heavens to Betsy. You've a storm brewing on your brow. What's the matter?"

"Other than questioning whether or not I *want* to be a reporter? Blossom who-knows-where? Donnie still not speaking? And Addie a spy in a war zone?"

"Heaven preserve us."

"And there's Cade, of course. Leaving him . . . his companionship, you understand. It's almost more than I can bear."

"'Tis more than friendship he's wanting."

"It can't be." For reasons I'll not breathe to a soul.

"Perhaps it's not the time, dear."

I gaze into space, imagining life devoid of the dear man. "If I turn down *Caller* and stay at Broadview, how can I resist him?" But how can I live without him?

"If his sister could choose, you two would be married tomorrow."

"He deserves a wife of quality, not a Sloat. I won't inflict him with such a burden."

She shakes her head. "Both of them know quality when they see it."

I pick at a hangnail, avoiding her gaze. Her eyes bore into my soul. "If I lived elsewhere, Sabina might come back. But then . . . if she mistreats you, I'd never forgive myself."

"'Twould be her work alone, dear. Not yours."

"I hope she finds contentment. For her sake and yours."

"'Tis my daily prayer."

"Why do I enrage her so?" I huff. "Sorry. I've a passel of questions."

"Questions are the portal to knowledge." She gives my hand a squeeze and focuses like a sure-set arrow. "But you'll never plow a field by turning it over and over in your mind. What does your heart tell you?"

"That I love you and Donnie and Addie. Ella and her family. And Cade. It tells me I need answers." I pause and pick at a hangnail "Should I accept *Caller's* offer? I told Addie I'd be doing so, but now that Blossom's vanished, my mind's whirling. Besides, I owe her everything."

"Love that's paid for—"

"Isn't love. I know. But you'll be alone here." I gaze at the high, deeply recessed ceiling. "Broadview's a big place for one person."

"I've plenty of household help."

"And Blossom?"

"Like the judge said, as a reporter with a press badge, you'll be in a position to ask questions."

Our lost loved one's words from three days past come back like a swat.

I want to snap pictures for newspapers . . . Never know when I might find something newsworthy.

My mouth falls open.

Of course.

I pop to my feet and run down the steps. Along the footpath. Over the rise. To the cottage. "Ella! The camera!"

CHAPTER 15

Ella meets me on the cottage's front porch.

"Blossom's camera. Where is it?"

"In Andrew's study. Why?"

"There might be clues inside that little box."

We race toward the twin rooftops peeking above shrubbery, Andrew's home office and Ella's gazebo, their Christmas gifts to one another a few years back.

I stumble into the study. "Here it is!" I point to the contraption atop the desk.

Chests heaving, we stare at the simple black box.

"How do we remove the film?" I examine its exterior.

She glances around and points at a rectangular, domed metal box with a hinged top. "If I remember right, that handle turns a roller inside. There's developing solution and trays. Fixing powder. Sheets of Velox paper and mounts."

"Do you know how it works?"

"No. But here's a manual."

Nabbing the pamphlet, I thumb through the pages. "No dark room required." I read the instructions aloud, and she manipulates the supplies.

By midday we have developed six photographs—three of Wally, two of a swarm of damselflies, and one aimed across the creek.

She adjusts her spectacles and points to a singular spot beside the haw. "Look at that."

I examine the snapshot at the east window. "It's Walter."

"And this?" She points to a black-and-white blur behind the haw.

"I can't make it out. It's just a smudge."

"The last picture my daughter snapped included Walter Sloat? What's happening here?"

Whatever the beast is planning is diabolical. He'll stop at nothing. But what does a thirteen-year-old child have to do with his plans?

She crumples into a chair, and her lips stiffen. "Walter's stolen my child."

What will satisfy the monster's need for control and cruelty? I won't voice possibilities.

I ease into an armchair. "A job awaits me in Fort Worth. According to Donnie, Walter's doing business in the same city. I can smell that man. And I can find him."

The next morning I wake with one question: How do I bid farewell to Broadview?

The previous days' horrid heat dissipated at sunset, but humidity oppresses today's early morning air.

Throwing off my nightgown and donning undergarments and a lightweight shift, I open my jewelry case and remove the tray, exposing my one treasure—the three-emerald forget-me-not ring. Shall I wear it one more time? No one's around to misunderstand.

It slips past my knuckle and settles into place as if it were meant for my finger alone.

In the wash room I splash scented water across my face and pat my skin dry.

At the stairs' bottom tread, a force—I know no other way to describe it—draws me, siren-like, into the parlor. The twilight before the dawn bleeds through the front window, nesting in a sheen on the chest's surface. I kneel beside the heirloom, and a sensation akin to the comfort of Ma's arms surrounds me.

Am I imagining it? I cross my forearms atop the trunk and lay my head on them. How would you advise me, Ma?

The good Lord saw fit to remove you from this sorry side of the creek, Lily. For His purposes.

Did my mother speak truth? Was my leaving Sloat sod part of some grand plan? Is Fort Worth the next leg of my journey?

Perhaps I should sit outside awhile before the sun rises. Take in the twilight sounds and listen for my feathered friends.

With my hair falling to my waist, free and unfettered as I prefer it, I steal onto the veranda with a church fan and settle into the swing. The sway stirs the air, multiplying the hand implement's cooling effect.

I stare into the darkness. A few stubborn night critters chirr. A breeze rustles the bittersweet vines, and a blackjack tree sways.

My eyes snap to movement in the shadows.

"Morning, Lily."

Cade. Can I bear his nearness?

He mounts the front steps in broad strides. "May I sit . . . beside you?"

I hesitate.

"As a friend."

Surely I can resist . . . his appeal. I pat the slatted seat. "Come."

The swing wobbles as he settles, but soon we rock in a steady rhythm. Heat radiates from his body. I fan my face and inch away.

"Surely you aren't heading to Texas. Or looking for Walter." His golden-brown forelock has fallen forward, grazing the brows that arch above eyes the color of buckskin.

"I can find him."

He inhales so sharply I start. "That's what I'm afraid of. It's too dangerous."

"I know Walter as no one else does."

He opens the arms he keeps for me alone. I ease toward him but allow only my head to rest on his shoulder. He's used Old Spice after shave.

"I'll go instead of you, Lily."

"No. You're needed here. Besides, your folks are in poor health." I lift my head and gaze at his beloved features. "What you have meant to me.

Thank you for . . ."

"No more than what love calls for."

I must steer us from talk of love. Pulling away, I sputter the first words that come to mind. "Why has that monster taken an innocent girl, a mere child?"

Frowning, he grows pensive-like and releases a sigh. He straightens his shoulders, seemingly resolved to my change of subject. "Won't know for sure 'til we find them."

"We will find them, won't we?"

"Bound to." He sucks in a breath and heaves it out. "There's something else." He turns and faces me. "I have no pride where you're concerned, so I'll ask again. Will you marry me?"

My core grows heavy, as if my chest has filled with rocks. "Oh . . . you deserve—"

"I deserve what I want. The woman I love. You." He sets his fingers under my chin and lifts my head. His intensity extends through his fingers into my core.

How I love this man.

"I'll build us a house on the west rise. It's my inheritance. Not wealth, but . . . "

My eyes widen. My mouth eases open as this fine man speaks of his dreams for us.

"We'll have a sturdy roof that holds the rain at bay. And a porch where the doves you love can nest on the eaves. I'll build us a swing of our own."

I hunger for such a life with my prince, a far cry from both my girlhood home and Broadview's wealth. His offer rips me in two. But the knowledge I withhold represents a chasm no one can cross.

Excuses are all I have in my arsenal. "There's Donnie to consider. Blossom. And the unrelenting hunger that's plagued me since I heard *not guilty*—a yearning for women on juries.

Other realities lurk, but I can't speak of them.

His hands tighten into fists. "Who knows what tomorrow will bring?

I want to face it together." He sets his jaw in a firm line and takes my hand. "It's time you know some happiness. I love you. Always have. Always will."

He runs his thumb over my fingers, and my body tenses. The ring. He mustn't . . . misunderstand. I slip my hand from his.

"Will you let me comfort you as your husband?"

I twist the ring, worrying the flesh beneath it, the singular band between knuckles where it seems to belong. "How can I pledge my life when every waking hour belongs to my brother? To seeking some kind of justice for Ma? And now to finding Blossom?"

"But Sheriff Dawson—"

"I'm just not free." How am I to endure this heartache? He's a part of me, and yet he never can be, not truly. "You must forget me. Find someone who deserves you."

"Don't want someone else. Never have." The brown in his eyes deepens.

"You will. In time."

His skin flushes ruddy beneath his dark, shaven stubble.

Will my heart forever skip at the sight of him? "My head's filled with questions. And my spirit with longings of every sort."

"*You* stay on my mind." He places my hand on his chest. "And in my heart."

I bend forward, and he moves his hand to my back, its warmth at once a soothing balm and agony.

I sit upright. "You've more important interests than the scandalous Sloat girl."

"You're beautiful within and without." He wraps a strand of my hair around his hand. "When God paints flashes of copper and the foxfire's light, I'm blind to all else."

If he knew the ugliness I hide, he'd turn away.

He runs a forefinger along my forehead and the blobs of freckles on either side of my nose. Brushing a fingertip along my lips claims my breath. His warmth brings to mind a fire's heat on a winter morning.

But, oh, so different.

I wiggle away. "This isn't right."

"Of course it is. I'll love you 'til I die. I believe you love me too."

I cover my face with my hands. Tears plead to be released, to trickle between my fingers . . . across my cheeks . . . over my chin, to drip like errant children onto my shift. But I've imprisoned them.

Bounding to my feet, I whorl, certain of my stance. "Is it right that I seek the warmth of your arms . . ." I inhale short, quick breaths and exhale in sharp heaves. "While our beloved young one's in Walter's hands? While women everywhere are denied justice and a voice in their governance? And criminals like Walter walk free?"

"But . . ."

Can I do what I should, the thing that's hard . . . but right?

Heart hungry for this noble man, I steel my mind and stiffen my will. My inner self numbs. I've waffled long enough. A man worthy of royalty stands before me. But I'm no princess. I must make the break

Resolved, I drop the three-fold symbol of his love into his hand. "I can never marry you. I'm sorry."

My beloved stares at the emeralds, as if unable to absorb the reality.

The twilight surrounding us is fading into the light of a new day. A sign perhaps?

Taking a deep breath as if resigning himself to what he cannot change, he jams the ring into a pocket and plods down the steps, his shoulders slumped.

I ease forward and lean on a pillar. Can I truly let him walk away?

Turning, he digs the heel of a boot through the turf. "I love you more than life, Lily."

Cade strides into the shadows.

And I let him.

CHAPTER 16

I call Ida Tate to inform her of our scheduled arrival in one week. She reports Germany has declared war on Russia, but Italy and Denmark are staying neutral, a bit of hopeful news.

Doc sets my brother's nose and gives him aspirin powder. He agrees we should take Wally with us, as the bond between boy and dog appears to be aiding recovery. He'll explain his prescription to Ida by telephone.

While the physician tends to Donnie, I snap up my valise and I bustle toward Sheriff Dawson's office. Tickled to find the lawman and judge together, I march in with an announcement. "We found a clue."

The sheriff motions to a chair beside his desk. "Have a seat."

"I found Blossom's camera at the creek the day she vanished but didn't question what it might contain. Until yesterday. Ella and I developed the film." I tug the photograph from my satchel. "Look who's in her last shot."

He examines the snapshot. "Walter Sloat?"

I nod. "And look over his left shoulder."

He squints through a magnifier. "Just a smudge."

Judge Fulbright peers over his shoulder. "Is it a person? Someone who moved just as the shutter clicked?"

"That's what it looks like to me." I extract a packet of photos from my valise. "Keep these for the search. We developed several." I pause to consider my position. "I'm not a lawman or a judge, but I know Walter, and I suspect he's connected to this. According to Donnie, they were bound for Fort Worth, which is where I'm headed."

"You'll speak with Ida Tate first?" The judge's brow has crinkled.

"Already have."

"I'll notify sheriffs in Texas." Sheriff Dawson jots on a tablet. "Gainesville. Denton. Fort Worth. Dallas."

Judge Fulbright nods, his expression pensive. "I'll do the same with judges."

The sheriff points at me. "The law will handle the situation with the Evans girl. Don't lose your head now."

"I appreciate your concern. But you needn't worry. As a reporter covering women's events, I'll simply watch and listen and ask questions—like how to find a businessman by the name of Sloat." I lift a shoulder. "Who knows? He might not be anywhere near Cowtown."

The sheriff grumbles deep in his throat. "Beware the man."

"No one knows him better than I, sir."

The judge shakes his head and frowns. "Your place is advocating for women. And the vote. Mr. Sloat's a job for lawmen."

I cross my arms and pace among a haphazard arrangement of chairs. "I admit I have more questions than answers, gentlemen. But I won't waste opportunities as they arise."

I step outside to the walkway.

The sheriff stands between me and my roadster. "Don't jump the gun, Lily. You'll miss your target if you do."

"Indeed." The judge runs his fingers through his thinning hair. "Don't let foolishness jeopardize your guardianship."

I've battled shyness always. A sense of worthlessness has plagued me. Even as an intern at *Caller*, I avoided public interactions, which relegated me to little more than an errand girl. But how can I sit by while others search?

An argumentative response would be futile—and disrespectful at that—so I hold my peace. "If Walter's still in Oklahoma, I trust you'll locate him, Sheriff. And bring Blossom home. I'll do the same in Texas."

He peers into my eyes. "I advise you to remain at Broadview, but it seems you're determined. Gather whatever advice you can from Ida Tate."

I stand and smooth my skirt. "I'll be on my way then. Donnie's at

Doc's." I step outside. "Thank you both for . . . caring for me."

Harness traces jangle and wagon wheels rattle, drawing my gaze to the feed store.

Cade. Dust billows and settles around him.

"Hello, handsome," a gussied-up young woman calls from down the street.

I shade my eyes. The daring daughter of Needham's newest business-man sends the McFarland nobleman a cheery wave.

He jumps off the wagon and tips his hat. "Afternoon, ma'am."

She grabs his arm. "You'll come to the Women's Club social next month, won't you?"

Even from a distance, I detect a flush on his face. My cheeks warm as well.

What's wrong with me?

Here I am, worried sick about Blossom. Preparing to move to Texas. Refusing the proposal of my dreams. Yet at the sight of this woman . . .

Can I continue to deny my feelings for Cade?

I shake off my misgiving. I must attend to business.

One week later, I hang a variety of frocks and ensembles in a travel ward-robe and clear the surface of my dressing table. Lotions and fragrances. Hand mirror and brush. Combs, hair and hat pins. Ribbons. And tie my cameo brooch around my neck.

The past week was chocked full of preparations overlaid with worries about the search. Maggie and I hovered near the phone extensions. I made unannounced visits to the sheriff's office daily. And to the post office to ask about telegrams. But my anxiety accomplished not a whit. If a worried mind could bring the child home, she would have been tucked in her bed the day she disappeared.

Snapping closed the last of my travel trunks, I survey my private abode. My armoire sits empty, save the heavy woolens I won't need for months. Surely I'll return before the first blue norther barrels into Texas.

I place Ma's Bible and the shuttle beneath the folderol in a travel trunk and nudge my crude sketch of the family tree into a side pocket. The original will remain in a pasteboard cylinder in my armoire. A photograph of Blossom and her snapshot of Walter slide into the journal, which fits into my satchel alongside the Brownie.

Never know when I might find something newsworthy.

Ella transports us to the train station in their Daimler limousine. Vernon, Cade, and Donnie pile into Addie's Cadillac with freshly bathed Wally poking his head out the window.

Dressed in a sensible golden-brown traveling suit, I stand on the depot platform between Ella and Maggie. My southbound train will depart at high noon. The wind whips our dress hems and nips at our hats.

We three ladies share farewell sentiments, and the man I love and can't peel my gaze from stands to the side with Vernon. Donnie and his canine shadow pose beside them. Yesterday's smattering of rain eased the horrid temperatures a bit. Our high-noon sky threatens a deluge but it has spotted only our shoulders.

Conversations hum around us. Strangers extend fond farewells. Gentlemen shout hearty greetings and bits of war news. Great Britain has entered the war, and Germany's advancing westward across Europe—invading and besieging and enlarging the circle of conflict. Ever-increasingly countries are issuing declarations of war, and others are countering. The news reports overlay our gentle goodbyes with stridency.

The train's whistle pierces the din.

I sling my handbag over my shoulder. The pistol-shaped bulge reminds me of Cade's target lessons years ago. I've cast aside my distaste of firearms with danger lurking.

Holding onto my hat, I reach for my friends.

"You've looked out for me since I was girl, Vernon. Thank you."

He tucks his chin. "You're like the daughter I never had, don't you know."

I take Maggie's hands. "You opened your mother arms to me. How

I've loved the hearth and home you've created."

"You're as dear as any daughter." She lowers her lips to my ear. "Your feet will bring you to where your heart is." She tips her head toward Cade and winks.

My cheeks warm.

Trust my fickle heart? It cries out for vengeance *and* for love. It longs for home and demands wings to fly. It shoves away an honest and true love while yearning for it as if for life.

I turn to my golden-haired friend with my eyes stinging. "You nurtured me so I could fly, Ella. I'll find Blossom. Your courage will be my example."

She presses her cheek to mine. "How I'll miss you. Trust the Lord's leading."

Am I to trust the One who let Walter beat Ma to death? Or the One who permitted the horrid abduction?

"Come, Donnie." Maggie heads to our passenger car with my valise in hand. "You're in the third car. Wally's riding with you, not the baggage car. The conductor approved."

My friends board the train with my limping brother and his cockeyed friend in tow, and our circle collapses.

Cade steps in front of me, his hat pulled down against the wind.

Fearful my resolve will collapse, I lower my head. The wind has sprinkled dust across his pant legs, but his freshly buffed boots shine.

"Bring your pistol?"

I nod and pat my handbag.

With a forefinger and thumb at my chin, he lifts my head. "I'll be here waiting."

My breath comes in gasps as I struggle for control. "You mustn't. I can't promise . . ."

He cradles my cheek in his hand. "I can."

"I can't rest until Donnie's where Walter can't find him. And Blossom's back home. There's the women's movement and the newspaper and . . . " Other realities will remain hidden.

He kisses my palm. "I'll wait."

"Who knows how long it'll take?"

"I've waited a lifetime. Can't remember a day I haven't loved you."

Nor I, you.

His eyes' golden brown deepens. My pulse skips a beat.

"I don't figure that day will ever come."

"All aboard!" The conductor steps onto the first car.

My suitor's shoulders slump.

My dear friends return to the platform. My brother, with dark half moons under his eyes, peeks through the compartment window, his expression blank. Wally smiles at the world.

I back toward the train. "I'll write. And telephone. Let me hear any news . . ."

The women wave handkerchiefs.

Ella cups her hands around her mouth. "We'll write."

"We'll be waiting." Maggie daubs a hankie to the corner of an eye.

I join Donnie in our compartment and lean my head out the open window. "Take care of each other." The train jolts forward, jerking me backward, and I right myself. "I'll miss you. Please stay safe."

The train chugs toward the first bend.

I stand on tiptoes to catch a final glimpse of the beloved foursome.

Cade raises his hat above his head.

Two handkerchiefs flutter and settle at the women's sides.

Broadview's faithful overseer lifts a bare hand and turns away.

The man I love moves his hat in an arc.

The tracks curve to the left.

And my eyes can feast on his form no more.

PART

Two

CANST THOU BY SEARCHING
FIND OUT GOD?

JOB 11:7A

CHAPTER 17

The train's steady clack-clack lulls Donnie and Wally to sleep, and I open the journal to the first entry. The pen strokes have faded, forcing me to read through my magnifier, a lovely cloisonné object Addie purchased in Venice, Italy. Still, portions of the script are unreadable.

Struggling to make sense of the message, I snap the book closed. Might the missing elements come to me by copying it in my own hand? I pull out a sheet of stationery and begin the laborious process. Sure enough, a young woman's account emerges.

May : ye : 27th : 1775

Aboard Nelly. Atlantic Ocean tween Ireland & ye Colonies

Sea & Sky devoid o Light.

Ship's Hold reeks o Disgorgements o Divers Sort. Me stalwart Davie be at Lantern with Bible. I be at Porthole with Thread & Shuttle.

Shabbat passed. No Kiddush Blessin. No Wine or Challah Bread. Davie be resolved we buried Loeb Name in Dumfries. We worship now with Christian Countrymen—on Sundays. I obey. But I be sittin Shiva in me Heart.

Fear attends me.

Rachel Loeb Lloyd
Daughter o Abraham

The screech of the train's whistle snaps me from my reverie, and we pull into the station at Ardmore. A mother and her son and daughter draw my gaze. The curve of the woman's back, the way the children focus on the ground, remind me of myself, of Ma and Donnie.

Do they live with a monster?

I squinch my eyes tight, my sole defense against persistent rotten images of a fair-haired girl and the cruel hands of a brute. I'm heading in the right direction. Something tells me so.

Peering at the landscape swishing past my window, I realize I identify with young Rachel Lloyd from a distant place and time. I too am heading to a new land, but I'm taking my name with me. I think Christians a bit strange at times, but I have yet to cast my lot with them.

Like Rachel, I'm fearful and harbor secrets.

The young wife overlaid her account of seasickness with her husband's stalwart bearing and her own misgivings, even fear and grief. Like her, I'm journeying toward the future, but the portal to my past stands ajar, the two pulling me in opposite directions.

But how are Rachel and Davie Lloyd connected to Ma?

The thought of my mother's shrouded past thrums a pang around my heart. Her history is my own, and I long to know it. Truthfully, my future might depend on it.

With curiosity burning, I leaf forward to the final entries. The handwriting is vastly different. The writer identifies herself with an R, and she's in love.

Surely my own ma was in love . . . once.

The engine shrieks at the Jackson depot, and I return the aged chronicle to my valise. I must see to Donnie's welfare. Then I can sniff out Walter. And Ma's secrets.

Philip, Ida's former student and now right-hand man, joins us on the platform. Muscled and fit, he swings our trunks from the baggage car into a Ford hack as if they're matchbooks.

With Wally hunched beside him, Donnie leans on his cane and observes from the platform. The older young man signals him to the bed of the truck, but my brother hangs back, frowning.

"What is it?" I clutch his shoulders. He's trembling. "You've nothing to fear. Philip's our friend." Coaxing Wally into the truck bed, I take my place in the front seat with the driver. And wait for my brother to make up his mind.

He refuses to budge. He stares. Frowns. But at length eases into the plank-sided bed of the vehicle beside the hound.

We arrive at the former Jackson Academy in the late afternoon. No more beautiful sight exists in all the world than the sun as it ducks behind this stately structure.

As our feet touch Jackson soil, Ida swings open the door. "Welcome."

She descends the broad steps with a hand on the railing, her back bowed but her gait steady. Her skirt hem grazes buckskin boots, and her belt buckle reflects the dusky light. What a fine figure she presents, this eighty-seven-year-old Chickasaw woman who welcomes us with a broad smile.

"Welcome, Lily. Who is this handsome fellow?"

I accept her outstretched hand. "This is my brother Donnie."

He recoils and hides behind me, but I tug him forward. "Meet our friend, Mrs. Tate."

He tucks his chin, worrying the knuckles of one hand with the fingers of the other.

Ida pats my shoulder. "Any news about Blossom, dear?"

"I'm afraid not."

She draws in a sharp breath and closes her eyes, her lips moving without a sound.

How does she pray with such spontaneous ease? As a ten-year-old, she endured the Trail of Tears. Her life has been speckled with trials, yet here she is, seventy-five years later, still praying.

A placid expression emerges on her bronzed features, and she extends an open hand toward the building. "Come. God has the answer to every quandary."

Donnie's brow smoothes, but acceptance has yet to settle on his features.

She ushers us into the walnut-paneled foyer. Laughter trundles above our heads, and the tap of hurried footsteps draws my gaze to the winding staircase. The black-haired crowns of two heads bob above the railing, and a pair of girls steps off the bottom tread. They curtsy and round the corner, giggling.

An unexpected wave of desolation rolls over me. Blossom is about these girls' age. Her mother taught her to curtsy and smile. Will she ever giggle again?

A piano plinks somewhere in the back, tugging my thoughts back to Jackson. "Sounds as if the school's still in session."

"My home is open to children in need." Her focus moves to the happy mutt, and tenderness flashes. "And their friends." Her gaze comes to rest on my brother. "Would you care to meet students, young man?"

He angles his eyes toward me.

"Go on."

She offers an outstretched hand, but he stands stubborn-like. Her focus snaps to his hound. "Come, Wally." She strides outside, and the mutt follows.

I ruffle the mop atop my brother's head. "You can trust Ida."

He ponders, gives a one-shoulder shrug, and wobbles out with cane in hand.

I peek around the jamb. Wally's minding his manners. And so is my kin.

Philip gestures for the pair to follow. "I'll introduce you to the boys in the workshop." He shortens his stride to match my brother's cockeyed gait, and the three lumber out of sight.

The dignified school mistress leads me into her office and points to two roughhewn chairs. "Those're students' handiwork. Have a seat."

Artwork decorates the walls. A depiction of the Trail of Tears has been painted onto a cowhide. A rug stretches its bright, woven threads across the wooden floor.

Leaning back in her worn leather desk chair, she cups her gnarled hands in her lap. "That jury performed a rotten deed. I'm sorry."

"Ma cries for justice while her murderer runs free. He attacked Donnie, and we've reason to believe he took Blossom."

She covers her mouth with a hand.

"But I intend to bring her home."

"Quite a load for fledgling shoulders like your own."

"Ma shouldered a heavier load all her life. And then there's Andrew and Ella . . ."

"How're they holding up?"

"They're on their knees."

She nods. "Any idea where the scoundrel has taken the child?"

"Donnie says he's going into business in Fort Worth, speaking of which . . . "

Her eyebrows lift, adding furrows of curiosity to her brow.

"*Caller* wants me to work the Women's Society desk. But now that I'm responsible for my brother, I'm in a quandary." I leave aside my uncertainty about my fitness for newspaper reporting.

"He's welcome here."

I drop my head in relief. "Thank you."

"How old is he, by the way?"

"Nineteen, but he's a bit simple minded. Judge Fulbright granted me guardianship."

She nods sagely. "The boy's slight of stature."

"A life of malnutrition. Depravation of every sort. And rickets."

"Healthful food and hearty work schedules have added to some students' height, even to twenty-one years of age. Has our boy attended school?"

"Never."

"He's a blank slate then. Who knows what he can learn?"

"You'll face a stiff challenge if he decides not to cooperate."

She waves aside my comment. "What of yourself, dear? How are you . . . really? I've been on my knees about you."

I desire neither sympathy nor talk of God, but what right have I to instruct Ida Tate? "Addie's off to Italy."

"With war brewing? Italy and Denmark have declared their neutrality, but Montenegro declared war on Germany today. The conflict is spreading."

"Her dream is the opera. War or no war."

"And what of your dreams?"

"There's *Caller*, so I'll have my own income at last."

"The Lord provides."

"Worry over the kidnapping is eating away at me."

"Pursuing Walter is a dangerous business, child."

"I can't sit idly by."

She steeples her fingers and brings them to her lips, her forehead a web of lines. "In that case . . ." She raises her eyes to the ceiling. "I've contacts in Fort Worth. Might you cover suffrage events?"

"I'll join the ladies of Texas anywhere." I pause and smile. "Cade says watching out for

Ella's like trying to get his hands around smoke. I suspect my life will be similar now."

"And what of that fine McFarland man, dear?"

I press a knuckle to my lips and look away. "He proposed, and I declined."

She lowers her head into one hand, kneading her brow. "One loved one off to a war zone. Another waiting at home, grief-stricken over a missing daughter. One aching for you to come back home. One spirited away by an abuser. And another here at Jackson, needing protection he denies he requires."

"Donnie's not spoken since Walter attacked him."

"It's the trauma. His mind's struggling to understand. This home'll be good for him." She gazes at the ceiling. "He's not yet reached his majority."

I snap open my valise and present the guardianship paperwork.

She scans it. "Wilson Fulbright and Doc called me about Donnie—and Wally. I'll keep all of you apprised of his progress. No one will know the boy is here, save those you tell."

I relax into my chair back, gratitude swelling. "Knowing Donnie's safe is a relief."

"We'll keep a close eye, but we can't watch him every moment, any more than you."

Taken aback, I straighten. "You can't assure Donnie's safety? I won't leave him then."

She reaches for a dogeared, leather-bound book. Her Holy Bible. "At some point we all must entrust our loved ones to God."

She can read me Scripture, but until she assures Donnie's safety, I won't change my mind.

Settling her spectacles, she flips pages as delicate as dried petals and runs a finger along lines of print. "Psalm One Hundred Forty-Six: 'The Lord watches over aliens and sustains the fatherless and the widow, but he frustrates the ways of the wicked.'"

She scrutinizes me over her glasses. "Do you believe that?"

I open my bodice to reveal the burl twisting from my collar bone downward. "With this and Ma in her grave, would you blame me if I don't?"

She sets her glasses into their case and leans back with her hands cupped in her lap. "Blame has no place in this household, my dear." One eyebrow peaks. "Nor in the Lord's."

I squirm but raise my chin and peer into her eyes' black depths. "What am I to think of a God who watched Walter smother the life out of my mother?"

"The evil in this world is great." She sighs and focuses out the window, as if her mind is traveling back in time. What yarns might she spin?

She blinks and returns her gaze to me. "Just look at the cross if you don't believe it." She leans forward, the light in her gaze piercing. "But the love of God is greater."

Chastised, I stare at my hands in my lap. "Ma needed a love that great. And so does Blossom."

"Let's pray, dear." She offers praise and petitions, but I squint at the rug. Her answer is to trust God with my brother and a frail thirteen-year-old girl. Where was His great love when Walter slashed my flesh open with a whip?

"Amen." Her voice corrals my wandering thoughts. She stands, and her chair whines against the floor. "You must be hungry. Supper's ready."

A sudden sense of ingratitude overtakes me. If Ida's God possesses a greater arm span than her own, can't I trust Him with my loved ones?

I ignore my quandary and follow her past an empty classroom and a sewing center no longer whirring. The aromas of roasted chicken, yeast bread, and bacon-seasoned beans draw us, magnet-like, down a hallway. Philip and Donnie, with Wally perched beside him, await us in the dining hall.

"Children, please welcome our guests, Lily and Donnie Sloat. And friend, Wally."

The handful of students rise to their feet. Philip urges Donnie to step forward, but he refuses. Will he ignore Ida's directions as well?

Applause brings warmth to my cheeks. I feel utterly embarrassed. How will I enter social gatherings armed with nothing but a pad and pencil? Honestly, the thought terrifies me.

Judge Fulbright's advice returns—*press pass . . . society circles . . . a reference from Ida Tate . . . working families' homes, tenements, hospitals, even prisons.*

Might I encounter more danger in the city than I ever dreamed? My imagination runs in circles, conjuring disasters and stealing supper's flavor.

Hungering for privacy, I choose not to linger for after-supper singing around the piano.

Philip is sharing his space with Donnie, and I take to the spare room. It's swaddled in moonlight. I close my door and lean against it. The moon casts a patchwork bit of the heavens across a bedside Bible. The open window allows the night creatures' chorus and lazy wisps of a breeze to dance through. Crickets continue their ceaseless wail, and cicada's tunes pick up. Their songs match those back home around Rock Creek.

Is Broadview's bachelor mockingbird still courting, or has he found a mate?

I don my nightclothes anticipating what awaits me: homespun sheets. Like Ma's. Setting Blossom's photograph on the bedside table, I bring the cotton cover to my chin. It smells of homemade soap. And comfort. As if Ma's reaching out to me.

Clouds pass over the moon, casting the photograph into shadows. How did Walter lure her away? She can't swim. Did he lay down a plank and dare her to cross? Ella fell into Rock Creek one Christmas past, all but freezing to death. If not for Vernon, she'd have perished.

Did Blossom meet such an end? Or will she even still?

I flop onto my back and run my fingers through my hair. I must stop this. A newspaper job awaits me, and I've a puzzle to complete. But the pieces lies in dark shadows still.

The Bible draws my eye. Who's Lily Sloat to question fine women of faith like Ma and Ida? Ella and Addie? And Maggie? Their God has shown them plenty.

The cloud scatters, as if heavenly hands have sifted it to powder. Moonlight stretches its fingers through the panes and taps me on the shoulder.

Straightening the sheet and laying my hands at my sides, I permit myself thoughts of God. Like a cattle prod, the Bible nudges me to consider one of Andrew's Sunday messages and the hymn "Purer in Heart." What if all I accomplish by opening the holy book is seeing how impure I am?

I asked for Ida's insight. But her responses affected me in unwelcome ways.

The Good Book pesters, as if picking at a scab, preventing the wound beneath it heal—a sore that will infect my soul without the proper ointment.

I try to see God as Father. But I've known nothing but cruelty at the hands of a father. Even my mother's love was stolen from me.

Punching my pillow, I flop onto my side . . . away from the holy book.

In the night I dream I'm standing at the edge of a wrinkled lake held in the palm of a great hand. Damselflies kiss the water, and rings expand into circles of babies.

Fair and dressed in yellow, one stands out from the others. She's laughing.

Blossom.

I awake with a start, one hand clenched. The moon casts a shaft of light across my body, and my fingers unfold. I eased into sleep with the shuttle clutched in one hand.

Resolved, I remind myself to keep my wits and train my eyes on the goal: Walter in jail. Ella's daughter back home. And women in their rightful places in voting booths and on juries.

I've yet to shed a tear, but I must find rest. A new world awaits me in Texas.

CHAPTER 18

*S*unday dawns with the thermometer registering in the low seventies, a welcome relief. With Donnie's place at Jackson assured, one less problem weighs me down.

My southbound train departs at noon. Philip will drive me to the station in time to return to lead the chapel service, a gathering I'm grateful to avoid. We're to depart for the depot at eight o'clock. I check the bedside clock. Six o'clock. Plenty of time for memoirs.

Squinting and angling the volume this way and that, I manage to decipher the aged and unfamiliar script.

> *May : ye : 28ᵗʰ : 1775*
> *Moon be stingy with Light.*
>
> *Christians speak Blessin over Bread & Wine on First Day o Week. Tis Lord's Day, they say. Strange Lot.*
>
> *I be watchin & wonderin.*
>
> *Rachel Lloyd*
> *Daughter o Abraham*

I sense kinship with this young woman—perhaps not by blood, but certainly by experience. I, too, consider Christians a strange lot. And I, like Rachel, will try to understand them.

I turn the page to the next entry, the print clearer than the last.

June : ye : 5ᵗʰ : 1775

Davie be on Deck, Men meetin with ye Cap'n. Passage Fee raised. Food & Supply Cost hiked. Davie to work at ye Port o Philadelphia to repay Debt.

Tis all a lie. Christian Lord's Supper be doin Cap'n no Good.

Rachel Lloyd
Daughter o Abraham

I would content myself with aboard-ship intrigues this morning, but breakfast in a working household like Ida's is served before the sun rises—-even on Sundays. The aroma of bacon and flapjacks refuses to be ignored.

Dressed for travel in a simple, high-necked dress, I step into the parlor and telephone Maggie, but news remains unchanged. *I'll find you, dear child. I'm on my way.*

I enjoy a breakfast of oats and fruit. Donnie devours his feast and scrapes up the last morsels and glances at me with a grin. A positive sign. I have just rinsed off my dish and cutlery when my brother joins the other boys washing dishes. He flings dishwater, behavior our mother would never allow.

"Donnie—"

Ida grabs my arm, holding me in place. "He'll learn from others. I'll intervene when I must." She gestures over her shoulder toward her private rooms. "Let's chat awhile."

Leading me to her parlor, she offers an upholstered easy chair. "What's troubling you, dear?"

My throat tightens, unexpected and unwanted. I haven't released a single tear since Ma died, and I won't start now. A torrent might result.

But I must answer this octogenarian with the respect due her. "I can't observe my brother from here."

"Won't you trust me?"

If Ma were in my place, would she be stewing? Or would she release her loved ones into this capable woman's hands?

"My insides are an ant bed this morning, simply teeming. I keep thinking about what you mentioned yesterday—-contacts in Fort Worth. As a reporter, I'll be developing a file of sources, sniffing out news tips. The sooner I arrive, the sooner I can begin my search."

She pulls a sheet of stationery from the lap drawer. "I listed them here. There's Sheriff Rae. And J. Frank Norris and his lovely wife. He's the firebrand preacher at First Baptist Church. There's Flora Zane, a firecracker suffragist with connections all over Tarrant County. And business leaders, owners of properties in an unsavory part of town who need a swift kick in the seat of their pants."

I scan the treasure trove. "What exactly is the unsavory part of town?"

She heaves a sigh. "Informally, it's known as Hell's Half Acre. A minuscule segment of the city's land area, it claims an inordinate portion of the community's commerce."

"What sort of commerce is that?"

"The sort that's seeded along cattle drives and railheads like Cowtown's."

"You mean . . ."

"I mean saloons and brothels."

Ida intends to send me into brothels and saloons? As Walter Sloat's child, I had a belly full of the agony whiskey and brothels wreak in homes.

Checking my brooch watch, I worry the inside of my cheek between my teeth. "Philip and I are leaving for the train station at eight o'clock. I've a few minutes to spare, but sitting and talking isn't accomplishing a thing."

She lays a gentle hand on mine. "Sometimes our most productive work is birthed . . ." She sweeps a hand around the room. "In parlors. Around coffee tables. With Bibles on our laps. And when we reveal secrets, often they take us where we never dreamed."

I heave out a deep breath. "So picking at wounds. Digging up secrets. And laying them out for others to view—"

"Just might accomplish more than running off before you're prepared."

I wanted to ask Ida's opinion on my mother's keepsakes, certainly not speak of saloons and brothels. But the sea chest and its secrets belong to Ma. Have I the right to expose them? Would she want me to share with Ida Tate?

An inexplicable sensation nudges my spirit, and I hear my mother's words. *Go on, Lil'.* "You see...I've stumbled across a mystery."

"Oh? Tell me more."

"Ma left me her one possession, an ancient sea chest some ancestor hauled across the Atlantic. A monogram and date are carved in the lid—RLD 1775."

"Oh my. That *is* ancient."

The telephone jangles, startling us both. Such a convenience is as rare in this countryside as it is around rural Needham. Ida answers and hands me the earpiece. "It's for you."

What news might be lurking at the other end of the line? I bring the gadget to my ear. "Hello?"

"Lily?"

"Maggie. What is it?"

"A telegram arrived for you." Not yet at ease on Broadview's telephone, she all but shouts into the mouthpiece.

Has the sheriff wired? The morning newspaper headlined the Battle of the Frontiers. And the struggle in Togoland. Has Addie been injured? Why can't everyone remain neutral like Switzerland? War would become obsolete.

"A telegram from whom?"

She clears her throat. "*Fort Worth Caller.*"

What in the world do they want on a Sunday morning? "Go on."

"I'm afraid it's bad news."

My spirits plummet. "What is it?"

"They've given your position to someone else."

Thoughts of the Jackson train station crumble to dust. A sense of rejection and something else—-perhaps relief—-sweeps through me. But what about my plans to sniff out Walter? And what about Blossom?

"You still there, Lily?"

"I'm here." How am I to respond? On the one hand, I'm relieved I won't be elbowing my way into social gatherings and questioning reluctant church leaders. But on the other, how am I to find leads to Walter?

"Excuse me . . . Madam?" A stranger's voice interrupts our conversation. "This is a party line. Get off."

I gaze at Ida with my mouth slightly ajar. "Something about a party line."

She grabs the receiver and speaks into the mouthpiece. "You can wait a few more minutes, Ishmael Bodman. My guest has an emergency."

She hands me the bell-shaped listening device, and I bring it to my ear. A click sounds. "You still there, Maggie?"

"Yes. But we better hang up." She speaks as if I'm hard of hearing.

"Thank you for calling. I'll contact *Caller.*" I return the receiver to its cradle and turn to Ida. "Looks like I won't be going anywhere today. I'm unemployed."

She eases into her desk chair with an expression of bewilderment.

Questions. Possibilities. A need for explanation. They stir like a rabble of butterflies in my mind. "No doubt they gave the job to a man. What now?"

"I have a suggestion."

I flop into the comfortable chair.

"As you know, I'm involved in the fight for women's rights. And legislation to protect females of every age from an abuse seldom spoken of in polite circles—white slavery. For corrupt purposes.

"My connections extend to Texas, but at my age, traveling is out of the question. I need an assistant to represent me at women's assemblies and rallies. Would you consider the position?"

My thoughts have deteriorated into a jumble. Can I form a suitable response? "I'm ignorant of the women's cause. I have nothing to contribute."

"You've known destitution, have you not? Abuse? Powerlessness? And a child you love has been kidnapped."

"It's true Ma and I lived in a tarpaper prison. And we bore Walter's abuse out of a mindset of powerlessness."

"You testified in a court of law, did you not?"

"With my friends' support and guidance. And I asked what difference might the vote—and one woman on the jury—have made. But I'm not capable of persuading the public. I could make matters worse."

"You're blessed with extraordinary friends who've educated you and expanded your world. Other girls need some of the same. And equality under the law. That includes the vote. And someone with a story like yours could hlep."

My shoulders sag. "Truthfully, I wonder if I'm cut out for society gatherings and public speaking and the like. I'm just a—"

"You're not *just* anything, Lily Sloat. You're a daughter of the King of Heaven. What're a few society ladies alongside a host of angels?"

If Ida knew how far I stand from the gates of the King's palace, she'd rethink her pronouncement. "How can I find Blossom if I'm galavanting all over Texas?"

"Do what you can to find her, with assistance from law enforcement. And then give her to the Lord, dear."

I feel as fickle as Oklahoma's weather in May. Can I ever possess a steady faith like Ida's? Or any faith at all? And will I ever find my true self?

Disappointment. Doubt. Old recriminations propel me to my feet. Shoving from my chair, I flee. To a place of quiet and solitude. Under a fringe of walnut leaves. At Jackson Creek.

A bullfrog belly flops into the stream, and I crumple into the creekside willow chair, crestfallen. My dream of a career in newspaper reporting—dashed? Granted, I've begun to wonder if the world of meeting news deadlines and breaking headlines, prying tips from reluctant sources, concealing and exposing without thought for the ramifications is what I'm cut out for. But I wanted to decide for myself, not have it forced on me.

I long to cry out to someone . . . something . . . higher, bigger, stronger than myself.

I need . . .

I long for . . .

What?

Have I tumbled down a rabbit's hole?

Meanwhile, the old sea chest's secrets nag. Why have they cropped up just now? It seems as if my mother's nudging me to investigate them, as if they're part of this swirling cyclone.

Ida's soft-soled footsteps announce her arrival. "You've come to a place for tears." She couches her words in a soft southerly breeze. "Hundreds have wept on this spot. Tears heal."

"Mine are bottled up. No way to uncork them. Will I never heal?"

"Healing follows its own road." A veritable bird's nest of life lines crisscross her sun-baked skin. It has taken decades for Ida to come to such beauty.

"What's your deepest longing, child? Beyond your love for your prince, that is. And justice and reclamation of a dear child."

"I crave something I can't name."

She nods. "I stepped onto this soil decades ago, searching for something I couldn't name. Jackson was a refuge at first, but it became my purpose. Now it's home."

"I've purpose aplenty—justice for Ma, health for Donnie, rescue for Blossom, safety for Addie, the vote for women."

"Why are you driven to these lofty goals, dear?"

Taken aback, I frown. "For the good in them, of course."

"Who determines they're good?"

"Everyone knows justice and mercy and reconciliation are worthy and upright, Ida."

"Do they?"

"I don't know what you're getting at."

Her head bobs as she gazes at her hands in her lap. "Good and evil must be measured by an objective standard. Otherwise what's good or evil to me or you can look far different to someone like Walter."

"Never thought of it that way. What does this have to do with my longing?"

"You'll answer that for yourself. At the right time, dear." She smiles and lays a palm against my cheek. "Meanwhile, I assume you won't be taking the train to Texas today."

I shrug. "Might as well return to Broadview."

"Will you consider my offer of an assistantship?"

"I don't know. I . . ."

"Give it a try. If you decide it's not for you, I'll understand."

"I have no idea how to stand up in public and advocate for women."

"You know much more than you realize. I'll give you pointers." She taps her fingertips on her chest. "But all you really need is what's in here." She moves her fingers to her forehead. "What's stored in your memory. And a tongue."

I dig a trench in the dirt with the toe of my shoe. "Representing you leaves me feeling . . ." My chin inches downward. "Small. The sensation is so heavy at times I can't hold up my head." My voice cracks, but tears continue to hide.

She sets a thumb and forefinger on my chin and raises it. "King David called God *the lifter* of his head. He'll lift yours if you'll let Him."

"I come from sorry seed, Ida. I'll never measure up."

"God plants new seeds and straightens crooked paths. But we must hand them to Him. He won't force us. The straightening requires pain, but He makes us better for it. Recognition of your smallness is a helpful starting place."

I peek at her from the corner of an eye. "Can't someone else do this?"

"Personal stories like yours can help achieve the vote and equal rights for women."

My story again. "My life . . . the things I've . . . People are cruel."

"Indeed. Sorrow and cruelty have speckled my life. But the Lord's used the grief in ways I never dreamed." She gazes to the heavens. "There's a gospel of sorts to preach."

I draw back. "Preach?"

"Paint a portrait, if you will. With words. About the extremes to which some men stoop when women like your mother are powerless under the law."

"Share my story with rank strangers?"

"With friends you've yet to meet, my dear." She smiles. "At women's clubs, temperance leagues, churches, and the like. But other gatherings, too, like rallies and picket lines. I can keep you informed of what I know is happening."

"I was swept into a picket line alongside Ella some years back, and we ended up in jail. I've no interest in repeating that experience."

"None of the women I'm speaking of are firebrands. You needn't worry."

But baring my soul can open old wounds. Mulling, I tuck a stray tress behind an ear. Jiggle a foot. And catch the inside of a cheek between my teeth.

I owe Ida full consideration of her offer. "I'll think on it."

She checks her pendant watch. "It's time for chapel. How the time has flown." She pauses with a pondering expression. "I believe we're doing the Lord's bidding where we are." She grins. "How about you?"

I raise open palms. "Don't ask me. You're the one with a straight line to Heaven."

She settles back.

"I've stumbled across a puzzle of sorts. Ma's one possession, an old sea chest some ancestor hauled across the Atlantic. I found mysterious items tucked into its bowels."

Her wide-eyed expression invites me to continue.

"Some were what I expected from an old chest—baby clothes, embroidery, a spool doll. And a cameo. But the objects in the false bottom intrigue me."

She leans toward me. "A false bottom?"

I glance toward the stately, red-brick building. "I brought some of the contents with me."

She sits erect. "What're we waiting for?" Barreling toward her home, she leaves me scrambling to keep up.

Am I opening a proverbial box of trouble?

Perhaps.

But I'll open it anyway.

CHAPTER 19

*R*etrieving my valise, I follow Ida into her private parlor. Setting my rolled sketch of the family tree on the coffee table, I hold the Bible and hand Ida the journal.

"What do you think about that old diary?"

Squinting, she handles its fragile pages with a feather touch, but they crackle like dry leaves. I fear they'll disintegrate.

She wipes her lenses and readjusts the eyeglasses on the bridge of her nose. "My eyes aren't what they used to be. You'll have to read it for me."

I move into the light of the floor lamp. "The first entry is an account of a transatlantic journey by a Rachel and husband Davie."

"And the year?"

"1775."

She draws in an audible breath. "What do the entries include?"

"Life aboard ship. Descriptions of life in the colonies. War. Prayers. And drawings. Over the years the handwriting changes. Some of it is faded and all but unreadable. And the ink has bled in places. But it's a fascinating account of the times."

I read the past two days' accounts aloud, and Ida sits nodding, her expression intense. She closes her eyes and rests her head against the davenport's back, motionless. Has she dropped off to sleep?

She raises a hand, her broad palm exposed. "Any entries by your mother?"

"The last entry is similar to Ma's hand, though. It's by someone who identifies herself with an R. Dated 1890. North Carolina. She'd fallen in love." I page through the book, reading tidbits but unsure what she's looking for. "On the last page is a drawing of a wild animal."

"May I?" Holding the book in the light, she adjusts the magnifier. "It's a panther. Looks like he's asleep."

"Why would Ma possess such a drawing? I'm realizing how little I knew about her."

"Surely she spoke of her life, even in snatches."

I sigh. "She shared nothing. But the monogram and date in the lid—*RLD 1775*—together with the memoirs . . ."

"Rachel and Davie Lloyd. There you have it. A lead, surely to family."

"There's a family tree also. I did my best to copy it." I unfurl my sketch and weight the corners with clay bowls. "Names are worked into the bark."

She squints at the print. "Recognize any of them?"

"The Lloyds are the tree's trunk. The other names in the diary are on branches. But Ma's not anywhere."

"Is there any other record of marriages and births?"

"There's the Bible."

She hands me the tome, and I open it to the Record of Marriages and Births. "The names are the same as those on the tree."

"More family clues, dear."

"You think so?"

"Why else would your mother preserve them?" She gazes upward, pensive-like.

"I guess you're right. She locked them up and hid the key in the chicken coop. I can't imagine when she read the Bible and made notes."

"Your father was abusive. How would he have reacted if he'd known she treasured these items?"

"He would've burned them. And made us watch."

"No wonder she kept them hidden. Did your brother know about them?"

"Only that Ma intended the chest for me."

"Any other clues?"

"Verses are underlined. Notations in the margins, some so old they're faded."

"Read some verses. Please."

Read Ma's Bible? Aloud? I hesitate.

"What is it?"

What has come over me? The book is . . . ordinary words. Isn't it?

I shake my head. "Let's see, here's one in Galatians. The sixth chapter. 'From henceforth let no man trouble me: for I bear in my body the marks . . .'" I cringe, horrified.

Ida nods. "The Apostle Paul bore in his body the marks of Jesus Christ. He was beaten and whipped, but he considered his scars brands for Jesus."

"Walter's cruelty branded me." But Jesus was kind and loving. Wasn't He? Where in the world did this Paul come up with the idea of being branded for anyone? I shudder.

"Whoever owned this Bible was a student of the Word. So were the keepers of the log. Did your mother speak of her spiritual background?"

Must God sprout in every conversation?

"She spoke of God, more to herself than to me. Matter of fact, she prayed. Walter would've punished us if he discovered she was teaching me. But she set a prayerful example. She was love, plain and simple."

"God is love, so you saw Him in your mother." She taps a her fingers on the open book. "Perhaps she wanted you to do something with the Bible."

"What?"

She peers at me over her spectacles. "Read it."

My cheeks flame, and I tuck my chin. Read about the God who failed my ma? Holding onto God is well and good for my mother and Ida and the rest, but not for me.

Best turn the conversation elsewhere. I pat my pocket and remove the tatting tool.

She holds it in an open palm. "It's a tatting shuttle. Looks like rosewood."

"Any idea what the symbols mean?"

She removes her spectacles and settles against her chair back. "This morning in prayer, the Lord brought someone to mind. Reverend J.T. Upchurch and his wife minister to women, unwed mothers, most of them former prostitutes."

Surprised, I await her explanation.

"Berachah Mission Home in Arlington is their ministry. The mothers keep their babes. They garden. Launder. Sew. Print *Purity Journal*. I've a copy in my office. "

"What has this to do with Ma's shuttle?"

"The home runs a small handkerchief factory." She plucks a kerchief from a pocket. "They tat the edges."

"Tat?" I reach for the folded square of cotton fabric, its edges trimmed in delicate lace. "I can't avoid the subject."

She holds up the shuttle. "This looks like Hebrew. J.T. might know the meaning."

I relax against my chair back, my foot tapping an insistent rhythm on the floor. "I'm bursting to be gone. It isn't too late to make the noon train, is it?"

She glances at a wall clock. "Chapel services are just letting out. Let's corral Philip and be on our way." Her eyes sparkle.

Twisting my gloves into cotton scrolls, I sit on a bench beside Ida in the Jackson depot and read Rachel Lloyd's next entry.

> *June : ye : 6ᵗʰ : 1775*
> *Quarter Moon out ye Porthole*
>
> *Davie be prayin Mornin, Noon & Night. Promised his Ma. Claims Peace in Present Troubles be comin thru Prayer. Ahead o Time.*
>
> *Reckon twill Trust me prayin Man.*
>
> *Rachel Lloyd*
> *Daughter o Abraham*

Peace. From the mid-Atlantic in 1775 to Austria-Hungary in 1914, the ephemeral concept dashes here and yon, avoiding capture even in the simple train station in Jackson, Oklahoma.

My folding fan stirs the thick, still air, but perspiration creeps down my spine. My orchid frock of embroidered lawn will be splotched with dark circles.

I run a finger around a skirt button. "Must be ninety degrees." I lift my bodice fabric and fan. Thankfully my simple straw hat allows air to pass through.

"You'll board in half an hour. Not long to wait."

Passing the fan to her, I whisk my ticket packet around my face.

"I'll be praying for you. Breakfast and supper. Noon and bedtime."

"Thank you. I need help from every quarter." I'm stepping out in blind faith, as Ida puts it. Don't know about the faith part, but I'm groping in the dark.

"I'll keep you apprised of Donnie's progress. You have my letter of introduction with instructions? And my phone number for anonymous messages?"

I pat my valise and nod.

"The Lord sustains the fatherless. Trust Him."

Surely my doubt is on display. I raise a hand to my throat. Under my high-necked bodice, scars. Back home, the body of my dear ma. At Jackson, my fatherless brother. But where's our dear, lost girl?

For now I must follow my employer's directions and keep my eyes and ears open. I'll be looking for clues to my past too.

I can't shake the feeling that somehow they're all connected.

"God loves you, my dear," Ida whispers, leaning against me.

The way He loved me when I begged Walter for my life? When I plead for Blossom?

Best take care. My wayward thoughts can destroy my good sense.

Ida removes a kerchief from her sleeve cuff and dabs moisture from her chin.

Conversations buzz around us. Travelers shout to loved ones, and someone yells, "France has declared war on Austria-Hungary!"

Ida and I lock hands. "Save Addie, Lord," she whispers.

Why would Ida's Lord allow someone as fine as Addie to enter a war zone in the first place? I imagine possibilities, and nausea swells.

Feet tramp, and trunks scrape the brick paving. The train's strident whistle and a blast of steam slash through the commotion and bring me up with a start.

I nab my travel case from beside the bench.

She clutches my forearm. "Promise me you'll talk to Him."

I stand and offer her my hand.

She shakes her head. "Promise."

"Ida, you can't—"

She snatches the ticket packet from me. "Try me."

My mouth slackens, and my brows scrunch into a frown.

Her expression grows fierce. "I'm not sending you off without *your* promise to pray."

I search for a rebuttal. What harm will praying do? I'll be talking to myself and no other. "All right. I'll pray."

She points a forefinger. "Morning, noon, and night."

I roll my eyes and raise a hand in a mock pledge. "I hereby promise that I, Lily Sloat, will pray morning, noon, and night."

She plops the packet into my hands. "Other women are telling their stories. It's time for yours." She smiles, and her eyes twinkle.

Reveal my story? My stomach twists, but a promise is a promise.

As I turn to the hissing train, a pair of friendly faces rounds the depot's corner.

Holding my hat, I hurry to Donnie and Philip. "Oh, I'll miss you." I give my brother a hug. "You're going to school. Mind your manners."

He grins. Perhaps he'll speak soon.

"Thank you for taking my brother under your wing, Philip."

He removes his flat cap and twists it into a roll. "We're pals." He cuffs his younger charge on the chin, and Donnie flashes a lopsided grin.

What a relief to know the young man will look out for my unschooled, inexperienced loved one.

"All aboard," the conductor calls.

Ida wraps her arms around me. "May the road rise up to meet you, my dear." She holds me at arm's length, and laugh lines form around her eyes. "As Maggie would say."

"Aye, and the same to you."

She urges me onto the train. "Call often. The Metropolitan is well equipped. Go with God." Ida raises her handkerchief. "I'll be praying."

I find my compartment with a common doorway to the adjoining berth and secure the latch. The train whistles and chugs forward, jerking me against the padded bench. I right myself with a hand on the window and take a seat.

The locomotive heaves from the station, coughing billows like dark prairie clouds. As the engine chugs forward, and we clackity-clack toward Texas.

Ida's life story—though speckled with sorrow—bursts with the one intangible I have yet to claim: faith. What will finding faith require?

Dabbing moisture from my forehead, I wonder at what Ida has managed to accomplish in moments. I've agreed to work as her assistant, and she's wrangled a promise from me to pray morning, noon, and night.

What was I thinking?

CHAPTER 20

*A*s the southbound locomotive rattles over the bridge spanning Red River, I let down the window for a better view. The river, named for the soil of its origin in the red sandstone of the Texas Panhandle, runs muggy green today.

I often crossed the span while a student at College of Industrial Arts, but it didn't interest me then as it does today. Has Blossom traveled across Red River?

I push aside dire possibilities and close *The Purity Journal*. Time to enjoy the scenery.

Texas. A land unto itself. And ahead, Fort Worth, the backdrop for my new role as Ida's assistant. I must perform honorably.

Elm, blackjack, and oak woods stretch east and west on either side of the tracks that traverse the cross timbers plains. The soil, reddish in places and darker in others, supports bluestem and buffalo grasses that wave a welcome.

"Dennison, coming up," the conductor calls.

The train brakes at the brick station to board a passenger with a small child and chugs toward Denton. Did blossom board a similar train? If so, to where?

A lovely landscape spreads on either side. Farmhouses here and there. Windmills. Corn in harvest. Ranch land. Dairy barns. Cattle in abundance. The famed stockyards up the way. And the old Chisholm trail.

A great expanse of rich green cotton plants, not yet ready for picking. At the edge of a small town sits a cotton gin with empty trailers in the yard, not a puff of smoke from the stack. All, unwelcome reminders of grueling labor in cotton fields and Andrew's accident—loss of an arm—

nine years ago. I refuse to let them stain this day.

The roof of an imposing structure juts upward in the distance. A cupola. CIA, my alma mater. The administration building rises in noble glory, its head aloft like the dormitory, built in large part with funds donated by Addie. We students enjoyed wagon rides and picnics. And field trips on the trolley.

I hadn't dreamed my education and training would come down to this—assisting Ida, advocating for women, the suffrage movement . . . and telling my story.

Serving as assistant editor of the yearbook, *The Daedalian*, inspired me to pursue writing. My brief *Caller* internship whetted my appetite for writing articles, but it accomplished not an iota in the art of sniffing out a story and elbowing my way into private lives and public gatherings. Yet here I am, chugging toward an assignment I fear will require the same.

Have I lost my mind?

And yet Ida insists I'll discover a level of fulfillment I never dreamed. Should I do so with Blossom lost? Addie unaccounted for. And Cade heartbroken . . . as surely as I?

I slip my reading materials into my satchel and gather my thoughts. Ida insists God cares for the fatherless and aliens. I guess we'll see about that.

"Denton, next stop." The conductor makes a final pass.

Clutching my hat, I lean out the window. The dark brick and granite depot rears its head, as imposing as ever. With bright yellow and brown trim, the structure sports pillars. Roof finials. Elegant window arches. And a copper-roofed tower straining for the sky.

The train chugs to a stop, but steam obstructs my view. I sit back with a vague sense of coming home. No time to visit the campus, but I can step off the train, stretch my legs, and find the ladies' facilities. I push aside the pocket door.

"Good day, miss." A gentleman stranger halts in the close corridor. "After you."

"Thank you, sir." At the exit, I glance over my shoulder. The man is standing closer than good manners allow, prickling my spine. The conductor offers me a hand down, and the dandified gentleman aims for the ticket window with derby hat in hand.

I toss aside the sense of disquiet the stranger engendered and stroll around the building's interior. I visit the wash room and enjoy a root beer.

The conductor issues his final summons, and I hurriedly purchase three picture postcards and scoot to my car.

Outside my compartment, goosebumps rise on my arms and neck. The adjoining cubicle's aisle door slides open, and the stranger leans out. "We meet again."

I pop into the privacy of my berth. And secure the lock.

The engine growls and hisses, and we inch away. The locomotive accelerates through a rural landscape toward Fort Worth. Buildings of varying heights etch an irregular skyline across the distant horizon. Some reach ten stories and others sit contentedly at one. Spires and towers and smokestacks prick the sky.

My *Caller* internship required me to work inside, mainly running errands, but I visited the city as a college student. Our well-chaperoned field trips utilized the interurban rails. Girls whispered the city's bawdy history of saloons, brothels, and gambling houses, but we spied not a hint of unsavory business.

This area has surfaced in conversation of late. I wonder . . . Will Cowtown answer some of my questions? Will the mission home in Arlington?

At the T&P Station, I don my gloves and stuff my belongings into my satchel. Snapping it shut, I stand and smooth my skirt. But I wait for the stranger to debark before I step off the train.

Away with self doubt—and everything sharecropper. I'll step into my new role with my head high.

First stop, the station's telegraph and telephone office. To let Ida and Maggie know I've arrived. I listen for the telltale clicks that signal someone in the Evans or McFarland households has picked up an extension.

But none sound.

"I've arrived, Maggie. Please let Ella know. And Cade, of course." I don't need a forget-me-not bauble to forget-him-not.

"Of course, my dear. God be with you."

A baggage handler checks my claim ticket, and I join him at the imposing clock tower out front. A depot hack driver agrees to deliver me straightaway to the Metropolitan Hotel.

We travel the short distance under a jumbled canopy of wires and cables for electricity, telephones, and the streetcars. The driver swerves to avoid automobiles and trolleys. I read the feisty Jitney automobiles have become a menace to public safety, weaving in and out of traffic and around streetcars to vie for riders' business.

Rather as my driver is doing now, I fear.

The man recounts over his shoulder—unnecessarily—the gruesome details of a streetcar-freight train accident. His soliloquy relieves not a whit of my unease. Nor the lingering effect of the stranger's stare.

I glimpse right and left and behind. No sign of the man. I cover my nose and mouth with my kerchief to ward off the dust. Layers of the nuisance cover the bricked street. And exhaust fumes choke riders in open conveyances like this one.

The three-story Metropolitan Hotel consumes an entire city block. Constructed of handsome red brick with white stone trimming, its straight, dignified lines represent understated strength and permanence.

The driver passes up the hack stand and delivers me to the awning-covered entrance.

Two porters whisk me and my luggage into the marble-pillared lobby. Grateful to be relieved of the city's din, I breathe in the lightly scented air. The expansive, marble and mahogany space is spotted with spittoons aplenty. The electric chandeliers and ceiling fans in the coffered ceiling rival the New York City hotels I visited with Addie.

"Welcome to the Metropolitan." The desk clerk spreads his arms wide. "Do you have a reservation?"

"Yes. Under the name Ida Tate. I'm her assistant, Lily Sloat. Do you have any messages for me, perchance?"

"I'll check." He rifles through a drawer. "Ah, a wire." He edges the yellow slip across the counter and continues his check-in process.

NO NEWS GOOD NEWS

Bless Maggie. No news *is* good news when one fears for a loved one's life.

Glancing around the lobby, I wonder where the infamous love-triangle murder occurred. How terrifying—

"Miss?"

I jerk around. The stranger from the train stands at my side. Is the man following me?

"Excuse me, but I've been wondering since I saw you on the train. Are you a friend of Adelaide Fitzgerald?" His tailored suit and polished dress boots denote affluence.

Sensing the need for circumspection, I hesitate. "Who's asking?"

He dips his meticulously groomed head, his expression conciliatory. "Please forgive me. I'm Chester Wainwright. I met Miss Fitzgerald at the last Cattlemen's Convention. I couldn't help but notice her fiery-haired friend." He clears his throat with a fist to his mustached lips. "If I can be so blunt."

Addie hasn't mentioned a Wainwright. The back of my neck tickles. "I'll tell Adelaide you asked after her." Following the porters up the broad marble staircase, I hazard a peek at the landing, and the hairs on my arms stand up.

The man is leaning against a pillar, staring at me. I shiver.

What's become of my newfound confidence? I better find it. Quickly.

I take dinner in the confines of my luxurious suite—bedroom, private bath, and sitting room with a telephone for local calls, desk, bookcase in reading corner, and an outside view.

Reviewing Ida's instructions, I make a note to contact the first name on her list, a Flora Zane. Slipping between luxurious sheets, I click off the electric lamp. The day's frantic tempo kept thoughts of loved ones at bay. But as I close my eyes and the darkness closes in, I remember my promise.

"Ida insists her assistant must pray," I murmur into the dark as if someone's listening. "Not sure to whom . . . or for what. But I'll start with this: Keep Donnie safe and well. Show me to Blossom. Let her know I won't be long. Help me figure out how I can serve Ida best. And please soothe my ache for Cade and his for me. And help me round up that villain, Walter."

I turn to my side, but my eyes refuse to close. Pushing aside my sheets, I return to the writing table. One more task for tomorrow: Wrest an explanation from *Fort Worth Caller*.

My eyes skim the flocked wallpaper. "With or without help from above."

CHAPTER 21

I wake with a hint of a breeze curling through my open window, supplanting Fort Worth's overnight street noises.

Tagged as *Where the West Begins*, the city and its storied Hell's Half Acre have become legend. I hope to meet the firebrand preacher, J. Frank Norris, who holds to account all associated with the unholy district. Ida provided his wife's contact information.

Recurring fears for Blossom and Addie—and a dream about Cade—robbed me of restful sleep. And waking at the stench of perversity and counterfeit gardenias didn't help. Exhaustion eventually overtook me, and I rested.

The plight of *Nelly*'s women claim the first of my morning.

> *June : ye : 14th : 1775*
> *Moon be full.*
>
> *Cap'n agreed men Labor aboard Ship and not at Port for Debt. They be workin round yonder Clock. Tis Unjust.*
>
> *Women folk gather at Portholes, grumblin. What can we be doin with no rights to our wee Names. I be organizin Women on ye Morrow. We be speakin with one Voice.*
>
> *Rachel Lloyd*
> *Daughter o Abraham*

Women speaking with one voice. The sentiment echoes these decades later, and it brings Berachah to mind. I'll call the Flora Zane on Ida's list and get directions to the home in Arlington. I'll ask her where to find the quarter no one admits exists——Hell's Half Acre.

Breakfast is served in my suite. I enjoy the creamy scramble egg concoction mounded with crispy fried bacon and venison sausage. But Rachel Lloyd's words—*We haven't a right to our names . . . We must speak with one voice*—replay like a phonograph needle stuck in a groove.

I dial Flora Zane's number, but no one answers. I'll try again later.

Examining my garments in a mahogany armoire, I choose an ensemble of soft lawn, a peach and green floral on ivory background. Its neckline displays the cameo nicely, and its trim waistline and soft, pleated peplum make a sweltering belt unnecessary.

Downstairs I question the concierge. "Sir, what was that egg dish on my breakfast tray?"

"*Migas*, ma'am. With cheese and corn *tortillas*. Our French chef has mastered Mexican cuisine."

"Delicious. Now, I need to make a long distance telephone call."

"There's a private cubicle down the hallway." He points to the right.

Entering the secluded, mahogany-paneled space, I sit in a worn leather armchair fit for a Texas ranch. An operator facilitates the calls to Jackson and Broadview, and I return to the concierge assured my brother is content and no catastrophe has befallen a loved one.

I excuse myself and aim for the news alcove where national newspapers and magazines are made available to guest. One headline in particular grabs my attention. *Child Abducted from Lake Erie!*

Snatching up the daily, I scan the article. Families frequent the amusement park between Fort Worth and Dallas, but it is considered safe and above-board. How could something like this have happened?

I check the reporter's name. Seems a visit to *Caller* is in order. Hoisting my handbag's strap over my shoulder, I proceed along the walkway with the sun on my face.

Like its rival, *Fort Worth Star-Telegram*, *Caller* is located a few blocks from the Met, but in the opposite direction. As an intern, I rode the interurban from Denton two days a week. My colleagues hopped streetcars for events around the city and occasionally took the interurban to Dallas, but as a student, I was confined to the office.

But I ignore the trolley stop. The five-block walk will do me good.

Wind gusts around the corner of the building, snapping the tail of my hatband ribbon. But my extra-long pins hold the headpiece firm.

Thank heavens I chose sensible walking shoes—my noontime prayer.

A young girl's lemon-custard curls bring Blossom to mind. *I want to snap pictures for newspapers. I could learn from you. On your job.*

Oh, dear one, I'll find you. I promise.

I slow my pace, catching my breath and gathering my thoughts. Can I uncover a single tip through club ladies? Perhaps not. But the *Caller* reporter who wrote the article might know a thing or two.

I pick up my pace.

Outside the three-story office building, a newspaper boy in a flat cap stands beside a stack of newspapers, shouting the latest headline. "Germany attacks Belgium! Britain declares war on Germany! Get the latest here!"

My gaze fixes on the bold type. The dreaded war has begun in earnest. Addie.

I stumble, and the paper boy reaches out to me. "Careful there."

"Thank you. One copy please." I hold out the pennies and devour the headlines above the fold. The war is mushrooming.

Has my dear mentor and friend found a safe harbor somewhere in Europe?

"Can I help you, ma'am?"

I focus on the lad, previously an insignificant detail on the periphery of my vision. A welcoming smile reveals misaligned teeth. Large, deep-set hazel eyes surrounded by a maze of freckles reach out to me, as if they know and understand more than I.

"You're a fine young gentleman. What's your name?"

He slides off his cap. "Name's McGregor. Tad McGregor."

I pull a small tablet from my handbag. "I'd like to compliment your mother on rearing such a fine son. What's her name? And where may I mail a note?"

"Ma's named Beulah. We live in Battercake Flats. But right now . . .

she's in the workhouse."

My mouth sags open. "Your father's in charge then?"

"Nope. Pa's dead. Just Ma and us seven young'uns." He flips off his cap and scratches his scalp. "I reckon you can address that note to Beulah McGregor in Battercake Flats. She'll read it when she comes home."

Left somewhat speechless, I stumble toward the building's wide entrance. A gentleman holds open the glass front door, and I flounder through, dazed. Sandy-haired and hatted, trim, and dressed in trousers, the man sports a vest and white shirt with sleeves rolled to the elbows. I vied for a position reporting on world events. Might this man have taken the job? And then the Women's Society page position vanished.

A receptionist offers me a warm smile. "May I help you?"

"Yes . . . I was an intern here earlier in the year . . ."

She angles her head to the side. "I thought you looked familiar."

"Might I speak with the Editor in Chief?'

"Do you have an appointment?"

I finger comb damp strands from my forehead. "I've come all the way from Oklahoma on business and would so enjoy renewing acquaintances."

Her delicately bowed lips draw up. "Hmm. Top staff are huddled at present—the war news, you understand."

"Of course. Dreadful."

"You're not a stranger, so go on up. You may catch Mr. Francis between meetings."

I thank the gracious greeter and skitter up the stairs. My sensible shoes have begun to pinch, but I must not allow my discomfort to show.

Outside the editor's office, I encounter a line of defense composed of one. She rivals Belgium's defense at Liege. The salt-and-pepper-haired secretary has received her marching orders. "Mr. Francis is not to be disturbed."

I repeat my *renewing acquaintances* line. "I'll just wait if you don't mind." Taking a stiff-backed wooden chair I figure no one will wrestle me for, I peruse the paper.

The wall clock chips away seconds. Minutes. I read every speck of the paper—even advertisements for liver pills and a new sanitarium for emotionally insane women. Does the same sort of facility exist for men? I cross my legs, rock my foot, and sigh.

I pace and examine the watercolor landscapes.

The editor's office remains barred, and his dour-faced sentry ignores me.

I approach the guarder of the door a second time. "I'm wondering . . ."

She pries her bespectacled gaze from typing. Her eyebrows rise, creating wrinkles.

"Berachah Mission Home."

She draws back with a snarl.

"Might you have the address and the interurban schedule?"

She looks me up and down and harrumphs. She consults a directory and scribbles the address on a pad of paper, ripping off the top sheet with a flourish.

I scan the arrival and departures times and check the clock. I'd missed the last afternoon trolley. The next available is the following morning.

A door opens and bangs closed down the hallway. A trio of gentleman step out and huddle toward the stairway.

"I believe that's Mr.—"

"As I said, Miss . . ."

"Sloat. Lily Sloat."

"Mr. Francis isn't to be disturbed." She straightens her spine and sets her fingers on the typewriter keys, her hand position pristine.

"He won't be back this afternoon?"

"Afraid not." She shoves the pad of paper toward me. "You may leave your name."

I print my name and Metropolitan Hotel on the back of Ida's calling card.

She flips it into a side drawer and returns to her task.

It seems Ida's assistant has struck out.

Settling my purse strap on my shoulder, I proceed down the stairs and step outside. Business is slow for the paper boy.

Returning to the Met, I consider a plan for making use of my time. My loved ones at home appreciate letters. Ida will be waiting for a call. According to her notes, the Rosen Heights women—The Rosen Irregulars—meet tomorrow.

An idea forms, one that originated on the street corner outside *Caller*. A comment Tad, the paper boy, spoke . . .

After a light lunch of chilled finger sandwiches and fizzy fruit drink, I approach the concierge. "I'm looking for directions to Berachah Mission Home."

He glances left and right, as if suspecting eavesdroppers. "The home in Arlington for . . . unwed mothers?"

I move closer with an elbow on the counter ledge. "That's correct. But why are we whispering?"

Again he sizes up the surroundings. "I'd advise you not to bandy around that name, not on a Wednesday."

"A Wednesday?"

"Wednesday Club assembles in the ballroom this afternoon." He points above our heads.

Ida mentioned the organization, but what is the man implying?

He straightens his vest and steps around the counter. "The cream of female society gathers each first Wednesday." Again he glances around. "Not everyone approves of that place."

I nod, but in truth I'm puzzled. Ida didn't hint at such. "I'll keep that in mind, sir."

The Met's front doors swing open, and a cadre of matrons makes a grand entry.

The concierge scrambles to greet the ladies. "Oh there you are, Mrs. . . ."

I step aside for the klatch to stroll down the broad hallway toward the staircase. Suffragettes are unexpected, but I'll avail myself of this opportunity. Berachah can wait.

The ever-so-accommodating concierge escorts the ladies up the stairs, and I follow at a respectable distance. I find the man waiting outside the ballroom.

"I'm sorry, but this is a private gathering, ma'am." He assumes a severe expression.

"I'm here under the auspices of a . . . member at large. I'm to meet a lady by the name of Zane." I hand him Ida's card and wait with a smile.

"Just a moment." He ducks into the ballroom and returns in moments with a bright-faced woman trailing him.

Attired in a tea gown of white eyelet and lace, the lady's as tall as I. She extends a hand. "Hello. I'm Flora. Welcome to Fort Worth." Bronze-colored waves escape her hat's asymmetrical brim. "Ida called our president last night. Told her to expect to hear from you."

I stare at her lush mound of hair. If mine is like copper, hers is bronze. With streaks of brass and a touch of the rich burgundy that graces Addie's crown.

I'm struck by our similarity. "We could be sisters."

"You're ever so much more beautiful than I, Lily." She ushers me into the ballroom. "I trust your journey was uneventful."

"I wouldn't dub crossing Red River uneventful exactly." I allow her to tug me into a well-appointed space crowned with elegant chandeliers and spotted with ladies' hats.

"Our president extends her apology for not greeting you herself." She nods to the speaker at the podium. "Tending to business."

The president, a picture of social dignity, speaks through a small megaphone that amplifies her whisper-soft voice. The group leans forward, as if locked onto her words.

"You're up next," Flora whispers at my ear, her doe-brown eyes irresistible.

"What? I'm afraid there's been a mis—"

"We're dying to hear about Indian Territory."

"But we haven't been a territory since '07. We're just plain ol' Oklahoma." Surely these women aren't expecting me to speak on such short notice.

"Our guest speaker has arrived." Mrs. President points to me. "Welcome, Lily."

The group turns en masse and applauds.

Thoroughly bewildered, I bend to Flora. "What is it I'm to speak about?"

"Why, the suffrage movement in Indian—I mean Oklahoma—of course."

"I see." But I certainly do not understand.

"You're bound to have a backstory. Everyone does. Don't worry." She extends both arms wide. "We're all friends here."

Open the storybook of my life? Now?

She nudges me forward.

I have a dream.

But girls need equality under the law.

What difference might a single jurywoman have made?

Forcing a smile, I step to the podium and eye the expanse of eager faces.

How much should I divulge?

Can I trust these women?

Or have I entered the Coliseum?

For all I know, newspaper reports have made it all the way from Needham. Perhaps the ladies have heard of the trial . . . and the lying sharecropper's daughter.

Ma's voice speaks to me. *The Good Lord saw fit to remove you from this sorry side of the creek. For His purposes.*

Seized with a sense of weightiness, I gather myself. "Hello. I'm Lily."

An ocean of smiles and head nods respond.

"Oklahoma is our country's forty-seventh state. But did you know we were almost the forty-seventh *and* forty-eighth?"

Heads angle to the side, and brows wrinkle.

"You see . . ."

Three quarters of an hour later, I've described the plight of certain sharecroppers and their children. Explained what the abuse of one man did to those of us dependent on him, in particular, the females. How the voices of his women folk were silenced with a fist and a whip. Like cream rising in warm milk, I've spilled my story of rescue and learning to read, lavender-scented sheets, and a graduation cap and gown.

I've looked these women in the eyes and reminded them the country's plastered with girls like me. I'm the exception, not because I'm more exceptional than the next girl. But because those who loved me are.

The ladies bound to their feet, not simply applauding but *whoopin' 'n' hollerin'*, as Ma would declare.

I pull a handkerchief from my handbag and dab at moisture above my top lip.

I've done it. Told my story. Part of it, at least. And a great chasm to the pit of Hell hasn't swallowed me. Matter of fact, Mrs. President thanked me. Her arm around my shoulder takes the shape of an angel's wing. If such a thing exists.

And then come the questions.

A dour club member raises a hand and calls out, "The women of Oklahoma failed in their mission to include equal suffrage in the state constitution. So what're you up to now?"

Heat surges at my neckline. I raise a hand to my collar, remembering the marks beneath it. What do suffragists proclaim? *Women have a right to participate in their governance.*

Blossom materializes before me. *What will you do about me?*

She and her sisters will be women one day. Who will safeguard their places in a world bent toward men?

Ma's earnest appeal from four Christmases past returns. *Make something of yourself, something I weren't able to do. Fly. For me.*

I straighten my shoulders and sweep my gaze across the expectant faces. "Ladies, the women of Oklahoma, like you Texans, intend equal suffrage to be a part of the United States Constitution."

The gathering bounds to their collective feet and applaud. My cheeks burn red hot, and my fingers quake. For heaven's sake, these women are cheering for the scandalous sharecropper's daughter, the one the Needham Women's Club barred, the one the jury said lied. The one scarred in ways this fine group can't imagine.

I cover my trembling lips with my hankie, thanking Addie for the elocution lessons.

Flora greets me with warmth. "Oh, my dear. You must visit one of the projects we support. It's a home for unwed mothers. In Arlington."

"The mission home?"

"Yes. You know of it?"

"I have intended to visit it. But the concierge . . . He . . ."

She flicks a dismissive hand. "He's like most men—and some women—who claim such places will soil their ladies." She leans toward me and grins. "But we know better."

A receiving line forms, refreshments are served, and a hint of an appetite for rich pastries develops.

Meanwhile, there's the matter of a bedtime prayer facing me.

And my feet are killing me.

CHAPTER 23

*T*he dawn's sun brings with it thoughts of Rachel Lloyd. With my wrapper tied snugly at my waist, I wash my hands and sit at the desk to examine the pale script. Thus far the sheepskin has remained supple. But delicate edges of the parchment have crumbled. Pages have stuck together. Using a letter opener, I loosen them and read through my magnifier.

> *June : ye : 22ⁿᵈ : 1775*
> *Naught but Quarter Moon in ye Night Sky.*
>
> *Women be longin for Home.*
>
> *Retched Coughs. Fetid Air. Abominable Heat. Mold.*
>
> *Leaks in ye Hull. Carpenter be workin. Men pumpin. Women too.*
>
> *We be sharin Load.*
>
> *Rachel Lloyd*
> *Daughter o Abraham*

The Lloyds' predicament weighs heavy on my mind, reminding me of my own frustration the previous afternoon.

Unable to speak with Mr. Francis, I returned to the Met with discomfort in more than my feet. I was caught in throes of anguish. For Blossom. And my inability to do a thing about it.

I called Flora near bedtime. "Might we visit the workhouse?"

"The debtors' prison? What in the world for?"

"The newspaper boy I met on the street—"

"The paper boy?"

"Yes. The one harking his wares outside the *Caller* building. I struck

up a conversation with him, blurted out a question. Curiously unchar-
acteristic of me."

"Have mercy. What question?"

"Where's your mother?"

"*My* mother?"

"No. The *boy's* mother. I asked him where his mother is."

"And you did this because . . ."

"Because the question popped into my mind."

"Curious."

"His mother's in the workhouse."

"So . . ."

"So I must visit the place. But where is it?"

"I thought you were traveling to Arlington tomorrow."

"No one's expecting me, so I'll visit another day. Visiting women in
the workhouse is appropriate as Ida's assistant."

"I'll see what I can do. At any rate, my bodyguard-drive will accompany us."

Why a bodyguard?

"The paper boy mentioned rocks at the workhouse. Peculiar, don't
you think?"

"We'll figure it out when we arrive. Pick you up at nine o'clock in the
morning." She disconnected with a click in my ear.

Settling the phone receiver into its cradle, I stared at the contraption
and wondered what had come over me.

As I close the journal, the morning news headline captures my attention. Austria-Hungary has declared war on Russia. And Serbia, on
Germany.

I call Maggie. She has nothing new to report, allaying my anxiety not
a whit.

A hearty breakfast of hotcakes and ham fortifies me for the day's
excursion.

At a sharp knock on my door, I check my pendant watch. Flora's a bit
early.

Pausing to submit to a promised prayer—*Take me where I can do some good, and I'll thank you*—I open the door and stand aside for my new friend's effervescence.

"Talked to the supervisor." My new friend's hat wiggles. "The guard will be expecting us."

"Thank you for arranging this. The city workhouse won't disappoint, I'm certain." I examine my reflection in the floor mirror. My muted nutmeg-colored ensemble will resist soiling. I snatch my handbag off the bureau and lock my valise in the room's safe.

As we make our way to the stairs, she chatters between breaths. "The men work chain-gang style around the city and the women in the laundry and sewing room." Her mink-brown eyes sparkle. A shock of her mane lazes in folds beneath her hat like sculptured bronze. "A handful work in the yard." Her simple camel-colored skirt and blouse will withstand our target's dust-laden byways

The bodyguard-driver carts us around the courthouse to Franklin Street and westward to the convergence of West and Clear Forks of Trinity River. He brakes the Packard sedan in a parking lot beside a twelve-foot stockade fence. Beyond the barrier sits a square-shaped building with a mission-styled facade. The workhouse. There's a section I read housed the city's stray animals—dogs, cats, cattle, and mules.

"There." Flora points to three women manhandling sledge hammers at a pile of rocks.

"One of them might be the paper boy's mother, Flora."

"I hear the women on rock duty are dangerous, Lily."

"We'll see. Come on."

She joins me with her diligent bodyguard in tow. Cade would be hovering as well.

Cade again? I must banish such thoughts..

The women wear skirts and blouses of coarse, ash-gray ducking. Dark semicircles line their underarms and leave ragged trails of blotches along their spines. Bandanas hold their hair atop their heads.

They lean on their hammer handles and eye us.

A guard nods and unlocks the gate. I step onto the barren grounds and survey the structure. The building measures no more than a couple hundred square feet, room for only a small contingency of debtors.

"How many prisoners?" I ask the guard.

"Sixty."

Shock pries my eyes wide. "Where do you put them all?"

"Got six cells, two for Coloreds."

"They must be stacked atop one another."

He scratches his head. "I reckon so."

I catch my bottom lip between my teeth, mulling. "Do you have an inmate with a son named Tad?"

"That'd be Beulah." He nods to the white woman breaking rocks. Sweat has soaked through her mud-colored hair, braided and wound into a tight knot at the nape of her neck.

I motion toward the building. "We'll check the facility first, sir."

"Suit yourself."

Stepping inside, we draw up with a start. Sunlight through the open doorway illumines the dark interior. The facility is far too small for sixty human beings, and the heat all but steals our breath away.

"How do they survive this heat?" I ask of no one in particular.

"I hear they strip down to skin at night and contend with the mosquitoes," she whispers. "Can't imagine." She tugs on my elbow. "Come on."

The three women have resumed their work on the stone pile.

"To the car, Flora. I'll be right there."

She and her guardian settle into the Packard, and I aim for Tad's mother. "Hello."

Her fair cheeks, blood-red in the heat, glisten with sweat. She swipes a sleeve across her face and offers me a scowl around hazel eyes.

I remember expressions like hers in cotton patches.

I'll not be daunted.

"I'm Lily. I met your son Tad yesterday."

She frowns.

"He was doing a grand job of selling newspapers."

She nods, but her scowl remains.

"I'm afraid I'm hopelessly . . . curious, I guess. Tad seems a splendid boy, a gentle lad, industrious and mannerly."

Her frown eases. "Better be."

I clear my throat and stumble on. "I thought . . . To tell you the truth, I wanted to meet his mother. He told me where you're staying . . . temporarily."

"He tell you I landed in the workhouse 'cause I ain't got no way to pay for damages my man done to a saloon?"

"No, ma'am."

"Husband died. They laid his fine on me. That sound fair?"

"It doesn't."

"I got rock duty 'cause I escaped, tryin' to get home to young'uns."

I'd read prisoners escape the workhouse with regularity. I remain silent.

"I refuse to work in a brothel—or give my daughter to them, though they'd steal her if they knew I wasn't home. I sweep out alleys and back rooms of businesses that wouldn't let the likes of me darken their front doors." She points toward the center of town.

"But I'm stuck here 'cause my shiftless, drunken man died in a brawl owing fines to the city. My young'uns are alone in Battercake Flats, and Tad's working barefoot on Cowtown's fancy streets." She huffs, scattering damp dirty-blonde strands off her forehead.

Memories flash. Ma and I in the cotton patch, laboring Saturdays and Sundays to pay Walter's debts. Walter who-knows-where, then absconding with payday coins.

My eyes come to rest on this mother's clear blue eyes. "None of it is fair. Don't know that I can accomplish a thing, but I can promise to try."

"Why?" She peaks one eyebrow.

"I've stood in similar shoes. Someone helped me. I'd like to do the same."

She stares, sweat dripping off her nose and chin. "Not interested in charity. We earn our keep."

"Everyone can use a hand up once in awhile."

She lifts her chin at Flora. "Who's your fancy friend?"

"Flora Zane."

She harrumphs but trusts me with her address. And I shuffle to the car.

"Next stop, Battercake Flats." Flora points from Ford Street to the confluence of Clear and West Forks of Trinity River.

I thumb toward the bluff above us—close to ninety feet high, surely. "What's up there?"

"Wealth, my friend. That's Quality Hill." She thumbs toward expansive rooftops above the wooded bluff. "Bankers and cattle barons."

"May we have a look?"

Maneuvering the Packard to Penn Street, the driver slows and I gaze at the mansions built on huge lots—ten palaces.

"The wealthy live this near the workhouse?" The stark difference stuns me.

"Six hundred feet as the crow flies. But a world away, if you know what I'm saying. Up here's tennis and teas. Down there's rock piles, saloon songs, and a campfire. And all the stray animals in the city."

I try to imagine how the genteel tranquility of this neighborhood's tennis courts and veranda parties blend with the sounds below—hammers on stone, barks, brays, raucous laughter, and bawdy songs.

The driver steers to Franklin and Bridge Streets. To Battercake Flats.

Bottom land caught between the bluff and Trinity River, the wedge of squalor squats virtually in the backyard of the Courthouse—Fort Worth's central bastion of power.

The slum's four streets are unpaved. Its main thoroughfare, Franklin Street, runs down the slope from the bluff to the river, more a track than a street. Prone to flood, the area is populated by Coloreds who can afford nothing else. And a few Whites.

In the deluges of 1889 and 1908 the flimsy shanties washed away with the owners' possessions, such as they were. Some residents moved on, but others tacked the shambles into shelters and carried on.

Like Tad's mother, I assume.

My neck tingles as I recall my morning prayer. *Take me where I can do some good, and I'll thank you.*

The driver aims toward the address I jotted down. We pass rows of shacks and end at a bare plot. Scrawny green growth tops a single row of tilled soil. Five children in rags run barefoot around a tent. A sixth child, a girl of no more than twelve, is tending the others. She straightens from an open fire pit where a creature is roasting on a spit.

Leaving Flora and the driver in the automobile, I step out. "Hello. I'm looking for the home of the McGregors."

The eldest girl nods, her laurel-green eyes steady on mine. "You've found it."

"I'm Lily. What's your name?"

"Opal."

How like me she seems. "Mind if I sit a spell, Opal?"

"Don't reckon." She points to a boy on a three-legged stool. "Move. For the lady."

I gather my skirt and accept my assigned place. "I met Tad. Selling papers. He here?"

"No. Out working."

"I visited your mother."

"Pa's fine was five dollars. She gets a dollar a day, so I reckon she'll be coming home in a couple days."

"What will you and your brothers and sisters eat?"

"Got wild onions over yonder." She gestures to the sole line of green and the roasting pit. "Don't know 'bout tomorrow, but today's a rat."

I suck in air and bring a fist to my mouth. We Sloats consumed plenty of 'possums, but never a rat. I must do something. Today.

"Any other source for food?"

She angles her head toward the next street. "Toby's. Scraps out back."

"Do you attend school?"

"Nah. Not for us."

The similarity to my own family strikes me in the gut. I yearn to whisk them from the squalor. But are they as proud as Sloats?

I must not steal their dignity.

I arrive at the Metropolitan completely spent from the emotions the workhouse and Battercake Flats unearthed.

I bathe. Enjoy a light supper. Curl up on the bed under the electric ceiling fan, one of the Met's modern amenities, and rehash the day's events.

I spoke with Toby, the cafe owner. He took my bills and agreed to supply the McGregors with more scraps than in the past and keep the dealings between the two of us.

Splinters of ideas dance in my head. Improving the destitute family's lot is in keeping with my responsibilities as Ida's assistant, but I need to concentrate on her list of suffragist leaders too. Achieving the vote will improve the lives of women like Beulah.

Which brings Blossom to mind. The stridency of traffic outside my window grates. I twist from side to side, but comfort eludes me. I sit up and notice my heart's fluttering.

Sweeping off the bed, I dial the front desk. "Any messages for me?"

"Letters. One just arrived. I'll have them delivered."

In moments a message boy knocks with a silver platter in hand.

Dressed in a proper wrapper, I receive three envelopes and thank him with a tip.

I settle at my writing desk. Maggie's letter bursts with details of Broadview and Needham. No word from Sabina, none expected. The Lord is sustaining Ella and Andrew.

Addie's wired that she made it to Naples through a circuitous route and joined Herr Romano in Rome. She brushed away concerns for safety, as Italy's refusing to enter the international fray. Still, will the Italian commitment survive with war on their doorstep?

Ella's and Cade's parents seem to be doing better, though Cade's despondent. My heart flutters at his name written in her neat hand. Despair knocks, but I mustn't dwell on my desires. I've others to consider.

The second letter is from Ella. The search teams' frantic forays into the outer reaches of Oklahoma have produced not a sign of Walter or Blossom. But Sheriff Dawson is communicating with Texas sheriffs.

Continuing to maintain a brave front, Ella insists her child's alive and the Lord will bring her home. Andrew includes a page of encouragement from Scripture.

My eyes flick to the old Bible on my bedside table. I'll keep my preacher friend's note in the Bible and look up the passages later. I owe him that much.

The final envelope is from Flora. She must have had it delivered by messenger in the last hour. It contains an invitation for an evening out— tomorrow. Dinner at the Worth Hotel. And a Fort Worth Symphony performance at Byers Opera House.

I accept the invitation by phone and scribble letters to Ella, Maggie, Ida, and Cade. Sitting at my lovely north-facing floor-to-ceiling window, I witness the city welcoming twilight. Off to the left, Tarrant County Courthouse's tower peeks above the rooftops. The sheriff's office is somewhere nearby.

I must speak with the lawman. Soon.

CHAPTER 24

I awake Friday morning with not a hint of appetite but craving a single sliver of news, one simple lead about sweet Blossom. Scanning Ida's notes, I locate Sheriff Rae's private extension and lift the telephone receiver. "LAMAR 9472."

"One moment, please." Metropolitan Hotel's switchboard operator, a plain and dour young woman, makes up for good looks with an abundance of efficiency.

The intermittent buzzes are cut short by a brusk reply. "Sheriff Rae."

"Hello, Sheriff . I'm Lily Sloat from Needham, Oklahoma. Ida Tate communicated with you about my visit to your city? And about a lost child we've searching for?"

"I heard from Mrs. Tate. And from Glover County's Sheriff Dawson." He pauses, and papers rattle. "A thirteen-year-old girl . . . fair-haired—"

"Like lemon custard, sir."

"That so? And blue eyes—"

"You'd think you were looking through pale blue crystals."

"Yes ma'am. I get the picture. It says here she's slight of stature. Disappeared from around Needham about a week ago. Is that correct?"

"This is the eighth day to be precise. She's exceedingly curious. Precocious. Articulate. Forgive me, but she's dear to me, to all of us. Have you heard anything? Any leads?"

"We've added this young lady to our list of missing persons. It's grown of late, a mighty troubling trend. But we're on it, rest assured."

"By 'on it' do you mean you're actively searching?"

"Just like for all those missing."

"You search everyday? Never quit? Where? How? Have you heard of a Walter Sloat?"

He clears his throat once. And again. "Whoa there. Sheriff Dawson tells me a certain Walter Sloat is suspected of abducting the child. Is he related to you?"

"Sadly, he is my father, but I don't call him Pa any longer. He smothered my mother to death. The jury ignored a woman's eyewitness testimony, my own, and acquitted him."

"I recall hearing about that. It's too bad. I see here in my notes Sheriff Dawson figures the no-good brought the girl to our fair city. That doesn't sit well with me as sheriff. Rest assured, if she's in Tarrant County, we'll find her. We'll let you know when something turns up."

"I appreciate that, sir. But can you tell please . . . *where* you're searching? I want to help."

He harrumphs. "I'm not at liberty to share our methods, not with private citizens. Only trained personnel are allowed into our dangerous investigations."

"I understand. Just one more thing. Might the search area include Hell's Half Acre?"

He sputters. "Why, the Acre's one part stretched-out truth and two parts myth. Don't you be worrying yourself about a . . ." He pauses. "Our police officers are all over that area of town."

"I see." Although truly, I do not. Looks as if whatever leads they uncover will remain for their eyes only. "Just in case, you may reach me at the Metropolitan."

The click of the receiver in its cradle bars me from further questioning. I'll have to look elsewhere.

I enjoy a noon meal from Room Service, a luscious cold asparagus soup with assorted fruits. What might be poor Blossom's fare today? What hands prepared it? Has she eaten at all? I can't bear to consider the possibilities.

Meals aboard *Nelly* were meager. The possibilities ruin my appetite for dessert. I push aside the tray and reach for Rachel Lloyd's ship's log.

June : ye : 30ᵗʰ : 1775
Ye Moon hidin. Calm Seas.

Back Home, Shabbat Lace, Tallow, Prayin passed.

Sailors be Merry Makin on Deck, Fiddle, Fife, Drum. Below Deck we
be needin Naught but single Invite to join them.

Tis Pleasant to Laugh.

Rachel Lloyd
Daughter o Abraham

Merry making aboard *Nelly?* Will Blossom make merry ever again?
How can the rest of us enjoy ourselves as long as she's gone?

Reminded of Flora's invitation to dinner and the opera, I force myself
to the carved mahogany armoire, gratified my evening gown—a jade-
green organdy over ecru silk with loose elbow-length kimono sleeves—
will be ideal for this warm Texas evening.

Is my precocious young friend still dressed in a play dress? Are her
stockings . . . Bend over and rest my head on the desk blotter. The images I conjure up, the possibilities are endless.

But grieving accomplishes not a whit. I've Ida's suffragist friends to
contact and a plan to lay out before dressing. Best begin.

The ladies on Ida's contact list include a group calling itself The Rosen
Irregulars. Peculiar. I place a call to the group's president, but a staff
member answers and takes my name and hotel contact.

Several back copies of *Fort Worth Star-Telegram* and *Caller* reveal the
heartbeat of Cowtown. Which of the establishments with ads conceal
secret business dealings.

Intending to visit the home for unwed mothers and their children
with an understanding of their mission, I examine *The Purity Journal.*

"Please . . ." What has come over me? I all but prayed out loud without planning to.

Just as well. Time for a promised prayer anyway.

If You're who folks say You are, You know Beulah and her girl remind me of Ma and myself. I've a plan and would appreciate your cooperation. If You're not too busy.

The day's headlines shout further developments in the European war. The Battle of the Frontiers is raging, and German forces are winning victories in France and Belgium. How long can Italy maintain a neutral stance?

I swat aside my dreary thoughts, as it's time to dress for an evening out.

A slender strand of jade beads, drop earrings, and a tortoise-shell comb will accessorize without garishness. Tucking my derringer into my clutch, I tug on my opera gloves and latch my door.

I check the time at the grandfather clock in the hallway. With a few moments to spare, I make my way down the hallway and around a corner to a large plate-glass window overlooking the south side of Fort Worth.

As a student intern for the newspaper, I was shielded from the city's night life. But I read infamous Hell's Half Acre squats mere blocks away. Where is the gaudiness I heard about? How might the scene have appeared decades ago when cowboys drove cattle straight through Cowtown on the Chisholm Trail? Saloons and brothels sprouted to satisfy the demands of the trail-weary clientele.

According to prohibition and women's rights advocates, liquor remains a scourge on the city. The firebrand preacher, J. Frank Norris, shies not a whit from calling out prominent businessmen for capitalizing on the rents they earn in the Acre.

Street lamps wink on, and I wrap up my musings. I must be on my way.

I halt at the top of the stairs, a hand at my bosom. How can I enjoy a single minute of entertainment with Blossom in Walter's hands?

I straighten my shoulders. By dedicating this evening to her. I'll not let an opportunity for questions pass me by.

Flora's waiting for me at the foot of the stairs. Her gold taffeta hob-ble-skirted gown and brown and gold hair feathers are impossible to overlook.

She grasps my gloved hands. "You're a vision. Turn around. That tortoise shell comb is divine. Come."

Her burly bodyguard stands to the side in the foyer, not at all a man to overlook. Tall and distinguished, he appears more than a decade Flora's elder.

"This is the brave woman I told you about." She tips her head toward me.

I peak an eyebrow. "Brave?"

"Journeying alone from Indian Territory is just the start of your bravery."

"Not brave. Just learned to be self-sufficient years ago."

"Didn't I tell you?" She grabs the crook of her guardian's left elbow and gestures me to do the same on his right. "I'd know a CIA graduate anywhere."

We stroll the awning-covered walkway to Worth Hotel in the next block. The evening temperature is tolerable, even pleasant, and the city's lights and traffic add a spark of excitement.

Our dinner in the ballroom is decidedly grand. Our shrimp cocktail, fillet of beef, and string beans with salt pork are seasoned with just the right amount of amiable conversation.

"Irish Potato Cake will top off this meal." Flora pats her lips with a linen napkin.

I lean near her. "What about Hell's Half Acre? Where is it from here?"

She flashes a bewildered glance. "Ladies steer clear of such places." She angles a hand at her mouth, whispering. "But adventurous ones like us—"

"Well, well, well. Look who's come to Cowtown. And asking about Hell's Half Acre, of all places."

At the sound of the familiar voice, I whip around.

Sabina.

My mouth eases open before I can lock it tight.

The woman I knew at Broadview has been transformed. Gone is her colorless, wispy hair. A thick midnight-back mane—in the latest cropped style—cups her head. A wig. Dressed in a gown of turquoise satin and chiffon with asymmetrical black lace overdress, she sports a matching wide headband, and a single black feather sticks straight up in front.

Her cheeks flash a subdued pink. Her eyes, a subtle kohl. And her lips, bright rose.

"Hello." She extends a hand to Flora's bodyguard. "Sabina Fitzgerald."

She's claiming Addie's name? "Of all the—"

"You two ladies acquainted?" My bright-haired companion bats her eyelashes.

The woman I know as Maggie's daughter waves away the question as if Flora's a pesky fly. "My sister Adelaide took Lily as her ward years ago. I was away back East and on the continent for years, so Lily and I . . ." She leans toward my friend as if to share a secret. "We're barely acquainted."

She moves her focus to me. "Too bad about that verdict."

Flushing, Flora lowers her eyes.

Sabina turns away with a flourish of chiffon, and I track her into the lobby.

"Interesting." Flora brings a water goblet to her lips. "She's a reporter?"

"She's wearing a *Caller* press badge, so I guess she is." She can parade around all she wants. And tinker with my life. But I won't allow her to besmirch Addie's name.

"Excuse me, please." I lay aside my clutch and push from the table. "We have some catching up to do."

I search the lobby, but the woman has vanished. The desk clerk can find neither a Fitzgerald nor a Gallagher on the register. Peculiar.

Flora and her guard escort me to Byers Opera House. She chatters, teasing my mind off Sabina. We enter the grand theater under a lighted awning and step into a festooned, carpeted interior decorated in greens, ruby-red, and golds.

Passing among theater goers in couples and small groups, my opera companion maneuvers the crowd seamlessly and introduces me to acquaintances. I spy a lovely staircase with fanciful balusters and finials. Might our seats be on an upper level?

She leads me to the orchestra section. Her gown's ruffled hem trails her.

Our position offers a one hundred eighty-degree view of the elaborate surroundings. Curved box seats create elaborately detailed mini-balconies reminiscent of *Romeo and Juliet*. The vaulted ceiling and fluted columns support carved arches that hint at Pompeii.

Ella and Maggie will ask for each detail.

The stage and heavy velvet curtain bring my opera-singer friend to mind. She would be impressed.

Help her find—I cover my lips with gloved fingers. Was I on the verge of praying?

Flora leans against my shoulder. "Your friend is sitting two rows back."

I turn and find Sabina's eyes trained on me.

"Will you excuse me?" I lay my clutch in Flora's lap. "I won't be long."

Stepping into the carpeted aisle, I stand erect and stop at my nemesis's row. "If it isn't Miss Gallagher. May I speak with you?"

Hiking a shoulder, she whispers to her male escort, and he glances at me.

Stunned into speechlessness, I stare. Her companion is Mr. Francis, *Fort Worth Caller*'s Editor in Chief.

Gathering myself, I aim for a lobby alcove and choose a settee for its prominent position, a subtle attempt to establish a dominant role. She selects a velvet chair and angles her body so that she's facing the teeming theatergoers.

"You're with *Caller*? How'd you manage it?"

She shows her palms and curves her shoulders, reeking nonchalance.

"I impressed them."

"In what department? Don't tell me. It's the Women's Society page."

"But I have plans to . . . spice it up a bit."

"Four days ago that position was mine. How did you do it?"

Her eyebrows angle in mock confusion, and her cheeks darken from pink to rose. Squinting, she points a forefinger at my chest. "I've a *résumé*. Unlike you."

I force a placid expression. "Under a false identity."

She stiffens. "Who are you to determine what name I claim? Or how I can dress? Addie and I nursed at the same breast as *sisters*. We grew up in the same home. We attend the same college. We opened Christmas presents around the same tree. I'm a Fitzgerald in every sense but one—blood. I can continue, but someone as . . . limited as yourself can never understand."

She stands and peers down her nose. "Be on your way, Miss *Sloat*. Good riddance."

Flouncing away, she leaves my old insecurities circling like biplanes. They advance in battle formation. They jeer and threaten and cast aspersions like grenades.

My shoulders inch forward, and my chin aims for my chest. My breath comes in short, shallow bursts. I return to my seat in defeat.

The evening's program consists of a piano recital by Rudolph Ganz, followed by the Fort Worth Symphony Orchestra. Schumann. Beethoven. Chopin. Ravel. Debussy. Liszt. The musicians perform with brilliance, and the audience responds with exuberance.

But I sit immune to the exquisite melodies and technical skills, listening instead to words spoken not so long ago.

You're fit for nothing but a cotton field. Was Walter right?

No matter how tall—or short—your parents and grandparents, you must do your own growing. Or is Maggie the astute one?

I'd be honored if you'd be my name bearer. How would Addie react to this woman purloining her name?

What had I told Sabina? *I towed a cotton sack . . . when I was a girl.*

Now I sport a hand-tailored dress. But either way, I matter. Same as you.
I straighten in the plush theater chair. Ella didn't endanger her life
to save mine . . . for nothing. Addie didn't give up her own dream to
prepare me for mine . . . for nothing. Ma didn't expose herself to winter's
elements, saving me from myself . . . for nothing.

No. Mr. Francis can deal with Miss Gallagher. And suffer the consequences. I'll keep my eyes on my goals and follow my roots wherever the
tatting shuttle leads me. And I'll broadcast my story with no help from
Caller.

Back in my room, I shrug off my wrapper and remember my promise
to Ida. Have I been praying a mere three days? Seems like three months.
Feeling rather like a child, I slip to my knees and place my elbows on the
bed, my hands clasped in front of me.

"I may be talking to a blank wall, but I promised." My focus wan-
ders to my surroundings. Ma's Bible reminds me of my instruction in
Scripture, a plethora of prayers.

My gaze tightens. "Time to speak my piece—again—and get to bed.
I'll show Sabina and everyone else what I'm made of. Ma's blood flows
in my veins too. I'll reach my goals with or without Your help. Amen."

CHAPTER 25

*J*ust as dawn's sun is painting liquid gold over the eastern horizon, I ease apart two delicate leaves and adjust the magnifying glass over the dim script.

July : ye : 1ˢᵗ : 1775
Night Sky be dark as Pitch.

Fellow Travelers— Man & Wife—be Dead. Cough. Orphaned wee Daughter be in our Care.

Travelers grumble. Women pen List o Demands. Will Cap'n listen?

Fear & Want reign. What be ye Future?

Rachel Lloyd
Daughter o Abraham

I knead the knots in my forehead. Human agony through the ages defies understanding. Blossom can be in nothing but agony. The poor child.

What were the words Beulah spoke about her daughter?

. . . they'd steal her if they knew I'm not home.

Will I sit in comfort, mulling over dreadful circumstances? Will I speak to women's groups and never *do* a thing?

I couldn't live with myself.

The wall clock bongs the half-hour. Breakfast will be delivered soon. Time to move.

Flinging aside my gown and wrapper, I dress with little care for how I wind the mound of copper strands at the back of my head or for the wrinkles lining my skirt. More important needs weigh on me.

I scrape the last crumbs of biscuit smothered in gravy and review my plans.

First, Flora.

"You want to what?" She yells over the telephone line.

I inch the receiver from my ear. "Help the children in Battercake."

"What do you propose?"

"According to Ida's schedule, the Rosen Irregulars assemble today."

"Yes. I know the leader."

"Can you wrangle us an invitation?"

"Don't need one. I'll pick you up at a quarter of ten." She dispenses with our conversation rather precipitously.

Best dress properly. I rewind my waist-long mane and secure a neat chignon with pins and mother-of-pearl combs. Dressed in a lightweight lawn skirt with embroidery and appliqués, I await Flora under the Met's front awning.

Her car arrives, and her driver opens a back passenger door. Does the man escort her everywhere? And why?

"You look divine." She examines my skirt as I settle into the plush back seat. "Those appliqués are exquisite. Brussels lace?"

I nod. My generous benefactor purchased the garment on one of our European excursions. "And you're fit for a bronze sculpture by one of the masters."

"Might we take a turn through Hell's Half Acre?"

She regards me askance. "What's gotten into you?"

I shrug. "I didn't find my little friend at the opera. And I don't expect to discover her at a coffee klatch. I figure I'll have to examine the underbelly of this city. Are you with me?"

She nudges her driver's shoulder. "Rosen Heights via Hell's Half Acre."

The man steers the car eastward, turns three corners going first one way and another. "But there's nothing but upstanding business along these streets."

"Hotels. Boarding houses. Men's smoking parlors. Such enterprises can conceal a multitude of sins."

My eyes roam left to right and behind. "I see."

The Rosen Heights ladies welcome me as warmly as the Wednesday Club. The president's home rivals those of Quality Hill. In former days, I would have admired the wood paneling, marble columns, and oil paintings. But today I can't wipe away the image of that lowly tent in Battercake Flats.

Can I find contentment in circles like this one? Will I ever belong? Do I *want* to belong?

Unworthiness lifts its ugly head, drowning my confidence. Phantom pain shoots beneath my bodice and sparks a moan. It's all in my head, I know, but what's to be done for it? My breath catches, and I reach for my throat.

"What is it?" Crinkled lines bunch above the bridge of Flora's nose. She tugs on my arm. "Come. There's a powder room down the hall."

I follow, struggling to regain steady breaths, and little by little my pulse quiets. "I don't know what came over me."

She pats my face with a lemon-scented towel. "I'll attend to introductions and explain your connection to Ida and Adelaide. Come out when you're feeling better."

Grateful for Flora's quick thinking, I nod, and she leaves me alone. I gaze into the gilded mirror, seeing not my present-day, powdered visage but the girl I once was—-with rust-water hair and butterscotch-toned teeth, the daughter of Ruby Sloat, who sacrificed herself on the altar of a mother's love, the field worker with red Oklahoma soil ground into her hands and feet.

I unbutton my bodice and hold aside the opening. A fat caterpillar scar burrows under my peach-fresh skin, collar bone to sternum. A cadre of disfigurements lie among patches of freckles. A whittler's hook in Walter's cruel hands gouged them into my flesh.

My image breaks into numberless shards, assuring me I'll be the same woman no more, not after witnessing that splotched and sagging tent.

I was reared in a tarpaper shack. Brutalized. And counted as no more than rubbish in an Oklahoma courtroom. But two women as fine as any who walk the earth washed and dressed me and seated me at their tables. The McGregors haven't been so fortunate, but I can change their unhappy circumstances.

As for my story, the telling will require every particle of will I possess. Perhaps a few will come to understand the powerlessness of women denied equality. And the utter tragedy of young girls snatched from their homes and made to participate in unspeakable acts.

I'll find the strength, the tenacity. No more delay. No excuses.

Have I a story to tell? Indeed. And tell it, I will.

I square my shoulders and turn the brass handle until it clicks. Striding with new confidence, I enter a Rosen Heights parlor of fine decor.

The women quiet, giving me their full focus. I hold up my head and speak of what Ma and I endured on that rotten horseshoe back home. I describe the workhouse and Battercake Flats. I articulate words that stun, even startle a few, but I speak the truth.

They honor me with hot-blooded applause. "That poor mother with seven children down by the Trinity." The president speaks with an earnest expression. "She needs our help."

"And the workhouse inmates could use a meal or two. Even the chain gang is fed bare bones—watery soup, beans, bread."

She focuses on each club member. "Why did we name ourselves the Rosen Irregulars? Because we approve the status quo?"

The group shouts, "No!" They murmur to one another in pairs.

"We can plan meals, can we not?" The leader hooks a thumb over her shoulder. "I've a kitchen staff and so does everyone else."

Plans for an evening meal to feed sixty hungry souls—plus the McGregor seven —materialize in minutes. A single member scowls. What's behind her disapproval?

We agree to gather at the workhouse at six o'clock.

At the meeting's conclusion, Flora and I return to the Packard. "Now to inform the workhouse." My earlier sense of panic has dissipated like prairie mist come sunup.

At the dreary facility, I inform the superintendent of our plans for the evening meal.

He scratches his head and scowls. "Don't know 'bout mingling with these folks."

"The Rosen Heights ladies understand your inmates have fallen on hard times. They'll feed them at six o'clock, nothing more or less. They'll use your tables and benches." I pause and fetch a five-dollar bill from my pocketbook. "Here's what Beulah owes you."

He growls. "This is irregular."

"The group calls itself the Rosen Irregulars." I chuckle. "Aren't you obligated to receive payment?"

He picks at an ear lobe. "Never been done before."

"First time for everything." I add a dollar to the five. "Now show me to her please."

He hides the currency in a drawer and stands. "She's in the laundry."

Steam barrels from the smoke stack, the interior heat so thick it chokes us. The man locates her, and she joins us out front.

"Your fine's paid." He offers no explanation. "You're free to go."

She glowers at me. "I don't take charity."

"I'm not offering it."

"What do you reckon this to be?"

"Payment for services to be rendered." I wave her alongside me, and we return to her cell. She changes into her own clothing and leaves her prison garb folded in a neat pile.

"What services?"

"You have a green thumb, don't you?"

"And what of it?"

"Green thumbs earn a wage in some quarters. I suspect we can locate such a place."

I point to the Packard. "We're taking you home."

Slack-jawed, she eases into the back where Flora moves aside and pats the plush seat cushion. The deprived but proud woman casts her gaze around the car's interior. "Never dreamed I'd be riding in an automobile. Nor talking green thumbs."

"You're likely to discover more than one surprise before Lily's done." Flora signals to her silent driver to steer us toward Trinity River.

Beaulah's brood stands outside the tent, staring at the Packard. She stretches her legs over the running board and holds out her arms.

The children run to her. "Ma!"

Their reunion sparks memories of my past. Forcing my thoughts to the present, I turn at the clatter of a vehicle's engine. A black, shiny Oldsmobile convertible eases toward the tent and parks near the Packard.

The car's brilliant paint finish flashes. The folded-down top reveals a female driver perched in the finely tufted, gunmetal-gray leather interior. She steps onto the car's running board and peers over the hood. Sabina.

"Look who the cats dragged in." Flora speaks in a mutter behind me.

The woman I knew in Oklahoma hikes her chin and raises a fist to her waist.

What business has she in a place like this?

She steps off the running board and aims straight for me. Something about her appearance strikes me as important, but it eludes me.

I shake away the sensation. Refusing to allow her to disrupt the family reunion, I waylay her. "What're you doing here?"

"Investigating, of course. That's what a reporter does."

I lace my arms at my middle. "Nothing to investigate in Battercake Flats."

"I'll be the judge of that." She shoulders past me.

Flora grabs her arm and spins her around. "This is as far as you go."

"Keep your hands off me, you—"

Flora's bodyguard materializes as if from a void, slipping between the women with his broad chest nose-high to Sabina.

She steps backward. "I have questions. For the lady of the house. Do you *mind*?"

Beulah strolls up and gives her uninvited visitor a once-over. "Depends."

"On what?"

"On the questions and who's asking 'em."

Hatless, wigged Sabina is dressed in a broad black-and-white striped and belted skirt, the one she donned the night she left Broadview. The sleeves of her white starched blouse are rolled to her elbows. She holds a pad and pen in hand. "I'm from *Fort Worth Caller*. Sabina Fitz—"

"Gallagher. Someone from back home." I insert the explanation without thinking first.

She flicks a casual shrug. "Sabina Fitzgerald, actually. At your service."

Beulah's gaze roams the interloper's form, as if taking in each detail. "You . . ." She pauses and squints. "You set my teeth on edge." She whips a turn and rejoins her children.

Sabina snaps her gaze to me, her eyes mere slits. "You're casting your tarpaper spell from the dregs to the cream of society. I can change that, but would it suit my purposes?" She taps a forefinger against her chin as if puzzling. "Perhaps not. Instead, I'd like to offer a proposition, a deal between . . ." She rolls her eyes from my head to my dust-covered shoes. "Friends."

"What sort of a deal?" And for what purpose?

"A chance to tell your oh-so-sweet story."

Should I involve myself with this woman? I vowed in the Rosen Heights powder room to find the courage and tenacity to share my story. And encourage other women to do the same. Must I do so through a shrew? "I'm willing to meet you in the Metropolitan lobby."

"You'll hear from me." Flipping her pad closed, she returns to her car and eases it over the rub-board roadbed out of sight.

I take a deep breath and expel relief with a hearty portion of emerging mettle.

CHAPTER 26

"What were you saying about a green thumb?"

I turn to Beulah with a smile. "Someone I know can't depend on her gardener's helper."

She sets her hands at her waist. "You think I can handle the job?"

"I've seen you work, and I assume you can follow directions. Worth a try, isn't it?"

She eyes me through a tightened gaze. "Don't take charity. What's in it for you?"

"Any help I give the ladies of Fort Worth will benefit women tenfold. I have plans."

"What plans?"

"Walk with me, will you?" I gesture down the road.

She nods and steps alongside me.

"As I said, I've been in shoes similar to yours. Someone helped me stand on my feet. I want to do the same for you and others. Are you aware of the women's movement?"

"For the vote?"

"Woman's suffrage requires approaches from different angles. I'm working for Ida Tate, an Oklahoman who knows women and children . . . in your situation.

"She provides me with contacts. But I've made a contact who's not on her list." I smile. "You. We can work together . . . in different arenas."

"Don't know 'bout that, but I do know work. I'm ready to start. Where and when?"

I tighten my arms around my middle and stare into the pale blue sky. "I'm not sure of the details yet." I return my gaze to hers. "But I will know them soon. Trust me?"

She peers at the ground where the play of light and dark mirror the good and evil I pursue at every turn. "I reckon I can. But there's something you need to know."

Raising my eyebrows and cocking my head, I gesture for her to continue.

"My sister's one of the women of the Acre."

"A barmaid or a prostitute, you mean?"

"Yes. One of *them*. She does both jobs."

I lay a hand on her arm. "I can help—"

"Sis won't leave. For fear of what they'll do to her. Or to us."

"Who are they?"

"A man named Simon Wilcox owns the property. He collects rents and wipes his hands of the transactions conducted in his building. Other supposedly upstanding men do the same. But in truth he owns the business too. And he claims more than rent for himself."

"This must be reported."

"Pastor Norris of that big Baptist Church has tried to make the city listen, but he's gotten nothing but trouble in return."

"The women are free to leave. Surely."

"Some have tried. And lived to regret it."

We stroll the hard-packed dirt road and return to her tent home as friends.

Sitting in a circle on the ground, her children scoot aside for their mother. The laurel-eyed daughter uncovers a pot on the open fire pit. "Got more than the usual at Toby's." She spoons a meaty gruel into four tin plates the children share, their filth-lined nails and knuckles ignored.

Promising to return, I join Flora to be delivered straight to the Met.

By late afternoon war headlines blaze across the newspapers, stirring my angst over Addie. The Battle of the Frontiers has begun in France.

I call Maggie and Ida to keep them abreast of ladies' club news. The Flats. And our planned supper for workhouse inmates. They've heard nothing from Addie and are as anxious about the war headlines as I.

Will a skirmish confront me at the workhouse?

Flora and I arrive at the facility at six o'clock. I've changed into a simple blouse and sturdy gabardine skirt with deep, buttoned pockets. I slip Blossom's creekside photo into a pocket and secured the button.

True to their promise, the ladies have shown up with food to feed a hundred. The inmates lay raw lumber across sawhorses to serve as tables. The women unfurl tablecloths and uncover fare as if for a church picnic.

Hostilities break out in the serving line.

"That's my chicken leg!"

"Your name ain't on it."

"I'll bash my name across your mug if you don't give it back!"

The women stand nose to nose with fists aimed at jaws. The super-intendent and a guard separate them and stick plates of beans in their hands. Poking the air with their fingers, they force the women inside the fetid building.

Intent on securing employment for Beulah, I step to the club president's side. "Did I hear you're looking for a gardener's helper?"

"Why, yes."

"I know a woman who can work like a man. Would you consider speaking with her?"

She raises a single eyebrow. "One of these workhouse inmates?"

"A former one."

"Would she happen to be the woman you brought tonight?"

I incline a nod.

She angles her head toward an empty table. "Over there."

I signal to Beulah. "Join us, will you?"

She sees to her children's plates at an out-of-the-way table. Their hands and faces have been wiped clean, and on their feet—shoes.

The club president points the less-fortunate but proud woman to the head of the table. "Lovely dress."

She runs her hands over her skirt. "I keep it folded in a trunk."

The socialite clears her throat and sets her elbows on the table's rough surface. "What experience have you had with physically demanding work like that of a gardener's helper?"

The former inmate points across the way. "See that pile of rocks?"

The woman turns and looks back. "Can't miss them."

"I broke them up. With a sledge hammer."

The society dame pales. "I read about women breaking up rocks here." She presses her lips together and brings folded hands to her chin, prayer-like. "When can you start?"

Beulah closes her eyes with her head bowed, but she returns the society dame's steady gaze in seconds. "Tomorrow. Where do you live?"

"Up on the bluff. In Rosen Heights. Do you have transportation?"

"Ma'am, I live in a tent down near the river. I get around on my two feet."

She inhales audibly. "You and your seven children live in a tent?"

"Yes, ma'am. We manage."

The woman slaps a palm on the table. "Well, that won't do."

Beulah bristles. "Why does that make a difference?"

"Our former gardener's cottage is sitting empty. I've been pestering my husband to find a use for it. It'll make a cozy home for your family."

The stunned and grateful mother brings her hands to her face and leans over, rocking and mewling.

"You alright?" I rub a hand across her back.

She nods, and the club president and I exchange glances. At length she swipes her dress sleeves across her face, her eyes splotched and puffy. "Better news has never come my way, ma'am. I'll turn in a solid day's work."

Filled with gratitude for this kindness extended to the least in Fort Worth, I leave the women to work out the details.

Aiming for Flora's table, I glimpse her champion conversing with a woman in the shadows. What's behind his perpetual presence?

The woman turns, and Sabina emerges wearing a press badge. She steps from the shadows and aims for the club president. How has she known my movements? Does she follow me and lie in wait?

Unease creeps up my spine.

"Hello." She offers the dignified club matron her hand and ignores the poor woman who broke up the rocks. "I'm from *Caller*. Have a moment?"

The club officer starts. "Why—"

"We're having a private conversation. If you don't mind." Beulah glares at the interloper.

"Aw, give a girl a break, will you?" Her smile bunches her cheeks but stops short of her eyes. "I can give your club some publicity."

The Rosen Heights matron glances between the two, no doubt measuring unspoken words. She steadies her gaze on Sabina. "Private conversations are . . . private."

The harridan harrumphs and twirls to me. "Something's brewing. I can feel it."

I shrug. "I'm clean out of answers."

She leans toward me with a cold gleam in her pale eyes. "Well I'm not. You and Mrs. Fancy Frock will regret this." She turns on her heels and stomps into the shadows. A car's engine roars to life, and headlights aim for the gates.

I flutter fingers her way and join Flora, but I chew on a pesky cud of considerations. She strikes me in an altogether different way today. What is it? Not her hairstyle. I've grown accustomed to her wig. A connection to the prisoners, perhaps?

I'm reminded of Rachel Lloyd. She and the other women were cooped up in *Nelly*'s hold like the workhouse women. They survived on meager rations without society ladies' bountiful spread. *Nelly*'s women suffered, but they supported one another, as we ladies did tonight.

Unlike Sabina. Bold and tenacious—even heartless—the woman no doubt can succeed in the newspaper business. I wonder . . . Do I possess qualities required for sniffing out news? Wedging myself between friends or foes appeals to me not a whit.

But writing an exposé represents a possibility.

First, I've a proposition for the mother of seven.

The Rosen Irregulars depart for their fine homes beyond the bluff, but Flora and I linger to allow the McGregors time to enjoy the merrymaking.

Beulah joins me at a table apart from others singing and dancing around the fire pit. The lines around her eyes have softened, it seems. And a grin plays around her lips. "What a fine couple of days you've given me and my young'uns, Lily. I'll repay that five dollars. What can I do for you?"

"You can give me some information. A bit of clarification."

"About what?" Her wizened eyes suggest uncommon insight.

"You made a curious remark earlier."

"I was irked. Coulda said most anything. What was it?"

"You said *they* would steal your daughter away if they could."

She forces a breath through her nostrils. "And they would."

"Who are they?"

She eyes me in an appraising way. "The women talk, and my sister's an able listener. But she can be as closed mouthed as a rusty lock too."

"Where do the women come from?"

"Some ask for the work, but those in dire straits are easy pickings. In depots and on street corners. They lure them. Drug them. Send them to far off places—New Orleans and who knows where else. We lived in St. Louis when my sister was abducted."

Might Blossom have been snatched for such a purpose? Questions teem, lava-like.

"Our father uncovered clues to my sister's whereabouts and moved us to Fort Worth."

"And where are your parents now?"

"Up in Oakwood Cemetery. Grieved themselves into their graves. I was married with a family by then."

"Your daughter's no more than twelve, isn't she?"

"Coming up on fourteen. Tad's fifteen."

"These dealers in human flesh aren't looking for grown women then?"

"Sure they are, but the girls bring more money."

Nauseous, I cover my mouth with a hand. How can human beings stoop so low?

"Do you have contact with your sister?"

"We visit over yonder in the City Park every Sunday before dawn." She points westward toward the river.

Stewing, I catch the inside of a cheek between my teeth. "Might she speak with me? On behalf of a girl much like herself."

She leans backward with a strained expression. "What're you getting at?"

Should I share the story with someone I just met?

"The girl I know is still a child. She disappeared from around my home in Oklahoma. I have a couple of clues—"

"Like what?"

I unbutton my pocket and remove the creekside photograph. "She loves photography. Found her camera in the spot where we assume she was taken." I point to Walter's image. "That's someone I know." I pause, considering what to reveal. "He's my father."

"Sounds like their tactics, using someone close to her. I can ask my sister tomorrow."

"May I join you?"

Her lips draw into a tight bunch, and she frowns. "Could prove dangerous. Sister never knows when she might be followed."

I glance at Flora's chaperon. "We'll have protection."

She raises a fist. "I've learned to protect my own self."

I smile with a nod. "A handy skill. You must teach me."

We chuckle, but a memory flashes, and my grin collapses.

I hand her the photograph and point to the smudges near Walter. "I believe that's Walter's accomplice, and they're in Fort Worth. Gotta figure out who it is."

CHAPTER 27

*O*utside my hotel window, morning's twilight holds sway while I open the book of recollections in the lamp's wide circle of light.

June : ye : 2nd : 1775

Shabbat be passed Sundown last. This be First Day. Christians take ye Lord's Supper. Again. They be Stubborn as Children o Abraham by Half & More.

No Rest in Nelly's *Belly. We be Cleanin.*

Ye sailor cornered wee Orphaned Ward with Evil Intent. Me empty Slop Bucket o'er his Head. He be Bathin.

Rachel Lloyd
Daughter o Abraham

Rachel Lloyd wrote an exposé of sorts, one that stirs questions this Sunday morning. How many stubborn Christians are taking the Lord's Supper today? Ida and her adoptive family and staff are doing so, no doubt with Donnie watching and puzzling as Rachel Lloyd did.

How often was Ma transported to a Lord's Supper observance through her memories? How I long to wrap my arms around her . . . sit beside her at her sea chest . . . or in Needham's Christ Church and . . . pray. Perhaps sing. Even partake of the flatbread and juice.

If I could, I'd ask Ma a boatload of questions. But today I'll query a woman of a different sort. Hopefully, the woman's answers will move me closer to women like herself.

I spout a half-hearted prayer and dress.

Flora and her keeper await me outside the Met at five o'clock a.m.

The sun has yet to rise. Flora remains with the children while we head for City Park.

The moon points us to a woman on a wrought-iron bench. "This is Lily." Beulah whispers. She motions me to sit in the middle and takes the space at the end.

"And what's yours?" I'm hopeful the woman will trust me.

"I like them morning stars up yonder." She points above us. "They're blinking bits of hope. I reckon you can call me Star."

"How long can you be away from . . ." How do I refer to her place of employment?

"The *boarding*house?" She gives a humorless chuckle. "Not long." She looks around in jerks. One leg jiggles up and down. "Three of us together can draw attention. Gotta hurry."

Moonbeams lie hard across the woman's features. A bruise at her jaw swallows the light, and shadows sink into the lines around her eyes and mouth. The stench of old smoke lingers around her. She could pass for Beulah's mother—ill and weak.

"Tell Lily about Simon Wilcox, Sis."

"He's a supposed upstanding businessman—a regular church attender—but we women know upstanding when we see it. And Simon Wilcox ain't."

"Has he been around long?"

"Worked the business for years, layin' low. Been stirring the waters recently."

"In what way?"

"Dealing in underage girls."

"Is this common practice? Do the authorities know? How's Simon Wilcox involved? And have you ever heard of a Walter Sloat?"

She hunches down, as if drawing her body into an invisible shell. "The underage girls thing is recent. A decade ago brothels wouldn't hire nobody but women. As a rule the lawmen turn their heads to the goings-on in the Acre." She speaks in a hoarse whisper. "Never heard of a Walter Sloat. But Simon Wilcox is in the newspaper now and again. Gives to charities and such. Lives over in Highland Park. No wife. Shows up at the big churches. I hear he's expanding farther south. With young girls."

Beulah harrumphs. "I'd like to expand his horizons, alright. Straight out of Fort Worth. And with a limp!"

I smother a chuckle, recalling the *Nelly* sailor and Rachel's slop bucket. "Can you describe him?"

Jittery, Star turns around and gazes into the darkness. "He's middle aged, I'd guess. Hair as black as coal but with streaks of gray. Ordinary size and groomed real nice. Wears dandified clothes. Got a hard edge. Heard it in his voice. Through the wall."

I slip the snapshot into her hand. "This shows a man from back home. Look it over and let me know next Sunday if anyone's seen him. I'm at the Metropolitan Hotel if you can access a telephone."

She conceals the snapshot in her bodice front. "What else you wanna know?"

"Can you learn how Wilcox finds and moves underage girls?"

"I can try. Gossip lines're buzzing 'bout one snatched from over in Dallas. They find their targets in places frequented by families. Trolley parks like Lake Como and the one near Arlington. Lake Erie, if I recall rightly."

"I plan to visit Berachah, the mission home in Arlington."

"The Upchurches have helped plenty girls."

"Why not you?"

She shrugs a single shoulder. "Others more deservin'."

What were the words I spoke recently? *He deserves a wife of quality, not a Sloat.*

"Who decides who's deserving and who isn't?"

She ignores my question and flicks her gaze across the dark landscape.

Leaving aside the subject of just deserts, I'll press her as long as I can. "Where does Wilcox keep the young girls?"

"His underground moves them south real quick." She looks over her shoulder. "Gotta go. They'll be missing me."

Beulah grabs her sister. "Same time next Sunday?"

"If I can." She skitters away and fades into the weakening shadows.

"If she'll trust me, I can remove her from that place."

"My husband worked at the water plan. We lived in a cozy house, small for the nine of us, but still home. Sister agreed to come to us. But liquor and brawling got the best of my man, and we lost everything. Ended up squatting on the river's bottomland. Survived the flood of '08. And sister went back to the Acre."

"Is she shielding someone?"

"She's charitable like that. So, yes. I'd guess she is."

We drive into Rosen Heights in silence. The sun spills over the horizon, erasing the shadows beneath the giant oak trees, welcoming the mother and homemaker to her new abode.

She points to the blaze of light above her rooftop. "First sunrise in my house. I've days of worthy work ahead. Unlike my sister."

"We'll figure it out."

She angles her brimming eyes to mine. "Thank you for caring." She squeezes my hand before she slips out. "And for your courage."

Ma would smile. So would Ella and Addie. They taught me to work and love, read and write, and lay a proper table. They showed me joy in sharing. And the shape of courage.

I've always been one for avoiding parties and crowds, stealing away to the creek or the gazebo with a book of poetry, a newspaper, or biography. Scared of looking people in the eyes. So I have trouble with a brave someone labeling me as courageous.

Slipping out of the cottage as Beulah enters, Flora settles into the back seat. "Those're the world's best children. I'd have a couple if I knew they'd behave like them. Tad and his sister are frying bacon. The others washed their faces and made their beds."

"They've learned to work together for their survival. And for their mother."

I share the information I gleaned from Star. "I can't explain why, but my gut tells me there's a connection between Walter and Wilcox. Birds of a feather perhaps?"

Silence consumes us. What sentiments fit such a morning?

Sabina comes to mind. She'll be looking for a lead for her next story. I can put her onto the scent leading south. Or I can follow the stench myself.

Back in the hotel, I call Ida and Maggie with the news about Sabina, and they promise to pray for further developments. I venture out mid-morning and hail a cab to the First Baptist Church on the corner of Fourth and Taylor.

Strolling past the imposing structure, I pause to listen to the song service. Is Flora's voice one of these? The congregants belt out "Shall We Gather at the River," much like Needham's Christ Church. Only this group sings with a piano.

Dr. J. Frank Norris preaches at this, the second largest congregation in the country. While a CIA student, I read about his forays into exposing "idolatry and wickedness," in Hell's Half Acre, tales that have become legend.

Perpetually mired in controversy, this former editor of *Baptist Standard* harangued the Texas legislature into outlawing racetrack gambling. And he chose Hell's Half Acre as his first battlefield.

Like a John the Baptist crying in the wilderness, he calls out leading businessmen for benefitting from the unholy transactions in the Acre. The target of a murder attempt himself, he killed a man in self defense, and arsonists set fire to both his home and the church.

I experience an urge to walk through the church's entrance but tamp it down. I'll steer clear of this assembly with thousands of members. Reporters eye the gatherings, and millionaire businessmen and cattle ranchers counter the preacher's fiery confrontations.

Pausing to take in the grand reconstructed structure, I'm reminded that certain prosperous members are property owners in Hell's Half Acre. I sniff. Is that smoke? No. Nothing but my imagination running wild.

As I stroll Fort Worth's tranquil Sunday morning streets, my insides are far from quiet. Questions, doubts, and longings war within me, my personal Battle of the Frontiers. I miss Cade. A fire burns in my gut for women's rights and justice. I want to follow clues to my family roots, but none such desires matter until Ella holds her daughter in her arms again.

Rachel Lloyd's Sunday memoirs come to mind. A placard in the hotel lobby advertised a Jewish congregation—Ahavath Sholom. When and where do they meet?

And where might stubborn Christians be observing the Lord's Supper this day?

Ideas for an exposé rattle like hail on a tin roof, refusing to be ignored. I'll search until . . . A Bible verse Ma quoted comes to me out of the Texas blue.

Canst thou by searching find out God?
We'll see.

CHAPTER 28

*C*hoosing a quieter way of tapping into J. Frank Norris's experience, I contact another of Ida's acquaintances—the pastor's wife.

We meet in an alcove of the Met's lobby mid-afternoon. She extends a warm handshake and a disarming smile. "I'm glad you called. Any friend of Ida Tate's is a friend of mine."

"I often find that to be the case, ma'am."

"How may I help you?"

Picturing the two sisters, I gather my courage and forge on. "I've read about your husband's courageous crusade to . . . redesign . . . Fort Worth's landscape."

First Baptist's new building opened just months ago, and so far no threats had been issued, but an air of uncertainty lingers that Sunday afternoon. Hopefully no fireworks will follow my conversation with his wife.

She chuckles. "My Frank's not one easily ignored."

"May I speak plainly?"

"Please do."

"A friend, a girl dear to me, was kidnapped in Oklahoma recently. We have reason to believe a nefarious neighbor is responsible. Searchers have scoured every inch of our state and found nothing. This man has been involved in business dealings in this city in the past and told his son he was headed to Cowtown."

She closes her eyes and gives her head a shake. "Oh, the baseness in this world."

"Indeed. I'm determined to locate the child. Ida hired me as her assistant, and I'm finding open doors. I've met someone who works in a brothel in the Acre."

"You must be careful. That crowd's capable of anything."

I nod. "I fear this woman is the one in danger. She's as skittish as a foal and in questionable health. I want to help her, but I'm not certain how to proceed. I thought perhaps you would have a suggestion."

"I'll pray about this, but please speak with the Upchurches."

The pastor and his wife. Again. "I intend to visit them tomorrow, but you're bound to have some advice. I'm just starting out on this mission. And a dear friend's life hangs in the balance—"

"Bathe yourself in prayer. Devilry is forever on the prowl."

Do three petitions a day qualify as a bath? Must I tack on a couple more? "I know wickedness. Firsthand." Should I share my story with this stranger?

She questions me with searching eyes.

I sense I can trust her. "Liquor enflames the man whose name I wear—no longer Pa to me. He beat me to the edge of death when I was just shy of thirteen. He killed my dear mother. I testified as an eye witness, but the all-male jury acquitted him. He's the suspected kidnapper."

She clutches me with her eyes. "There's no limit to a godly woman's influence. Like yours."

Mine? If this preacher's wife truly knew me, she'd use an entirely different adjective.

"My husband's mother was as strong an example of this truth as I've ever known."

"I'd like to hear her story if you're willing."

She closes her eyes and clasps her hands as if in prayer. "Mary Davis Norris possessed the strength of will of ten ordinary persons. She endured Frank's father's battle with liquor as long as she lived. Her courage one day in particular marked Frank forever.

"His father Werner had squandered his pay check in a saloon, his habit on Saturdays. Mary sent Frank to the establishment with a note asking the bartender to keep whiskey from her husband, as the family was hungry, and their pantry was bare.

"The man threw Frank out, and the boy walked the four miles back home with the unhappy news."

I imagine Ella or Addie in a spot like Mary's. Neither would stand for it.

"Mary told her son to prepare the carriage, and they headed for the saloon. She pointed to the bartender. 'Is this the man who laughed and cursed you, son?'"

All, including Frank, remained silent.

"Sweeping her eyes over the drunken scene, she spied her note crumpled in an empty whiskey glass. That's all it took."

I lean toward this storyteller, hungry for the rest of the tale. "All it took to . . . what?"

"Mary chased off the liquor dispenser with a horse whip. Actually, he fell and crawled out."

"Oh my."

"She didn't stop there. She used the whip's wooden handle on the bottles. Smashed them to bits." She eyes me under a raised eyebrow. "I don't expect my husband to back down a minute. He got his courage from his mother.

"But that's not all you and my husband have in common. One Christmas when my husband was a boy, he and his mother emptied his liquor bottles. The man took the whip to his son. Beat him to unconsciousness. Frank woke to his father hugging him and crying and begging God to send his son across the land to fight the curse that wrecked his life."

I possess no control of my hands as they rush to my chest, to the marks my bodice covers and to the grown-together hole in my throat.

"Rest assured, Frank won't be backing off from the fight to clean up this city. He learned his hatred of that sort of sin as Werner Norris's son."

I escort my newest friend outside to a waiting cab, and we wave as it drives away. My fingers itch to record my impressions as Rachel Lloyd did. I ascend the marble staircase and enter my room with plans for an exposé twirling like whirligigs.

The stench of a slop bucket accompanies me.

Alone in my room, I write letters to the business owners on Ida's list. Mrs. Norris's story evoked innumerable memories. And spurred me to reason with these men. Who knows if they'll note a single word, but I write the words anyway.

The telephone rings at six p.m., and I bring the receiver to my ear.

Sabina's bold voice tumbles through. "Got time to talk business?"

I tap the end of my writing pen on my chin. I'd best learn what she has tucked under her wig. "I'll be in the lobby in a half hour."

Smoothing my blouse, I pat stray strands into my chignon and hurry down the broad marble staircase.

A police officer strolls the hotel's main hallway. "Evening, ma'am." He flourishes his hat, gentleman-like.

"The same to you, sir." The officer's polished brass badge flashes the light of the wall sconces, drawing my eye to a figure embossed on its surface. "Is that a panther, sir?"

"Yes, ma'am," he replies with a nod. "Fort Worth's known as Panther City. Back in '73 a Dallas lawyer thought this city was doomed. Claimed Cowtown was so quiet a panther slept on Main Street.

"The *Democrat* editor took it as a challenge. Designed a new masthead with a crouching panther." He points to his badge. "The Police Department adopted it as a symbol of strength."

"Interesting bit of local lore. Thanks for explaining. And thank you for your service."

He gives a half bow and strolls on, but I stand staring at the floor. A recollection teases the fringes of my memory, but it's veiled by time.

"See *Caller*'s Sunday edition?" She claims a conversation grouping and I join her. She offers me a rolled-up copy of the paper and a sly grin. "Women's Section."

I open the heavy Sunday edition with trepidation. My fingers halt at the society section's header: *Rosen Heights Handouts for Criminals*. By Sabina Fitzgerald.

Unable to stifle my outrage, I toss the paper aside as if it has burned my hands. "How dare you undermine those women's gracious act. Or the unfortunate ones serving their time—for no more than unpaid debts!"

"That creature in the Flats doesn't know quality when it's standing in front of her."

I clamp my eyes shut. Returning her venom with venom of my own will move me no closer to a loved one, nor to an exposé. I need to find that serpent wisdom Ella spoke of in Addie's kitchen. But can I wrap it in the gentleness of a dove?

"Quality resides in the heart, not in clothing or mansions or titles."

"Don't preach to me. I know where you come from and what you're made of."

I ignore her scorn. "You asked to talk business. What is it?"

Twirling a leather key fob, she taps a foot on the marble flooring. "I hear you're working for Ida Tate."

"Where—"

"Don't deny it." She runs her thumb over the leather fob. "I'm a reporter. With sources. Remember?"

I return her smirk with a wary gaze lingering on the fob's embossing. It's the shape of . . . "Why are you interested in me?"

She lifts a shoulder, and the corners of her mouth slide downward, nonchalant-like. "I'm interested in what local women are up to. From someone with *insider* information. Besides, you can tell your honey-sweet story through me. My lady readers will lap it up."

"Why would I provide you a single tip?"

"For your puny brother's sake."

My body slackens, and my interest in her key fob vanishes.

"The last thing you want is for your oh-so-loving father to know his pitiful son's with Ida."

An explosion wracks my insides, and I grab her arm. "You're in contact with Walter? Where is he? Explain yourself."

She snarls and pulls away. "Don't touch me!"

This heartless woman has stoked smoldering embers of dread in my core. "He's wanted by the law. If you know where he is, you're harboring a criminal. I'll contact the sheriff."

She glances around. "Not an eavesdropper in sight, but I advise you to keep your voice down. Remember this is your word against mine. Who's Sheriff Rae going to believe? A fine Fitzgerald employed by *Fort Worth Caller*? Or a disgraced false accuser?"

"What do you want from me?"

"In exchange for keeping your brother's location to myself, you grant me exclusive access to the women's movement in the city."

Is she guessing? I'll admit nothing and put her off as long as I can.

"Why would I leave Donnie at Ida's when he has a perfectly wonderful home at Broadview?" I hesitate, considering my choice. Can I make a deal with the devil? "You know, I think it's best we not try to work together."

She chuckles and stands. "If I haven't heard from you by noon Wednesday, I'll inform Walter and write whatever I jolly well please in Thursday's *Caller*."

As she sashays out the Met's entrance, I slouch against my chair back. How did she learn Donnie's at Jackson? And does she indeed have contact with Walter?

I must contact Ida. Now.

CHAPTER 29

"Ida. Oh, Ida." My voice jostles off the telephone alcove's wood paneling.

"What is it, dear?"

I lower my tone to a whisper. "Sabina knows you have Donnie."

Silence. "You're sure?"

"For all I know, she's guessing. I denied it, of course, but still . . . It concerns me."

"Indeed. To be safe, we'll take him away as soon as we can gather our things."

"Where?" Has notifying Ida endangered my loved one further?

"I'll keep that private, dear. For your own good."

"All right . . ."

"Meanwhile, I'll notify Tarrant County Sheriff Rae and ask him to give you a call."

Ida's voice, strung tighter than piano wire, rattles my nerves.

She disconnects with an abrupt click, leaving me staring at the receiver. What may I reveal to the sheriff? Must I keep my sources confidential? As a newswoman, I must.

I skirt the desk and flurry up the stairs. The phone rings just as I enter. Seated at the desk, I expel a series of deep breaths. "Hello?"

"Miss Sloat? Miss Lily Sloat?" A man's bold voice.

"Yes. And this is . . ."

"Sheriff Rae. Just talked with Ida 'late. What's goin' on?"

I scrape my bottom lip between my teeth. "A girl is missing."

"A Tarrant County child?"

"No. Oklahoma. But I . . . We have reason to believe she was secreted to Fort Worth."

"When did she go missing?"

"The thirtieth of July. It's taken us awhile to figure out—"

"Wait a minute. Is this the girl Sheriff Earl Dawson wired about a couple weeks ago?"

"It is. But since then, I've discovered some things you might find helpful."

"It's not safe to talk on this contraption, not with elephant-ear operators listening in." He harrumphs. "Too late to meet you in the Met lobby?"

"Don't want to make a certain someone suspicious—"

"I've a better idea . . . There's a quiet corner in the bar and a bartender I can trust. I'll see you there in a half hour."

"All right, sir." I replace the receiver. My plans have taken an altogether unexpected turn—into a bar, of all places.

The rich tones of the hotel tavern's stained-glass sign strike me as daring. I peek inside.

The bartender is replenishing his stock of glasses and bottles.

Feeling bold and somewhat racy, I enter and look around. A lone customer, his head on a far table—certainly not the sheriff—appears to be sleeping. I ease toward the finely carved bar.

"What can I get you, ma'am?"

Perhaps I can garner some information before the sheriff arrives. I open my pocketbook and remove a dollar bill. "A little information."

He slips the currency into his vest pocket. "This establishment has rules, you know. Like non-drinking customers taking up space at the bar."

I look around. "I'm your sole customer." I thumb over my shoulder. "Except for that . . . sleeping gentleman."

He shrugs. "Are *you* a customer, ma'am?"

"Alright. I'll have a maraschino lemonade."

He gives the surface a final swipe. "Coming right up." He swirls red liquid into pale yellow liquid and drops in a maraschino cherry.

"About that information . . ."

He sets the pink-tinged drink on a small square napkin. "A dollar's worth of information, eh? What would you like to know?"

I sip. "Know any bartenders in the Acre?"

"What if I do?"

Lifting a shoulder, I offer him a second bill. "There might be some . . . remuneration."

He harrumphs. "A dollar at a time?"

"Depends on the information."

He frowns, and the corners of his mouth dip downward, tugging his mustache into a quarter-moon. "What'd'ya wanna know?" He polishes a whiskey glass with a cotton napkin.

"Can you tell me about Cowtown's panther?"

He canters his head to the side and raises his eyebrows.

"I've seen it on the policemen's badges. Anywhere else?"

He continues to twirl the rim of a whiskey glass in a napkin. "Ever hear of Black Panther Saloon? It's a . . . uh . . . private gentlemen's club."

I muffle a gasp in a fist, pretending to cough. "Oh, my."

He shrugs and sets the glass on a shelf. "The 'private' means upstairs."

"Know of any working girls . . . women of the night . . . changing their stripes?" I sip the sweet concoction and eye him over the glass rim. "How about underage girls?"

"Whoa." He holds up a palm, the napkin squeezed between a thumb and forefinger. "Know nothing about that." He resumes his buffing of the glassy surface.

Touchy. Interesting. "I'm willing to pay for information."

He considers me out of the corner of an eye. "Who are you? Can I trust you?"

I give a huff through my nostrils. "How do *I* know I can trust *you*?" I hand him a card with Ida's telephone number. "This number accepts anonymous messages." Snapping my pocketbook closed, I slide off the stool.

The door swings open, and a tall, trim gentleman enters. He hangs his

Stetson on a rack and heads my way.

I slip off the stool with lemonade in hand. He gives his head a snap to the right, and I follow him to an alcove with table and benches. Plenty private.

The sheriff positions himself with a clear view of the door and leans toward me with his elbows on the table, spearing me with his gaze. "You're poking at a mighty dangerous critter, Miss Sloat. Step back and let the law handle this."

I twirl the bottom of my glass in a circle of moisture. "Happy to, Sheriff. But I intend to be involved." I solidify my gaze on his. "And write an exposé when it's done."

He grimaces. "You a newspaper reporter?"

"I was supposed to work for *Caller*, but one of the players in this story snatched the job from me. Meanwhile, I have sources . . . I'm not at liberty to share."

Besides, I recognize a certain odor.

He sits back with his arms crossed. "What do you know?"

Packing a bag with several days' changes of clothing and toiletries, I pause to call my adventurous new friend. "I'll be at Berachah for two or three days. Mind checking my mail when you're at the Met for Wednesday Club? If there's anything from home, I'd appreciate a call." I hand her a card with the home's phone number.

"Glad to. Any other way I can help?"

I consider her offer. "Your guardian angel ever venture into the Acre after hours?"

"I can ask him." She pauses for a silent beat. "What do you have in mind?"

"I'm wondering about the supposed legitimate businesses—"

"*Supposed?*"

"I've heard some aren't all they claim to be? A boarding house or two.

Hotel. Billiards parlor. Gentlemen's Club. And a saloon or two doing business on the side."

"If you mean business owners working secret commerce, there's been talk."

"Perhaps your bodyguard can investigate? Maybe tail Sabina, learn where she lives, her comings and goings?"

"My husband would lock me up if he knew what I'm up to."

"And while you're at it . . ."

"Oh my. What else?"

"If you don't mind . . . If you feel comfortable asking . . ."

"Out with it."

"Would you ask him about Black Panther Saloon? Is it a private gentleman's club?"

"I've heard whispers now and again. We'll ask around. See you Thursday?"

"Or Friday. Thanks ever so much, friend."

Crawling between my sheets, I feel smug. My time in Fort Worth has produced results. I spoke to two small gatherings and met society's cream. Made friends. Flora. Beulah and her family. Star. Mrs. Norris and Sheriff Rae. Even a bartender, an associate of sorts.

I whisper a quick prayer, my duty done. A rabble of puzzle pieces flit about my head. Sabina's knowing—even guessing—where I placed Donnie troubles me. As does her threat to publish a tawdry article in *Caller*. However distasteful, could contact with her work to my advantage?

Then there's Ida's sudden flight from Jackson. Where has she taken my brother? Have I made a mistake, coming to Texas and depending on someone else to care for my loved one?

No. I must rest on the assurance I felt back home. I'll trust Ida with my brother. Flora and her guard with the Black Panther Saloon tip. The Met bartender with news about not-so-upstanding businesses. And Sheriff Rae with the investigation into Blossom's kidnapping. His phone number is printed on a card in my valise.

"Prospects are looking up." I speak into the darkness. "Just in case You're arranging things. . . Thanks."

CHAPTER 30

A shaft of morning sunlight creeps through an opening between the drapes, and my eyelids pop open. Flinging aside my sheet, I lower my feet to the carpet. I'm heading to Berachah today. But first, the journal.

> *June : ye : 3rd : 1775*
> *Moon be hidin.*
>
> *Traveler Man slap ye Wife. She be a-feared. Me warn ye Man, now mine Enemy. Ye Wife be me Friend.*
>
> *Cap'n Call me to Quarters. I refuse, save with me Man. Cap'n grill me. Davie Watch & Listen. Cap'n be worried I be Trouble. He be right. I halt Davie fore he lay out the Man.*
>
> *Ye sated Man have no Understandin o ye Hungry. Cap'n Belly be full.*
>
> *Rachel Lloyd*
> *Daughter o Abraham*

I pause to consider Rachel Lloyd's astute observation: *The sated man has no understanding of the needs of the hungry.* As a girl, I discovered layered implications of this truth. What stratums remain to be mined?

Will I allow Rachel's thoughts to invade my own? Time's fleet of foot.

Sliding the chair to the desk's kneehole, I find my gaze wooed to a triangle of white peeking under the door. The morning paper. Have I time for it? No, but I can devour the details on the interurban.

I peek out. No one's in sight. Snatching up the daily, I snap the door closed and secure the lock. As I'm tucking it into my valise, one bold headline claims my focus.

Battle of Stalluponen Begins!

Submitting to curiosity—and anxiety—I unroll the paper. Far more than a regional conflict, the European war is becoming a conflagration. Daily the fires of war rage, and our nation—and Addie—inch closer to the furnace.

What benefit are my thrice daily prayers? Moments of peaceful contemplation. But nothing else.

I flutter through the remaining pages, intending to save them for my trip. But the Women's Society page grabs my attention. I spread the pages flat and focus on one heading. *Oklahoma Visitor Comes to Cowtown, by Sabina Fitzgerald.*

The woman hasn't waited to stir the cauldron. She's agitating the brew Monday morning.

Scanning the article, I pause at key words and phrases: *mysterious . . . dubious purposes . . . courtroom . . . jury . . . perjury . . . checkered past . . .*

I cover my mouth and slump. What will the Rosen Irregulars and Wednesday Club think of me now? And what will it do to Ida's reputation?

Shall I give the counterfeit reporter's elixir a whisk . . . offer *Caller* a rebuttal . . . and inform them of their writer's true name. Will I let her manipulate my plans, control my days?

No. I'll not put off my trip to Arlington any longer. No doubt the society page will be strutting to a different tune in a day or two.

I snatch a traveling ensemble from the armoire. Shaking out the skirt, I wrap it around my waist and force the buttons into their holes. Shove my arms through bodice sleeves. Force the opening closed. And secure snaps, hooks, and belt. My fingers tremble. How dare Sabina claim Adelaide's name and besmirch it!

It's enough to leach the last iota of my patience.

I yank a brush through my hair and chuck it into my travel bag. Twist my hair into a knot. And secure it with pins. Wrenching a rolled-brim hat over my crown, I imagine forcing Sabina's head through a stock. Would even that teach her a lesson?

Shall I take my pistol to a home inhabited by mothers and their children? I think not.

I place the firearm in a box and tie it with string. Snapping my valise closed, I lock my door and tread down the stairs.

I hand the boxed pistol to the clerk. "Will you keep this in your safe? I'll be away."

"Of course." He tucks the package into the small safe beneath the array of guest mail slots and gives the combination dial a twirl. "And where might you be going this fine day?"

"Arlington." I tug on short cotton gloves.

"Don't tell me you're off to that . . . that *place*."

I answer with a shrug and flounce toward the electric-powered interurban at the corner of Ninth and Main. The conveyance ekes eastward, snail-like. Through the city's burgeoning outskirts. And into rural countryside.

All the while, I sit like a fence post and seethe at Sabina's audacity

At Handley's Lake Erie, couples and families bound from the trolley at Handley's Lake Erie. Festivities at the fun park and pavilion await them. I read the North Texas Traction Company created the lake for an electric generator to provide energy for their trolley line. Their recreational trolley park idea proved brilliant. The bright-white buildings with red roofs surrounded by a park of lush, flower-strewn greens invite travelers to join the family fun.

The trolley's overhead electric wires snap and buzz now and again, mirroring my ire. But images of joy elbow into my thoughts. Will I permit Sabina Gallagher to snuff out this jaunt's potential? What can I achieve for any cause in such a state of mind? The exuberance of families and the laughter of couples douse my exasperation.

With my thoughts corralled, my breathing slows and the burn in my stomach eases. I step off the trolley at Arlington's depot on dusty Abram Street. A full-faced young woman greets me. Her sable-brown braids are twisted into mounds on either side of her head. Her wide-set brown eyes hint at a lively disposition.

"I'm Bessie. Excuse my attire, ma'am." She indicates her sweat-stained bodice and work-spotted skirt. "I was plowing. Jumped off the tractor just in time."

"Thank you for meeting me." I offer a hand. "Please call me Lily."

"Glad to make your acquaintance." Her callused palms attest to her familiarity with physical labor. "That bag all you brought?"

"That and my valise." I nod and reach for my satchel.

"Whatever suits you is alright with us." She grabs my bag and heads to the mule-drawn wagon. We climb aboard for the mile-long trip into the country.

A lovely, two-story white clapboard home appears, and my breath catches. This moment in time won't be like others—fleeting. No. Somehow I know this one will endure.

"It's beautiful, Bessie. How long have you lived here?"

She smiles. "Ten years now. I was one of the soiled doves in Fort Worth. Got myself with child, and the Upchurches took me in. That was '04. My boy Joshua's nine now."

Stunned that my new acquaintance speaks easily of her past, I gaze at her in wonder. She appears to care not a whit that the brutal Texas sun beams on her freckled skin. Her demeanor leaves no question as to her state of mind. Bessie is happy.

"Pastor and Mrs. Upchurch are fine folks." She flicks the reins and directs the mule between modest entrance pillars onto property that extends as far as I can see. Full oak and pecan trees, elm and ash. Plowed fields. A barn. Outbuildings. And the home.

Arrested by the placid beauty, I reach out a hand. "Can you give me a moment to take it in?"

"Why, sure." She reins the mule to a stop.

"What's the large building?"

"Whitehall Tabernacle. For Sunday church. Wednesday nights are optional."

She moves a pointed forefinger from building to building and to patches of green. "That's the dormitory where we mothers and young'uns live. Over there's the garden and orchard. The sewing center. We make handkerchiefs to sell. We're a self-supporting endeavor, so we all help."

"I read your publication. Impressive."

"Over yonder's the printing shop's where we print *The Purity Journal*. That's the schoolhouse next to the clinic." Bessie parks at the barn and hops down. "The Mrs. is waiting for you." She points to a two-story clapboard home. "At the big house."

At once eager and dubious, I halt beside the team and look around. What is it about this place that sets it apart from other locales? I've a sense I've . . . come home.

Tossing aside my wonderings, I enter the abode nestling among shade trees with an impression the house knows me, and I know it. Odd.

Bessie strides off to notify my hostess, and I look around. White shades hang on wood-sashed windows set in papered walls. Framed prints of Jesus in Gethsemane and in the midst of children assume prominent positions between windows.

A piano sits in a corner, and mismatched upholstered furniture on a worn, patterned rug. Embroidered pillows and footstools. Oil lamps. Side tables.

I examine a framed photograph. A group of a dozen women are gathered in the parlor, some on chairs, others standing, and a few kneeling. A gentleman and a lady stand on the left. Children are scattered throughout the group.

The women sport Gibson-girl hair styles and are garbed in white dresses or dark skirts and blouses with puff sleeves, stylish a decade ago.

"That's our first group of mothers at this location." Someone speaks at my back. "1904."

I turn, and a woman's kind expression greets me. Her mahogany-brown hair is mounded at the back of her head with combs taming stray wisps.

"You must be Lily."

"Yes. Thank you for receiving me."

We latch hands. "I'm Mae Upchurch." She stares into my eyes. Her gaze moves to my hair, and the silence stretches to discomfort. I snap a nod. "Ma'am?"

She blinks, as if her mind has returned from a distant place. "Yes. Welcome to Berachah." She gestures to the settee. "Have a seat. Tell me about yourself."

CHAPTER 31

Straightaway, I'm to lay my life bare? I traveled to Berachah to question this woman. Perhaps I can do so as I ease into my own story.

I alight on the settee, a worn velvet Victorian, and my hostess, on the chair beside it. A tea table consumes the space between us.

Her gaze lingers around my head. "Your hair color . . ." She shakes her head and flicks a hand, as if shooing a pesky bee.

"Someone back home describes it as . . . like copper."

"Indeed. It's beautiful."

I pat the mound at the back of my head. "From my mother's side, I guess, though hers was darker . . . before she turned gray."

Her gaze strays from my hair to my eyes. "Ida tells me you're from Needham."

"Lived there all my life. Which reminds me . . . I've—"

A girl enters with a tray of juice and cookies and sets it on the table. Pouring the pale juice into two tall glasses, she serves the pastry on dainty china plates and exits.

I sample the potion and crumbly pastry. "This is delicious."

"We grow our own pears. And pecans."

I munch on the delicacy shot through with nuts and drenched in finely sifted sugar. "Don't know when I've tasted anything so luscious."

"Mexican wedding cookies. We maintain a small dairy and churn our butter. The sugar is a gift from a supporter in New Orleans."

I dab my lips with a simple cotton napkin. "You have a beautiful place here."

"Thank you. It requires all of us."

"Bessie identified some of the outbuildings. But I wonder—"

"Would you like a tour?"

"I'd love it."

She sets aside her napkin. "We'll get acquainted as we stroll." Rising, she gestures to the front door.

I follow my hostess with my pocket-sized tablet in hand.

She steps onto the porch and halts. "You grew up in Needham?"

"Yes. My mother never . . . We . . ."

She lays a hand against my back. Her gentle touch, perhaps the warmth in her eyes, communicates trustworthiness and inspires me to open up.

"My family's story is . . ." A breaker of cold swells over me. Am I to yank dark memories into this bright, lovely day? "It's sad."

"Sad stories abound here, but so do happy tales." She gazes across the landscape, as if lost in thought. "You were saying?"

"My mother is dead. My father . . . was . . . is cruel."

Her forehead wrinkles. One eyebrow scrunches downward, and her lips draw into a pouch. "I'm sorry, dear. You have siblings?"

"A younger brother. He's with Ida."

"He's blessed to be in that fine woman's care."

How is it I'm opening my storybook the third time in as many days? And to a complete stranger, trustworthy or otherwise? "Mind telling me about your ministry?"

She eases us into our stroll. "Our mothers learn they need not be victims. They develop strength and self reliance, as well as job skills."

Smiling, she motions to a gentleman standing at the open window of a hut. "And then there are men like my husband, Tony."

Pastor Upchurch's oval face cracks into a broad grin. "Welcome, Lily." He spreads his arms wide, encompassing the shop. "We'd stop for a visit, but we've work to do." A thatch of dark curls sprouts from his crown.

Two young women wave from either side of a work table. Behind them stand shelves of printed materials and supplies. An aproned young man perches atop a stool at a printing press controlled by a foot pedal. I learned to use the same type of press at CIA.

My guide speaks with a boy in a khaki shirt and dark trousers, and he skitters away

We return to our stroll. "We send the *Journal* to our contributors, businessmen in the Dallas and Fort Worth area." She nods toward a red-brick two-story structure. "We've a medical clinic and a dormitory."

"And those children?" I point to a group playing in the shade of pecan trees.

"We believe mothers and their babes belong together, so they tend their children a full year before considering adoption. We've not had to work out the details of an adoption yet."

"Do they live here indefinitely?"

"It's their home as long as they want. They're free to leave anytime. They develop marketable skills." She points to two outbuildings. "In the laundry and handkerchief factory. So if they leave us, they can support themselves."

I'm reminded of Ida's hankie. "May I see them?"

"Come. Let me show you."

The gentlewoman leads me to a purity-white wooden cabin with shamrock-green trim. Curtains flutter out open windows. Six women work at sewing machines, four at a table.

The handwork draws my eye. "They're trimmed in lace?"

"We tat the edges for ladies. The plain are for gentlemen."

I gaze at the instrument in a girl's hand. "I have a shuttle in my satchel. It's rather a mystery—the family kind."

She gathers me into a deep gaze. "I love a good whodunit. Don't you?"

I chuckle. "Especially when it's solved."

Just as I'm edging closer to leads to the abduction of girls—perhaps even Blossom—the old implement calls, and family secrets take over. Perhaps I'll unravel one troubling knot soon. But what if I chase answers and find more heartache? Or discover I come from sorrier stock than even Walter?

I'd best follow the bread crumbs.

Returning to the parlor settee, I unbuckle my my valise and extract the velvet pouch. I release the strings and hold up the tatting tool.

My hostess stares for a long moment. "Where did you come by this?"

"Found it in my mother's things. After her death."

She holds the instrument in her palm and traces the letters with a forefinger. "Where did she come by it?"

"I've no idea. Ma wasn't allowed to speak of her life before I was born."

She raises her eyes under pinched eyebrows. "How old are you?"

"Twenty-two."

"So you were born in . . ."

"'92."

"Where, my dear?"

I raise my shoulders and let them collapse. "Truthfully, I'm not sure."

"Your mother tatted?" She strokes the shuttle as if caressing a friend's hand.

"Never saw her at it. Not once."

She stares at the instrument with an expression akin to a painted doll's, frozen in place. She flicks her gaze to me. "We deliver garden goods to elderly folks this afternoon. And we're going to Lake Erie tomorrow. Can you stay awhile? There's an extra bedroom upstairs."

This lovely woman's reaction has given me pause. I followed bread crumbs to this place, but I'm the one being questioned. Flora's waiting for me to return to Fort Worth to question Star further. But I sense I belong here. For now. "I'd be delighted. But may I stay in the dormitory?"

"You're welcome under any of our roofs."

The remainder of the day is spent in the dormitory kitchen with my hostess overseeing meal preparation. I catch her staring at me time and again.

At length, she puffs out a breath and gives her head a half shake. "Let's sit outside."

I follow her to a simple bench on the shaded back porch.

Her eyes drift skyward. "I'm calling up memories. Not sure . . ."

I shrug. "In the meantime, mind answering some questions?"

Seemingly tossing away her disquiet, she refocuses on me. "Of course not."

"I'm in Texas as Ida's assistant—calling on contacts, speaking to ladies' groups, looking for ways to support the drive for the vote—but my key mission is to find a loved one—a thirteen-year-old girl. Kidnapped."

She closes her eyes and bows her head. "I can only imagine."

"The daughter of my friend, Ella Evans, was abducted from their home outside Needham two weeks ago." I pause to consider my explanation. "I've learned even underage girls are forced into prostitution."

She rests her elbow on an arm of the bench. "Tragic but true. The seizure of innocent daughters for wicked purposes is a scourge on our society. Congress passed the White Slavery Act in 1910 to curtail travel across state lines for unholy purposes—interstate commerce, you understand."

"Yes. The Mann Act. If this child I seek was brought from Oklahoma to Texas for such a purpose . . ."

"The federal legislation would apply."

I flick open my notepad and scribble with the exposé in mind. "I'm told the women in Cowtown's Acre are all but imprisoned. And that you've been rescuing women like them for years now. How have you reached them?"

"They aren't locked in cages. They mingle in public, some as well as you or I, but most consider themselves enslaved. They believe they have no choice. In time shopkeepers and waitresses and cab drivers notice them and notify us. We've developed an underground railroad of sorts. Spirited away dozens."

"And the impact?"

"Minimal. Our private investigator found eighty brothels in the Acre alone."

"In such a small part of the city?" I gape at the breadth of the problem.

"They hide behind legitimate enterprises. Wealthy businessmen are property owners who insist their renters' business dealings don't concern them. The almighty dollar rules."

I tap the end of my pen on my chin, and focus on her doe eyes. "Ever looked for the connections between property owners and those who run the brothels?"

She offers me a knowing grin. "You'd be surprised at the network we've uncovered."

Perhaps she can speak to the whereabouts of Wilcox. But will I be trespassing on confidential territory? "The problem's magnitude astounds me."

I promised Star I'd protect her identity, but who better than this couple to help her? And provide a lead to Blossom? "I met someone who works in the Acre, a prostitute."

She tucks a wisp of hair behind an ear. "That's risky business."

"Her sister introduced us. She thinks she has no choice."

"That's where we come in. With options."

"Do you have knowledge of underage girls plied in this city? And can you put me in touch with your investigator?"

"Yes." She grins with mischievousness sparkling in her eyes. "And yes. I'll give him a call. But we must be careful. Very."

CHAPTER 32

July : ye : 11ᵗʰ : 1775
Eve o full Moon

Cap'n Call Below-Deckers to Merrymakin. We be suppin with ye Crew.
Refuse Game o Chance.

Sailor with rovin Hands best steer clear o Me & me Ward.

Rachel Lloyd
Daughter o Abraham

This new morning I dine on oats and apples, but side dishes of Rachel Lloyd's defense of her ward and news of the foreign war transform the sweetness to the bitterness of bile. Montenegro has declared war on Germany, and France has done the same against Austria-Hungary. The Battle of the Frontiers rages while my treasured friend traipses around Italy.

Back at Broadview, I would've retreated to the gazebo—not to pray, mind you—but to ponder. To what end, I can't say. I only know this: Cade possesses my heart and deepest longing. Broadview holds my fondest memories. And the ancient roots that burrow in Ma's sea chest nag.

But nothing compares with the pressing need of an abduction. Perhaps I'll find another moment to speak with my hostess on this day of recreation at the Lake Erie fun park.

At the trolley stop in downtown Arlington, Bessie sits smiling alongside Joshua with ball cap in hand.

"I'm sorry you had to wait for me."

"Don't worry yourself a smidgen. We enjoy watching people."

Summer recreation seekers such as ourselves board the trolley along the way to Handley, and we riders scoot aside to make room for them. Soon the red rooftops of the Lake Erie recreation area peek above trees' full crowns.

I stretch for a better view. "Lot of families."

"Should've seen it Independence Day. Folks were thicker than overcooked grits." The morning sun highlights the robust young mother's rich strawberries-and-cream complexion. The freckles enhance her appeal—like nut topping on a sundae.

We debark and join the promenade traversing the pier with boat dock. Wide-brimmed hats and parasols steal the show. My white cotton, sporty dress mirrors fun seekers' sailor attire. On a day that should reach one hundred degrees, I welcome the cut of my loose, elbow-length sleeves.

A potpourri of aromas greet us. Popcorn and roasted peanuts. Taffy and cotton candy. Braised beef and frankfurters on sticks. My stomach growls.

Ragtime music wafts across the emerald-green lawn.

A flash of bright white draws my focus to a couple at the edge of the lake. Both wearing hats, they huddle with their backs toward us and their heads all but touching. They strike me as familiar. Is that . . .

"Over here!" A mother waves us toward the pavilion, and the lakeside couple is forgotten.

Our group enjoys popcorn and the penny arcades. Mrs. Upchurch and I sit at a picnic table while the mothers tend the children and the lively notes of "The Saint Louis Blues" dance from a Victrola.

"A supporter is treating the children to this outing." She nods to a pair of boys at the pinball machine. "Even the pennies."

I look around and smile. "It's a treat to observe scenes like this. I never enjoyed such frivolities as a child. My life was . . . limited."

"Want to talk about it?"

Is an amusement park the place to speak of my life? Perhaps the buzz of activity around us will afford a measure of insulation.

"I was a sharecropper's daughter. My mother tended crops. My father was no good."

"I'm sorry. Daughters need their fathers."

"He was fond of liquor. And a horse whip."

"Oh, Lily . . ."

"He beat me to the edge of death when I was just short of thirteen."

"How in the world did you get to where you are today?"

"The daughter of the farmer whose acreage we worked took me in. Now she's a dear friend. She started Broadview School for Girls and helps women in need.

"I witnessed my father murder my mother and testified for the prosecution. But a jury of twelve men chose to believe the murderer over a mere female."

Reaching across the table, she squeezes my hands. "You're a woman of substance, dear." She gazes toward the fluted ceiling, as if considering an idea, perhaps a daring one. "I'm a member of Arlington's Thursday Club. We're close to a consensus on the suffrage issue. A story like yours might tip the balance. Would you consider speaking to our group?"

"I told my story to two women's clubs, fine society ladies who were kind. Still, I'm the offspring of a shiftless drunk who made our name a byword."

"You're ever so much more." She pauses. "Your eyes . . . Out here they're brighter than emeralds . . . as if the sun's shining through."

I chuckle. "A friend back home compares them to the foxfire's light."

Running a fingertip around the rim of her red-and-white striped soda cup, she stares into the distance. "Most unusual."

Stillness creeps between us.

"J.T. and I began our ministry in Waco, a town south of here, back in the '90s. Worked among women in need."

"Of all people in the world, it should be church members who help them." I run a thumb over my left knuckles. "Bessie introduced herself as a former soiled dove. Is that what you mean?"

She chuckles. "That one's a straight talker. Let's just say some Waco churches decided our work was shameful and removed their support.

But the Lord provided our present site."

God again? "Where did you come by the name of your mission?"

"Ah, you've reminded me—"

"Help? Come quick! It's Joshua!" A towheaded boy runs to her side, pointing to the roller rink.

Intent on determining Joshua's condition, I enter the rink alongside Mrs. Upchurch. The music halts, and skaters move to the sides, silent.

Joshua lies sprawled on the rink's hardwood floor, his mother on her knees, shaking him. "Joshua? Son?"

The matron of Berachah crouches beside Bessie, and I stand to the side.

Squatting, the manager presses a finger to Joshua's neck and bends to the boy's face. "Let's take him to the medical clinic." He and Bessie hike Joshua to a sitting position.

The boy sputters and swats, striking his mother across a shoulder. "Wh—. Where?"

Bessie latches onto his shoulders. "You fell, Joshua."

He reaches for the back of his head. "Ooo."

The manager grabs Joshua under an arm. "Gonna have a goose egg, young man. Can you stand?"

"Sure you can." Bessie grabs Joshua under the other arm.

"Easy now." The overseer maintains a steady hold on Joshua as they exit the rink.

I remain with the mothers and their children.

A girl in ringlets and party dress perches at a table before a cake with candles glowing. "Mother, what's going on?" Dozens of similarly attired girls and boys encircle her.

She sticks out her bottom lip and scowls. "It's time to sing 'Happy Birthday'. And all anybody can do is stare at that clumsy boy."

Her mother pats her shoulder. "Some ragamuffin was careless. Forget it, love." She raises her arms as if directing an orchestra. "All together now . . ."

My mind races backward in time to a former birthday gathering, my sixteenth. In Addie's garden. With the county's socially elite. Accustomed to working alongside Maggie, I mixed the punch in the crystal bowl, and Sabina stepped up with two friends.

"Got dirt under your fingernails?" She spoke with a snarl.

I scrambled for a fitting response.

"Cat got your Sloat tongue?" She served up a jaunty lift of a shoulder.

"There you are." Addie had appeared at my side. "Come, Lily, there's someone I want to introduce you to." She took my hand and led me away.

Did anyone notice my clean, trimmed nails?

Today's birthday song brings me back to the present.

Remembering where I am, I take in the group. "Time for our picnic."

One mother steps forward. "I'll get our baskets. Watch my little girl, will you, Lily?" She skitters off with another mother.

"Spread out our things," I call to the raven-haired six-year-old. Our group gathers under an ash tree on a slope between the pavilion and lake polka-dotted with boats.

When the women return with the baskets, my charge's mother looks around and frowns. "Where's my girl?"

I turn a full circle, my eyes raking the lawn from the pavilion to the lake. "She was just here."

"The lake!" the mother cries and runs toward the water.

I snap my head left to right in a frenzy, all but pleading for someone to— "There she is!" A black-haired girl is accepting a mound of cotton candy from a man in a Panama hat.

"No!" I yell and run toward the girl, her mother in tow.

The girl's blue eyes latch onto her mother's. Her face crimps, and she wails.

Her mother falls to her knees, clasping her daughter, both bawling. "Scared the life out of me. You mustn't wander off. That stranger . . ."

We look around, but the man has evaporated.

The hairs on my neck stand on end. I retreat to a shaded section of grass near the pavilion. Leaning my head backward, I take deep breaths, and my mind flies away to Oklahoma.

"Mama! Oh, Mama!"

"Blossom's disappeared."

"Where could she have gone, Mama?"

"We've looked everywhere."

As I relive the terror, my heartbeat quickens, and I pant. Where are you, child?

"You're pale as snow."

I open my eyes. Mrs. Upchurch has appeared beside me.

"We had a scare." I point to the mother and daughter. "We lost the girl. And then found her . . . with a stranger—"

"Dear God." She runs down the slope toward the pair.

Our appetites—and enthusiasm for frivolity—drain away. The day is ruined. We pack our baskets and trudge up the slope, slogging along the pier, past the boat dock, to the wait station.

A family of five awaits the trolley in the three-sided kiosk. The mother fans a flyer advertising an upcoming Lake Erie event. Her full cheeks have flamed in the heat, and perspiration has pasted milk chocolate-colored strands across her forehead.

Her elder son has inherited her pointed nose and the younger son, her faded blue eyes. Both are tall like their plain-featured father. The girl's hair mimics her mother's.

Whom do *I* resemble? Not Walter, although I can be as stubborn as he. I wish I possessed my mother's rock-solid faith and gentle nature in spite of my lot.

Each branch of Ma's family tree springs from a root and the root from a seed. How will I find the seed of my beginning with disaster my persistent companion?

For now, I'll trail the abductor's brutish scent. But then I'll search for that seed.

I traveled to Texas to do some stalking—with the struggle for women's equality stirred into the mix. But I check over my shoulder at every turn. As if someone's following.

I reckon it began with that stranger on the train. Has he been tailing me ever since?

Flinging aside my sheet, the sole bit of covering the summer heat allows, I dig into my travel bag for a card of hat pins tucked into a zippered bag for hair combs. I promised I'd keep a weapon nearby, and a seven-inch pin will do nicely.

I place it on the side table and return to bed. In my haste, I forgot to offer thanks over breakfast. But I bowed my head for the noon blessing at Lake Erie and again at supper. I'm bound by my promise to speak the three prayers myself. Best be done with it.

A sturdy honeysuckle outside the dormitory's second-story window climbs a trellis that arcs over my window. At my *Amen*, it scratches against the pane, signaling a bit of wind.

A long and lonely keening pierces the night, and a walloping whack sets me upright in bed, my pulse racing. A second creak and a staccato swat . . . The barn door is dancing in the wind. Best secure it.

With my dressing gown assuring my modesty and the hat pin threaded through its wide lapel, I creep outside in my house slippers. The moon, full and bright the night before, wanes tonight, but its vivid glow lights a pathway straight to the barn.

A baby cries out in the dormitory. A swing rattles, and a dog barks in the distance. I skitter toward the barn, feeling at once . . . exposed.

A gust wraps itself around me and lifts my nightgown and wrapper, baring my knees. All the more reason to hurry.

The barn stands wide open. One swings on its hinges, complaining. The other flaps against the clapboard siding. A hasp assembly keeps the doors closed. Has the wind rattled the wooden pin out of place? Hardly seems strong enough. Odd.

I find the wooden pin in the dirt and wrestle the wind until the hasp and pin clunk into place. A flurry all but flings me back to the house, bringing to mind *At the Back of the North Wind*, a favorite book of Ella's girls. The story whetted Blossom's appetite for seeing the world.

Stumbling up the back steps with her fair-haired image knotting my middle, I remind myself to telephone Ida tomorrow. She might have news.

As I enter, the wind dies down as suddenly as it picked up. The night lies still, as if a shroud has fallen over the world. The hairs on my forearms stand straight up, and I rub my arms, elbows to wrists.

I cross the kitchen and up the stairs. The treads grouse beneath my feet. A clock chimes. A rustling draws my gaze over the railing.

"Can't sleep?" Bessie's silhouette is backlit by the moon.

I sigh. "Today was rather upsetting."

"For me too. Talking it over might help."

"Surely you need your rest."

"Joshua has a headache, so I prepared a packet of aspirin. He's asleep now. Care for a tepid cup of tea?"

"I'd be delighted."

Our table conversation reminds me of Broadview. Maggie. And Sabina.

Two women couldn't be more different than Bessie and Sabina. *Since she returned from her wayward life in Fort Worth, her bitterness has deepened.*

"Do you mind if we discuss your life before this home?"

"Don't mind a'tall. Best not hide it."

"Was Joshua born here at the Home?"

"He was. I lost my job at the boarding house—or disorderly house, as the brothel was called, my belly being so big and all. The girls made fun of the Upchurches as you might imagine. But I was desperate, so I took the train to their mission in Dallas. They told me they were moving to this place, and I tagged along."

"Do you keep up with any of the . . ."

"Working girls?"

"Yes."

"Some are dead, and others moved away, but there's a few still around. I write to them every month."

"Ever run across someone from Oklahoma?"

"Sure. More than one. Got a name?"

"I hesitate to . . . you know, gossip."

"Describe her."

"She's thirty-two, I guess. Returned to Oklahoma some months back, supposedly from wayward living in Cowtown. I never wondered what her life might've been until now. I ran across her in Fort Worth. Wouldn't have known her. She's changed."

"In what ways?"

"I knew her hair to be rather colorless. Thin and wispy. She depended on hair frames and padding. Her natural complexion hasn't a touch of color, and her figure's what I'd call rawboned and boyish. But now . . . She's altogether different."

"Women of the Acre have learned some tricks. Plumb bewildering."

"Now she wears a wig in a rich dark color. It's cut in a modern bob with perky curls. Her skin's now a rich color, and she's rather curvy."

"And her dispostion?"

I can't suppress a sigh. "She's no longer allowed in her mother's home."

Bessie threads her fingers behind her head and stares at the ceiling, as if calling up a memory. "I recall one girl fitting your description. Back in . . ." She lifts her eyes to the ceiling, enumerating on her fingers. "Around '03. Always brawling. Gave management one too many head-aches. They sent her packing."

"What was her name?"

"She was known as Jasmine. But we girls didn't use our real names. She reeked of a perfume from Paris she claimed was made from her fa-vorite flower . . . a cousin to jasmine." She snaps her fingers, as if to coax the word to her tongue. "It's that white flower. You know . . . It turns brown if you touch it."

"Gardenia?"

"That's it!"

Could this be Sabina? If so, the wayward life her mother spoke of was a brothel. A prickling sensation brings me to a shiver. Unable to draw a deep breath, I'm silence stricken.

"That sound like the woman you know?"

I blink away my momentary muteness. "It does. But if she's one and the same, I grieve for her mother. I'd love to facilitate a reconciliation."

"You've an unspoiled heart, Lily. But my guess is the Lord can do a better job of reconciling those two than you can." She slaps her hands on her knees. "I'd best be on my way. Need to check on my boy."

I tidy the kitchen and return to my room with Ida's voice playing like a Victrola.

The Lord sustains the fatherless . . . Jesus knew the children He'd place right here—in the palms of my hands.

Berachah, like Jackson Academy, has assumed the shape of a pair of hands. But what of those who haven't been swept into the loving palms?

Sabina is fatherless. And her mother grieves.

Bessie's assessment of my role in reconciling mother and daughter pokes at me. Doesn't her Lord care to reconcile flesh and blood?

Thankfully Beulah and her fatherless seven have begun to know peace and security. But Star is imprisoned in a gilded cage without bars.

Above all, sweet, guileless Blossom is lost to us. Who knows how many others suffer the same fate?

I might not reconcile Maggie and her daughter, keep Addie safe at war's front stoop, or move a single stone from Star's pathway.

But I'll do what I can to find Ella's daughter and return to her mother's bosom.

CHAPTER 33

While tending to my morning prayers, I'm reminded Berachah's Wednesday evenings are devoted to prayer. Perhaps I'll attend. The service can fulfill this day's prayer obligation.

Meanwhile, I'll speak with the resident mothers. Rachel Lloyd would do the same. Her leather-bound chronicle draws my gaze, and I rise from my knees to the bedside table.

> July : ye : 19th : 1775
> Port o Philadelphia
>
> Men topside preparin to Dock.
>
> Women below Deck. Put me in Charge. I be toleratin no Mistreatin from ye Sailors or Cap'n Himself. Women submitin Complaint to Sailin Comp'y. Fee Hike twas Lie. Cap'n be pocketin Coins.
>
> I be holdin Christian Bible o'er me Heart. Ye Jesus, Man o Peace, be stirrin Pot in me People's Temple, taggin Moneychangers as he saw em—Thieves. I be doin same.
>
> Best I thank ye Jesus for Good in ye New Land. Ahead o Time.
>
> Rachel Lloyd
> Christian

Thanking Jesus ahead of time requires a solid faith in the Provider. How does one capture such assurance?

A blank page follows. Turning the crackly leaf, I find an entry in a different hand on a date twenty years in the future. I thumb through future entries, all but overcome with curiosity. The War for Independence. Homesteading in western Tennessee. A general store in Missouri. The

War Between the States.

Mere glances at the writings in a half dozen different hands capture me, magnet-like.

What am I thinking? I haven't the time for this.

Pondering the enigma of firm assurance that steps into the unknown on the wings of faith, I chat with eight mothers and jot notes. Ask questions about sightings of underage girls. And help around the grounds.

I'll revisit the old diary this evening rather than attend the prayer service. The sound of voices rises from outside, and I part the window's lace sheers.

The residents are required to attend church on Sundays, but from the looks of the line entering Whitehall Tabernacle at seven o'clock, no one misses mid-week evening service either. Glancing at the ancient tome, I admit to myself a different sort of curiosity consumes me. With reluctance, I slide the book aside and dress for the gathering.

I enter the large space alongside Bessie. Side panels are rolled open for cross ventilation. How pleasant, the mild evening temperature.

Pastor Upchurch stands before the group with a solemn expression. "You ladies experienced a scare at Erie yesterday."

Heads nod.

"A girl celebrating her birthday was snatched from the play park last evening."

The birthday girl? Whatever has become of our world?

Dignified in posture and demeanor, he calls us to prayer. Heads bow, and some women drop to their knees. I lower my head, but my gaze lingers on the little diary I've begun carrying for note taking. If I'm to write an exposé, I'll need detailed notes.

Shortly, the rustle of clothing and murmurs spread from the back. Brother Upchurch bounds up the aisle and we congregants turn *en masse* toward the commotion.

Beyond the last row of pews, I glimpse the backs of two heads—the pastor and a stranger. A flash of ruffles and strands of blonde hair. The men bend over a girl.

"Give us room." Mrs. Upchurch motions the crowd aside and squats, blocking my view.

"Who are they, Bessie?" I ask.

She raises her shoulders and shakes her head.

"Let's move her to the clinic." Pastor Upchurch signals to Bessie, and she returns with a stretcher. The men roll the girl onto the litter.

As they exit, I catch a glimpse. Sunflower-bright hair covers the girl's face. Looks like the birthday girl. I stumble to the doorway and strain for better view, but it's darkening outside.

Mrs. Upchurch leads the group in prayer, but I wait at the back.

Soon Brother Upchurch returns and stands at the front. "The Lord has brought a missing girl to our doorstep."

The birthday girl? Like others, I choke back a gulp, stricken to silence.

"A friend found her near Lake Erie," he continues. "Doc's here, and sheriff's on his way. Meanwhile, we'll pray."

Mrs. Upchurch spins toward the entrance.

I follow close at her heels. "May I come?"

"You may." She answers without stopping.

Arriving out of breath, Mrs. Upchurch enters the exam room and takes her place beside the injured girl. I observe through the opening between door and its facing, but all I can see are the child's feet.

She's lying on a cot, her bare, grime-crusted feet bleeding. Mrs. Upchurch removes her dress and tosses it aside. A simple cotton shift takes its place. Torn and blood spotted, the discarded garment hangs haphazard-like from a straight-backed chair.

The sight unearths memories. My eyes clamp shut, and I lean against the jamb.

I mustn't allow recollections of Walter's heinous acts to restrain me. I creep forward, and Mrs. Upchurch clears a space, revealing . . .

The child's countenance, equally grime-ridden as her feet, claims me.

I move to her side, trance-like. Mrs. Upchurch hands me a porcelain bowl of warm water and a wash cloth. I wipe the girl's face and hands, and a long-forgotten tune rises up.

My mother sang it to Donnie. No doubt to me as well. Unnamed babes in the woods . . . a long time ago . . . night falling . . . The lyrics elude me, but the tune returns as accompaniment to these unexpected ministrations.

Her lip is split and swelling. I daub blood from the corner of her mouth.

She flinches and swats. Groans.

"You're safe now." I heard similar words from Ella years ago. *You're a brave girl . . . Walter won't harm you again.*

The girl's lids flutter open.

We stare, this child and I. Her body relaxes, and her head lolls sideways.

Mrs. Upchurch sets a bowl of clean water in my lap, and I tend bruised and bleeding feet. The act brings to mind Bible passages Andrew used in a distant sermon. An outcast woman washed Jesus' feet. And He washed his followers'.

What other memories will this night exhume?

"No broken bones," Doc announces. "But she's walked through mud and briars, even crawled. I've given her a sleep medication."

The sheriff arrives, and Doc and Mrs. Upchurch join him out front.

I remain cot-side, caught up in wonder.

Mrs. Upchurch enters on tiptoes and crumbles into a chair.

My task complete, I cover the girl with a sheet. "Berachah lives up to its name."

"We're in the blessing business, but who would do this?"

I glance around. "Who's the man who brought her tonight?"

"A friend, his identity confidential. Like us, he's in the rescue business."

"What does he know about her treatment?"

"Not much yet. She was confined near Erie, so we assume she's the missing birthday girl. She escaped and followed the gleam of lights above the treetops to the park."

Brother Upchurch returns and speaks a prayer of gratitude.

Mrs. Upchurch inhales audibly. "This must be the girl snatched from Erie yesterday."

Her husband scratches his pate. "Appears so."

"No." I give my head a shake. "This isn't the birthday girl."

Puzzlement scratches a line in Mrs. Upchurch's brow. "How can you be sure? I didn't get a good look at her. Did you?"

"I did. But that doesn't matter."

He points a finger. "It'll matter to the girl's parents. I'll call them."

"Don't bother."

The couple eyes me with twin frowns. "And why not?"

"Because this girl . . ." I hold the child's small hand. "She's Blossom Evans."

The Upchurches stare, agape.

Astonished at my calm, I wonder why a dam of tears hasn't crumbled.

Aside from sensing the clues to Fort Worth are bread crumbs scattered for my benefit, it's almost as if I expected this turn of events.

"Will you excuse me, please?" Slipping outside on unsteady feet, I lean against a post.

"Are you Blossom's sole rescuer? You must give Blossom to the Lord . . ."

My gaze traces the darkened grounds, the lights twinkling in windows. And the sparkling canopy above me.

You're there, aren't You?

You must be.

With Bessie watching over our reclaimed lost one, I call Ella. A click on the line tells me Maggie has picked up Broadview's extension.

"Blossom's safe, Ella. She's with me in Arlington."

"Thank you, Lord! Lily's found her!" Ella hollers to her brood. A series of thumps and clunks tell me she has released the receiver to dangle and bang against the wall. Her sobs and the girls' riotous clamor render further conversation indistinguishable. Knowing my feisty friend, she'll board the train to Fort Worth tomorrow.

"God be praised." Maggie whispers into her extension.

"If I knew how to contact Ida, I'd give her the news."

"No need. I'll find Ida."

I disconnect, thankful—to whom I have yet to decide.

Mrs. Upchurch invites me to meet her in the parlor with Ma's keepsakes.

I arrive with tablet in hand, pencil lodged chopstick-style through my drooping bun and the shuttle swinging in its pouch from my wrist. I've tucked the journal and Bible into the crook of an arm. And wedged into the Bible, the family tree, photograph of Blossom, and her snapshot of Walter.

Smoothing her skirt front and back, my hostess sits on the davenport and motions me to a companion easy chair. She pours us each a glass of chilled fruit juice. "Your devotion to your lost loved one . . ." Her voice catches, and she clears her throat. "It inspires me."

Holding my keepsakes on my lap, I extend a playful swat. "*You're* the inspiration."

"Just an instrument in the Lord's hands." She pauses and runs a fingertip along the rim of her glass. "I've a story for you, Lily." Her forehead puckers.

"Excellent. An effective exposé includes stories." I flip a tablet page and position my pencil for note taking.

"This may not be a tale for your exposé."

I cock my head to the side. "And why not?"

She inhales a breath that seems to fortify her. "My story concerns Berachah's beginning."

"Of course I'll include it. This home will play an important role."

"I'd very much like for you to put down your pad and pencil and listen."

"All right." I close the pad, my curiosity lined with a touch of dread.

"It won't be easy to hear—"

I fear I've gone pale. "Something's happened at home. Is it Addie?

Or—"

"No, dear." She raises her hands, halting me. "Nothing like that."

I release a deep breath. And another.

"As I said before, the seeds to our story were planted in '94 in Waco, but in time . . ." She shoots me a mirthless grin. "We opened a soup kitchen in Dallas. It drew similar unfortunates. Some were widows; others, prostitutes with children. The idea for this mission took shape in that kitchen."

She points to a framed portrait of Jesus in Gethsemane. "That piece of art was a gift from a generous contributor. He hopes it'll serve as a reminder that the Lord suffered for everyone——even the least among us."

This story might amount to no more than a rabbit trail, but I'll follow it. "Please continue."

CHAPTER 34

"*B*rothels draw men and desperate women both." Mrs. Upchurch smooths her skirt and lays her hands in her lap as if to gain composure. "Ranchers drove Longhorns across Texas and Oklahoma to Kansas for years. The Chisholm Trail came through downtown, which is how Fort Worth came by its nickname, Cowtown."

"I hear Hell's Half Acre grew up near the stockyards because of cowboys and all."

"And greed. Many Forth Worth businessmen have profited from the unholy 'trade.' Saloons, gambling houses, brothels. They were on every corner and in between. They're more hidden now, but landlords receive their rents even so."

"Aren't brothels a form of slavery?"

"In their own way. We've worked alongside Dr. Norris in trying to wipe them from Fort Worth. Have you heard of him?"

"I've spoken with his wife."

"You're resourceful." She pauses, tapping a fingertip on her bottom lip.

At the sound of an engine, our eyes snap to the bay window. "Wait here." She pads to the porch, and I take her place at the window.

The car comes to a standstill, and a man climbs out. He and Pastor Upchurch stand talking at the arbored gate.

The gentleman strikes me as familiar, but in the dark I can't be sure. They join Mrs. Upchurch on the porch, and the threesome stroll into the house.

Mrs. Upchurch instructs the visitor to leave his hat in the foyer. Their footsteps draw near, and I move forward to greet them.

Mrs. Upchurch enters and steps aside for the guest.

"Mr. Wainwright." I steady myself against the chair.

He tugs on his vest and squares his shoulders. "At your service, ma'am. I'm Chester."

I point. "We met at the hotel. What's going on?"

Pastor Upchurch motions to a chair. "Have a seat. I'll explain."

The four of us sit around the tea table, but I'm perched on my chair edge, ready to pounce. "I'm in no mood for chit chat. I've a feeling you've been following me. Why?"

"Chester is Flora's husband." Mrs. Upchurch explains in a conciliatory tone.

I gape. "But her last name is Zane."

Chester chuckles. "Kept her maiden name when we married." He flicks a wrist. "Women's rights and all."

I can imagine Flora making such a choice. "What's your business, sir?"

"I own a private investigation firm."

Pastor Upchurch clears his throat. "He works for us and Frank Norris. And Ida Tate."

Ida? And the Upchurches? Even Dr. Norris? "Investigating what?"

"Ultimately, the white slavery business. Daily I watch for unaccompanied female travelers, particularly those with no one to meet them. Like yourself."

"You were stalking me."

"Only watching out for you."

I blink away astonishment. No wonder the man struck me as a Pinkerton type.

The mysterious gentleman gazes at me with an expression of earnestness. "I'm tailing a ring of criminals who deal in prostitution and forced servitude of underage girls. I was in Oklahoma at Ida's request, looking for your friend's abductors."

I collapse into the chair back and stare at the patterned rug.

Mrs. Upchurch gathers my hand in hers. "Chester found Blossom."

I grab the man's gaze with a questioning glare. "But how, for heaven's sakes?"

"Tailed you to Lake Erie. I must admit you're a challenge to avoid."

"I'm observant. Can't be a reporter otherwise."

"And apt to change your mind . . . rather precipitously." He chuckles. "Ida tells me you suspect Blossom's abductor is a man named Walter Sloat. Your father. From Needham. And that you believe he relocated to Fort Worth."

"That's right."

"The same Walter Sloat who was acquitted of the murder of his wife in Oklahoma."

I nod.

"Describe him, please."

"First, call me Lily." I heave a breath and picture the abuser in my mind. "He's middle aged. Medium height and build. Ace-black hair, worn scruffy-like. Unkempt in dress. Unrefined in speech and behavior. Cruel. A drunk who deals under the table."

"The man I'm thinking of doesn't fit your description, but I'm following a solid lead at present.

"Then there's a special someone . . . Did Flora tell you about Beulah's sister?"

"Not necessary. Star is working for me."

"What?" Astonishment rings in my voice.

"She uncovered the southbound smuggling ring. Into Mexico."

I startle. "Might Blossom . . ." I push away the dreadful thought.

"There's more." Pastor Upchurch leans forward, glancing at his wife and friend.

Ignoring the pastor's comment, I press Chester. "I have a photograph of Walter. It's poor quality, but it might help."

"I'd very much like to see it." Interest lights the man's eyes.

I thumb through the Bible. "Here."

Adjusting his eyeglasses, he holds the snapshot under a light. "Too unkempt for Wilcox." He squints and brings the photo nearer. "Could be brothers, though."

Chester turns to me. "I suspect he and Wilcox are in league."

"How in the world?" Recollections somersault in my brain. "Walter was often away from home. In court, he appeared to have grown prosperous. Still, I don't have to stretch my imagination to picture him as part of a band of knaves."

Chester returns the photograph. "An idea or two are percolating." He gazes at the floor, his fingers scraping his whiskers. "But I must be certain. Anyone else making trouble for you?"

Matter of fact . . .

As fidgety as a June bug, I bound to my feet.

"Sabina." Pacing the worn-patterned rug, I'm determined to stitch together the scraps of what I've learned. "She's from back home."

Chester's forehead crimps. "Who's she?"

"A *Caller* reporter. Goes by the last name Fitzgerald—"

"The one who wrote about you recently?"

"One and the same. But her last name's Gallagher. She grew up at Broadview alongside Addie. Her mother was Adelaide Fitzgerald's wet nurse, then housekeeper, and, over time, a substitute mother."

"And what brought her to Fort Worth?"

Piqued, I halt my pacing and cross my arms at my bosom. "All I know is she lived a wild life in Cowtown for a decade. She returned to Broadview earlier this year, but now she's banned from the estate. I ran across her. She's claims she's a Fitzgerald."

Pastor Upchurch sits erect. "The *Caller* reporter whose articles brought the newsmen to our front gate?"

I nod. "She has her ear to the ground like no one else. Seems to know what I'm doing before I've decided." I poke a thumbnail between my teeth.

Chester harrumphs. "I've connections of my own. Meanwhile, please describe Miss Gallagher."

I picture her as I knew her at Broadview. "Pale hair and complexion. Used hair frames and padding. Rawboned, boyish figure. But she's altogether different now."

"Some women have learned tricks." Mrs. Upchurch shakes her head. "Plumb bewildering."

"She now wears a wig in a rich dark color. It's cut in a modern bob with perky curls. Her skin's now a rich color, and she's developed curves."

"I'd like to work with you if—"

A door's swat stops Chester mid-sentence, and we four gather at the bay window. So engrossed in our conversation, we haven't noticed a car's arrival. A man steps through the arbored gate, and Brother Upchurch eases toward the porch.

The latch clunks.

"How do you do, sir."

"Philip!" I scamper out and embrace him.

"Excuse me, but Ida and Donnie're out yonder in the taxi."

I slip past Philip and run to the car.

My brother steps out with Wally on his heels. "Brother mine!"

He acquiesces to my embrace with his exuberant companion slobbering between us.

"Come into the light." Under the porch lamp, he's aglow with good health. "I believe you've grown." I laugh from my belly and scratch behind Wally's ear.

He squares his shoulders and smiles.

I circle him. "Have you filled out at Jackson's table already? No overalls. A fine suit of men's attire. Groomed, even to your fingernails. And shoes . . . Wait, what's that, Donnie Sloat?"

He pulls his pant legs to his knees.

"Are your legs straighter?"

He tucks his chin.

His transformation in three weeks astounds me. "If Ella were here, she'd be weeping. But then Ella cries when she's happy and sad. And when she's mad. So pretty much all the time." I laugh. "Oh, I'm just plain happy!"

"So are we all." Ida emerges from the shadows of the back seat.

Exhaling my relief, I embrace her. "I've been worried sick. Where've you been?"

"We planned to head to Tulsa, but I sensed Berachah calling. What's the latest news?"

"You haven't heard. Blossom's here!"

Donnie's body tenses, soldier-like.

Ida gazes toward the starry sky. "God be praised." She takes Philip's arm, and we rejoin the others inside.

My brother tugs on my arm, and I know he's asking after Blossom. "Come on."

Mrs. Upchurch shoos us toward the back of the house. "We'll wait here."

Philip and I guide our elderly companion across the unfamiliar acreage to the clinic. My brother tromps, heavy footed, alongside me and rushes ahead into the clinic. He looks around, wild-eyed.

"In here." I open the exam room. "She's sleeping."

He steps inside and draws near to his friend, his treads soft as whispers. His hands graze the crown of her head, and a teardrop shatters on her cheek.

She jerks her head sideways and opens her eyes.

I scoot a straight-backed chair behind my brother.

He takes the seat and folds his arms on the edge of the cot. "Blossom."

Had I a needle and thread, I'd tie off a knot. Donnie has spoken at last.

PART

Three

SHALL MORTAL MAN BE
MORE JUST THAN GOD?

JOB 4:17A

CHAPTER 35

The mooing of cows and the clatter of pots wake me at daybreak. I turn toward the window where a morning breeze billows the curtain sheers. The sun brushes a dim square of light on the rug, and fingers of breakfast aromas crawl up the stairs.

The journal draws my gaze, but I leave it undisturbed for another time. The entries I've read thus far suffice. For now.

Most of last night I rested in the clinic on a cot. But mulling over the recent revelations kept me tossing and turning. Doc returned at four a.m., and I took to my bed here in the dormitory.

How I'd love to hide away in my room, exploring the old tome and scribbling ideas for the exposé, but Mrs. Upchurch and I are attending the Thursday Club meeting at noon. According to Flora, the group is a bunch of firebrands, and some follow Sabina's articles as if they're Gospel. Might the women link to the reporter herself?

Chucking aside the sheet, a tangled mess between my feet, I gather my mane into a tail and dress in a simple shift.

If I'm not mistaken, Fort Worth's Wednesday Club's Executive Committee assembles for breakfast at the Met the third Thursday of each month.

Bustling down the stairs, I pause at the kitchen wall calendar and nod. "I'm going to the big house to make a phone call."

Bessie lifts her focus from the dough board where she's rolling out biscuits. "We'll eat in twenty minutes."

I scurry outside and over the grounds to the kitchen at the back of the house. "Mrs. Upchurch?"

"Yes, dear." Her voice wafts like a pleasant breeze from the dining room.

I find her at the sideboard pouring her morning coffee.

Ida enters from the hallway. "Did Blossom sleep alright?"

We touch cheeks. "She was asleep when Doc arrived at 4 a.m."

"Then you haven't rested much yourself." She sets her cup into its saucer.

"I'm returning to Fort Worth this afternoon."

"So soon after Ida and Donnie arrive? And with kidnappers afoot?" Our hostess stirs cream into her coffee, but distress lines mar her smooth brow.

No need to worry these two with my plans. "I'll catch the trolley after the meeting. But I need to make a call. I'll reimburse you the cost. That alright?"

"Why, sure." She points toward the hallway. "You know where it is."

I lift the receiver, and an operator responds, "Number, please."

"Lamar 4355."

"Metropolitan Hotel. I'll connect you." Decided efficiency edges the female voice.

The desk clerk answers after a single ring. "Metropolitan Hotel, European luxury in downtown Fort Worth."

"Hello. This is Lily Sloat."

"Yes?" He stretches the single-syllable question like a fat rubber band.

"I believe the Wednesday Club's—"

"They meet on Wednesdays, ma'am. This is Thursday."

"Of course." Did the man consider me a dolt? "Their Executive Committee has breakfast on the third Thursday of each month, if I'm not—"

"You are not."

"I'm not what?"

"Mistaken."

"Of course. I need to speak with Flora Zane."

"I'm afraid she's unavailable at present, ma'am."

"I know she's in a meeting, but I really must—"

"She's been out of town since Tuesday, Miss Sloat."

How does the desk clerk know Flora's movements? "I see."

"If that's all then—"

"Wait. Do you know when she's expected back?"

"Tomorrow, I believe. But I've a guest requiring my attention. Good day, Miss Sloat."

A click resounds in my ear, and I return the receiver to its cradle with more questions than when I picked it up.

Whatever can Flora be up to? She's due back tomorrow. Meanwhile, I've a group of formidable strangers to win over.

Mrs. Upchurch ushers me to her Model T Ford at a quarter to twelve. "The flivver kicks up dust." She ties scarves around her head and over her nose and mouth, bandit style.

I follow her example, and we bounce out the drive.

A wisp of a woman, she handles the three floor pedals as effectively as a man. Arriving with a layer of grit over our skirts and blouses, my hostess produces a clothing brush from the back seat, and we enter the town hall morning fresh.

The club members have gathered in small groups, their voices subdued and their expressions troubled. They've apparently left their Sunday hats at home.

Mrs. Upchurch greets the nearest grouping. "What is it?"

A sturdy matron with silver-streaked hair rolled at the nape of her neck turns to us. "A lost child." She holds a handkerchief to her nostrils with one hand and extends a *Fort Worth Caller* with the other.

My Berachah hostess gestures for me to join her, and we read the headline together: *Search Still On for Kidnapped Girl!* The daughter of one of our prominent businessmen and seventy-five of her friends were celebrating her birthday.

"It's an article about the birthday girl."

"God help her. And her parents."

Remembering our near miss at Erie and the elation over Blossom's rescue, I release a breath of relief tinged with empathy. "Perhaps today's not the best time for us."

"All the more reason for them to hear your story."

Calling the meeting to order, the president dispenses with housekeeping details, and Mrs. Upchurch introduces me.

One dour matron stands and points. "We know all about you. From *Caller*. Miss Fitzgerald's article."

I tamp down a swell of defensiveness. "Will you hear my side of the story?"

A few nod, and the assemblage quiets. "I've felt the bitter sting of a cruel man's hand. I know the tragedy of illiteracy and exclusion from my own governance. Such powerlessness robs women of their voices, even in courtrooms. Recently, I'm acquainted with the abduction of young girls for unholy purposes."

The ladies appear duly stunned. A rural bunch, they show a different sort of enthusiasm for the drive for women's equality than those in Fort Worth.

And a different opposition.

"Women belong in their homes, not galavanting around the countryside!"

"We belong in our homes *and* galavanting around the countryside!"

"No. We'll trust our husbands to vote for us! That's the Christian woman's way."

"Poppycock! We Christian women won't give legislators a day's peace until they act."

One member stands and waves a book. "I just returned from New York. A representative of the national women's organization insists we unite around a holy book."

Heads angle toward the speaker. "The *Holy Bible* degrades womanhood from Genesis to Revelation. I move we adopt *The Woman's Bible* as our official holy text. Unite around it and influence others to do the same!"

Elizabeth Stanton's *Woman's Bible* was an effort to produce a version that reflected her sentiments for women's rights. This speaker sparks an ember in my gut, and soon I'm as hot under the collar as a Texas farmer in August.

I step from the lectern and raise my hands to quieten the group. What has birthed my boldness? "If you ladies believe the King James version of the *Holy Bible* is the Word of God, isn't it good enough for the club?"

"I agree!" The group's president bounds to her feet. "The *Woman's Bible* doesn't belong in our organization."

The opposing sides assume battle lines, and pandemonium ensues.

"Order!" The president hammers her gavel on the lectern. "Ladies, sit down! This meeting must come to order!"

The attendees quiet, and she continues. "I'll abide no more outbursts. We've been grumbling over this subject long enough. We'll end it once and for all. Now.

"One representative from each group has five minutes to explain their positions concerning one question: Will our organization adopt a platform that references the *Holy Bible's* 'degrading of women from Genesis to Revelation' and adopt Mrs. Stanton's work, *The Woman's Bible*?

"You have thirty minutes to prepare. Following the presentations, we'll vote. During this process, I will allow no unladylike behavior. Violators will be removed."

How has a simple club gathering degraded to this? I turn my eyes to Mrs. Upchurch, and she covers a grin with a hand. The woman with connections to the national women's organization offers to present the affirmative position.

Against my protests, the president of the club insists I present the opposing view.

"Men have subjugated women throughout history." The proponent of *The Woman's Bible* concludes with a flourish. "The supposed 'infallible' *Holy Bible* is at the root of this subjugation. I, therefore, move that Arlington's Thursday Club adopts a platform that endorses *The Woman's*

Bible."

As I walk to the lectern, I imagine my mother on the front row. In my mind I flip pages of Ella's English grammar text, recalling the rules.

"I submit *The Woman's Bible* has no place in this organization's platform. My mother was as fine a Christian who ever lived, and according to her, Holy Scripture elevates women to places of honor, not dishonor."

I pause to consider my position more fully. "Why must *direct* references to Scripture be a part of this club's platform anyway?"

I haven't a speck of faith, but I can speak for my mother. "Doesn't the power of Holy Scripture lie in its ability to change the human heart? If so, it attends meetings like this one encased in believers. Political platforms, spurious attacks, or degrading publications cannot change this one whit.

"Therefore, on behalf of the opposition, I move Arlington's Thursday Club disallows any reference to *The Woman's Bible* in its platform. Your positions speak for what's in your hearts, the Word of God."

My motion carries by a single vote, and the opposition glowers.

"Proceed with your story, Lily." The speaker has stood from the back row.

I settle my thoughts. "The injustice of women denied the vote and barred from juries affects more than I imagined until I heard the awful pronouncement 'not guilty'."

Bare heads move side to side.

"Speak out. Talk with your husbands. Win them over to our cause. And perhaps not too many election days in the future, we'll be casting votes alongside the men."

"You can count on us, Lily Sloat!" some call in agreement.

But others chatter among themselves, frowning and seemingly less decisive in their stance on the vote. One rises to her feet. "We heard you out. Your reasoning about adopting *The Woman's Bible* makes sense. But why should we hear further from someone barely out of girlhood? And not even from Texas?"

I return her steady gaze. "Back home I heard similar sentiments. I was nothing but a sharecropper's daughter, not to be trusted in the court-room or town square."

A club member stands. "The rest of us hear you, Lily."

"Thank you. But there's more."

The group quietens, and I scan their faces. Their hearts must change. "I met a woman who works in Hell's Half Acre."

The ladies produce a collective gasp.

"I saw her fear and hopelessness up close. She and many others are trapped. They fear for their lives and the lives of their families. And, frankly, sharp tongues."

Silence blankets the room.

"The Upchurches and Berachah can accomplish only so much. But what an impact ten homes can have. Or a hundred."

The club members sit stock still.

"Imagine the effect a collective public outcry could produce. If prop-erty owners refuse to let the brothels operate—"

"Every quarter of the state can be cleaned out!" a cheerleader shouts.

"Which brings me back to the recent event." The ladies lean forward, peering at me. "Underage girls are nabbed in cities across our nation and forced into prostitution with regularity. This is why Congress passed the White Slavery Law in '10."

The whites of their eyes shine, and they scowl, grumbling.

"Consequently, I'm on a mission." I pause, considering what else to reveal.

"What can we do to help you?" someone calls from the back.

"Education is the first step. You can educate your families and friends, fellow church and club members. A great swell of righteous indignation, as my dear friend at home would call it, can sweep your great state and from here encompass the entire nation.

"The sooner our U.S. Constitution includes an equal suffrage amend-ment, the sooner our votes can help shape our destinies—and those not welcome in Thursday Clubs."

A few expressions tighten, but the bulk nod their agreement.

I hold Mrs. Upchurch's gaze before continuing. "Furthermore, you can welcome Berachah's mothers into your homes and stores and women's clubs."

Sharp inhalations sound from one corner to the others, but postures gradually relax, and corners of mouths lift. Frowns smooth, and heads nod.

The leader stands. "We'd be honored to have the home's mothers to tea." She turns around and sweeps an open palm in a half circle across the assemblage. "We're turning over a new leaf. Plan for Berachah mothers and their children at next week's meeting, ladies."

All but a few cheer. The frowning handful stands en masse and moves toward the exit. Their leader turns and spears me with her gaze. She mouths three words: *You'll be sorry.*

They flitter away like a cluster of hornets, leaving their stingers. And a nagging unease that Sabina has something to do with the tumult.

CHAPTER 36

$\mathcal{B}$ack at Berachah, I catch sight of a Daimler. "It's Ella!"

"Praise the Lord." Mrs. Upchurch brakes at the barn.

I find the clinic empty, save Bessie, who nods toward the big house. "They're over yonder."

Running headlong to the grand house, I throw aside the back door. "Ella!"

My friend receives me with her arms wide. "You found Blossom!"

I hold her at arm's length. "I didn't find her. It was—"

"Chester Wainright, I know. But if it hadn't been for you . . ." Her voice cracks, and she dabs a kerchief at her nostrils. "I just knew you'd find her."

"And who have we here?" My hostess and matron of Berachah has followed on my heels.

I hold out a hand. "Mrs. Upchurch, this is Ella Evans, my dearest friend in the world."

"Welcome, my dear."

We follow her into her kitchen, and I look around. "It's quiet. Where is everyone?"

Ella gestures toward the parlor with a smile that reaches way past her eyes.

I all but stumble to a stand-still in the sitting room. Sipping iced tea, Blossom sits ensconced on the settee with a semi-circle of sisters and Wally on the floor around her. Losing in chairs, Donnie and Andrew pop to their feet. Philip and Pastor Upchurch, who are enjoying cool drinks at a library table with Ida, follow suit.

From the corner of my eye a figure emerges from the entry hall and leans against the piano as casual as can be. I turn, and my gaze rests on Cade.

I know without benefit of a mirror I present the picture of stupefaction.

He points to his rescued niece. "Couldn't wait to see that girl."

Bereft of words, I stare, my eyes drifting back to Ella's six daughters, sitting quiet as baby doves. Donnie. Ida. Pastor Upchurch. And back to my beloved.

The initial shock settles, and my knees weaken. I reach for the rocker, and Cade lends me a hand as I drop into the chair.

Ella perches on a footstool beside Blossom.

Mrs. Upchurch joins Ida at the window table, and the men take their seats.

My persistent suitor claims a chair beside me, and his gaze angles at his sister and her girls. "Couldn't let loved ones head for Texas without me. Not again."

I've been hungering for his rich baritone voice without realizing it. My skin warms, and I tug my eyes away from his. I must gain sufficient control of my faculties to speak. I clear my throat. "That's nice."

Conversations restart as if the past few moments haven't occurred, as if the love of my life isn't sitting beside me in Arlington, Texas. As if my heart isn't swelling out of my chest. And the old scars aren't throbbing.

Am I to crumble in this man's presence? Melt like chocolate in the summer's heat? Nabbing a hand fan from a side table, I give it a twirl. My foot taps against the worn rug. Have I not learned to control extremities after all this time?

I toss the fan aside and slip my jittery fingers under my legs.

"Care for a walk?" Cade speaks as leisurely as you please.

A walk? The outdoors would provide the oxygen—and space—I crave. "Yes. I would."

I lead the way to the pecan orchard where the broad, full branches produce an abundance of shade. Strolling with my hands clasped behind me, I wrest a semblance of nonchalance but fail miserably, I fear.

He clears his throat. "What are your plans now?"

Plans? "Now that you mention it, I do have plans."

Did I perceive a lowering of his shoulders?

"Care to share them with me?" He angles his head and eyes toward me.

I marshal my thoughts. "My two loved ones are safe. But the felons are still out there."

He nods. "The sheriffs in two states are investigating."

"But I have an advantage on them."

He halts, his gaze piercing. "And what advantage is that?"

I tap a finger alongside my nose. "I can smell them."

He chortles. "What does that mean?"

"It means, dear . . . friend . . ." I point and smile. "I know both of them in ways no one else does. I know their stench."

"Their stench? Of what?"

"Of Evil. Walter reeks of whiskey. Sabina, five-day-old gardenias."

He places his hands on my shoulders and turns me to him. "Listen to yourself. You've received the worst from those two. Leave it to the law."

"I'm not standing in the way of the law, for heaven's sakes."

"But you can get hurt."

"My friend Flora knows important people. I have a plan."

Reaching down, he plucks a rotten pecan off the close-cropped sod and pitches it three trees over. "Who are these important people? And what does your plan involve?"

I stare at this man I've loved as long as I can remember. My longing for him knows no bounds. "Flora and I know a confidential informant. An officer of the law would spook her, but she'll trust me."

"Who is this person?"

"I can't reveal her name." I roll my eyes. "It's *confidential*."

He taps a finger tip on my nose. "Confidential can mean trouble."

I whip around, but he grabs my shoulder. "You're going to listen to me if it's the last thing you do. You've talked, and I've listened the past five years. Now I'm gonna talk, and *you're* gonna listen."

Startled by the harshness in his tone, I stand with my arms crossed tight against my middle. My chin has inched upward, and my backbone has stiffened. But I listen.

He makes sense, I must admit. He's exercised more restraint than called for. And more patience and understanding than any woman deserves, least of all myself.

Didn't I expect him to understand? Even when I rebuffed his proposal and returned the ring? And when I hitched a train to Fort Worth, leaving him standing there, soaked clean through with love?

It's time. To trust the man I love.

Back at the house, those previously populating the parlor have cleared out. Bessie is clearing away cups and napkins. Cade has excused himself to move the Daimler behind the barn. An automobile as valuable as the one Andrew shipped from England would bring a hefty sum on the black market.

"Where's everyone, Bessie?"

"Blossom and Ella are resting. The rest are touring the grounds."

"I see." I help her with the last of the parlor litter. "They'll want to visit the print shop later."

"You reckon them women's hearts are in it?" Bessie apparently makes a habit of ignoring preambles. Rather like Blossom.

I stop mid-kitchen, frowning. "What women?"

"The Thursday Club. Can we trust 'em?"

I lean against the kitchen counter with an elbow resting on the arm I've crossed over my middle. "I understand your reticence. You've known little kindness from women like those in the club. But I believe I saw sincerity in their eyes."

She crumbles into a chair and jabs a pointed finger at me. "And I've seen something else."

I've a pinch in my midsection for Bessie and the other mothers. I've known such pain.

"I believe you. Truly I do." I pause until her eyes settle on mine. "But doesn't everyone deserves a second chance?"

Bessie looks away, and I wonder what stories she and the others would reveal if they could. Which reminds me . . .

The screen swishes open, and Cade steps inside.

"I need to use the phone." I point him toward the phone box.

He nods and accompanies me to the hallway.

"Lamar 7493," I inform the operator. The Arlington club member's warning replays with each ring once . . . twice . . . a third time in my ear: *You'll be sorry. You'll be sorry. You'll be sorry.*

A shiver passes through me.

"Wainwright residence," a voice answers.

"Hello. With whom am I speaking?"

"I'm the housekeeper, ma'am."

"I'm Lily, Flora's friend. Chester's too. May I speak with Chester?"

The woman responds with a muffled cry, sniffling and blowing her nose.

"What's going on?"

She clears her throat. "You haven't heard?"

"Heard what?"

"Mrs. Wainwright disappeared on Tuesday."

"How? Her bodyguard doesn't leave her side."

She lets loose a hacking cough. "When he isn't drugged."

"Drugged? I was just speaking with Chester last night."

"The bodyguard wired yesterday morning, ma'am. But Mr. Wainwright was incognito somewhere. He didn't read it until he returned home last night. Mrs. Wainwright slipped her guardian something in a glass of iced tea. And absconded for Brownsville."

"Brownsville? Why, that's all but Mexico."

"Yes ma'am. But that's not the worst news."

Fire ignites in my middle, icy-hot. I tamp down an urge to hang up and turn away, pretend worse news wasn't awaiting me.

Cade's hand tightens on my waist, and his eyebrows arch.

"What news is that?" I sputter.

"I'm sorry, but Mrs. Wainwright passed."

"I . . . I don't understand."

"A call came this morning. Mr. Wainwright's headed south. To escort her home."

"Where exactly?"

"It happened at a stop in a small town called Raymondville. Right there in the little train station. She was shot, ma'am. Right in the heart. And the murderer got away."

I wrestle words to my tongue. "Please convey to Chester . . . when he returns . . ."

"I'll tell him you called, ma'am. Check the newspaper for funeral arrangements."

Replacing the earpiece, I lift my eyes to my loved one. "Flora is dead."

He holds me in his arms, but my body's stiff. I push him away, battling for a breath. "Not beautiful Flora, so full of life." I drop my forehead to his chest.

"I'm sorry, Lily. How'd it happen?"

"Come with me." We slip outside to the porch swing, the housekeeper's awful news clanging in my ear.

The door screeches open, and Ida joins us. "Bad news, Lily?"

"Chester's wife, Flora . . . She's dead. I . . . I'm . . ."

Ida gasps.

"What happened?" He slips his arm over my shoulders.

"According to the housekeeper, Flora outwitted her bodyguard—"

"Bodyguard?" My friends respond in unison.

I sigh. "Chester kept a bodyguard with Flora at all times. I don't know why unless it has to do with his profession."

"His private investigations?"

I nod. "Perhaps he's received threats."

"I'm sorry, dear. I know what her friendship has meant to you."

My insides roll. "Flora eased my adjustment to Fort Worth. She knew everyone. Accompanied me on my forays and always lent an ear. She was a delightful friend. I don't know what I'll do without her." Tears have gathered, but they retreat.

"I'll get you a cup of camomile. And give the Upchurches the news." Ida rises with a frown of concentration. "We'll check on funeral arrangements too."

Cade nudges me to his side, and I rest my head on his shoulder. He breaks out in prayer, reminding me I must tell Ida I've kept my promise.

At his *Amen*, I sit erect. "I'm going back to Fort Worth."

"For what? Blossom's safe, and so is Donnie."

"Until those responsible are exposed, there's still work to do."

"What work do you have in mind?"

"I need to contact someone who can help."

"And who is this person?"

Flora's gone, and Chester won't be any help for awhile. Didn't I tell myself just today it's time I trust Cade? "Her name's Star. And she works in a brothel."

"A brothel? What—"

"It's a long story. You see—"

Jarred to my feet, I scamper out.

CHAPTER 37

I scurry to the big house with Cade beside me. "I must speak with Blossom,."

"What if she's not ready? Ella says her lips are locked up tight."

"Gotta use the right key."

Ida has taken a spacious guest room on the lower floor of the big house, and Ella and Blossom the other. Andrew and the girls are tucked into rooms upstairs, and Philip and Donnie are bunking in the dormitory with Wally.

I tiptoe down the hallway and peek into the second of two guest rooms. Dressed in cool cotton wrappers, Ella and her child are lying on the bed. Blossom's eyes are closed, but her mother's are wide open and directed toward the ceiling. The cross draft has coaxed a breeze through the windows, stirring the lace sheers.

"May I . . ." I whisper and thumb toward my suitor at my back. "May we come in?"

He gives a head shake. "You ladies need privacy. I'll wait downstairs."

Ella sits up and swings her legs over the side of the bed. She indicates chairs beside a tea table between two windows. Donning slippers, she takes one and I the other.

I lean forward. "No one knows me quite as you do, Ella. I'll never forget your reassuring words as my tattered rags fell into strips on the floor, exposing the truth I now hide.

"You sat beside me those nights, coaxing me to hold onto life moment by moment. To breathe. To live. I credit you for each breath today."

Ella plucks a handkerchief from her wrapper and dabs at moisture in the corner of her multi-colored eyes. "I credit you, dear Lily . . ." She turns to her sleeping daughter. "For each breath my child takes."

"She's who I'd like to discuss with you."

She glances at me and then the floor, but she nods her assent.

I take a deep, fortifying breath. "I've mulled over what's transpired—the trial and horrid verdict and my earlier life, too. Like my days on Sloat land. The field work. Walter. Ma's stoic endurance. My fight for life and her releasing me into your care. And learning to read at your knee."

I chuckle. "Our ventures into the countryside, building a business. My thirteen-year-old eyes beholding the wonder of you and Andrew falling in love. Addie's arrival and transporting me to Broadview with all its finery.

"My enrollment at CIA and your letters. That Christmas Ma and I shared in the old shack, her running away. My returning to CIA to 'make something of myself.' Her death and all that's come since.

"It's like a giant button box has spilled and I've been scrambling to put them back where they belong. Just as I gather up a handful, another wad takes its place.

"Until now."

"I've met certain individuals in Fort Worth . . . who've helped me. I'm certain Walter—"

"Kidnapped me."

We three jerk around, agape. My gaze rests on Blossom's hollow cheeks. She scoots back against the headboard. "I'll tell you two and Papa, but that's all. I won't announce what they did to me to the world, won't speak in a courtroom, won't identify a single person. It's going into a drawer, and I'm locking it up tight."

Ella moves to her daughter's side. "Of course not, dear. We wouldn't—"

"But other girls haven't been found yet." The words escape my lips before I've given them a thought. "What about their parents?"

She shakes her head and muffles her sobs in her pillow's feather stuffing.

Ella turns to me with a scowl. "We don't expect her to testify in a court of law. Do we?" She emphasizes each word with an eye spear meant solely for me.

Will I allow my fear of jeopardizing Ella's friendship to stand in the way of what's right? Can I hold my tongue while a mere child decides what will haunt her the rest of her days?

I settle on the mattress beside her. "Your mother taught me to read. And to be brave. She pushed me from my comfortable nest at Broadview, told me I had it in me to move crowds. Taught me how to grow from victim to victor."

Stillness creeps in. The wall clock ticks. The window sheers flutter. And a mockingbird trills outside. We three bits of humanity remain silent, steeped in wordlessness.

Blossom raises her head. "I'd like to speak with Lily alone, Mama."

Ella's eyes snap between her daughter and me. "I'll wait outside." Her shoe heels mark her steps to the porch.

"What is it you're planning?" Blossom has centered her gaze on me.

"When that jury found Walter not guilty, justice was denied my mother."

She nods.

"That can't be undone. By law. Ma's justice will be found solely in justice for other women. And girls like you."

Moisture fills her pale blue eyes to the brim, and twin tears roll through her thick, blonde lashes. They drip from her jawline and puddle on her gown. "But Mr. Sloat is Donnie's pa. He loves him. And I don't want to hurt my friend."

"No matter who's connected to the business of selling girls as slaves in Mexico, can you turn away?"

She shudders and shakes her head.

"Then straighten your spine. Prepare to tell what you've experienced. I have an idea for working together."

"What?"

"We can describe consequences of women being denied a voice in their governance."

"The vote?"

"Yes. And other rights that are dependent on women's votes. Like serving on juries."

She stares beyond me, as if she's watching a movie film. "What do you need?"

"No details regarding your treatment. Not yet, anyway. I understand the pain such revelations can cause. But we do need to know how your kidnappers managed your abduction."

She lifts a single shoulder. "Mr. Sloat laid down a plank and dared me to cross over Rock Creek."

I nod. "And how did he spirit you away with no one knowing?"

"He pinned my arms behind me, and someone pressed a wet cloth to my nose. Smelled rank, like rubbing alcohol or gasoline. But sweet too."

Ether. On a handkerchief, perhaps one belonging to one of Walter's ladies of the night?

"I blacked out. And I woke in darkness on a dirt floor, musty smelling."

"A basement?"

"Maybe. Reminded me of Mama's cellar."

"Did you hear anything?"

"There were street noises. Car engines and horns. Rumbling, like the trolley in Fair Valley. Voices far off. Must've been there days."

"You were gone three weeks, dear."

"Just a couple days ago a man pressed the cloth over my nose again, and when I woke I was somewhere else, like a gardening shed. One window, boarded over. Stifling hot. I used the heel of my shoe to break the glass and hammer the nails out. Then I just crawled to freedom. Left my shoes on the floor. Saw lights in the distance and ran.Mr. Wainwright found me near that Lake Erie."

"How were you fed?"

"Someone delivered a pitcher of water and a bowl of food scraps. After dark, never in the light, so I never saw them."

"Did you hear names?"

She raises her eyes toward the ceiling. "Now that you mention it, I heard a name. In that first place they took me." She brings her gaze back to mine. "Will something-or-other. No, Wilcox."

"Somehow Simon Wilcox is connected to brothels and the stealing of girls. There's more, but what is it?"

Cade and I are taking in the evening coolness on the dormitory's porch. Everyone else has retired, and he and I are laying out a plan. He has promised to trust me. And I, him.

"Star works in . . . one of those places. Feeding Chester Wainwright information, but now that Flora's . . ."

I release a groan and lean forward with my head in my hands. "I still can't comprehend it. I can see Flora—as tall as I, wavy hair the color of ginger. And skin like . . . apricots, but with a sprinkling of freckles."

"Did she look like you?"

I lean into the wicker chair back, pondering. "Except for her brown eyes, Flora and I could have been sisters." Struck with a new realization, I bound to my feet. "Was *I* the target of the murderers? And Flora was mistaken for me?"

"Are you suggesting we're looking for murderers too?"

"I wouldn't put it past child nabbers."

"But why you?"

I tap a thumbnail against my front teeth. "Bitterness is behind it."

"That's a far cry from the hatred required to murder someone. You're not going back to Fort Worth alone. I'm going with you."

An idea raises its head. I lower my chin and angle a gaze at him. "A woman like me can't enter a brothel. But you can."

His mouth eases open. "You want me to visit a brothel and do what?"

"Not partake of the . . . wares, of course. But search for clues." Something nags. What am I missing?

He gives the porch swing a gentle shove, and we sit in compatible silence. I gaze above the treetops at the thousands of stars glistening above our heads, reminding me of the last Christmas I shared with my mother. In 1910.

I returned home for Christmas and found Walter had abandoned her to die at the old shack. Broken in body and spirit, she welcomed the prospect of moving to her heavenly home. But I refused to give in. So I tended her.

My friends delivered household goods from Broadview and stocked the kitchen, even brought a Christmas tree and ornaments. The firebox flames cast light onto crystal stars that sent showers of rainbows across sharecropper drabness.

Heavenly lights.

Think you can count the stars, Ma?

No more'n ol' Abram could. Reckon I'll have as many offspring as Father Abraham? . . . Time for you, Lil'.

I longed for Cade, but I waved aside her suggestion. *"No beaux for me. No marriage. I'm preparing for a career."*

She frowned, and her eyes flashed a knowing that flickered and dimmed. *"Providence'll decide 'bout family and fancy career, Lil'. Just like He'll count out my days, my breaths."*

Thinking I was gifting her that Christmas morning, I announced I'd drop out of CIA to tend her. But I had yet to understand love without measure.

I awoke the next morning, groggy with the sleep Ma's potion forced on me, and found her gone. She left a note scribbled on a scrap of paper wedged between Christmas boughs.

Go back to that fancy college, Lil'. Make something of yourself, something I weren't able to do. Fly. For me. Don't never forget I love ya beyond measurin'.

I had no desire to count out my mother's days and breaths. Wouldn't. But Walter did. And he got away with it.

Four years later, Ma's dead at his hands, and a jury of twelve men have found him not guilty. He's working devilry, and I'm sitting in a porch swing in Texas beside the one man I'll ever love, gazing at the same stars that're twinkling over rotten Sloat sod in Oklahoma.

This unexpected rescue has nudged me closer to believing God exists. I've learned to speak to Him rather easily, but tonight I'm cogitating on my mother. Girls like Opal. And poor Flora.

Donnie's safe. So is Blossom. Berachach and the origin of the shuttle tug at my curiosity, but I must postpone them for now.

"Walter's up to wickedness. He isn't far, though. I can smell him."

CHAPTER 38

A deluge greets us in Fort Worth, washing into the gutter our plan for a walk, perhaps even toward the bluff. But the temperature cascades with the rain, settling in the upper sixties, a welcome respite.

Cade insists rooming at the Metropolitan would be unseemly, so he boards at the nearby Worth Hotel.

We meet in the Met's lobby, both of us with the day's *Caller*. We select a conversation grouping near the check-in counter, and he reads aloud the front-page headline. The Battle of the Frontiers continues. Germany attacks Russia in East Prussia. I scan the reports for any mention of Italy, relieved to find not a hint.

A front-page article screams Flora's death. She'd complain that they refused to use her preferred last name— Zane. I note the arrangements for her funeral the following week and remind myself to send flowers.

If I'd not come to Fort Worth, Flora would be alive today. If I hadn't forced my way into her Wednesday Club . . . or insisted she introduce me to others . . . or stayed away from the workhouse and Battercake and the notoriety, my new friend still would be flittering around Fort Worth with her bodyguard in tow.

I hang my head in regret.

"What is it?" He has lowered his newspaper into a heap on his lap.

"Just remembering Flora and wishing I'd never come to Fort Worth."

"You can't blame yourself. Someone else murdered her. Not you."

"Speaking of that someone . . ." I leaf to the Women's Society page. "Look at this." Turning the paper around, I point to a prominent piece. "Our former neighbor has written an article intimating a white slavery ring is operating between Fort Worth and New Orleans. She's bound to be throwing the scent in a different direction altogether."

He stands and looks out the front plate-glass windows. "Sky's clear." He turns to me. "Let's visit your friend, the gardener's helper."

"It just rained, so she's either working in the greenhouse or tending her family."

"I'll call a cab for Rosen Heights." The desk clerk calls his offer from his counter.

We turn to him. The man has been eavesdropping. Furthermore, how does he know the identity of my friend? Or that she lives in Rosen Heights?

"Thank you—"

"No." I give the clerk a piercing glare. "We'll hail one outside."

Settled into the freshly swept back seat of a Tin Lizzy, Cade cocks his head toward me. "What's up with the desk clerk?"

"Just a feeling. At first he couldn't be bothered with my requests. But after I met with the Wednesday Club, he's seemed *too* helpful. Supercilious. Far too informed of my doings."

"A *male* busybody? Didn't know they existed." He chuckles, and I give him a playful swat on his arm.

The cab delivers us to the Rosen Irregulars president's home. The rain has left the lawn a deeper green and the beds richer reds, golds, and purples. The soil is fresh turned. And a wheelbarrow of potted plants awaits someone's attention.

"This is a grand place. A woman is responsible for it all?"

I scowl at him. "She's the gardener's helper. But why not a woman? She's as able as any man. Why, I witnessed her breaking up rocks at the workhouse—"

He pulls away in mock astonishment. "A convict's your friend? What's next for our Lily?"

I give his shoulder a playful tap. "Not a criminal. A widow living in a tent with seven children. Unable to pay her deceased husband's debts. Thrown into the workhouse and handed a sledgehammer. Told to break up rocks or suffer a stiffer sentence."

He pays the driver to wait and offers me his arm. "I take it Battercake Flats is no Rosen Heights. You and your widow pal are cut from the same bolt of cloth, in Mama's words."

I grin. "That's a compliment. To me."

Running to greet us, Beulah flings aside her work gloves and finger-combs damp tendrils from her forehead. "Oh, isn't it terrible about Flora?"

We share our shock and angst in an embrace of friends. She gestures toward her little house where wicker chairs sit out front. "Come and sit awhile."

I introduce the two, and children peek from the front windows. She motions them outside. "These are five of my seven young'uns. My two oldest are out selling newspapers."

"So Opal's working with Tad now?"

"He looks after her. Every penny counts." She eyes me, speculatively. "But I suspect you haven't come to chat about my offspring." She shoos them into the house.

"I . . . We need to talk with Star. Can you arrange it? Before Sunday?"

Her facial features scrunch, and she leans on an elbow. "Tad can deliver a message."

"Where is Star this time of the day?"

"Sleeping . . . in the disorderly house . . . upstairs from the saloon."

"Which saloon?"

"Black Panther."

A clue here and one there snap together, magnet-like. Ma's panther drawing. Fort Worth's moniker. The policeman's badge. Sabina's key fob.

But what picture do the clues form?

Beulah frowns. "You look like you've seen a ghoul, Lily—or maybe a panther?"

"I'm putting clues together. Speaking with Star might help. Cade has agreed to present himself as a potential customer. Can Tad get her a message?"

"He's outside the *Caller* building. I'll write a note." She whirls into her cottage.

"What's this about a panther saloon?" Cade's expression has turned wary. "And clues?"

"Found a drawing of a panther in the old trunk. Fort Worth's called Panther City."

"Why? No panthers around here."

I flick a dismissive hand. "It goes back decades to an article a Dallas newspaper man wrote. The moniker stuck. Even the policemen's badges sport the animals." My thoughts return to the key fob. Why embossed with a panther?

Beulah returns with a folded paper scrap. "Tad will understand."

Cade settles beside me in the taxi and gives our destination to the driver. Setting my gaze on the road ahead, I ponder where the jaunt might lead us.

To Star and exposing Walter?

Or to an end akin to Flora's?

We're not dealing with amateurs. It's professionals we're after.

We wait in the Met lobby for an answer from Tad, but we choose a pair of chairs far from the desk. The clerk glances our way, and I speak to Cade behind a hand. "He's watching. Don't trust that man a whit."

"Tell me about your mother's journal, Lily."

"I'll do better than that. I'll bring it down." I whisk along the broad marble-floored entry to the stairs and retrieve my valise.

He handles the old tome with care. "This is fine leather, but it's very old."

"The first entry is 1775."

He sucks in a breath. "The handwriting reminds me of the founding fathers' script. What a remarkable piece of history." He reads silently. "Rachel and Davie Lloyd were originally named Loeb. Jews." He turns page after page. "They converted to Christianity."

"Appears so. Look at her notations concerning the treatment of women on the ship."

His eyebrows rise. "This Rachel didn't back down to anyone."

I nod. "She wouldn't've sat still for Walter's abuse."

His head snaps up. "You don't know what she might have done in your situation. Each person has his or her unique story. She had hers and you have yours."

"See Rachel's last entry in Philadelphia harbor? Someone else's handwriting picks up later. And so it goes over the decades, ending with the panther. This old record has wooed me since I first laid eyes on it."

"It's no wonder." He turns pages with care.

"But what in the world does it have to do with Ruby Sloat?"

"You mentioned a drawing."

I turn to the back page. "Here."

He examines the artwork in the light. "It's a panther. Fort Worth is Panther City. They have a panther-ready police force and Black Panther Saloon."

"It's all so mysterious. I embarked on a journey of discovery just weeks ago, sensing my past and future were pulling me in opposite directions. Now I'm convinced the past is speeding to catch up with the present. And a collision is inevitable."

He places his hand atop mine. "You been praying like you promised Ida?"

"I have." I answer with a grin. "Matter of fact, I suspect it's done some good."

His fingers tighten. "Don't quit. Providence'll lead us and take us back home."

Us? We won't be making a home together. "Sounds like my mother."

He nods, knowingly. "She was wise in ways few of us can claim."

"I realize it more everyday." I run the tip of a forefinger over a wet spot on the tea table. "There was an old tatting shuttle in Ma's trunk." I slide the pouch from the valise and dump it into my hand. "It's carved from rosewood."

"What are the symbols?"

"She recognized it as Hebrew."

His eyes rise with frown lines between them. "Hebrew. That would fit with—"

"Rachel Lloyd."

His eyes snap toward movement at the windows.

Tad, his hands cupped around his eyes, peeks through the plate glass. He smiles and nods.

I grab Cade's forearm. "He made contact with Star."

Standing, he hesitates. "We need to notify the sheriff."

"Star doesn't want to involve the law."

He bends toward me. "Chester had the muscle and fire power to back us." His whisper sounds as if gravel lines his throat. "But he's out of pocket. We have no other choice."

I pop upward. "How about Flora's bodyguard."

He pauses before answering. "Know how to reach him?"

"I can't call." Striding toward the stairs, I glance back. Out the front window Tad's handing Cade a square of folded paper. My faithful companion slips it into his pocket.

CHAPTER 39

The Wainwright housekeeper reports Flora's bodyguard is to arrive home at ten a.m., and I leave an invitation to join Cade and me in the Met lobby.

The man arrives precisely at three o'clock, and we explain our newly begotten information. "Law enforcement's already apprised." He indicates the bartender with a head nod. "He's working undercover, matter of fact."

I sit straight. "I've met him."

Cade flashes an expression of feigned horror. "The tender of a bar?"

"Snooping for information." I give a shoulder a casual lift. "The point is I know him, and if he's in undercover work, I believe he'll cooperate with us."

Our muscled companion expels a deep breath. "I'll be getting back then. Mr. Wainwright's returning tonight. With Flora." He stands with hand extended. "I'm glad to have met you. Perhaps we'll meet again."

A wash of tears threatens, but I hold them in check. "Please give Chester my love."

The man's posture is less than erect as he exits the Met's front doors, and together we approach the bar.

I peer at the stained-glass sign. "Someone's been holding out on me."

He grabs the brass handle and jerks it outward. "You been hanging out in a bar, Lily? What's come over you?"

"Just using my voice. Like *your* sister."

He arches one eyebrow. "One Ella is enough to keep up with."

I lead him to the rich mahogany bar and plop onto a stool. It's mid-afternoon on a Friday, not a peak time for drinking customers.

"Afternoon, folks." The barkeep greets us as he wipes down the sparkling-clean surface. "What can I get you?"

Cade thumbs toward a distant table, and the man follows with order slip in hand.

"We're here for information." No one's around to hear me, but I whisper all the same.

"We're friends of Chester Wainwright."

The man glances around and shoves a neighboring chair to our table. He sits backward with his arms crossed over the ladder back. "Terrible thing about Mrs. Wainwright."

"Yes." I give my head a shake. "We're determined to uncover the murderer."

His eyebrows peak. "How can I help?"

Cade leans forward with his elbows on the table. "Chester told us you work for him—undercover."

The man jerks back with his palms shining. "Whoa!"

I touch fingers to his forearm. "Please don't worry. No one will learn of your involvement from us. We need information, and Chester's beyond our reach due to poor Flora. According to her bodyguard, you can help us."

He returns his arms to the back of his chair. "I'm listening."

Cade assumes a clandestine pose. "Do you know the bartender at Black Panther?"

"What do you have in mind?"

"Call him. Give him my description. Say I have 'undamaged merchandise' for sale."

His eyes move to mine and back again. "I can do that. But I can't call on a hotel phone."

His declaration puzzles me. "Why?"

He head-nods toward the front desk. "Desk clerk knows more than he should, given his place in society. I believe he listens to guests' phone conversations."

I jerk backward. "I spoke openly with Flora on the phone. Made calls to Oklahoma. And Berachah. I even spoke about Donnie at Jackson."

"Have you noticed a curious knowledge of your comings and goings? Perhaps your cable messages and mail?"

My mouth eases open. "I have."

"I'd wager the leak lies right out there at the front counter."

"We'll speak in person from now on then." A storm is brewing on Cade's brow. "Or use another establishment's phone. I noticed a public phone box down the street."

The bar man stands and scoots the chair into its place. "No skin off my nose." He pauses as if to ponder. "Except where Mr. Wainwright's concerned. Horrible about the Mrs." He walks away as if dazed.

I seize Cade's arm. "The desk clerk is how Sabina's known about my movements."

"I'm afraid you're right. We'll have to be very careful from now on. Meanwhile, there's this to consider." He holds up Tad's note.

"Look here." I point to the scribbling. "Star wants to meet her sister and me tomorrow morning, usual spot and time. That means five o'clock at City Park."

"You two can't be out alone at that time of the morning."

I swat away his protest. "No need for concern. Flora . . ." Words fail me in the reality of my friend's death. "Oh dear. I've depended on Flora for transportation. Now . . ."

"I'll hire a cab."

"We'll need to leave here at four-thirty to pick up Beulah in Rosen Heights and make it to City Park on time."

He nods. "Here in the lobby at four-thirty then."

I return to the lad's note. "Opal has a plan and has talked with Star."

"What's that mean?"

I catch the inside of a cheek between my teeth, cogitating. "Knowing Opal, it can mean most anything. Growing up in poverty has taught her life lessons other girls her age haven't learned. She's a lot like me."

Cade takes my hand. "You're one of a kind, Lily."

My heart slips onto its side. "Wait 'til you get to know the sisters." I chuckle.

"I must admit, Star will be the first . . . lady of the night . . . I've met."

"You won't forget her. But I'll need her permission to include you in the conversation. Be prepared for the cab to drive around while I talk with her. Star fears being followed. An idling cab might draw undue attention."

"I'll do what I must."

The golden streaks in his brown irises gleam in the lamplight, bringing to mind the warmth of our fireside chats over the years.

I push aside such thoughts. They're helpful to neither of us.

CHAPTER 40

"Wilcox buys girls." Standing in a deep shadow, Star speaks soft and low. Her night-black pupils reflect the Saturday morning shimmers overhead. "Others snatch and deliver. Wilcox gives a yea or nay. Gotta be undamaged, mind you."

I'm seated on a bench between Beulah and Opal, imagining Blossom in a similar position. I shiver, not from cold, for the twilight is hot and steamy, but from anticipation and trepidation

"How do you know this?" I must be certain I can trust this woman.

"I keep my eyes and ears open. Wilcox's Cowtown Cafe turns into Black Panther Saloon after sundown. I'm a waitress and a bar maid. Then there's the Wild Gardenia upstairs where we girls . . . work." She glances at her sister, who's hanging her head. "But a more profitable business is transacted in the basement where the girls are bought and sold."

"How does he escape detection?" Squatting beside us, Cade speaks just above a whisper.

"Wilcox eats his Saturday noon meal at his cafe. Claims a table by a window. Most Saturdays, a stranger and his lady stroll past."

The space between my eyebrows crinkles. "By strangers you mean—"

"Folks I ain't seen anywhere but outside that window. The woman wears all black. A hat with a veil, so I ain't seen her face. The man dresses dandified—in eye-catchin' colors. A vest over a pot belly. And a bowler hat over hair the color of mud.

"The man joins the boss inside, and the lady goes on her way. They talk private-like, and when Wilcox wipes his mouth and loosens a vest button, the stranger walks out."

I lean forward with my arms crossed at my waist. "Sounds like a message of sorts."

Star gazes overhead, as if her words are etched among the morning stars. "An alley—wide enough for Wilcox's Cadillac and delivery trucks—separates his establishment from a fortune teller—a psychic, she calls herself."

Cade harrumphs. "I know the place."

"That alley door opens into the bar's storage room. Stays unlocked for deliveries."

Our four heads nod as one.

"But the alley on the other side of the building is different. More like a passageway. Cramped and dark. A hack or delivery truck can squeeze through, leaving little space on either side. No street lights at either end. That door's always locked. 'Cept for special deliveries."

Cade runs his knuckles along his jawline, as if ruminating. "I've scoured the neighborhood and know both alleys."

"What sort of special deliveries?" Beulah flashes her sister a pointed stare. "For heaven's sakes, sun'll be up soon. Get on with it."

The woman of the night draws a deep breath and releases it through pinched lips. She clenches her hands at her sides. "Last Saturday night I claimed I was down with stomach cramps. Watched and listened from my upstairs windows. Patrolman strolled by just before midnight and stood not on the corner under the street lamp but at the entrance to the wide alley.

"Boss man arrived at straight-up twelve o'clock. Parked near the delivery entrance. Patrolman met him at his car. They chewed the fat awhile, and the lawman strolled away, twirling his billy club, and whistling. I'd wager he sported a newly padded pocket."

"He buys off patrolmen." Cade speaks from deep in his throat.

I reach out to the courageous woman. "Were you able to keep track of him?"

"I claimed I was going for a soda water to settle my stomach. Took the back stairs to the bar. Place was so busy no one noticed me."

Cade stiffens. "And?"

"The door to the basement was standing ajar."

My eyes widen. Are the whites shining? "Did you follow?"

"Scared plumb outta my boots, but I did."

I give her hand a squeeze. "What'd you find?"

"A hallway stretches under the building from one alley to the other. It ends at stairs that lead to the narrow passageway."

I cogitate. "This is Saturday. If the couple shows up a noon, Wilcox will expect a shipment tonight. He'll park in his usual spot. And unlock the special delivery door."

"Oughta work out that way." Star looks over a shoulder and fidgets.

"What else is below the saloon?" Cade runs his fingers through his hair.

"Rooms on either side of the hall. One's for storage, all kinds of cast-offs from upstairs. And empty crates. Marked *Liquor*."

"But isn't liquor delivered through the wide alley and kept behind the bar?" Opal speaks up with an observation the rest of us missed.

"That's right, my young detective." I turn to Star. "Why are liquor crates below?"

She glances around in jerks. "Bein' out here with you folks scares me plumb silly."

"Answer us!" Beulah's tone has assumed a commanding edge.

Star's mouth scrunches tight, and she scratches her scalp. "Light showed around the jamb to the other room, so I took a peek."

We four lean toward her, expectancy silencing us.

"Wilcox was with that couple—the strangers. The men were working with crowbars. On a crate marked *Liquor*."

I tighten my hold on her hand. "Did you see the merchandise?"

Star drops her chin. "No, but I heard . . . whimpers. A girl—drugged, I'd wager."

We expel a trio of sighs, our breaths absorbed by the humid air.

Our burly companion stamps to his feet. "What're we gonna do?"

"What *can* we do?" Beulah's voice trembles.

"I been thinkin' 'bout somethin'." The child sleuth gives her mother a steel-like stare. "Planning. Has to do with me and a crate labeled *Liquor.*"

A memory blinks to life—Walter's liquor-bottle graveyard back home . . . his bootlegging business . . . and the evidence of his tawdry trysts just yards from our home.

Can we trust Star with our lives? With Opal's?

My companions think so.

But can I?

Beulah draws back, and the whites of her eyes shine bright. "You're a child. You have no business around Wilcox."

Star's gaze zips between her sister and niece. "Your ma's right. I seen what he does to women."

Cade nods his agreement.

The girl's hands draw into fists. "I'm thirteen years old, but I feel like I'm full grown. Ain't never backed down. Don't intend to start now."

"But—"

I tender a halting signal to our male companion. "Girls like Opal are at risk daily. I stood up to Walter at age thirteen, and Opal no doubt can stand up to Simon Wilcox. *If* we have a plan to keep her safe. But her mother should decide."

"Let's hear it." Beulah slouches cross-legged on the graveled path.

Opal sits straight, her chin lifted and protruding. "First, Tad and me peddle newspapers all over Cowtown, including the Acre.

"Second, I'm undamaged goods. Ain't gotta be told I'm purtier 'n a spring day. God made me this way for a reason. A girl with eyes like mine'll bring a hefty price.

"And third, I ain't got a scared bone in my body. Battercake has taught me plenty."

I point at her. "Your *mother* taught you, Opal."

Mother faces daughter head-on, and seconds creep by. What will this mother decide?

"Ain't gonna keep you from doin' what I'd do myself. But you can bet your britches I ain't gonna be nowhere but beside you. *Inside* that crate."

Astounded at her response, I stammer on. "But . . . How will we accomplish it? It's daring and dangerous."

Cade folds forward, his elbows on his knees. "We want to free any captives in that basement. But ultimately, we want to expose the underground that transports girls to Mexico. That requires law enforcement."

I nod. "Police need to raid the place while Wilcox is dealing."

He runs a palm over his beard stubble, a match-on-striker grate. "Sheriff Rae won't allow untrained private citizens—certainly not a thirteen-year-old girl, tough and brave though she may be—to conduct an undercover operation alone."

"Does Sheriff gotta know what we're up to from the outset?" Our young partner has raised her hands toward the sky. "Can we wait 'til the time's right?"

Her aunt stares, pensive-like. "Tad can carry messages."

"Sheriff Rea knows my boy's an enterprising lad. Honest. And dependable."

Cade peers past me to Star. "We'll need to know if that pair shows up at noon today. Can you send us a message through Tad?"

"Yep. Send him my way at one o'clock. I'll buy a newspaper and tell him yea or nay."

I'm growing increasingly uneasy. "Then what?"

Our little group sits in silence. "The sky's brightening. We don't have time for chit chat. This is a rare opportunity to work from the inside. But how will it play out?"

Star bounds to her feet and paces. "Depends on that couple. And if they show up at noon, Wilcox'll open the basement at midnight."

"In that case, we'll have time to alert Sheriff Rea to raid the place." What a relief that would be.

"But if they don't show at noon, the boss'll be with me." Star flashes a glance at her sister. "All night."

Beulah snaps her eyes shut. How her sister's words must wound her.

Cade mimics Star's hard-scrabble pacing. "In that case, I can pose as a seller of untouched liquor."

She halts her pacing. "Good idea. Best you deal with the bartender. He can be bribed."

"Won't he be suspicious?" The longer I consider my beloved's part in the plan, the tighter my stomach knots draw.

"I'll claim you're a former customer with a special brand of liquor, Cade." She scratches her scalp. "He'll understand."

"What time should I arrive?"

"'Bout eleven, I reckon. I'll lure Wilcox upstairs 'fore then."

"I'll approach the barkeep and ask for you. You'll be busy, so I'll wait."

"Untouched whiskey's worth the wait." Opal flashes a Cheshire grin.

"Offer some bills for his trouble." She catches a lip between her teeth. "But he can't leave the bar unattended. So when Wilcox is asleep, I'll take the back staircase to the storage room.

A grin shows Cade's well cared for teeth. "Where there's also a way to the basement."

"What's the point in all this?" I jump to my feet, fearful of where the plan might end. "To identify the players—Wilcox and the stranger couple? Then what? You overcome the villains with your superior strength while Opal's locked in the vipers' nest? Her mother too?"

Cade paces, his boots kicking up blasts of pea gravel. "We'll have to ponder this, Star. We'll wait in Lily's suite at the Met. Send Tad with a *yea* or *nay* message regarding the couple. So we'll know how to plan."

She nods and scurries away. We return to the cab, quiet and pensive.

I'll remain a voice of reason, a watch woman atop a tower. If it kills me.

CHAPTER 41

$\mathcal{M}$orning and noonday meals at the Met pass without incident for us four—Beulah, Opal, Cade, and I—but we're as skittish as foals. News that Germany has attacked Russia magnifies our anxiety over Addie.

We all but wear out the rug in my sitting room, pacing and adjusting details to what we hope will be a fail-safe plan. We wish Star could've stayed with us, but she's expected back. Ladies of the night sleep away their days.

Tad delivers a one-word message from Star shortly after noon.

"Nay," I read aloud.

Staring out the window, a frown clouds Cade's expression. "That couple didn't show. So we're left to playing our parts for an audience of two—the bartender and Wilcox."

"Got a message for Aunt Star?" Tad shifts from one foot to the other, eagerness permeating his fine frame.

Cade turns to us. "Are you all sure about this?"

Beulah stands, her hands on her son's and daughter's shoulders. "We McGregors are sure."

I sit at the desk and scribble a one-word reply: *Yea.*

Beulah sees Tad out.

"Wait." I follow him into the hallway. "Where will you be tonight?"

"Around. You won't see me. But I'll keep track of you."

His mother joins us in the hallway and stares at her son's scurrying form, her expression chiseled stone, the sort I often spied on Ma's countenance.

"Don't worry. You taught that boy to care for himself."

She closes the door behind us and pauses with her forehead pressed against the wood, whispering to herself—or to her God.

As jittery as a June bug, I join Cade at the window with my arms laced at my middle. "Am I to stay back in perfect safety? I need a part."

"You played your part years ago." He gazes beyond my eyes into my soul. "You're why we're here. Soon the villains will be rounded up and the damsels rescued. Because of you."

Beulah sets her hands on my shoulders. "Generations of women yet unborn will benefit from this night you've led us to. You may never meet them and the world may never notice." She gathers her daughter in a one-armed hug. "But we will."

I battle a threatening storm of tears. "All the same, I want to take part tonight."

Cade returns to staring through the window, his hands in his pockets and his fingers jangling loose change. He excuses himself without explanation and returns with a camera.

"Where'd you get that?" I take the Kodak in hand, remembering the similar piece of equipment in my valise.

"Belongs to our friend in the bar downstairs. Has an adjustable aperture set for daylight now, but you can flip it to low light. See here?" He points to a switch on the frame. "I'll snap Opal in case the Panther bartender quibbles about her . . . potential. And our barkeep friend downstairs will develop it. He has one of those simple devices."

Leading Opal into the sunlight spilling through the window, Cade snaps and hurries away on what he calls a hunch.

We're left to wonder what else he has planned, watching the clock, and imagining.

He returns after nine o'clock. Attired in dandified garb, garish in fabric and color, he's sporting a bowler hat, not at all his usual dress.

"What happened to you?" Opal rakes her gaze over his peculiar attire.

He tugs on his plum velvet lapels. "My disguise." He offers me a brown-paper wrapped bundle. "This is for you."

I tear away the paper to reveal a lady's black-veiled hat and a matching drawstring bag.

"I'm to accompany you?"

He gives a half-hearted grin. "Nearest I could find to Star's description of the stranger's lady. Got a depot hack for our use tonight. It's parked at the delivery entrance. Removed the last seat to make room for a liquor crate."

Opal's eyes widen to the size of the garden-green tea plates back at Broadview.

Cade assumes a reassuring stance with one hand on the mother's shoulder and the other on the daughter's. "I've attached a hasp latch. To get you out quick when the time comes."

They return approving nods.

"Lily, dress in black and cover your face with the veil. Do whatever you want with . . . whatever that is."

"It's a lady's evening bag." I stretch out the drawstrings and peer inside. "Reminds me of the shuttle pouch."

He sets the Kodak on a side table. "Take this along just in case. I've already set it for low light."

In the adjoining bedroom, I dress in my single black ensemble—a suit I keep on hand for funerals. A flashing memory of Flora's infectious laughter tempts me to give in to grief, but that will come later. I must keep a clear head.

What might I need?

My derringer fits into the bag.

The shuttle? For what, I haven't an inkling, but why not? It fits alongside the pistol with barely a bulge.

I rifle through the valise. Coins jangle, and I drop them into the bag with the sheriff's phone number written in his neat hand.

Blossom's camera? *Never know when I might find something newsworthy.* No. I'll take the Kodak.

Securing the hat with an eight-inch pin, I lower the veil and tie it in back. When I enter the sitting room, my friends smile their approval.

"I insist you both carry one." Cade extends an open palm topped with two pistols.

Beulah stares at the derringers. She slips one into a skirt pocket and buttons up.

I hold up my evening bag. "Mine's here."

Would I be capable of using the firearm? I glance at Opal. If necessary, yes.

I slip the Kodak's strap over my head, and the body rests just below my bosom. Tightening the purse strings, I tie them to my belt loop, pistol out of mind.

Cade proceeds with my instructions. "Sit up front with me. When the bartender steps out, show yourself, as if you're the usual seller's lady. You'll add credibility to my claim."

We exchange encouraging smiles and nods, and he reaches for the door knob.

"Wait." I touch his arm lightly. "Let's pray first."

What has come over me in these brief weeks? Has my promise to Ida become so routine it's habit now? Or might . . . something else . . . be at work?

Cade calls on his God for protection, especially over Opal. He prays for wisdom and strength for himself and—surprisingly—thanks Him for answering his prayer already.

He's thanking God for answering prayers ahead of time? My silent query brings Rachel Lloyd to mind.

Me man claims Peace in Present Troubles be comin thru Prayer.
Ahead o Time. Reckon twill Trust me prayin Man.

Peculiar.

I glance around, wondering what I might have forgotten. "Got the snapshots of our beauty?"

He pats his coat pocket. "Yep."

I sweep through the doorway, and we head to the Met's little-used back staircase.

The hack's canvas siding hides our load, but the front seat is doorless. "I feel as exposed as a flag atop a pole."

Cade adjusts mother and daughter in the crate and secures the latch. Without warning, the thunk of metal on metal dredges up buried horror.

> *Walter raised a hammer and pounded the head of a rusty nail. His half-hearted repair of the chicken coop would last no longer than the next stiff gust of wind.*
>
> *He jerked me to him, his whiskey breath repulsive. "See this?" He raised the hammer and flashed me a loathsome grin. "I can use it on your ma's skull too. So not a peep outta ya." He dragged me into the coop.*
>
> *The hens squawked.*
>
> *Baby chicks peeped.*
>
> *Peep. Peep.*

I raise a fist to my mouth, stifling a mewl. I haven't thought of that day in years, not even when I found the old trunk in the chicken coop. What's coming over me?

Cade cranks the engine, and I shove aside my memory of abomination.

I stare into the shroud of darkness. Danger and potential terror await us. But I must maintain a clear mind. For all our sakes.

Cade parks in the cramped alley with the tail gate just shy of the locked door. The hack's sides all but scrape the brick walls. Slipping sideways out of the hack, he rounds the corner toward the saloon's front entrance.

I snap open my battery-lighted pendant watch and point it toward the wooden prison. "It's eleven o'clock," I whisper-shout. "Wilcox'll be asleep upstairs in an hour. Can you two breathe back there?"

"We're fine," Beulah answers.

We chat in whispers to pass the time, but if their insides are as jumpy as mine, they won't last long in that cage.

At midnight, I peek into the back. "Won't be long now."

"Heart's beatin' outta my chest." The girl's words are encased in a smile. Thankfully.

I'm tempted to speak a prayer, but haven't we already thanked these folks' God? Am I learning to trust Him too?

A latch clicks. My body stiffens. Heavy metal scratches over hard-packed dirt, and the bartender steps out. The white of his shirt all but glows. Ladies' garters encircle his biceps.

The man looks both ways and ventures out with Cade. "There's a rock." He points into the shadows. "A doorstop."

I stand at the tail gate, silent.

The man glances at me and turns to Cade. "Where's the beauty in that photograph?"

"The crate," Cade answers. "Got two, matter of fact. Both are out cold."

"Too dark," the man notes. "Get 'em inside. If one's the beauty in that photograph, Wilcox'll thank me for making the deal."

The two men grunt and snort, lugging the crate from the truck to the ground.

I stand, silent as a stone.

The barkeep hefts one end of the crate and backs toward the doorway. He kicks the rock aside, letting the door swat against Cade's backside. A horse and carriage whiz past one end of the alley and automobiles putter at the other. Horns blare, and a trolley rattles past.

"Whoah!" Cade hollers, letting his end rest on the top stair step.

"What's the matter, mister?" The man's heaving breaths carry over the night sounds.

"Two are mighty heavy. Take it slow." Cade kneads his lower back and stretches side to side, glancing back at me and nodding.

As the men descend the stairs, I wedge the rock in the threshold. A faint glow creeps through the opening around the jamb, and an idea dawns. Cade instructed me to stay put, but what's my purpose out here in the dark?

I'm disguised. So why not join Cade? The basement light could be bright enough for photography. I can slip inside and record the transaction.

I force the door open, and the heavy metal gives a bass screech. I wait, my senses razor sharp. Manly grunts rise from the hallway below. The crate scrapes over floor planks. The tender of the bar complains, and Cade urges him onward.

I click open the collapsible camera and ease down the staircase.

The hallway's dark as sin. The room on the right stands open, its innards a black mystery. Lamplight burns around the jamb to my left where the men have settled the crate.

Pressing into the shadows, I slide one eye past the casing, relieved to find the men facing away from me. An overhead lamp illumines an empty room, save the crate hiding two brave females.

"Open this." The dispenser of alcohol whacks the box with a crowbar. "I wanna see this beauty."

"I'd rather wait for—"

"I said we'll open it, and that's that!"

Cade rubs his fingers over his chin stubble. "No transaction without the boss."

The man holds out a hand. "I'll get 'im. *After* I check the merchandise."

Sighing, Cade slaps two bills across the man's palm. Metal gives a thin screech as rod slides from hasp, releasing the latch. He lets the lid bang against the side of the crate.

"Well, lookey here." The crass man gloats. "We got us *two* beauties."

I imagine the pair cringing in a corner of the crate, Beulah's arms around her daughter, as if to shield her from the man's leers.

Like my mother and me.

"Stand up." The man demands as if he's a military commander.

"Now wait a minute—"

He shoves Cade aside. "Stand up, you women! Now!"

Beulah's head inches up. Her torso. And under an arm, Opal whose persimmon-pink cheeks glow with perspiration. Damp tendrils lay plastered against her temples, but her eyes hold steady, as if daring the man to touch her.

Good for you, Opal.

"The young one'll bring a hefty price. Best not touch her, but the older one looks like my type." The foul man guffaws.

"Wait." Cade grabs him around the shoulders, and the men scuffle.

A trolley roars past outside, and I depress the shutter button, capturing the moment on photograph film.

A latch rattles at the opposite end of the hallway. Someone's coming.

I've no hiding place but the back throat across the hall. Tamping down my fear, I slip inside and press against the wall. I open my throat wide to allow air to pass without a sound. My pulse quiets.

A man grumbles, deep and packed with gravel. From the far stairs.

The gravel . . . The voice . . .

A bit of ice pokes at the base of my spine.

Boot heels clatter down the stairs and into the opposite room.

"Why—"

"Lookey here." The man growls, masking Cade's response.

Gravel man answers with a phlegmy chuckle.

That chortle . . .

A pistol hammer clicks, readying a weapon for firing.

Cade and my friends are in danger. I'm armed with nothing but a pistol the size of my palm, ineffective from a distance—or against two men. Unless . . .

Never know when I might find something newsworthy.

I lay a hand on the Brownie around my neck. I'm armed with a camera shutter . . .

Surely the rumbles of Saturday night traffic will muffle my movements. Creeping across the hall, I position the lens at the edge of the door frame . . . Lower an eye to the view finder . . . And stare, stock-still, at the back of a head.

A head I loathe.

Walter's.

"Tie him tight, man." I shudder at his graveled, commanding voice. Each sliver of past defeat comes rushing back. Each cruel expression on each society girl's face. Each whispered word and name I was called. Each slap of Walter's hand, pound of his fist, slash of his whip.

Each moment in the chicken coop.

I stifle an outcry with a fist between my teeth, my feet bolted to the floor.

No way can I withstand Walter.

I haven't the courage.

CHAPTER 42

"Well, if it ain't Cade McFarland. In a brothel." Walter howls laughter.

"Why, you—"

Boot heels scramble, scuffle.

Squawks. Grunts. A body falls to the floor with a groan.

"Tie him up and gag him. Gotta talk to the boss. Need a go-ahead on these two ladies."

Sounds like Walter. He works for Wilcox?

Movement could draw attention my way. I freeze in place.

"Aw, I was gonna have a little taste of this . . . liquor first." The bartender chortles.

Mother and daughter must be cringing in the crate.

"Time for that later." Boots drub toward the door. "Get back to the bar."

"You're a heartless taskmaster, Wilcox."

My breath catches. *Wilcox?* Walter is Simon Wilcox? And there's a boss above him?

Stupefied, I back into the storage room and press against the inside wall.

"Hurry up!" Walter shouts from atop the stairs. "Gag those women and latch the crate. Hammer in the rod."

"Got no hammer." The barkeep shouts back.

"Use the crowbar. And hurry!" A door slams shut.

"Open your mouths, ladies." A scuffle ensues. And a yowl.

Beulah must've bitten him.

Slap! "Open your mouth. Or I'll have my way with your girl."

The scuffling ceases.

"That's more like it."

Muffled groans, protests. He must be gagging them.

Two whacks of metal on metal. "That oughta do it." His footsteps track Walter's up the stairs, and a distant lock click-clacks.

My thoughts eddy and purl.

Cade mumbles across the hall, and my thoughts settle. I find him on the floor, leaning against the far wall. Rushing to his side, I tug down the gag.

"Thank God." He turns backward. "Untie me."

I examine the tightly-drawn knots and hold up the shuttle with its sharp point.

Cade's shoulders relax. "Leave it so that it looks like I'm still restrained but loose enough to break free."

"No." I slash through Cade's binding "I'm getting all three of you out!" I turn to the crate and pound the crowbar against the rod. It slides through the hasp and drops into my hand. I lift the lid. "Hurry!"

Beulah stands inside the crate, and I pull down her gag. She shakes her head. "Let's think this through. There's a boss over Wilcox. They'll return soon. Things need to appear as they left them."

"She's right," Cade adds. "I can overpower Walter—"

"That'll be two against one."

Opal stands, mumbling through her gag. I tug it down, and the girl's words tumble out. "Not with us able to help."

"She's right. Wilcox wants to show the boss the merchandise."

"Oh no, you don't. You two aren't going to—"

"Listen!" Beulah slaps a wooden slat. "If I can break up a rock pile at the workhouse, I can manhandle a measly weasel like Wilcox. And his boss." She unbuttons her skirt pocket and retrieves the pistol. "Besides, you and me both have these."

"And I strapped a pistol inside my boot." Cade whisper-shouts.

Relief floods me. I wrap my fingers around my evening bag. "Need to call the sheriff."

"You're right." He glances toward the far stairs. "Alley door's wedged open, isn't it?"

"Yes. The Met's blocks away."

"Can't trust that clerk. There's a phone box around the corner. It's painted bright red. Got a nickel?"

"I've plenty of coins."

"Sheriff's number's in my shirt pocket. I've memorized it."

Pulling aside his velvet lapel, he runs his fingers into a breast pocket and pulls out the snapshot of Opal and the paper scrap with Sheriff Rae's phone number. "Now pull up our gags and skedaddle."

Repositioning the three gags, I return the lid to the crate. Exiting, I look back. "Take care of yourselves."

Cade nods. Two taps sound on a crate slat. I retreat to the hallway and up the stairs.

I'll return with pistol drawn. But I must hurry.

Of all times for a phone to be out of service!

Slamming the receiver down, I search right and left for a spot of red. Why don't they install more phone boxes?

A cab nears, and I step to the curb with my hand in the air and the veil thrown backward over my hat.

"Lily?"

I jolt around and stare, as if at a wraith.

Sabina slips her hand from her potbellied escort's arm. "What're you doing around here this time of night? Folks might talk."

My hands swoop to my chest. Thankfully, I'd tossed the camera into the hack. I lift a forefinger. "I . . . You see . . ."

She plants a hand on her hiked hip. "Lily Sloat, tongue-tied?" Flashing her companion a lopsided grin, she juts her chin at me. "Speak up, girl."

"I . . . I . . . I couldn't sleep. Thought a walk might . . ." I look around. "I had no idea I'd wandered so far. Where am I?"

She lowers her chin and scrutinizes me. "You don't expect me to believe you don't know here you are. Surely." She eases toward me with her attendant following on her heels.

I back up, but she draws nearer, forcing me toward the brick wall. "What're you doing out here, Lily?"

My eyes widen of their own accord, my tongue immobile.

Her man friend presses against me, and she fumbles in her handbag. Liquid sloshes and splatters on the sidewalk. A hand as big as a skillet clamps a wet handkerchief against my nose and mouth. I struggle against the stench of . . . kerosene . . . No. Ether . . .

Cade. Beulah and Opal. I can't fail them.

Darkness encloses me, and I collapse against a barrel chest.

I wake in darkness. On a hard floor.

My head pounds.

My hands are tied behind my back, and I'm gagged.

The heat is insufferable, the air stale and still.

I'm slumped like a sack of cotton. Gotta move, figure out where I am. A car honks far-off, muffled. I must be in the basement. Where's Cade? Beulah and Opal? They must be somewhere around.

Wiggling to my knees, darkness swirls around me. I hang my head as a wave of nausea overtakes me. I inhale a series of deep breaths, and the sensation abates.

How to free my hands?

The shuttle's point can tear apart my bindings as it did Cade's. But it's in my evening bag tied on a belt loop in front.

Forcing my hands as far to my right side as I'm able, I gather a handful of fabric and tug. My skirt waist inches backward. A second tug. Another, and I'm holding the evening bag. I work the drawstrings apart. And reach inside for the shuttle and pistol.

I must free my hands before I can handle the pistol. Ignoring the tiny firearm, I snag the shuttle and lie on the floor. If I drop the shuttle while I'm working on the binding, it'll fall where it lies—at my waist, in easy reach.

Patience. Just a bit of patience.

Jabbing the pointed end through the cord, I experience a sharp flash of pain. I've stabbed the heel of my left hand. I muffle an outcry and return to my task, picking at a single fiber. A second. And a third.

Shifting the shuttle to my left hand, I attack the cord binding and gouging my right hand. Trembling, I drop the shuttle. It falls into the folds of cloth at my backside, but I retrieve it.

Again, I pierce one minuscule thread. And another.

At length the cord gives way, and my arms collapse on either of my body. My hands are sticky with blood. I curl my fingers and make fists. I can still use them.

Standing, I remove the gag and turn my skirt around so that the evening bag is dangling at my right. I return the shuttle to the bag and pat my chest, searching for my pendant watch.

I release a breath of relief. Click the silver timepiece open. Press the button. And light floods the dark space.

I'm struck by the effect a single pinpoint of light produces in total darkness.

Cast-offs, no doubt from upstairs, and empty crates line the walls. This is the storage Star spoke of, where I hid earlier but never explored.

Two crates labeled *Liquor* sit in the center of the room.

I bend over one. "Anyone in there?"

Was that a moan?

I tap against the wooden slat. "I'm here to help."

A screech. A scratch.

"Lie still. And quiet. I'll get you out of there."

Exploration reveals an old trunk tucked into a corner. A velvet settee. I stumble over a footstool and take hold of the love seat. My timepiece dangles at my bosom. I snap it open and shine the light. My hands have left bloody palm prints in the plush pile. And on my blouse.

Here, an old floor mirror. There, hatboxes. Feathers. A milk can. A seamstress's dress form. And a dusty sewing machine.

I tug on the top drawer. It releases in stop-and-start coughs but opens sufficient space for my hand. My fingers shove aside spools of thread. A measuring tape brings back a haunting memory of the Christmas Ma and I shared in the old shack.

Love can't be measured.

Pushing aside the recollection, I extract the yard-long measuring tape and lay it on the machine cabinet's surface.

My fingers wrap around a sharp-pointed instrument with a blunt hook below, like a bird's claw. A seam ripper. Setting it beside the measuring tape, I continue my search.

I grasp a soft, round object. Pin heads. A needle pricks my skin. A pin cushion. Setting it atop the machine, I open the lower drawer.

Inside, pinking shears. The heavy implement joins the other finds.

A paper packet crackles. A pattern. And a broken-point pencil. I lay them beside the other discoveries.

Now how to utilize what I've found?

CHAPTER 43

"Can you speak?" I whisper at the crate.

Mumbles. A muffled voice. Must be gagged.

"Tap or kick if you understand me."

A shoe heel raps against a slat.

"Good. The wood's lightweight, even a bit flexible. Kick harder."

The rap intensifies to hammering. Fearing the noise might alert someone, I extend my arms across the top of the crate to steady it, and metal objects clatter to the floor.

I kneel with my watch light aglow. A crowbar and a hammer.

Of course. Both are needed for crates nailed shut.

I return to the captive. "Two slats have bent outward. They're weakened. But I found a crowbar, so I'll have you out in no time."

Soon I'm helping the child out of the broken crate and wrapping my arms around her. "What's your name? And where do you come from?"

She stiffens and stares, reminding me of Blossom—and myself. She needs time.

Mind swirling, I lead her forward to a trunk. "Sit here. If someone comes in, at least you'll be hidden."

I shove her opened crate against the sewing machine to hide the broken slats and turn to the second container with crowbar in hand.

Inside, a girl younger than the first—around eight years of age. I drag her onto the floor, as lifeless as a sock.

I press an ear to her chest and fingers at the pulse point in her neck. She's alive, but her heartbeat's weak.

How utterly unspeakable.

I lay the child on the settee and turn her crate backward.

How can I maneuver the girls outside? And what then?

I pause, mulling. The first victim isn't speaking, and the other is still unconscious.

Slipping to the second girl's side, I slap her cheeks lightly. "Wake up." A far-off memory returns. Ella and her mother found me unconscious. Ella scraped a fingernail across the bottom of my foot, which brought me awake.

Untying the girl's shoe, I throw aside a stocking and dig my thumbnail into her sole's soft flesh. She jerks and moans.

I shake her by the shoulders. "Wake up!" I shine my watch light into her eyes.

Her lids flutter open, and she covers her eyes with a hand.

"I'm Lily. I'm here to help, but you must follow my instructions precisely."

At length she jerks a nod and sits up.

"You're in a basement, but men who would do us harm can return any moment. Both of you must remain quiet." I hand the first girl the crowbar and the second, the hammer. "Strike at anyone who comes near."

I tear open the sewing packet. Unfold the patterned paper. Cut out sections of white space with the pinking shears. Grabbing the pencil point's wooden fibers between my teeth, I tug them away to expose the lead.

HELP! I scratch onto the pinked rectangles. *Black Panther basement.* And the sheriff's number.

Pinning the messages to the inside of the girls' skirt hems, I whisper to the younger. "Put on your stocking and shoe."

She nods, and I turn to the door. How am I to unlock it?

Perhaps the seam ripper will do. I retrieve it and stuff the measuring tape into a pocket. They might come in handy.

I poke the ripper's sharp end into the lock and turn, but the tool bends under the pressure. I remove it and reinsert, feeling for the lock's inner workings. At last the lock's mechanism clicks open, and the ripper joins the measuring tape in my pocket.

I kneel with my hands on the girls' shoulders. "I'm taking you to an alley outside. Run as fast as you can to the right. Look for a boy named Tad. Show him the notes. And trust him."

The girls nod, and I lead them up the stairs.

The alley door remains ajar. The rock at the threshold has done its work. Outside, the fresh air revives us, and my headache abates. The dark alley is deserted, occasional vehicles meandering the streets at either end.

A single garbage bin is wedged into a corner. But no sign of my targets.

Wait.

There . . . a shadowy figure rises.

Tad.

With a girl tucked under each arm, I scramble to Tad.

"Where's my mother and sister? And Mr. McFarland?"

"Not sure. I was out cold for awhile. I'm going inside to look for them. But you must get these girls away now."

"Where to?"

"The Metropolitan. Go through the back."

He nods.

"Walk inside as if you belong. To your right is a delivery entrance. Tell the bartender I said to hide them."

"But—"

"No buts." I lean forward with my nose all but touching his.

He snaps a nod and grabs the girls' hands.

"Tad's taking you to safety." I whisper to the girls. "Walk alongside him as if he's your brother. Mustn't raise suspicions." I run my fingers through their tangled hair. What might I use to tidy them?

Strips of cloth.

Using the seam ripper, I tear away two strips from my skirt hem and tie the girls' manes into tails. Neat enough for nighttime.

I return the ripper to my pocket and press my hands against the girls' backs. "You're going home, girls. Stay with Tad."

They gaze up at the boy, and the trio turns to the right. Beyond them, a streetlamp glows. An automobile purrs past. A horse and buggy clip-clops by. The girls look back, and the three round the corner.

Now to find Beulah and Opal. And Cade.

A snarl twists in my stomach. What will I find in the basement? What depravity faces me? I haven't time to ponder.

I must find my loved ones.

All's quiet inside.

With my watch lighting my way, I tiptoe downward, my senses as tight as baling wire.

The door to the storage room we escaped stands ajar, dark and still.

I focus on the other end of the hallway, my ears attuned to sound overhead. Footfalls in the saloon. The plink of a piano. Bawdy laughter.

Inching across the passageway, I press an ear against the closed door. Silence.

Extracting the pistol from my evening bag, I turn the knob and step inside.

The crate Cade labeled *Liquor* sits in the vast, dark emptiness.

I steal toward the bin. "Beulah? Opal?"

My words bounce off the walls, unanswered.

The crate is empty.

I flash the light in a left-to-right arc. No sign of Cade.

I'm alone. And I haven't the vaguest idea how to proceed.

A clunk startles me into a turn. Someone has locked me inside.

Light glows around the jamb. A gaggle of whispers crawls along the threshold.

Words and phrases are hurled in deep-toned, guttural whispers. The utterances are strands of cotton, jumbled and knotted, bandied with force.

"Oh, have it your way. But don't claim I didn't warn you."

A key is inserted into the lock, and I back up, gripping my pistol and the shuttle behind my back.

The knob turns, and Walter enters with a kerosene lantern in hand.

A dark figure slithers into view with pistol drawn. Fabric rustles, taffeta-like. The person wears a hat with a heavy, closely woven lace veil.

The mysterious female gestures to Walter, as if to prompt him to speak.

He sets the lantern atop the crate and scratches his scalp. "Girlie, it seems your hero and friends're . . ." He considers me with an lewd grin.

She whispers at Walter's ear, sprinkling a fragrance . . . of . . .

He steps toward me. "Your gentleman farmer's bound for a gallows. And the women folk're on their way to Mexico. The young'n will bring a pretty penny. And the older one'll keep the brothel owner and his friends entertained." His chest rattles phlegm.

Pain daggers my chest, and weakness washes through me. I fall to my knees with my forehead pressed against the hard floor planks, moaning. "No."

Walter guffaws. "'Fraid so, girlie."

The shrew lets out a gleeful shriek.

I sit up, gaping. "You're . . ."

She holds stock-still, a shoe tapping a steady rhythm on the floor. At length she thrusts her head back. And lifts her veil.

Sabina. And she's wearing bold black-and-white striped suit.

I realize in a flash what struck me as familiar about the smudge in Blossom's creekside snapshot. The black and white smudge. This woman left Broadview in a bold, black-and-white striped suit. And the fragrance I'm all but choking on is . . . gardenias.

Devoid of wig and face paint, the true character leans against the wall with a hand hiked to her waist. She twists the edge of her veil around a forefinger. Her lips peel back, exposing her teeth, canine-like.

"Thought you'd fool my bartender by wearing the garb of the mystery woman you heard about?" She speaks in a hiss. "And then sending your friend Flora to the Valley dressed like you, as if you could fool my crew."

"Flora? You've—"

"You're both slow learners. Easy pickings."

"You had Flora killed?"

She waves away my question. "Save your shock for someone who cares. As I was saying, you haven't the imagination or the guts to pose as me. And now you're my prisoner. To do with as I please."

I turn my gaze to the man I once called Pa, clean shaven but for a trim mustache and sideburns. "How can you treat your own flesh and blood like this?"

He guffaws. "I reckon it's alright, you not callin' me Pa no more, since—"

"You haven't been a pa to me my whole life."

He leans forward with a 'possum grin. "Don't get it, do ya, girlie?"

"Shut up the bickering." She thrusts a kerchief at him.

He bends over me, forcing the gag between my teeth and tying it behind my head.

He tugs a length of cording from a jacket pocket and bends to wrap it around my wrists, his chest rattling. "I've got plans for you, girlie."

You're fit for nothing but a cotton field.

They'll rewrite their bylaws to exclude riffraff like Lily Sloat.

Would my Sloat blood and sharecropper past forever define me?

As Walter fumbles with the cording, Sabina presses the pistol's barrel end against my skull. "Now you're gonna listen, you piece of trash. Walter and I are business partners."

He snorts. "You're so stupid you told Sabina about meeting with the judge. Why else would I wallop my boy like I did? To keep him in line. And his mouth shut."

I'm the reason Walter struck Donnie, broke his nose, traumatized him?

She preens like a peahen. "Even got us a helper over at the Met's desk. So I've known where you took my young'un all along."

They're partners in the saloon and brothel business. And claim a spy at the Met. No wonder she's known every move I've made.

"What do you think I've been doing in Cowtown all these years? Waiting tables? Teaching brats?" She expels a brittle laugh. "I've been a lady of the night, but the business side is where money's made."

The key fob . . . the panther embossing. Black Panther Saloon.

"Bought me part interest in the business." Walter straightens but wobbles. Addled by whiskey, he leaves the cording loose. He produces a cigar from a coat pocket and bites off an end. Striking a match on the sole of his boot, he lights the stogy and expels a foul cloud.

"Been trading for new and different for years." Sabina chortles. "Snatching spoiled urchins from their yards. Almost got away with that black-haired beauty from Berachah. But we grabbed us an even better catch. A whining, yellow-haired minx. "

"You took the birthday girl at Lake Erie. How can you be so cruel?"

"Nothing but sniveling brats under fancy ruffles and lace, no better than me."

I shake my head, but at my back I'm twisting my wrists, loosening the cords.

"Why'd I join the Needham Temperance League and Woman's Club? Why'd I cultivate followers in the Rosen Irregulars and Arlington's Thursday Club? To know what the opposition's up to, of course."

What was it the sour-faced woman in Arlington's Thursday Club said? *You'll be sorry.*

"You've been to Arlingt—"

"I haven't been sitting on my backside, that's for sure. Why, just the other night Walter and I did some exploring right there on Berachah property."

So I hadn't imagined someone was stalking me.

"How'd I snatch your job out from under you? By blackmailing Mr. Francis, a former customer.

"And why did I care if you left Broadview or stayed? Because you brought dishonor to the household?" She hollers with laughter. "You're little more than a pesky gnat to me.

"More importantly, why'd I return to Broadview in the first place? For a sweet family reunion with Mother?" Her bitterness sharpens her message to a fine point.

Walter guffaws.

"Hardly. Six Evans girls are growing into beauties. Right before our eyes."

CHAPTER 44

*M*y longings crumble to dust before the depravity. Ella's daughters sit in the crosshairs of this woman's wickedness.

Her moves have led to this revelation. She returned to Broadview months ago not to reconcile with her mother but to stage the abduction of Ella's girls. She stole my *Caller* job in an underhanded way, and her press badge admitted her to ladies' clubs and suffrage events. She cultivated connections to stay informed of the investigation into abductions.

I never would have guessed she's the kingpin of the brothel and child slavery ring. And Walter, a chess piece in her hand.

No! I snap my head side to side, mumbling around the gag. Behind my back I tug at the binding, loosening it further.

She forces my head against her thigh and presses her revolver deeper into my flesh. "I know exactly where your precious Evans bunch is. Your brother. And besotted admirer. They're with that bunch of mealy-mouthed nobodies at Berachah."

She bends toward my ear. "When the Evans family returns to that ridiculous cottage, they'll have nothing but a one-armed weakling to defend them." She spits the words.

Walter harrumphs. "I *own* four of the jurymen, by the way. They're waiting for word from me to haul six bits of Evans cargo off that stinking land."

I picture the foreman in the jury box, tugging his vest over his belly and announcing the verdict: not guilty. And the jurymen skittering away.

The vile felon's face cracks into a sneer, and his glee nips at my spine, rodent-like. "My ol' pal's gotten to be an expert at snatching girls from their own backyards. He'll cart them Evans beauties to Matamoros, across the Rio Grande from Brownsville. A certain brothel owner is waiting to get his hands on 'em."

I moan. No.

I must find a way to stop this wickedness. I can't let harm come to Ella's girls. But how?

"You're staying right here." Malevolence distorts Sabina's features. "Too scarred to be of use upstairs in Wild Gardenia. But you're fit to do our laundry in the basement. Until I figure something more rewarding. Like a cotton field farther south."

"Drop your guns. And put up your hands!"

The criminals wheel around, and I pull my hands free.

Sheriff Rae, the Met's bartender, Chester Wainwright . . . and . . . miracle of miracles, Cade enter with rifles extended.

Devoid of a firearm, Walter raises his hands above his head.

Sabina throws me aside and aims her pistol at Cade. "You can take me out but not before I wipe that silly look off Lily's face with a bullet between *your* eyes."

She's an expert shooter. I've witnessed her precise aim. Cold and calculating, she's steady as stone. She'd rather murder Cade, my one love, than live another day.

From where does such hatred sprout?

I tucked the seam ripper and measuring tape into my pockets, but the derringer and shuttle are in the evening bag. I ease the drawstrings apart.

Armed with a pistol in one hand and the pointed lace-making implement in the other,

I creep toward the villainous female whose gaze is locked on Cade. I shove the barrel end of my derringer into her mid-back where the bullet will lodge in her shrunken heart.

She stiffens. Wrapping my right arm around her neck, I press the shuttle's fine tip into her neck, bringing blood. But she holds her pistol steady on Cade.

"I could slice clear around your neck and finish you off with a bullet."

I imagine the scene—her crumpled body, the blood seeping in a dark circle around her. The ruby-red flower on her chest, enlarging ever so surely.

"Don't do it, Lily." Cade's words reach across the six feet between us, a chasm even he can't traverse.

My eyes snap to Walter, who has crumpled inward upon himself.

My image of retribution rattles around my empty, steel-plated heart.

I bring my gaze back to my tormentor's colorless mop, each fine hair devouring the light.

My thoughts pick at the embers of a fire that once burned hot—revenge and justice. A passage of Scripture comes to mind, blurring my sight.

Shall mortal man be more just than God?

Job, the man of old. God pointed out his goodness to the devil himself. That ancient conversation opened a spoiled can of spinach. Folks like me have questioned God about the stench ever since.

This pair deserves the harshest judgment a court can pronounce. But my mother and brother. Blossom. Flora. They deserve nothing short of God Almighty's justice.

Am I the one to dispense it?

What of those whom they sold into prostitution? How will my stopping this pair of wicked hearts bring God's justice to those girls?

Ma's purity soars above their malevolence. Someday this villainous twosome will be rotting in abandoned graves, but goodness like Ma's will be told to tens and thousands . . . *if* I step away and let Sheriff Rae . . . and God . . . see to both of them.

Good and evil must be measured by an objective standard.

But where's such a measure?

Vengeance belongeth unto Me; I will recompense. Ma's long-ago words clang like a poorly-cast bell.

The elation I imagined at subduing Walter and Sabina, wreaking havoc on their bodies, sputters to nothingness, as deflated as a motionless windsock.

Sheriff Rae puts a bullet through Sabina's hand. She screams, and her pistol falls with a thud. Chester pins her against the wall.

Walter scrambles for the gun, but the Met's bartender, an undercover deputy, kicks it aside. Throwing Walter to the floor, the man presses a knee into the criminal's back.

Looking up at me, the deputy nods at the measuring tape dangling from my pocket. "Wanna do the honors?"

I wrap the tape around Walter's wrists, picturing Ma's hands at Christmas time four years past. And her words—*Love can't be measured, Lil'.*

I must remember Ma's words.

The deputy snaps handcuffs over the measuring tape and tugs Walter to his feet.

Soon Sabina is shackled beside her partner, and the two responsible for the shackling of untold others are on their way to jail.

Perhaps Mr. Francis will write the news himself.

Suddenly aware of Cade nudging me near, I sag against his sturdy frame. "Thank you for coming." I jerk away. "Where are Beulah and Opal?"

"They're safe."

"Where?"

"I'll let others share the details."

Outside, the morning sun shines bright. Cade hails a cab and directs the driver to the Met. Within the hotel's sturdy surroundings, I sense I've awakened from a dream. Just blocks away, a vile province of human depravity brims like a festering boil.

I note the lobby's marble and filigree adornments, the plush carpeting and sedate lighting. But the elegance is overlaid with a glaze of other scenes. Battercake's depravation. Hell's Half Acre's wickedness. Sabina's and Walter's villainy. Wild Gardenia's hopelessness.

The scenes roll past like a moving picture. I bury my face against Cade and follow his lead up the plush staircase toward my room.

I pat the evening bag hanging at my waist. "I haven't a key, Cade."

With a shrug of nonchalance, he knocks, and the portal swings open, ushering in a chorus of unspoken words I vowed to remember—*Love can't be measured.*

Dumfounded, I stare. Here, Ella and Andrew and their six girls. There, Ida and Philip. Mrs. Upchurch. Donnie and Wally, his tongue lolling to the side.

I stretch out my hands, and my loved ones rush to me. With Cade's strong form at my back, the air around me swishes and swirls with flurries of cheer, a gusher of love.

My legs threaten to give way, and Cade carries me to the divan.

Ella points to the darkening red spots on my blouse. "You're hurt!"

"No." I hold up my palms. "Turned myself into a pin cushion."

Sighing in relief, she fluffs a pillow for my head. Mrs. Upchurch unbuckles my shoes and kneads my feet. Seated in a nearby chair, Ida pats hydrogen peroxide onto my pricked palms and fingers.

Donnie and Wally and Ella's girls flounce to the floor in a line facing me. Andrew and Philip pull down the window shades, easing the squint lines between my eyes.

The girls chatter like baby chicks as their sister regales them with her tale of danger and rescue, a much-repeated story, I suspect. She often glances at Donnie, and he chimes in, his arm around Wally's neck and his voice deeper than I remember it.

I startle at a thought. "The Brownie. Where is it?"

"In trusted hands." Cade smiles. "Film's developed. Copies made. For the trials."

Moisture threatens the backsides of my eyes.

"That's what I meant before." His eyebrows curve into arcs.

"You said they're safe."

Nodding and smiling, he opens the door to my bedroom and lets it ease backward with a gentle tap.

Into the empty space at the threshold steps Opal. Beulah.

And Flora.

CHAPTER 45

*A*ir gushes into my lungs, and I'm unable to exhale. No one need tell me I've paled, for the warmth in my cheeks has melted into my chest.

Flora. Dear, life-filled, bright-haired Flora glides toward me. A vision?

She's beside me, and my hands are touching her cheeks. "You're alive. How?"

She tosses a grin over her shoulder, and her bodyguard enters. "A man with eagle eyes and biceps like his would let no harm come to Chester Wainwright's wife."

"But . . ."

She pats my hand. "Long story, Lily. Suffice to say, it was all a ruse."

"But Chester . . ."

"He knew all about it. While you were still at Berachah, my trusty guardian and I were leading Wilcox's team on a wild goose chase. To Waco and points beyond.

"You and I look enough alike to be sisters. So I dressed like you. Arranged my hair like yours. Even found a hat like one of yours. Bought a train ticket to Brownsville under the name Lily Sloat, and the crooks followed the scent."

"But you were reported dead."

"We suspected they caught onto us around Kingsville. Chester's men got the best of them in Raymondville with a rancher friend's help. We sent the wire about my death, and in the confusion, shipping the crate was delayed. At T&P Station.

"We arrived back in Fort Worth just before you and Cade met with my trusty guardian." She shoots the man a wink. "Being the wife of a private detective with a host of enemies warrants a body guard. Mine's the best."

Her gaze rounds the gathering. "Chester contacted the sheriff. And here we are."

My eyes flick to Cade who's standing at the cold fireplace with an elbow cocked on the mantel and an ankle crossed over the other. "How did you escape?"

"They gagged and tied me up in Panther's storage room. Drugged Beulah and Opal and carted them to the train station. Sheriff turned up with Tad—"

I sit straight up. "Tad and the two little girls are alright?"

He nods with a satisfied grin. "Star's at home with him and his sisters. She's made a break. And those two little girls are in their parents' arms. The notes you pinned under their hems saved them."

I flash a glance at Ella. "I thought of how you use the inside of your hem to dry your tears. Figured I could do the same for notes."

Ella chuckles. "You've shown real courage, Lily. And a heap of creativity."

"So everyone's in their places." I point a finger at Ella and Andrew and the girls. Ida and Philip. Donnie. "Even Wally." My finger moves from one precious soul to another.

Heads nod around the room.

I ease into the divan's back, pensive. "What will happen to Walter and Sabina?"

Snapping a glance at my brother, Cade clears his throat. "Up to the law now."

Awash with gratitude and . . . emptiness, perhaps . . . I force my gaze away from Cade, though my eyes pitch a mighty battle. I focus on my hands, swollen from the shuttle pricks.

Veins crawl across the backs of my hands like blue earthworms. "Walter's blood flows through my veins, no matter what the law decides."

"Lily?" Mrs. Upchurch's expression of anticipation is laced with dread. "May I speak with you in private? Ida and Ella and Flora are welcome, too."

Puzzled, I watch the room grow still. "Of course."

Seated in my bedroom's conversation nook, I gaze from Mrs. Upchurch to Ida and from Ella to Flora.

"Whatever can be so important—and momentous, I assume from your expressions?" I've laid aside my evening bag and changed into a loose-fitting morning dress. I twist the ends of the satin waist ribbon around a finger, curious but leery too.

Mrs. Upchurch scoots to the padded edge of her straight-backed chair. "Your shuttle . . ."

"My mother's tatting tool?" I'm careful to be precise.

"May I examine it?"

I remove the pistol from my bag and upend the pouch. The lace-making implement drops into her palm. The rosewood's patina reflects the the lamp's golden glow, as gentle as mist.

Flora startles. "That's Hebrew."

I can only stare.

She shrugs. "I'm Jewish. Family name's Zinn. My great-grandfather changed to Zane when he emigrated from England and converted to Christianity. He wanted to avoid the bias some show toward Jews, even here in America."

Silence slips between us as I gaze into my new friend's eyes. "I have an old diary of sorts—a multi-generational chronicle of the past century and a half. I think you'll find it interesting." What other commonalities might await us?

Mrs. Upchurch takes the shuttle in hand and inhales deeply. "Surprises have become commonplace recently. Speaking of which . . . I've seen a shuttle like this, and I've been chewing on how the rare creation could've been duplicated. I've come to the conclusion it couldn't. One such tatting shuttle exists. I believe I know its origin and how it came into your possession."

I sense a life-altering moment descending like multicolored gauze. "Go on. Please."

Setting the shuttle aside, she leans toward me. "Remember our Waco mission and the Dallas soup kitchen?"

I nod, wondering what either has to do with me.

"One of the Waco women was named Rowena. She had suffered beatings. We offered her shelter, but she wouldn't accept. Said doing so would put us in danger. We explained our planned Dallas mission and invited her to accompany us."

She heaves out a deep breath. "In '94, shortly after we moved to Dallas, she showed up on our front porch. With a two-year-old daughter."

My eyes cling to her gentle countenance. Must I draw the story from her? "What became of them?"

"We tended them. Rowena was delirious at times, mumbled about coming from North Carolina. Something about a planter's son and getting his tobacco to market."

"Was she a prostitute?"

"Never knew for sure. But when she recuperated, we shared the details of our plan for a home for desperate women."

"How did she react?"

"She said, 'What a blessing.' And to thank us, she drew up a house plan."

"A what?"

"She was an artist. She drew the plan for our mission grounds. The dormitory, Tabernacle, and outbuildings. Her little girl played with tiny dolls atop the drawing, a dollhouse of sorts."

A pained expression passes over her face. "She ran away while we slept. In '96."

I recall the sensation of having come home in this woman's house. I close my eyes and shake my head. A memory reemerges. I spilled a tin of Ma's buttons, and they scattered across old floor planks, some mounding and others rolling away. A few fell between the boards, lodging just out of reach—spots of color like paint dribbles.

Has an old button fallen into a crack in my memory, hiding just beyond my reach?

"Why should Rowena and her daughter interest me two decades later?"

She grips my hands. Her palms are warm, but mine have chilled.

"The little girl was bright and precocious and her beauty equally captivating. Her complexion was the color of peaches."

A flush travels up my neck and over my cheeks. The scar beneath my bodice throbs with each heartbeat. Phantom pain. But misery all the same.

"Her eyes were extraordinary." This godly woman—and mother herself—gazes from my hands to my hair and eyes. "They were no ordinary shade of green, mind you. Brighter than emeralds." Her features congeal with her wide brown eyes staring into the past.

"What is it?"

"Like how you said Cade describes yours . . . the foxfire's light."

"It's possible . . ." Ella holds my focus like a magnet. "Rowena and Ruby are one and the same. And you're that little girl."

I give a startled gasp. "You're suggesting my mother lived all those years with a false identity?"

Mrs. Upchurch's eyebrows arch above her rounded eyes. "Knowing Rowena, she would have wanted a fresh start for her daughter."

"So Walter was one of her customers? And I'm the result?" If Ma was caught in a web of darkness, she believed she had no other choice. Full of grace even then, she did it for me. Nothing can change my love for her. But to think Walter begat me under such abusive circumstances adds another layer of revulsion for him.

"Don't know that for certain." Mrs. Upchurch squeezes my hands, as if to reassure me.

"Just because the child's hair and eyes were like mine doesn't mean . . ." The initial shock gives way to denial. "You can't know Rowena was Ma. The whole thing's outlandish." I retrieve my hands. I need them to think straight. Twisting the ends of my waist ribbons around my forefingers, my fingertips throb.

She sits back. "Tell me more about your mother. What was her maiden name?"

"Her name was Ruby. Don't know her maiden name. She married Walter Sloat before '92, the year of my birth. We moved to Indian Territory when I was maybe four years old."

I release a memory-sodden breath. "Never made anything of herself, not even her appearance. Her back was crooked from work in the fields. And poor nutrition."

"And her features?"

"Her hair was the color of a scuttle pot in need of polishing, tarnished-like. Her skin was rough like leather left out in the rain, abandoned to the hot sun. But then she washed in the creek with homemade soap. Her eyes were hazel, sage-like. Her mind was quick, her spirit fiery. Loved me with her life."

My questioner nods. "Did she ever speak of Texas?"

"No, but there's a drawing." I open the old tome and thumb to the back. "Here."

She draws her magnifying glass closer. "That's Fort Worth's panther."

"Ma could've seen it in a newspaper."

She takes the shuttle in hand. "You won't find a tatting shuttle in every home nowadays. Certainly not one carved from a solid piece of rosewood. Or inlaid with Hebrew."

I imagine the implement not in the bright light of the electric lamp, but in a ship's dark hold, in the hand of a woman who spoke Hebrew, a woman named Rachel.

"Rowena was a masterful lace maker."

"I never knew Ma to tat a day in her life."

"Rowena held this very shuttle. And I know the meaning of the Hebrew."

Desperate to clear my mind, I shake my head. How could Ruby Sloat have come into possession of this object? "What does it mean?"

"Blessing."

"All right . . ."

"But spoken in Hebrew . . . It's *berachah*. Rowena suggested it for our mission home."

I lean against my chair back and knead my forehead. A sense of awe and serendipity like the lining up of planets washes over me. My thoughts agitate, churn-like. "Did this woman from your past possess anything besides the shuttle?"

"An old trunk."

I wrap my arms around my belly. "Describe it."

"It was a dark wood. She called it—"

"Bog wood?"

"That's it. Said it soaked and hardened in a bog long ago."

I know without asking, but I must. "Any identifying marks?"

"If I remember right, a date and a monogram were carved in the lid."

"And its contents?" A button tin rattles in my memory.

"Other than clothing for herself and her child. And the shuttle, I wouldn't know."

"Did she read a Bible?" I glance at my mother's on the bedside table.

"Indeed. Morning and night." Tapping a forefinger on her chin, she focuses on the ceiling. Then points at Ma's old tome. "She wrote in a diary. Like that one."

Lost buttons emerge from cracks and fall into straight lines, but I can only stare, bewildered.

"Have you found any birth records?"

"Only in the Bible. I don't recognize the names."

"Rowena's last name was Maddox. But then most of the women took on aliases. For their families' sakes."

"What am I to make of this?"

Ida smiles at my question. "I'd suggest you have family you've never met."

"And your mother meant for you to find the shuttle." Mrs. Upchurch smiles, this time with mirth. "And knock on Berachah's door."

Goosebumps tickle my skin. "I'm going to get some answers from Walter Sloat if I have to pull them from him."

CHAPTER 46

Sheriff Rae's eyes widen, deepening the crevices in his forehead. "You want to speak to Simon Wilcox, ma'am?"

"He's Walter Sloat to me, sir. I called him Pa until he killed my mother."

Cade, who accompanied me to the sheriff's office, punches the air with a fist. "An Oklahoma jury believed his lies over Lily's eye-witness truth. Judge called the jury's ruling profoundly shameful. Ever hear a judge make such a pronouncement?"

The sheriff gazes at his feet. "Don't reckon I have." He switches his focus to me. "So you want to speak to the prisoner."

I nod. "I'd've been in here yesterday if you weren't out of town. I have some questions for that man."

One of his eyebrows peaks, and the other slouches toward an eye lid. "What sort of questions?"

"Family questions. No one can answer them but him."

"Be seated, Miss Sloat." He offers me a straight-backed armchair and relaxes in his cracked leather desk chair. He taps the end of an ink pen on a blotter, as if musing over my request. "The man might be willing to . . . cooperate with the district attorney . . . provide the answers you're seeking. For consideration of leniency."

"What do you mean?"

"We're looking for names. Others in that underground he's aligned with. He answers your questions—and mine—and the DA might lighten his sentence."

"It rankles that Walter would avoid a single hour he's earned in prison."

Sheriff Rae stands at the window with his hands in his pockets. "Your snapshots provide evidence we can use at trial. We might get a confession and names of others involved without making a deal."

"I can't imagine how."

"I take it neither of you has much regard for the other."

I harrumph. "You can say that."

"And you know how to rile him up?"

I release a brittle chortle. "Oh, I riled him up enough to beat me to the edge of death."

The sheriff mulls, rocking on his boot heels. He turns to Cade. "You're deputized, but Wilcox doesn't know it. How 'bout you sit in with Miss Sloat and when he's hot enough under the collar, throw some fuel on the fire. Maybe he'll put out some names without intending to."

Cade's cheeks pucker in glee. "When do we start?"

"Now's fine with me. How 'bout you two?"

"Been waiting a lifetime to see justice done." Growling, I stand.

"Come on." The lawman leads us to a separate cement-block building for lawbreakers.

Inside, a deputy sits with his feet on the desk. He slams them to the floor and stands, soldier-like. "What can I do for you, Sheriff?"

"Bring the Wilcox prisoner to the interview room."

"Yes sir," the man replies and scurries away.

Sheriff Rae ushers us into a windowless space with a table bolted to the floor. Cade and I sit in secured chairs on one side of the table. The deputy leads in Walter and chains him to a bolted chair on the other side. Leaning on a shoulder with his booted feet crossed, Sheriff Rae assumes a casual stance in a corner.

Walter's grooming has deteriorated in two days. His foul breath spoils the air. "What'd ya want?"

"Answers."

He grimaces. "Don't owe none of you answer one."

Sheriff gives a single-shouldered shrug. "It might be to your advantage to answer."

Walter eyes us, suspicious-like.

I cross my arms atop the table, and my mind circles for ways to stir up the man. "I've done some digging here in Fort Worth. Found some interesting records."

"Yeah? Like what?"

"Like the two ladies of the night found murdered and floating in the Trinity. Summer of '96." Sheriff Rae runs his fingers over his beard stubble. "And a certain slouch who hung around Hell's Half Acre, the last one seen near those ladies. A good-for-nothing fitting your description."

Walter sits up straight. "Now wait a minute. I ain't got nothing to do with no killing of soiled doves. I weren't in Fort Worth in '96."

"Someone's willing to testify that you were. Someone from Wild Gardenia."

"That's a lie!"

My eyes draw into slits. "I'm to believe a word you speak when I know you as I do?"

"Why should I care, girlie? I knew your ma back in the '90s. Them do-gooder Upchurches found her on a street corner and took her in. Got her in at Black Panther and Wild Gardenia in '96. If not for me she'd've been stirrin' up business along Cowtown tracks or at the stockyards. I gave her what she deserved in the end—a hole in the ground."

"You admit to killing my mother?"

"Can't try me for the same crime twice. So, yeah, I smothered your beanpole ma. Had all I could take of 'er. But I ain't never killed no harlot."

"So my mother wasn't a harlot after all."

"Uh . . . Well now . . ."

"That's what I thought. If she was working at Black Panther and Wild Gardenia, she was doing the laundry. You haven't a single bone of compassion. Hadn't been for Betsy and Ella, I'd be dead at your hand."

"Earned it. Girl as impertinent as you deserved ever' lick you got."

Cade bolts from his chair and grabs the neck of Walter's prison garb, pressing him against his chair back. Sheriff Rae pries Cade off him.

I recognize telltale signs of Walter's ire reaching fever pitch, so I bore in. "My mother was made of better stuff than you. Fine stuff. How'd you convince her to marry the likes of you?"

His neck flushes. The redness rises into his cheeks and forehead. "Your ma was nothin' but a common—"

"She was a queen among women." I spout spittle with my words.

Sheriff plants his hands on the table, glaring at the prisoner. "You admitted involvement at Wild Gardenia in '96."

Walter's eyes widen, crazed-like. "Naw. . . uh . . ." He jerks his gaze around the room. "I reckon that was later on . . . '98, it was."

I point a forefinger at his nose. "You were sharecropping in Indian Territory in '98. Your wife was doing the crop tending, and I was towing a sack alongside her. Six years old."

He smirks. "Your fancy words don't mean nothing to me. I know where you come from."

"The deepest sorrow of my life is knowing your blood flows through my veins."

"You're slow, girlie. Why . . ." He halts mid-sentence, his eyes flicking side to side and his upper lip raised, as if chewing on a bitter cud. He laces his fingers together in his lap, prayer-like. "You're mine, Lily girl. Won't nothing change that." He flashes a licentious grin. "Peep. Peep."

Memory's fingers prod, but I shoo them away, ignore his barbs. "My mother was an artist. She drew the plans for Berachah, and I played house on them."

"There's plenty you'd give your right arm to know, but . . ." He examines his fingernails, trimmed and clean and bearing not a hint of Oklahoma soil. "My memory's not what it used to be. Might need some priming."

"You forced Ma and me into Indian Territory."

He chortles. "Ruby would cooperate or I'd sell you to a brothel."

So that's how he controlled her.

"I was four. I lay on quilts in the old trunk in the back of a creaky wagon. The lid was wedged open. I remember a lullaby and pretending

I was in a fancy cradle. Trees were russet colored. Nights were cold. It was the fall of '96. You're not smart enough to make me believe anything else."

His mouth turns down at the corners. "I shoulda killed ya when I had a chance."

I smile. "Looks like you should've."

"Come on." Adjusting his Stetson, Cade eases me to my feet. "Can't bear the stench."

I turn back to the evil doer. "I know about Waco. Wild Gardenia. And you dragging us to Indian Territory in '96 after those poor women were found in the Trinity. We sharecropped for the McFarlands until you absconded with my mother and brother in '05. I know about you and Sabina here in Cowtown. And your partners farther south—Johnson and Villegas."

Rearing back, he guffaws. "You know nothin'. Never seen hide nor hair of my real partner. Why, Jeremiah Stone and his bunch . . ." He halts, having spouted two words too many.

I expel a deep, satisfied sigh. "Get that, Sheriff?"

The lawman nods. "Jeremiah Stone."

"Thank you very much, Walt." I speak with satisfaction but no joy. "I'm going on with my life. In Ma's words, may God have mercy on your soul."

CHAPTER 47

$\mathscr{T}$hree days later, the North Texas landscape passes in a blur outside my train window and with it, clouds of memories. I've achieved my goals. My loved ones are safe. But family recollections have coalesced in a mire murkier than ever. Only the colors have changed.

What am I to do with the bewildering stew?

The morning *Caller* reported battles in far-off places with strange names—Etreux, Le Cateau, Komarow, and Tsingtao—and an Allied retreat, as well as a victory in China. Rachel Lloyd came to mind as I read reports of the conflict, wondering what battles she fought, what agony she endured so long ago. And what lies ahead for me, even still.

Grateful Walter and Sabina are in the hands of the law and Mrs. Upchurch and the Berachah mothers are free of fear, I consider my traveling companions, each safer than ever before.

Donnie and Blossom sit side by side, their heads all but touching, no doubt whispering secrets. My two loved ones are homeward bound.

Ida sits to my right. Her back's bent, but her smile lights her features. Philip's driving the Daimler back to Oklahoma. He's but one of scores of young people Ida prepared for the high road of life. And he's returning her love and grace.

Ella and Andrew are seated in front of the others. She leans against her husband, her head resting on his strong shoulder, heedless to her beloved's shortened arm as an amputee. She saved my life, and her husband has enriched it. No finer man walks Earth's sod.

Six girls stretch out beyond the beloved couple, their heads four lemon drops and two chocolate bonbons. They giggle and tease, oblivious to their scrumptious beauty and spirit. Someday they'll realize the great bounty of the love into which they were placed.

More than sense, I *feel* Cade's nearness. His hand grips my seat back, warming my left shoulder. His breaths are audible and stir a wisp that's escaped my hat. He hums, and the rich baritone envelopes me like velvet wrappings.

I know without shifting around that the stubborn forelock that falls carelessly across his forehead is daring me to turn and swipe it back. My fingertips tingle.

How am I to batten my heart against this onslaught?

My brother slips into the space beside me. "Been thinking."

I pat his knee. "About what?"

He runs a forefinger and a thumb over his chin stubble, reminiscent of Cade. "Broadview."

I smile my satisfaction and relief. "Isn't it wonderful? You and I can live under the same roof again—and what a glorious roof it is."

Frown lines mar his smooth forehead. Freckles clump. "Do I belong there?"

I note through the far window the road that runs parallel to the tracks. A shiny new roadster speeds around a jiggling jalopy.

"You belong wherever I am, brother mine."

"When Miss Addie comes home, her society friends won't take a hankerin' . . . That is, they won't approve of a Sloat like me."

"I understand, but I hope you won't let others determine your course in life. Besides, Addie wants you at Broadview."

"Yea, but Miss Addie's nice. Those society folks ain't . . . aren't."

I hold his callused hand. "Remember Broadview's hens?"

"I do. We walked out back to the chicken yard. Behind that stand of sumacs. Broadview's hens ain't . . . aren't like ours back home."

"Broadview's chicken yard affords a rooster and his harem space to roam. We watched awhile, and I pointed out certain of the hens. Remember?"

"Sure do. Those black-spotted ones were fat and sassy."

"They've enjoyed Broadview's bounty a long time."

"And the plain browns were new to the place. Scrawny."

"We talked about how the spotted hens treated the brown ones."

"Not at all friendly."

"The brown ones are a fine breed of chickens. Given time, they show it."

He sits in silence, his tightened jaw muscle a sure sign he's ruminating. "I know what you're saying, but a hen can grow fat and sassy only so long—"

"Remember, brother? One brown hen in particular was mangy and foul tempered as a hornet, the sorriest looking chicken that ever flapped off the delivery truck. The others tried to push her aside, but she stood her ground, and before long, she was Mr. Rooster's favorite companion. She's given him more baby chicks than all the others put together. I'd wager he's glad she stayed around."

He peers into my eyes. "She's grown a heap of feathers. I can round out nice, too, with Maggie setting the table. But there's one thing that hen's got that I ain't . . . don't."

"What's that?"

"Straight legs."

Hidden away in a tarpaper shack, how can he be anything but guileless?

Voices blend amiably around us as I search for a response that fits. Daunting. Perhaps I'll leave the subject of bowed legs for another time.

I stretch an arm around his shoulders. "What have I heard, brother mine?"

"Don't know. What have you heard?"

"Proper grammar."

"Oh, that. Ida's gotten hold of my tongue and taught it some lessons."

I squeeze his shoulder, and silence returns.

He leans toward the window glass with his nose all but smashed against it. "You figure our mother can see us from Heaven?".

I shift on the bench seat. How am I to know? "Maggie says she can. So do Ida and Ella." Andrew nods and points to Scripture. And Addie claims it's knowing Jesus is watching her that keeps her on her toes. "Does it matter?"

"Been wondering what our mother would tell me." Air whistles between his lips and through his teeth, as if forcing extra drafts into his lungs. His pulse throbs in his neck.

Gazing at his chipped-tooth grimace of concentration, all at once I know. "She'd speak the same blessing she spoke over me. 'The Good Lord saw fit to set you on the other side of the creek. For His purposes. Best you seek Him.'"

Donnie cants his head sideways. "That what you're doin'? Seeking the Lord?"

My brother's innocence slaps me across the face.

I crossed Rock Creek years ago. Traveled at Addie's side for a decade. Beheld innumerable sights outside train windows, carriages, and coaches. Memories clickity-clack.

I journeyed to Fort Worth in search of Blossom and dreams for women. I longed for answers to the questions my ma's old chest unearthed, and Mrs. Upchurch brought me closer. I helped the McGregors. And saw Walter and Sabina brought to justice.

Was I seeking the Lord? Or was He tracking me?

Another ball of yarn to unravel.

Ida debarks at Ardmore, and another of the Jackson boys waits to drive her back home. We continue to Westwood where Philip meets us in the Daimler. A solid rain yesterday left the roads rutted and tricky to maneuver, but our exceedingly crowded journey to Broadview is studded with incessant chatter and laughter.

Maggie greets us in Broadview's circular drive. Before I have a chance to speak a word to Ella and Andrew—or Cade—she sweeps Donnie and me to the veranda. I stand with an arm wrapped around a pillar and my eyes trained on the Daimler, humming toward the cottage and Cade gazing at me out the back window.

Wiping her hands on her apron, Maggie comes to my side. "You and I are blessed—"

"Your daughter's locked up, likely for the rest of her life. That's blessed?"

She releases a weighted sigh. "I've feared this for years. Lord's been preparing me. Consumed with envy, bitterness, hatred, my daughter could come to no other end." She dabs a tear from an eye. "I can only pray for her."

I slip my hand into hers. "I love you."

"Aye. And I, you." She halts at the front threshold. "You're my household of blessings."

After supper I show Donnie to his suite in the downstairs hallway. He shoos me out, feigning exhaustion. Surely he's ruminating on where he belongs.

I return to the kitchen and find my breath stolen away by Cade, leaning at a jaunty angle against the door jamb, his thumbs hooked into his pants pockets. We've not been out of one another's sight for days, but gazing upon him . . . at home . . . is indefinably thrilling.

I gawk, slack-jawed and unable to find my voice. How am I to keep my thoughts straight with Cade McFarland near?

"Got chores." Maggie scampers out as if she's a list of tasks as long as her arm.

I know better.

Cade and I lock gazes.

Does his heart skip a beat like mine?

Does his breath come in short, rapid spurts like mine?

He rights himself and opens his arms. "Mighty fine, having you home."

"Yes." I step toward him, and he does the same.

His arms surrounded me, and he lays a hand on my head.

My fingers move across his back, absorbing the glorious, heart-stopping feel of him.

He cups my face in his hands. "Is it proper for a friend to kiss a friend on the forehead?"

I nod.

His lips leave a spot of warmth on my brow.

"May a friend kiss a friend on the cheek?"

I nod.

His lips are cool against my heated skin.

"And the nose?'

"Hmm. I reckon."

His lips hover above my mouth. "Is it proper for a friend to kiss . . ."

I wrench away, stunned at my boldness.

"What is it?" Cade holds me, as if claiming me as his own.

"Well, I. . ."

"Let's talk outside." Applying pressure to my back, he guides me to the back garden and points to a wicker chair. "Sit."

"For heaven's sakes, Cade, what's gotten into you?"

"It's important." His tone has turned serious.

I take the wicker, leaving the iron for his substantial frame.

"How'd the crops fare while you were away?" I experience a sudden case of chills.

"I'm here to discuss you and me, not the crops."

"All right," I answer, fearful of what comes next.

"As I told you before, I have no pride where you're concerned."

"Cade . . ."

He holds up a hand to halt me. "Hear me out, Lily."

My insides churn.

"I'm repeating myself, but I love you. Always have and always will. I want you to be my wife. I want to build you the house you've dreamed of but never would admit. I know it's there in your imagination, Lily. Draw it, and I'll build it."

Riveted, I'm speechless as Cade McFarland—once again—asks a murdering beast's daughter to be his wife. The last time he proposed, I blamed my reticence on caring for my brother. Broadview. Blossom.

The war in Europe. The women's movement. And women making a difference in courtrooms.

What words will I speak?

Disfigurement lies between my heart and Cade's. One man scarred me. Another seeks to banish the pocks. But even Cade McFarland can do nothing of the sort. He can cover them, but nothing can erase them.

Or change the color of my Sloat blood from black to red.

He slips the three-stoned emerald ring from a pocket.

Can I accept it when I hide unspeakable ugliness. But how am I to live without the man who owns my heart?

He reaches for my left hand, but I shove him and the love bauble away. I bound to my feet, thrust aside the wicker, and scramble inside. Up the stairs. To bed.

CHAPTER 48

I can't. Can't expose the scars. Can't even acknowledge them. I've not an iota of strength to reveal what a husband needs to know.

Securing the lock, I rip blouse buttons from holes. Fling slippers aside. Scatter my traveling attire to the far corners of the room. And tug a cotton nightgown over my head. Shucking aside bedcovers, I slip between lemon-scented sheets and force them over my head.

Boots, surely composed of steel, buffet the staircase. Was the balustrade shaking?

A heavy hand pounds. "Open up, Lily!"

I sit up. Cade? Outside my bedroom?

"I'm fed up with your running away. Open up! Not leaving 'til you do."

Cade's passion . . . his fury . . . astounds me. "Go away," I squeak.

"I won't. Open up, or I'll break in!"

Has the man gone mad?

Flinging aside the sheets, I stamp to the door. "You'll do nothing of the sort." I spout with my nose all but pressed against the oak. "You *will*, however, *leave*."

Silence, save Cade's bellowed breaths and the call of the mockingbird outside. I hope the feathered bachelor has found a mate. What a farcical thought at a time like this.

Cade rattles the brass knob, the jamb. "You've not heard the last from me. I'm finished with your hide-and-seek garden-party game. Hear me? Finished!"

His boot heels pummel the carpeted hallway, sending tremors through the floor.

I step into the hallway and squint as he rounds the corner, all but swearing with each tread. He slams the front door, and the beveled glass rattles.

I stumble to bed, my innards splintered.

Hours melt into days like lard in a hot skillet.

Cade shows up on Saturday, and Maggie extends an excuse.

Others see to daily routines. Maggie gardens. Ella tends house. Blossom snaps photographs and writes stories. Donnie copies her, and Wally loafs beside him, slobbering.

Sunday morning arrives. The downstairs bustle. The Cadillac coughs and sputters, then purrs. The household's headed to Christ Church.

The heat is abominable. I steal from my bed and open the door, allowing a cross draft.

Ladies' hand fans are aflutter at the church, but life has gone out of me. My heart's sore. My monthly courses have come with all the pain I've endured for years without speaking a word of it to anyone.

For what purpose? My womb will produce nothing.

The heat intensifies as the noon hour nears. The family returns, and Maggie delivers a tray of chilled fruit and clabbered milk. Mercifully, she leaves me to my misery.

"I'm sorry, Cade. She's feeling no better." Maggie's unwelcome words steal upstairs.

Curiosity gains a toehold, and I sneak into the hallway.

"But it's been three days. What did Doc report?" The lament in Cade's voice reaches inside me and twists.

"Not much, really. He'll return in the morning."

"Will you give Lily these?"

"Ahh, they're from your mother's garden. Beautiful."

"Tell her they're passion flowers. And I love her."

A hand flies to my chest where misery is building.

"I will, Cade. Maybe tomorrow." Her tone conveys her own dismay. Devoid of the strength, I droop to the floor. A sob elbows my chest walls, but I tamp it down. Last time I wept was for my dear mother. I'll not shed a tear for myself.

Back in bed, I flutter my top sheet. "Be gone, heartache.," I whisper.

Footsteps tread the stairs, and Maggie enters with a tray. "A row between friends—even bitter . . . 'Tis never long." Her homespun wisdom provides little comfort.

Pressed against the headboard, I remain as silent as stone.

Thunder grumbles in the distance.

She pours, and steam curls above our cups. A square of sugar for her. A spot of cream for me. Our silver teaspoons create a symphony of clinks against china.

A bolt of lightning strikes nearby, brightening the room. A clap of thunder follows, rattling the china and jolting us upward.

"Heavens!" She races to the window. "Sky's cobbled with black clouds." She returns to my side. "Looks like it's moving on though." Her eyes find mine. "Whatever's forced you to bed, you must answer Cade."

I bury my face in a pillow and groan.

"A wren has need of naught but her nest." Whispering a prayer, she leaves me to my turmoil and heartbreak.

She's right. Cade deserves an explanation. But how will I speak the words?

At length, a soft knock sounds. The knob turns, and the door eases open. "Lily?"

Ella. Now I must withstand Cade's twin? I tug the sheet over my head.

The mattress lowers with a faint squeak. "I wouldn't intrude under ordinary circumstances, but this isn't ordinary. Am I right?" She speaks in her uniquely kind tone.

My silence replies.

"You don't have to look at me, Lily. Stay where you are, and I'll explain what I'm thinking. If I'm wrong, please forgive me and forget I ever spoke. But if I'm right . . . Oh, Lily, I pray you'll hear me."

She clears her throat, nervous-like. "Mama and I found you on the verge of death. I tended your wounds. Bathed you. I know what Walter did to you. All of it."

Ella knows the worst? And still wants me for her beloved brother?

"On my wedding day," she continues, "Mama spoke of my gown's symbolism and tradition. You listened, as quiet as a dove. Her words touched you in ways we never dreamed.

"I believe your love for Cade is so true you'll deny yourself a world of happiness to spare him what you imagine will crush him."

Beneath the lemony sheet, I snap my eyes shut, and my thoughts tumble like a whirligig.

"Hear me, sister-of-my-heart. If I'm right, you don't know Cade." The mattress wiggles upward. "I pray you'll give him a chance to show you what he's made of."

With a gentle click of the knob, Ella treads softly away.

I know what Cade's made of all too well. That's why I must turn him down.

Crawling for the light, I scratch at a wall of darkness and open my eyes.

"Welcome back." Ida's silver hair glows. Subdued sunlight glimmers through window panes kept sparkling with vinegar water.

"You came."

She nods and seats herself beside me.

"What time is it? What day?"

"Monday morning." She points to the wall clock. "Ten o'clock. Overcast sky."

I run fingers over my brow. "I've been in bed three days?"

"You escaped into a deep sleep. Ella visited. And others called."

I sit up and swing my feet to the floor. The room twirls around me. "Whoa."

She fluffs the pillows and eases me against them. "Three days abed with no food, and you can expect your head to spin." She stands with her fists at his waist. "Maggie's stirred up a bite to eat. Promise to stay where you are?"

"I promise." What choice has one as frail as dandelion down?

Ida's ever-bending form fades into the hallway.

Faint kitchen sounds trickle upward. A clink of glass. The swat of a cabinet door.

I wonder . . . What might I hear over yonder, where I come from?

Ida reenters with a food tray, the aroma of chicken broth preceding her. "Soup's on."

"Chicken soup?"

She nods and sets the tray on the bedside table. Steam rises from the bowl. "It's hot, but you'll draw strength from it." She snaps open a cotton napkin and tucks it under my chin. "The Lord has brought you home."

But can Donnie view this grand estate as home?

And—oh—the home Cade longs to build us. Can I bear to live with him so near?

Thunder grumbles long and low in the distance.

"Rain's coming." She arranges pillows at my back. "I've yet to see you weep. Tears clear the soul of poison." Setting the tray on my lap, she swipes her face with her apron and murmurs words of a different cadence, a different tone. Soothing. A Chickasaw prayer.

Ladling soup to my lips, she speaks of the mysterious nature of God's divine loom, how He weaves colors—the brights, the dulls, and the blacks—into a stunning tapestry of life.

I bite back a sharp-edged retort: Why're some—like Ma's—nothing but dull threads?

Broth dribbles down my chin and onto the napkin.

I snatch the spoon. "I'm not a complete invalid."

She grunts. "Could've fooled me."

Moving to the bay window, she turns her head left, right, and above. "A solid rain would do for the crops what you did for the women of

Fort Worth and Arlington. Even Dallas. Sabina's articles only whetted readers' appetites for more about you.

"Your talks at the women's clubs. Your foray into Battercake Flats. Closing down Wild Gardenia and the kidnapping ring. Exposing Sabina sand shutting down the opposition in Arlington's Thursday Club. You lit a fire under women's skirt tails."

"Delicious." I drop the spoon alongside the bowl. "As far as news stories and women's rights . . . I'm plumb tuckered out, as Ma would say. Finished with it all."

She sets the tray aside. "It's time to tell you my story."

I straighten against the pillows, wide eyed.

"I married a fine man from Ohio. Had a baby boy. My husband fought in the War, alongside my tribal brothers. He was imprisoned at Camp Chase. Died there."

"Oh . . ."

She smiles. "But not before leading fifty men to Christ."

"But what about you all that time?"

"I raised stock alongside my mother's brother. And took my curious four-year-old all over the land that would be his. He called the trees by name. Found rabbit burrows and birds' nests. Knew which snakes to avoid and which were harmless.

"The two of us crossed a log bridge over a creek a time or two, and he pestered me to teach him to swim. But caring for stock and pastures pushed swimming into the background."

My insides heat up. I fear where the story is headed.

"One day we followed the creek to the south pasture. The horses were together, all but one little filly with more spirit than she could hold. I whistled to her, but she whipped around and raced away.

"She tripped over an old broken fence and went down. I dropped my boy's hand and shouted over my shoulder, 'Run!'

"I fell to my knees beside her. Her front legs were broken. I laid my head on her side and talked to her.

"'Gotta put her out of her misery, son.' I reached for my boy, but he was nowhere in sight. I called. And circled the pasture. But down in the marrow of my bones I knew . . . My boy had run to the creek."

Closing her eyes and releasing a heavy sigh, she presses her hands against her mouth, stifling hoarse, racking sobs. The veins in her neck protrude.

Dread holds me still.

"I found my little boy. Floating face-down. My uncle heard my wails and came running. He found me promising my son I'd teach him to swim in the morning."

"My heart's breaking." I mumble the words as tears threaten.

"But then I received an invitation to work with Chickasaw orphans. Rather than rattle around in my little house and on my tear-soaked land, I packed up a wagon and headed for Jackson. That was 1865. Forty-nine years ago, and it seems like yesterday."

"How could you survive it?"

"*I* couldn't, but Jesus *in* me could. No longer my own, my life belonged to a God of love and the children He sent me. Haven't regretted a moment."

"A husband, a child, both taken from you. How is this a picture of love?"

"My boy ran out of my sight, but he never left God's. His Father in Heaven watched him jump in. Held him while his lungs filled with water. And embraced him as he passed into Glory. Did the same for me as I entered Jackson Academy's gates."

I dab at an eye. Is that a tear? "I understand comfort in sorrow, but why allow the sorrow in the first place?"

"Can't explain His reasons, but Father God knew each little one He would place in my palms." She raises both hands. "Forty-nine years of young ones with no one to hold them but me. By God's grace, I'll embrace my boy again. We'll swim in the River of Life first thing."

She turns her raven-black eyes to me. "Love is from God. Your love for Cade and his for you come from your Heavenly Father. You can't know His plans for your love if you deny it, bridle it, or bury it. You'll know His plans for your love by living it."

I examine my palms. Will I ever look at them the same way again?

A bolt of lightning strikes nearby, brightening the room. A clap of thunder follows, rattling the china plates on the wall and jolting us upward.

"Heaven preserve us." She scrambles to the window. "Hail's pelting the grounds."

Out the bay window lightning daggers a sky cobbled with billows of gunmetal gray tinged with green.

"Looks fierce, Ida."

She nods.

A sudden commotion commences below us, and foot treads pound the staircase, drawing our eyes toward—

"Twister!" Maggie shouts and flings aside my door.

CHAPTER 49

A chill greets us in the utility room. Lightning flashes in an ominous, green-tinged cloud bank to the southwest. A heavy darkness descends.

Nabbing a shawl and with a lantern in hand, I open the cellar door. "Maggie? Donnie?"

"We're all here." Her voice brings a wave of comfort.

We descend into the cellar Adelaide's grandfather built beneath the original house, a fine root cellar and storm shelter.

A musty scent hovers, the air thick. We draw our shawls tight against the chill.

"The cold of the south wind means rain." More Irish wisdom.

"Let's pray that's all it brings." Ida's voice remains steady and sure.

Vernon and three household staff members huddle on a bench against a far wall. We gather beside them, clutching one another.

Thunder booms, and we cover our ears at the rumble of a train bearing down.

"Dear God, spare us." Maggie's plea is little more than a croak. "And our loved ones."

Crashes sound above. Glass shatters.

What lies in store for us?

The storm resounds above our heads. Great whirling roars reverberate. Is the world disintegrating above us?

We tighten our grips.

I look to Ida. Her eyes are closed, her lips moving. Her expression remains placid.

Years ago a twister took the lives of twenty citizens of Glover County.

Reduced homes and barns like the McFarlands' to piles of lumber. Ravaged pastures and crops. Corkscrewed picket fences around trees. Peppered the landscape with chicken feathers. And cast livestock into the next county.

Surely the creator of heaven and earth won't allow a storm to descend on the McFarlands. Not again.

My mother's God . . . Ida's . . . Maggie's and the McFarlands' will spare us. Won't He?

The tumult ceases abruptly, and we survivors snap our eyes upward.

"It's over," Ida proclaims.

But what has it left behind?

Vernon holds the lantern aloft. "I'll go first."

We fellow survivors ascend the stairs behind him.

Hail the size of figs and glass fragments cover the utility room floor. A breeze ruffles tattered curtains.

I inch toward the kitchen, and glass crunches.

The kitchen lies in shambles, utensils strewn around, the table and chairs pitched over. Cupboard doors hang open, the stoneware shattered. The water spigot drips into the sink.

Maggie's eyes arc from one corner of the room to another. "At least the walls are standing."

"God be praised." Ida has taken her place amid the disorder.

We steal into the dining room. The ruthless wind has flung hail and hapless leaves through the shattered windows. A velvet drape hangs at an odd angle. The sideboard is littered with hail and broken crystal. The elegant crystal chandelier, mere shards on the mahogany table. Each of the sixteen chairs sit in their places as if the world hasn't shifted.

Other than shattered lamps, the hallway, entry, and staircase bear few marks.

We venture into the parlor. Portraits hang at awkward angles or have fallen, the tea service overturned on the settee. Furniture has rattled across the floor and settled in a haphazard arrangement. More hail and broken lamps—some, untouched.

A breeze carries a heavy mist through the windows. Rain splatters increase.

"I'll see to boarding up the windows." Vernon scurries away with the gardener in tow.

Opening the front doors ushers in a misty draft that tugs on my skirt and twirls strands of hair about my head.

Outside, the sky has brightened to china cup blue.

Hail carpets the veranda. The wicker, whisked away. Bittersweet vine, ripped from the trellis. A piece of siding flaps.

"The house is intact. The porch preserved the interior."

"A wise man's house stands when the winds beat upon it," Ida declares, "for it is founded upon the unmovable rock."

Considering my paternity, I wonder about the old shack across the way. And . . . "Daisy!" I bolt down the steps toward the horse barn.

"And Addie's Majesty." Maggie huffs behind me.

My horse and Addie's have kicked their stalls open and run off.

A housemaid and I head toward the pasture. The mares stand grazing on Indian grass.

"Look at that," the girl exclaims.

"You'd think a storm hadn't come near in years." I halt with a start. "Ella's family. And the McFarlands." I lope toward the sun that's fast slipping toward the horizon.

Cade meets me on my way to Ella's. "It missed us and the cottage. What about Broadview?"

"All's well."

"But look at this." He guides me over the rise.

My head snaps northward, and I stand stone still. My eyes fasten on a scene as fanciful as any made-up story. A wide, barren swath stretches before us. The thicket has been swept clean. And in the distance, beyond the creek . . .

I whip around for the car barn. "I'm going to check the old place."

"I'm coming too." Cade huffs alongside me.

Taking my roadster, we find Needham's Main Street coming alive. Townsfolk mill around the square, their expressions stunned. Flowered hats and bowlers bob along the walkways. A boy runs into the road, and a mother retrieves him. A bald head pokes out a doorway. A puff of cigar smoke through the bank's front window. A wave from inside McFarland's General Store.

We motor through town, past the post office, to the horseshoe. Venturing to where the fence stood, we step out, and our jaws slacken. The land lies barren, swept clean.

Dazed, I clump forward, and Cade comes alongside me.

Halting at the plot where the old shack once stood, its form materializes as an illusion and a vision of myself with it. The screen has fallen off and lies on its side, blocking my way. I push it aside and step into the shanty I once called home.

Don't reckon Pa can object to a judge paying a visit.

The imaginary table has fallen over with the chairs and upended logs. A different tomato crate hangs on the bare wall.

I reckon we can sip on cool well water, if you're of a mind to.

In my mind a pale rectangle forms where the old cupboard sat.

A burlap sack in the corner, torn and leaking its last few kernels of corn.

No wood in the firebox, but plenty of ashes.

A yellowed-glass bottle above the fireplace, its wildflowers dried to dust.

No mattress. No mother. *Her love for her young'uns was stronger than any fist.*

No Walter.

No Donnie.

But memories aplenty. They rattle in my head like nails in a tin box.

I startle at the sound of flour sack curtains, frayed to uselessness, flapping in a breeze.

Shaking my head, I realize my mind's playing tricks.

I sweep my gaze across the now-barren parcel. No old shack. No coop or shed. The well's just a hole in sorry soil. Indian grass and wildflowers, picked clean. No more sycamore, nor blackened circle where Donnie cooked beans and Walter heated his poker.

Filled with nameless emotions, I follow what once was an overgrown footpath.

"Lily, I'll wait for you here."

Grateful for Cade's sensitivity, I keep moving.

At the mossy outcropping, I stare across the creek at the clear, unobstructed landscape. To the right's the McFarland farm. Straight ahead, the cottage. And to the left, the wide expanse of Fitzgerald land crowned by Broadview.

The cyclone has cleared the boundary between my old and new lives. Even the creek critters have gone silent.

Where does such power reside?

Gooseflesh prickles, and I shiver in the humid heat.

I kick off my shoes and sit on the mossy outcropping, my toes skimming the water and stirring up a damselfly couple newly hatched.

Creek comes alive like a simmerin' pot when they dance.

You're free of the sorry life on this side of the creek.

Alone and beyond prying eyes and listening ears, I lie prone on the moss. The pain I've carried inside stirs and seems to seep through the blotches on my body. I pound my hands and moan. And call out . . . to whom?

To God, I hear my mother whisper. Ida and Ella echo her words. So does Cade.

"Take my pain, O Lord. Heal me." My eyes burn. I'm filled with longing and loss. And need. "Come, Jesus. Wipe me clean, deeper than my skin. Make my heart and soul Yours." I claw the mossy carpet and wail.

At length, my ever-faithful suitor joins me, his shoes and socks tossed to the side and his feet in the water. I run the backs of my hands over my nose, and my skirt hem soaks my tears.

The spring at the McFarland property line gurgles a new tune.

"I hear these are healing waters, Cade."

"I wouldn't argue that point."

I swirl a toe in the stream. "I watched you baptize folks when I was a girl. Up yonder behind the church. You and Andrew and your pa. Will you baptize me, Cade?"

He stares into my eyes, as if searching for a hidden gem. Seemingly satisfied, he slips into the creek and helps me down. "Do you believe Jesus is the Son of God?"

"I do. Truthfully, I've believed always, but I let life come between Jesus and me."

"Do you trust Him to blot out your sins? And your scars?"

Cade knows about my scars? I picture the quirt tracks, the poker burns, the slashes.

"The scars on your soul. Those in your mind. And the ones on your body. Do you trust Him to wash you so clean that when You stand before God at the end of time, He'll see you dressed in the perfect righteousness of Christ—simply flawless?"

"Oh," I stammer. A spring of tears—a lifetime of them—gushes from their hiding place, sheeting my cheeks and dripping off my chin. "Oh, to be flawless."

He holds me against his sturdy body, but below surface, our feet are treading water. That's what I've been doing all my life, yet never coming clean.

Cade prays and sets a hand on the crown of my head. "I baptize you in the name of the Father, the Son, and the Holy Spirit." He immerses me, and when I rise, his features seem to glow. "Your sins are washed away. Every inch of you is flawless, Lily."

We crawl onto the ledge. Water drips from his nose and hair onto his shoulders. I swipe my hands over my face, flinging droplets into the creek, and a puddle of tears gathers in the hollow of my throat.

Now I understand what Ida meant about good and evil. Only God is good. And only He has the answer for wickedness.

"Oh, Cade, I've carried a nameless longing inside me all my life, an empty place that nothing could fill. It's gone now. Something happened to me in that water. Peace seeped through my pores and filled the void. Filled it with Jesus."

"You've learned He's the healing waters."

I close my eyes and pray silently for strength. "I've something to share with you."

He nods, knowingly. "I've been waiting."

I unhook my top blouse button, exposing the burled hollow, soaked with tears. "I've many more besides." I hesitate and pray for strength to speak the full truth. "Doc says I'll never bear a child. That's why I can't marry you."

Tears well in his rich brown eyes and crawl down his cheeks, great lobs that put the creek water to shame. "If Jesus were to show you His scars, what would you do, my love?"

I puzzle over my answer.

Beaten and whipped, Paul saw his scars as brands for Jesus.

Once I shuddered that a person would be branded willingly. Now I understand.

"I'd kiss his scars."

"So would I." He brushes his lips, feather light, along the burled welt in my throat. "Ready to go home?"

I nod, and we retrace our steps.

Just past where the old chicken coop stood, Ma's voice turns me around. *The good Lord saw fit to spare Lily's life and set her on the other side of Rock Creek.*

I give the barren horseshoe one last glance. "Nothing can steal my mother's love, but this place has always belonged on a trash heap, not among my treasured memories. The Lord's swept it clean."

CHAPTER 50

We meet in Addie's gazebo just as the sun is ducking behind distant hills, leaving a purplish glow. "I've something for you." Cade hands me a large envelope. "Came in the mail from Mrs. Upchurch. She thought I should be with you when you read it."

"What is it?"

"Won't know 'til you open it."

Slashing the pasted tab with a fingernail, I clutch a stack of documents topped with a letter.

> *Berachah Mission Home*
> *August 22, 1914*
>
> *My dear Lily,*
>
> *The Lord reminded me of Rowena today. After she disappeared, I received a packet in the mail. Postmarked Indian Territory.*
>
> *She asked me to keep it safe. And if anything happened to her, I'd know if and when the time was right to share it.*
>
> *I'd forgotten it until I cleared out some old files, and the bundle plopped into my lap. Your face appeared, and I knew the Lord intended it for you.*
>
> *I pray this knowledge will bless you, body and soul, and new vistas will open before your eyes.*
>
> *God be with you, dear Lily.*
>
> *Mrs. Upchurch*

I lay aside the letter and gaze at a North Carolina Marriage Certificate for Rowena Simpson and William Maddox dated October 23, 1891.

Boarding stubs for Mr. and Mrs. Maddox on *Swift Swan* from Belhaven Harbor, North Carolina to Jamaica.

A newspaper clipping about a fierce storm striking our southeastern coast and the West Indies.

A Galveston, Texas Port of Entry document for Rowena Maddox dated November 6, 1891.

A Harris County Certificate of Birth for Lillian Cathleen Maddox, born in Houston, Texas on July 29, 1892. Mother, Rowena Simpson Maddox. Father, William Maddox, deceased.

A church bulletin from a congregation in Waco.

A placard for a soup kitchen in Dallas.

An Indian Territory marriage certificate for one Walter Sloat and Ruby Moore dated November 10, 1896.

A drawing of a tatting shuttle inlaid with the now-familiar Hebrew.

A sketch of a family tree, same as the one back home. And at the tree's crown, a single name—Lillian Cathleen Maddox. And above it in pencil . . . Lily.

"I'm the Lillian who played with dolls on the house plan. That's why Berachah felt like home." Gooseflesh tickles from my feet to my crown.

Examining the backs of my hands with new sight, I trace the blue lines with a fingertip. Not a drop of Sloat blood flows in my veins. I turn my hands over and examine my palms, my fingertips. "I consist of not an iota of Walter. If not for the scars, you'd never know he exists."

Cade kisses my forehead. Reaching into his trouser pocket, he extracts a ring. Sun rays ignite the gemstone, a blaze like the foxfire's light. "I'm asking again, Lily. Will you marry me?"

How can I sentence Cade to childlessness, Lord? "But Doc—"

"Shh. First things first."

Can I give Cade all of myself, even the blackest corner? "The scars—"

"Jesus has tucked you into the palm of His hand. His scars have healed yours." He raises my left hand to his lips.

I smile with a joy I'm just getting acquainted with. "You sure you want to marry a girl from the other side of Rock Creek?"

"Always have." He encases my hands in his and lays them on his heart. "Will you marry me, Lily Maddox?"

I release a sigh threaded with the joy of new birth. "I thought you'd never ask."

He chuckles and slips the ring into place. "You never answered my question."

My mouth eases open as I gaze at the jewels. I shake my head, clearing my brain of cobwebs. "What question?"

He wraps his still-damp arms around my shoulders and draws me close. "Is it proper for a . . . man who's going to marry—"

"Oh, for heaven's sakes, Cade. Kiss me."

And he does.

Down the way, Rock Creek gurgles. In that singular, glorious moment I'm a fine, well-bred woman with a porcelain complexion and a life story as flawless.

Jesus has made it so.

EPILOGUE

May 26, 1916

$\mathcal{C}$ade and I stand on a wooden arc over Rock Creek, a bridge at last.

Leaning on the sturdy railing, I tuck my body against my husband's.

"Happy?" His breath stirs wisps around my face.

"Very." The gentleman mockingbird twiddles on a branch overhead, now a song of celebration as he and his mate, like Lily and Cade, feather their nest.

"I'm proud of you, Lillian Cathleen Maddox McFarland. Your exposé shocked the nation. Your newsworthy photographs presented a case no one can ignore. You revealed the kidnapers, which led to the discovery of dozens of girls."

"Even the birthday girl's back home."

"You raised awareness of the need for women's votes." He kisses my forehead. "By claiming your Hebrew roots—"

"A heritage Flora and I share."

"The two of you highlight Jewish contributions to our nation."

"Thanks to Rachel Loeb Lloyd."

Cade lays a hand on my protruding belly. "Won't be long now."

"Our miracle child."

"Couldn't come at a sweeter time." He nods northward, and my gaze follows.

A grand, three-story structure rises to the sky where the old tarpaper shanty once stood. Around it sit outbuildings, a car shed, a barn with cows and chickens and pigs, and one for horses. A fine garden peeks through the soil, and the laundry snaps on the clothesline.

"Are we not blessed, Cade? Donnie's healthy and strong at Broadview with Wally at his side. Even learning to dance. The women's movement is gaining momentum.

"And today we officially dedicated this home for destitute women and children. Nell and Philip glow with newly wedded joy. They'll manage the home well. Even Ella's girls are volunteering with the children." I expel a satisfied sigh. "Come. Let's take another look."

Cade submits to my tug over the bridge, chuckling at my pretended exertion.

We stand staring at the building's wide entrance, our eyes drawn to the name carved in stone above the grand portal: *Rowena Maddox Home for Women and Children.*

And beneath it, three words spoken by Jesus: *Come unto me.*

An underlined passage in Ma's Bible comes to mind. . . . *my words . . . teach them to your children . . . write them upon the door posts of thine house.*

"Ma would approve."

Cade nods. "And so would Rachel Lloyd."

"Ahh. Because of Rachel, I know I'm the physical *and* spiritual seed of Abraham. And I can tat now." I lean against my husband with both hands on my belly. "She kicked."

"She?"

I turn my eyes to his. "I'd like to name her Maddox."

"Maddox would suit a boy too."

"Yes, but I want a daughter."

"Why is that?"

"Because I won't send a girl off to war." I release a core-deep sigh. "Now Great Britain is drafting married men like you, dear. Just a matter of time until we're all going to war." I grasp my belly. "If only Addie were home."

Cade kisses the tip of my nose. "Why must you borrow trouble, dear?" He smiles at a face peeking out a window. Other heads rise above window seals, and mothers join them, waving and smiling.

"Forgive me, Cade. It's just that I love you so. You mustn't leave me, never to war."

I take his arm, and we turn toward the creek. Beyond it our sturdy new home, the one Cade promised, sits like a gentle wren on McFarland soil. It's fit for a family. An Oklahoma twister. Or a war.

As Cade bounds off the bridge, I halt with one hand gripping my belly and the other my back. "Better get me home. Maddox is on her way."

About the Author

*L*inda Brooks Davis was born and reared, educated, and married in Texas. Her children and six grandchildren were born in Texas. She devoted the bulk of her 40 years as a special educator in Texas schools. But her mother and grandmother hailed from Oklahoma, the setting for Linda's 2015 debut novel, *The Calling of Ella McFarland*, which won the 2014 Jerry Jenkins Operation First Novel Award and the 2016 American Christian Fiction Writers Carol Award. Linda continues to write from her home in San Antonio, Texas. She and her beloved husband Al worship and minister at Oak Hills Church. Readers may contact Linda through her website lindabrooksdavis.com.

HISTORICAL NOTES

*I*n *The Mending of Lillian Cathleen*, I continue my mother's and grandmother's storytelling tradition through the circumstances of certain characters' lives, as well as historical realities and my ancestors' overcoming of tragedy and loss through faith and grit. I alone am responsible for any historical errors. They result not by design but by frailty.

In the Oklahoma scenes, Needham, Westwood, Fair Valley, Glover County, Jackson Academy, Rock Creek and its rural environs, Broadview, and Christ Church are imaginary, as are most of the characters themselves.

Imaginary Jackson Academy is based on the true Burney Institute of Lebanon, Oklahoma, which existed while the Chickasaw Nation controlled the land prior to 1907. Some fifteen years ago, Park Ranger Gary Carter showed my husband and me the grounds, the school's collapsing remains, and the outbuildings, and he explained some of the boarding school's history. The idea for Rock Creek came to me as I stood at the creek behind the school. Thanks to the Chickasaw Nation, Burney has been restored to a grand representative of its former self. You may view the restoration process at https://www.westernspecialtycontractors. com/western-project/burney-institute. Ida Tate is the product of my imagination.

College of Industrial Arts in Denton, Texas—my deceased mother-in-law Charlotte Camille Lane Davis's alma mater—truly existed and lives on today. Established in 1901 by an act of the Texas Legislature, it became known as Girls' Industrial College in 1903 and conferred its first degrees in 1904. The college changed its name in 1905 to College of Industrial Arts and today is known as Texas Woman's University.

In the Fort Worth and Arlington scenes, Black Panther Saloon and

Fort Worth Caller are imaginary, as are Flora Zane, Star, and Bessie. Beulah McGregor and children are inspired by a historical newspaper account of a mother and seven children living in a tent on Trinity River.

Fort Worth's history includes its *Cowtown* moniker; the sleeping panther legend and resulting mascot; Trinity River floods of 1889 and 1908; Hell's Half Acre; Metropolitan Hotel; Worth Hotel; Byers Opera House; Sheriff Rae; Dr. and Mrs. J. Frank Norris; First Baptist Church and its destruction by fire in 1912; City Park; Battercake Flats; the workhouse and its female inmates breaking up rocks. I extend my gratitude to *Hometown by Handlebar* for a wealth of historic newspaper accounts. Reference: https://hometownbyhandlebar.com

I took artistic liberties with this couple by involving them with a private investigator to uncover human trafficking and in Mrs. Upchurch's membership in a women's clubs. Any inaccuracies in their portrayals result from my frailty alone.

Berachah Industrial Home for the Redemption of Erring Girls truly existed in Arlington, Texas. Pastor and Mrs. J.T. Upchurch established it in 1903 to shelter unwed mothers and their children. Reference: https://legacy.lib.utexas.edu/taro/utarl/00112/arl-00112.html

The idea for the human trafficking subject matter, which was birthed in my research of the Mann Act of 1910, otherwise known as the White Slave Traffic Act. Reference: https://www.encyclopedia.com/history/united-states-and-canada/us-history/white-slave-traffic-act

Author Acknowledgments

One story sprouts readily while another requires the heart to break, the spirit to bend, and a spring of tears to flow. This is one of those. It originates in the true-life story of a family member of another generation. Waiting in the shadows for close to a century, it is now exposed to the healing power of the light of Jesus Christ. May He accomplish His purposes on these pages.

Thank you, Sharon Bales of Elmore City, Oklahoma. Fifteen years ago, you welcomed Al and me to the State Bank where I caught a glimpse of my grand- and great-grand- parents making deposits at the same teller's window.

Thank you, Julia Embree of the Pauls Valley Library in Pauls Valley, Oklahoma. You graciously showed me around the historical section. You whetted my appetite.

Thank you, J.R. McCaskill, a newly discovered cousin who showed Al and me around the land our ancestors once inhabited. The old cemetery where our common great-great-grandparents, Samuel and Catharine Pyle, are buried returns in my memory as I write these words. Your hospitality and graciousness remain with me.

Thank you, Evelyne Labelle of Carpe Librum Book Design for the beautiful cover. Not only are you proficient, but you're patient beyond measuring.

Thank you, authors Caryl McAdoo, Kelly Irvin, Allison Pittman, and Ann Tatlock, for your endorsements of my work.

Thank you, reader Becky Gifford Smith, for your discerning eye and encouraging words. And for your inspirational contribution to HeartWings Women's Fellowship.

Thank you, Caryl McAdoo, for your generosity of spirit, keen editor's eye, and on-target suggestions that made this story better. You inspire me and many others.

Thank you, friend and mentor, Allison Pittman, for your vision for the big picture. While I fixate on a tree, you see the whole forest. Not only are you a gifted author and inspired mentor, you are real in word, action, and spirit. Thank you for caring, for finding the time to critique my work, and for encouraging me in my quest to edge just a tad nearer to the skill and inspiration that permeate your writing.

Thank you, Brookstone Publishing Group, for taking me on. You are providing me with the level of expertise and support I've longed for.

Thank you, Mother—Goldie Leona Banks Brooks. Nowhere in God's creation did a truer, nobler, nor fuller human love exist than yours. You insisted on what I needed, not what was popular. Looked out for me like the ever-hovering blackbirds over the cornfield. And hesitated not a moment to appear unannounced and uninvited at events for which I'd gone past curfew. Your unfeigned faith in Jesus Christ dwelt first in your mother, Ella Jane, and in her mother, Louisa. I pray I'm handing down a faith no less true, honorable, and brave. Your love of family roots and your stories have waited patiently to be told. I hope this story meets your approval. My heart remembers. It always will.

Thank you, Al Davis—husband mine—for your love that mends and sustains me every day of life.

Above all, thank You, Lord Jesus. You alone are the Eternal Mender.

TO THE READER

*Y*ou first met Lily Sloat in award-winning *The Calling of Ella McFarland*, a story set in 1905 Indian Territory prior to Oklahoma statehood.

In *A Christmas Measure of Love*, Lily stood on the cusp of womanhood and her mother at the nadir of her life. Lily was as straight as her starched collar, but Ma was as bent as a shepherd's crook. Joined by blood and separated by circumstance, mother and daughter reunited for Christmas 1910. But they found more than they reckoned for in the old shack where their sweat and tears once mingled.

I hope *The Mending of Lillian Cathleen* blesses you. The import of reader feedback can't be overstated. So I thank you in advance for your review on Amazon and Goodreads and your recommendations on social media.

Inspired by my mother's love beyond reckoning—and by knowledge of the marks abuse leaves even on well-loved souls—I tithe from the proceeds from *The Mending of Lillian Cathleen* and *A Christmas Measure of Love* to causes benefitting children of abuse.

Sign up at lindabrooksdavis.com for my weekly blog with author interviews and give-aways and my quarterly newsletter. I love to hear from readers on my Facebook Author Page, Linda Brooks Davis; Twitter @LBrooksDavis; and on my website.

Linda

"I have not stopped giving thanks for you ..."
Ephesians 1:16

DEAR READER,

I thank you sincerely for purchasing *The Mending of Lillian Cathleen.* By doing so you have validated the story of one young woman's quest to rise above the scars of her past and to welcome the flawlessness found in Jesus Christ. I thank you in a tangible way by offering at no cost to you in digital format the companion novella, *A Christmas Measure of Love.*

To access this Christmas novella, follow this link:

lindabrooksdavis.com/ebookbonus

and enter the promo code:

LillianChristmas